Book 3 of the Talion Series

J.K. FRANKO

Published in the United States and the rest of the world by
Talion Publishing

Cambridge, UK

A catalogue record for this book is available from the British Library

ISBN 978-1-9993188-9-5

This book is dedicated to my Grandma Laura,
who never took shit from anybody.

That corpse you planted last year in your garden,
Has it begun to sprout? Will it bloom this year?

The Waste Land
T.S. Eliot

PROLOGUE

Death is always several seconds and a few footsteps away. Look around you, wherever you are right now. How many things are there within five feet of you that could kill you? An improperly grounded electrical outlet plugged into your tablet. A slippery, wet bath tile that sends your head smashing into the side of the tub. An invisible virus silently multiplying in your lungs.

From the moment of conception, we fight to cheat death. The majority of what parents do for most of a child's life is simply keep them from dying. And much of what parents teach kids, from avoiding strangers to keeping their fingers out of their mouths, is about staying alive.

Although the odds are stacked against us, we get very good at cheating death. So good that, maybe out of misplaced pride or just to maintain our sanity, we tell ourselves that death is far off.

But it never is. And it comes for us all.

Given my profession, I have always feared death at the hands of a patient. For years, I imagined an unhinged, unmedicated client lashing out at me. Hopefully with a gun, not a knife. When I met Susie and Roy, that changed somewhat. I feared death at their hands not because they were unstable, but because I was expendable.

I must say that after the murder of former Congressman Getz, I believed that I finally had that situation under control. Susie, Roy, and I—and all of our incentives—were finally aligned. We were on the same team, so to speak. I foolishly believed that my life could simply return to normal.

But as I look back on everything now, with twenty-twenty hindsight, I can see that even as Roy was drowning Jeff Getz in the Bay of Pollença in Spain, the rough outlines of our tragic ending had already been sketched—all of the pieces were in place. Death was watching, and planning.

As you must appreciate by now, my story is inextricably intertwined with the stories of others. This is, of course, fundamental to the human condition. We are all part of a larger whole. Seemingly unrelated people and events, distant in time and location, weave their way in and out of our lives like the threads of a tapestry.

I have told you two stories from the past that directly impacted me, Susie, and Roy. I shared with you the tragic tale of little Joan's death and how she was finally avenged. And, I shared with you the evil done to Billy Applegate and how Jeff Getz paid the ultimate price for that crime.

To complete the circle, for you to understand everything that happened to us, and so that you can take from all this the same cautionary lessons that I have learned, I need to share one final story with you. It is about a woman whose life was irreversibly impacted by our actions.

It is a story about love and death. And, in this case, depending on your point of view, you might even say that her story had a happy ending.

PART ONE

Rebecca Forsyth
Turks and Caicos
2020

My work as a therapist requires imagination. To help someone, to really get inside their head, you have to have some sense of what they are going through. If you haven't experienced what your patient is suffering firsthand, you must imagine.

For example, I have never had a panic attack. But then, only five percent of humans will experience a panic attack during their lifetimes. A pretty low number. So, how can I relate?

I must imagine.

From what my patients tell me, a panic attack closely resembles the feeling of claustrophobia. This is something that I have experienced. What gets me there instantly is that scene from *Kill Bill*—the one when the heroine Beatrix is buried under six feet of dirt in a coffin and left to die. Do you know it?

Indulge me.

Imagine that you wake up and open your eyes, but you can't see anything. It's pitch dark. So dark, you're not sure your eyes are even open. You're lying on your back. The air you're breathing feels warm and slightly humid, the way it does when you're sleeping with your head under the sheets.

You don't know where you are, but you don't hear the usual sounds you would hear in your bedroom. No ceiling fan. No A/C blowing. Everything is silent around you. Muffled.

You try to sit up and immediately feel a thump as your

forehead hits something. Your hands automatically react and reach up, discovering that something dry and smooth—heavy, immovable—is laying on top of you, just inches above your body. Right above your face, your torso, your legs.

You try to stretch your arms out to either side, and you feel the same barrier just inches away from your elbows, from your shoulders. You move your legs, spreading them apart and lifting them up. They are able to move only inches before, again, you feel something boxing you in.

Your nose itches, but you can't reach your face to scratch it. You clear your throat and can hear that the sound doesn't travel. It's close to you, stifled by the box you're in. The box is made of wood. There's maybe six inches between you and the box, all around your body. It's so close you can smell it. Damp wood. You can also smell soil.

You're in a box that's been placed in a hole, six feet deep. On top of it, and on top of you, are six feet of dirt. That much dirt weighs over two thousand pounds. One ton.

The weight of the dirt prevents you from opening the box. The lid won't budge. And even if you could break out of the box somehow, the dirt above you would fall into it, suffocating you before you could dig your way up to air.

There is no way out.

No hope.

As you realize this, your heartbeat accelerates—firing more rapidly. Your breathing speeds up. You struggle to take in air. You're not sure if you're already running out of oxygen or simply panicking. You can feel the silent, blind weight of two thousand pounds of earth above you crushing down onto your body. Your legs are tight, anxious. Your body fights for more space... to move, to stretch out, to stand, to run. But on every side you are closed in. You know that out there, everywhere, there is air, freedom. A universe of wide-open space.

But not for you.

You scream. The sound is muffled by the box. The only one who can hear it is you, and you know it. And you remember, as you scream, that there is a very small supply of oxygen in the box. With each breath, you are depleting it, converting it into CO_2.

You're going to suffocate. And there is no way out.

That feeling of being closed in, of paralysis, of heart-racing suffocating hopelessness, is what a panic attack feels like. Just like being trapped in a coffin.

My patients say that this is how you will feel when you're about to die.

When I try to imagine how Rebecca must have felt, 120 feet underwater with an empty scuba tank strapped to her back, I draw on this image.

* * *

Rebecca Forsyth was floating, weightless. Free as a bird. The feeling was otherworldly. And the view was breathtaking. Above her in every direction stretched a majestic canopy of bright blue. Looking heavenward, her eyes traced dancing beams of sunlight up and away until they converged into a round disc of shimmering white firmament. As she gazed downward, the world fell away from her—the bright blue and the light fading, everything becoming darker the further she looked. The only sound she could hear was the too-close, too-loud in-and-out of her own breathing, which she tried to control—relaxing, breathing slowly.

In: *one-two-three-four-five-six-seven-eight-nine-ten.*

Out: *one-two-three-four-five-six-seven-eight-nine-ten.*

She reached up, pinching her nose, and gently blew, equalizing the pressure in her ears—the Valsalva Maneuver.

Scuba diving was something Rebecca enjoyed, to a point. She was no expert, though she was open water certified and dove several times a year. She loved the feeling of weightlessness. And she liked being able to explore the ocean without having to bob up and down for air. She'd never quite mastered using a snorkel—she always had trouble clearing it of water. Scuba was much more convenient. No bobbing up and down. That being said, she had not done many deep dives.

Today was different.

Alan, Rebecca's husband, had talked her into diving a wreck. A sunken ship. It was all perfectly safe. Alan was an extremely experienced diver. A certified instructor. He had spent numerous summers working as an instructor and had logged hundreds of hours. In fact, he was the one who had gotten Rebecca into the sport.

The plan was for Rebecca and Alan to follow standard protocol and stay close to one another, buddy diving in case of an emergency. As Rebecca floated about 40 feet underwater, Alan was signaling for her to follow him down toward the wreck, which at its deepest was 165 feet below the surface. They weren't planning to go down that far. The bow of the ship was at about 110 feet.

Although Rebecca wasn't crazy about diving so deep, she reluctantly followed. They were on vacation, trying to relax. Trying new things to reinvigorate their marriage. After five years married, they'd hit a rough patch. They'd had some issues. Nothing insurmountable, she would have told you.

Part of their problems stemmed from the way they approached things. Rebecca was more conservative in her thinking. Alan was more of a risk-taker. Of course, for her to have chickened out of this dive would only have served to underscore the differences between them.

She checked the air pressure in her tank and noticed that it was dropping a little faster than normal for her, given the amount of time they'd been underwater. But, she knew that she was stressing over the fact that they were going to dive so deep, and she was breathing a little more rapidly than usual. She reached up and slightly reduced the buoyancy of her BCD, then gently frog-kicked her legs to conserve energy and air, following her husband down into the dark blue depths.

Rebecca swam about ten feet behind Alan and a bit to his left. The bow of the wreck still lay another 70 feet below them and hadn't come into view. Rebecca couldn't see it yet. She also couldn't see that, in addition to the bubbles that drifted up and away from her each time she exhaled, a stream of tiny bubbles trailed behind her. Air was escaping from her scuba tank through a small leak in the line to her backup regulator. As she descended into the depths, the water pressure around her grew, increasing the rate at which air was bleeding from her only tank.

Rebecca followed after Alan, taking in the immensity of the ocean floor that lay before her. The vastness of it was almost overwhelming. She tried to focus on keeping pace with her husband, and on breathing slowly.

In: *one-two-three-four-five-six-seven-eight-nine-ten.*

Out: *one-two-three-four-five-six-seven-eight-nine-ten.*

She scanned beyond him, hoping that the wreck would soon come into view as she gently kicked and followed. As they descended, they were following the natural slope of the ocean floor off the coast of the island. The seabed was spotted with seagrass, kelp, small fish, and here and there a lobster. She saw several lionfish as well.

Rebecca enjoyed fish-watching. Although, for her it was always secondary to keeping an eye out for sharks. The Caribbean is home to a great many species—nurse sharks, lemon sharks, reef sharks—which are generally harmless. But now and again, you will see more aggressive bull sharks and hammerheads.

Rebecca followed behind Alan, staying close, but she couldn't help being entertained admiring the seascape. She regularly pinched her nose to clear her ears. After what felt like just a few minutes, a shape began to take form ahead of them. Alan stuck his arm out to his side and gave her a thumbs-up. It was the wreck. A few more kicks, and she could clearly see the silhouette of the freighter sitting on the ocean floor below.

It was a tranquil day and the water was clear. There was still very good visibility as they passed 100 feet, though at that depth the water filtered out most of the reds and yellows in the color spectrum. Everything was draped in shades of blue and green.

Rebecca and Alan were diving just off the coast of Providenciales in the Turks and Caicos Islands. The wreck they were approaching was the W.E. Freighter, a 100-ton ship that was purposely sunken just north of Turtle Cove to create an artificial reef. The plan for the reef had been for the ship to settle in somewhat shallow waters to create an attraction for recreational divers. The ship had unfortunately ended up much deeper than intended and required a bit of expertise to reach.

Once at the bow of the freighter, Alan stopped and gave Rebecca the "okay" sign. She responded in kind, indicating that she was fine. She checked her depth gauge and saw that they were at 110 feet, just what the guidebook had promised. Alan and Rebecca had agreed on the surface not to go inside the vessel. There was always danger of collapse or of getting trapped due to gear catching on something. There was also the risk of getting cut since what remained of the ship was decaying metal that tended to be sharp and jagged. A cut meant blood in the water. And blood in the water attracted sharks.

They hovered for a moment by the bow of the wreck.

As they looked about them, a small school of fish swam out of the boat through a hole in the hull. They were silver with what appeared to be yellow fins and tails, though the color was muted and dull due to the depth. Most were about two feet long. Rebecca recognized them as horse-eye jacks. They shimmered in the water as they swam past the husband and wife, less than three feet away. Alan reached out and touched one of the fish as it went by. It didn't seem to notice or care.

Rebecca watched the school of fish briefly, then her focus shifted. Always scanning for sharks, she'd seen a shadowy movement not far from them—maybe forty feet. Whatever it was had whipped its body and quickly disappeared into the dark, murky distance. She kept scanning as the small school of fish swam away from them.

Suddenly, her peripheral vision registered a rapid movement coming from their left. She focused just in time to see sparkling glints of silver—a large barracuda rocketed in from the murkiness and sank its teeth into one of the jacks as the remainder of the school scattered. Thin wisps of black blood trailed behind the barracuda as it swam off, chomping and chewing on its prey. In the wake of the attack, the remaining jacks re-grouped and continued on as if nothing had happened.

It was not the first time that Rebecca had seen a predator make a meal of another fish. It never ceased to amaze her how an underwater scene could turn from completely tranquil to suddenly violent and bloody, and then return once again to the prior calm as though nothing had happened. She turned to Alan, who was shaking a hand back and forth as if to say, "Holy crap!" She gave him a thumbs-up in reply.

Rebecca continued to scan. Now there was blood in the water. And she was nervous—looking for sharks. As she looked around, Alan drifted a bit deeper examining the wreck. Rebecca was about to follow when a strange shape on the seafloor caught her eye. She felt her belly tighten and reached for her dive knife. She froze and watched carefully. Her patience was rewarded.

A sludgy-looking grey rock, which had apparently been laying low waiting for the barracuda incident to pass, decided that the coast was clear. Rebecca marveled as the rock changed color and texture, turning back into an octopus. The little guy half-swam half-crawled away, in the opposite direction of the barracuda. Rebecca smiled to herself. She loved those smart, creepy, eight-legged mollusks.

The octopus gone, she turned and saw that Alan had drifted about twenty feet away from her, deeper, exploring the hull of the wreck. He looked back at her and waved her towards him. Apparently, he'd found something of interest. Rebecca gave him a thumbs-up, and as she began to move, she looked down at her depth gauge.

Still at 110 feet.

They had agreed not to go below 130 feet, which was the official cut-off for recreational divers. Realizing it had been a while since she'd checked, she also took a look at her air pressure gauge.

Red.

A cold claw of panic squeezed Rebecca's chest when she saw that the needle was in the red zone, between 200 PSI and zero. Almost empty. The gauge had to be wrong. She and Alan had both checked her tank in the boat. It was full then. And they'd not been diving that long—certainly not long enough for her to have used up a full tank of air.

She tapped on the gauge with a gloved finger. The needle didn't move. Still red.

She carefully reached back behind her head with one hand to make sure the tank was fully open. Sometimes a not fully open tank would give a bad reading on a gauge. She turned the air valve in one direction and the flow of air stopped. Then she turned it in the other direction, fully opening the valve, and air flowed. She checked the gauge. Still red.

Rebecca looked up and saw that Alan had swum farther away from her, about thirty feet. And he was still moving. She fought down the panic and breathed out slowly: *one-two-three-four-five-six-seven-eight-nine-ten.*

Then in: *one-two-three-four-five-six-seven-eight-nine-ten.*

She had two choices.

She could try to ascend. If she did, she'd be abandoning Alan—leaving him at risk. She also had no idea if the air in her tank would get her to the surface. If it didn't, she'd have to make a "controlled emergency ascent." She remembered from her training what that meant. Possible decompression sickness. Possible pulmonary barotrauma—essentially her lungs exploding. And, of course, she could drown.

Her other option was to get Alan's attention and return to the surface using his backup regulator—an "alternate air source ascent."

She had to choose quickly. Given her options, Rebecca decided she had to get to Alan. She frog-kicked gently, trying not to accelerate her heart rate or breathing, conserving air, swimming down deeper into the cold sea after her husband. As she swam after him, she removed her dive knife from its sheath and used the metal ball on the end of the hilt to bang on her tank, making a high-pitched metallic *clink clink clink* hoping to get Alan's attention.

Alan continued to descend. He was too far away to hear her. She was still breathing. She still had air.

But her brain began to work against her. Fear gripped her

throat like a noose slowly tightening. As Rebecca swam deeper into the sea, the ocean began to collapse in on her. Tunnel vision. Panic began to rise in her belly. She felt boxed in.

Trapped.

She fought the fear, trying to keep her breathing slow. Kicking gently, trying to get to her husband. He had air. He was only thirty feet away.

Life was only thirty feet away.

She began to feel desperation. To lose hope.

Is this it?

Is this how I die?

Alan didn't hear the continued and more desperately rapid *clinking* of her knife on her tank. He wasn't turning. He was swimming deeper, and she was barely gaining on him. She began to kick harder, knowing that her heart rate would increase. And her breathing as well. She had to get to him. He was still too far away.

Rebecca kicked and breathed.

Kicked and breathed.

Kicked and…

...she breathed in, and three quarters of the way through the breath she hit a wall—it was like she was sucking on a rubber hose that was closed at one end. There was nothing. She was out of air.

She couldn't fight the panic any longer.

Sheer panic.

The feeling of being closed-in, of paralysis, of heart-racing suffocating hopelessness hit Rebecca Forsyth like a brick wall.

CHAPTER ONE

Detective Eddie Garza loved it when a case came together. Sure, his job was mainly about catching bad guys and doing good. But part of it was just plain competitive: a battle of wits against the crooks. That was the part that really motivated Eddie—winning. He loved the challenge. And he hated to lose.

Frankly, many of the criminals Eddie dealt with were not too bright, and not too difficult to catch. Maybe this is why he was fascinated by Roy Cruise. In the initial investigation of Joe Harlan Junior's disappearance, Roy Cruise won the battle, hands down. Eddie was the first to admit it. He felt in his gut that the guy knew more than he was telling, but Eddie couldn't find any holes in the man's story; no holes big enough to pursue legally anyway. Which is why the recent evidence he'd unearthed was all the more exciting. After months and months of dead-ends, Eddie was finally making progress.

Cruise may have had the first laugh, but I'll have the last one.

Eddie's first break came with the surveillance video from the Cruises' house on Halloween night. Two people entered the house that evening. Only one came out.

Though they had a decent quality image of the man who entered via the front door, facial recognition searches yielded no hits. So, Eddie focused on identifying the two people by figuring out how they'd gotten to the house. No cars were visible on the video, but the Cruise house was in a gated community off of Old Cutler Road. There was no public parking anywhere nearby.

Eddie obtained the guardhouse records which listed the license plate numbers of all vehicles entering and exiting the subdivision that evening. After discarding the ones that belonged to residents, seven license plates remained that belonged to Ubers. Further investigation revealed that one Uber in particular had delivered a woman named Kristy Wise to the Cruise property—apparently dressed up as one of the Mario Brothers. That was extremely interesting. Eddie added her to his list of persons of interest.

Unfortunately, none of the other vehicles' license plates on the guardhouse list accounted for the man at the front door. As there was no surveillance footage of the man leaving the property, Eddie ran a search for police reports of abandoned vehicles in the area. Nothing turned up in the relevant timeframe.

On a hunch, Eddie got a junior cop to start calling rental car companies, beginning with the big guys and working their way down, to see if any had picked up an abandoned vehicle in the area sometime around Halloween. See, Eddie understood how cops work. If a police officer came across an abandoned vehicle, they would call it in and write up a report. But, if a cop came across an abandoned rental car and could identify it as such, he would most probably call the agency directly and have them pick it up—because by doing that, he could avoid doing paperwork... no police report required.

Bingo.

On November 2, 2019, Magic City Car Rental picked up a Hyundai Elantra one block from the gated entry to Cruise's subdivision. The car was rented to a Ronald Clayton—who had picked up the car at Miami International Airport on October 29th. Eddie obtained a copy of Clayton's car rental agreement from the company, which included his email address, mobile number, home address, and driver's license. Clayton was apparently from Georgia. Eddie accessed the man's photo ID online—and knew from the image that he had found the mystery man at the front door.

Eddie called Clayton's mobile number—no answer. He left a voice message. Twice every day thereafter, he called the number and left a message.

Meanwhile, Eddie ran a background check, and with a bit of research determined that Clayton's only next of kin was a distant aunt in Minnesota. He spoke with her by phone, but she had not spoken to or heard from Clayton for years.

Eddie also learned from the background check that Clayton held a private investigator's license in Georgia.

After ten days leaving messages on Clayton's mobile phone, Eddie began to receive a "mailbox full" message. Eddie called the local authorities in Georgia and connected with an Officer Gary Nunn.

"You play the guitar, Gary?"

Nunn chuckled. "Nope. But I get that a lot."

Eddie gave Nunn a high-level rundown of Harlan Junior's case—the alleged rape, the disappearance—and explained his interest in Ronald Clayton. Nunn was happy to help out and did a drive-by of Clayton's house.

"No one home," Nunn reported via mobile phone from the property. "Quite a bit of mail backed up in the mailbox. Most of it's addressed to Ronald Clayton. And there's some junk mail addressed to 'Resident.' So, my guess is he's still occupying the house—he hasn't rented it out, I mean."

At that point, Eddie prepared a Missing Person Report on Ronald Clayton and submitted it to all the relevant national clearinghouses including the National Crime Information Center and the National Center for Missing Adults. He also sent a copy of the report to the Georgia State Police and the local police in Clayton's hometown.

Given that Clayton had rented the abandoned Hyundai at Miami International Airport, Eddie obtained air travel information for Clayton from Homeland Security. Clayton had made several airplane trips during times relevant to the investigation, which allowed Eddie to begin to put together a timeline.

On December 9th, when Eddie called Clayton's mobile phone for the second time that day, he received a message indicating that the number was no longer in service.

Suspended for non-payment, no doubt.

At that point, Clayton had been last seen over a month earlier. That, plus the overflowing voicemail, cancelled mobile phone account, abandoned rental vehicle, and the condition at his home—uncut lawn, the mailbox continuing to overflow—was enough for the local police to obtain a warrant to enter Clayton's home, not based on probable cause relating to a crime, but simply exigent circumstances. The man might be injured or dead inside.

After a cursory look through the house, Officer Nunn called Eddie.

"No dead body. No signs of foul play. But you need to come up here in person."

The next morning, Eddie flew to Atlanta, then drove south to Clayton's house. He was met outside by Officer Nunn.

Nunn showed Eddie into the house. It was a small home, neatly kept except for the overgrown lawn, sitting on an acre of land just off the highway.

"Wait 'til you see this."

The wood floor creaked as the two walked through the living room and down a dark hallway.

"I don't smell *eau du* corpse. That's a plus, I suppose," Eddie chuckled. "Lights?"

"No power," Nunn replied. "Unpaid electric bill. I called and confirmed."

Eddie followed Nunn through a doorway.

"Holy shit!"

Eddie was standing in what appeared to be the master bedroom, but was set up as a home office. Taped to the wall before him were photos of Joe Harlan Junior, Joe Harlan Senior, Roy Cruise, Tom Wise, David Kim, Kristy Wise, Debra Wise, and two young men who looked somewhat familiar to the detective. There were numerous yellow sticky notes on the wall next to the different photos, each covered with tiny scrawl. Eddie peered at them.

No motive.

Motive—revenge.

Out of town alibi.

Highly unlikely.

Dead.

On the desk were file folders, neatly stacked—apparently

one for each person on the wall. From these, Eddie concluded that Frank Stern and Marty McCall were the two young men on the wall whose faces he didn't recognize.

Eddie opened desk drawers searching for further clues.

He spent quite a bit of time flipping through a large drawer in the credenza.

"Looking for something specific?" Nunn asked.

"Well," Eddie put his hands on his hips, looking up at the wall of photos, then around the room, "it's pretty clear to me that he was investigating my case—the one I told you about. But why? There are a bunch of investigative files here," Eddie pointed at the credenza, "and most of them have one of these."

Eddie handed Nunn a sheet entitled *Client Intake* that listed general information about a client, and a short summary of the scope of work to be done. Nunn was looking at one from a file belonging to a Beatrice deWitt, who was apparently interested in *Mr. deWitt's alleged marital infidelity.*

"I don't see one of these for the Harlan file," Eddie said. "Or any accounting documents. Time sheets. Bills. There's no client name on any of this." He looked at Nunn who was idly flipping through the folders on the desk while he listened, apparently looking for a *Client Intake* sheet. "If Clayton was hired to investigate this case, there'd be some indication somewhere of who hired him, right?"

"Well, let's go on down this way," Nunn suggested. "Maybe what's behind door number two will shed some light on that."

Eddie followed Nunn back through the living room to the other end of the house. Nunn stopped at the doorway to what appeared to be another smaller bedroom.

"After you, amigo."

Eddie entered. He'd seen a lot of weird shit in his days, and this was by no means the strangest, but it definitely made the top ten list. The room was a small bedroom and contained only a bed, a cot really. Military style. On the floor next to it was a length of black rope, maybe two feet long. Aside from not wanting to contaminate the scene, intuition told Eddie not to touch it.

On the wall next to the cot were photos and news clippings.

Most appeared to involve national politics—conspiracy theory stuff. Though there was one section devoted to clippings of articles and photos of Senator Joe Harlan.

"This guy could give Alex Jones a run for his money," Eddie chuckled, studying the wall.

Nunn chimed in, "You're missin' the best part."

Eddie turned to look at Nunn and saw that the officer was looking up over the cot.

Eddie got closer and craned his head. Taped to the ceiling, there were—he counted—twelve different photos. All of them of Kristy Wise. They appeared to have been taken from the internet. There was a large photo in the center that looked like a school photo. Then smaller photos all around it.

"What. The. Fuck?" Eddie studied the images for several moments, then asked. "Has anyone else seen this?"

"Just you and me, Detective." Nunn smiled, then added, "You're the second one to know."

CHAPTER TWO

Upon returning to Miami, Eddie obtained a warrant to access Ronald Clayton's phone records. Going through these, he discovered that Clayton had been in regular communication for several months with someone at an Austin, Texas mobile phone number. Clayton's contact name for the number was *Cherry.* No email address or physical address. Just *Cherry* and the phone number. The phone log history showed that the first contact between the two was a call from *Cherry* to Clayton in late August.

While there were several calls back and forth in the phone log, there were only two text messages—both incoming—from *Cherry*.

Urgent. We need to talk.
URGENT. ABORT.

Eddie added these messages to his timeline. He also searched through his case file. *Cherry's* phone number did not match any of the mobile phone numbers Eddie had for the people associated with Joe Harlan Junior's case. Eddie tried calling the number for *Cherry*, and received a message indicating that the voicemail for the phone had not been set up.

Eddie found one other text message *from* Clayton's phone to another Austin phone number.

Mission accomplished.

That message was sent to a phone number that did appear in Eddie's file—Senator Joe Harlan.

Eddie also obtained location data from Clayton's phone. The locations logged on the phone were consistent with the missing man's travel information. From analyzing this information, two things stood out to Eddie. The first was that the man regularly turned off either his phone or the *Location Services* function, as there were gaps in the data where the phone could not be located. The second was that the last use of the phone triangulated to coordinates placing the phone in Florida, in the ocean, offshore in the Florida Straits just east of Biscayne Bay on Halloween night.

Eddie compiled all of this information in preparation for a meeting the following day with Spencer Shaw, the prosecuting attorney he'd been working with on the investigation into Roy Cruise. As he was finalizing his notes, an alert appeared on his computer screen—an email from Liz Bareto. Eddie hit *Print* on his notes for Shaw, then opened Liz's email.

Hello Eddie,
I hope all is well with you. It's been a while since I had any updates from you on Liam's case, but I know that you're very busy.
I did want to alert you to something that popped up that I thought you might find interesting. Now, who do we know that was in Mallorca recently???
Link below.
Former Congressman Found Dead
Talk soon.
Liz

Investigative Notes

RE: **Cruise surveillance**
DATE: December 16, 2019

On October 31, 2019, two individuals entered the subject's home. The first, Ronald Clayton, entered via the front door. No video captures him leaving the property. Clayton's rental car was found abandoned two days later on Old Cutler Road.

Preliminary investigation of Clayton yields the following additional information:

Ronald Sherman Clayton
1902 Highway 81
Hampton, Georgia 30228
470-632-8743
rsclayton@hotmail.com

Clayton has not been to his home for weeks. Mobile phone, electric, and water bills are unpaid. Clayton's home office contained documents and photos relating to the disappearance of Joe Harlan Junior. Clayton appeared to be investigating the case. See attached photos of office and bedroom.

Ronald Clayton Timeline

August 29, 2019	Call for 2 minutes—from *Cherry*
October 12, 2019	Flight from Atlanta to Miami
	Call for 3 minutes—to *Cherry*
October 18, 2019	**David Kim "hit-and-run"**
October 19, 2019	Flight from Miami to Austin
October 27, 2019	**Tom Wise suicide/homicide**
October 28, 2019	Call for 8 minutes—to *Cherry*
	Msg rec from *Cherry*: *Urgent.*

	We need to talk.
October 29, 2019	Flight from Austin to Miami Rents Car: Magic City Car Rental Msg rec from *Cherry*: *Urgent. ABORT.*
October 31, 2019	Last seen on Cruise property
November 1, 2019	Location: 25° 39.524' N 80° 4.852' W Call for 23 seconds—to *Cherry* Msg Sent to Harlan: *Mission accomplished.*
November 2, 2019	Rental car found abandoned—Old Cutler Rd. Kristy Wise leaves Cruise house

The second person entering the home, Kristy Wise, was filmed leaving the property on November 2, 2019.

Persons of interest:
Roy Cruise
Susie Font
David Kim
Kristy Wise
Senator Joe Harlan

CHAPTER THREE

Eddie met Spencer Shaw the next morning at the State Attorney's office. He gave Shaw a rundown of everything he'd discovered about Ronald Clayton. He also updated Shaw on the fact that the unknown Austin mobile number—*Cherry*—had been traced back to a prepaid phone. Most likely a burner.

Eddie decided against mentioning anything about former Congressman Jeff Getz's recent drowning in Spain. It was only a tip from Liz, and he hadn't had any time to look into it.

He sat quietly as Shaw reviewed the notes Eddie had prepared for him.

"Okay, Eddie." Shaw looked up. "What's next?"

"The way I see it, we need to interview Senator Harlan next. Based on what we've got—especially that 'Mission accomplished' text message that Clayton sent him—he's got to know something. My most likely scenario, he hired this Clayton guy to investigate his son's case. Clayton got close to the truth—too close—and Cruise took him out."

"But you didn't find any evidence of that? That Harlan hired him?"

"No."

"No payments, no references to Harlan in his file, nothing?"

Eddie shook his head.

"But, you think this Cherry number belongs to Harlan? The burner phone?"

Eddie nodded.

"Cherry... that's a weird fucking nickname, don't you think? Especially for someone like Harlan."

Eddie continued nodding.

"But if Clayton got 'too close to the truth' and Cruise killed him, then why would Clayton text Harlan 'Mission accomplished'? In fact, why text Harlan 'Mission accomplished' at all right after talking to him on the burner?"

Eddie shook his head. "I know. Not all of it makes sense. There's something missing."

"Unless—what if that Cherry phone number belongs to someone close to Harlan? Maybe that's it!" Shaw loved gaming out scenarios. "What if Harlan got someone else to bring Clayton onboard, so Harlan could keep his hands clean? And this Clayton guy *called* to let *that person* know 'mission accomplished,' but then wanted to make sure Harlan got the news too. So, he texted Harlan."

Eddie pursed his lips. "Could be."

"I like that scenario better," Shaw sat staring into the middle distance, licking his lips.

Eddie nodded some more.

"Could it be Kristy Wise? Cherry sounds more like a girl. Not that she was working *with Harlan*—this is a different scenario. Maybe Clayton was working *for her*, but thought Harlan might have an interest and wanted to curry favor with him?" Shaw shook his head answering his own question in the negative. "But, what would she want from Clayton that Harlan would consider 'mission accomplished?' And I just don't see them being aligned here, do you? Wise and Harlan?"

Eddie shook his head, "I don't, either. No way."

Shaw looked back down at the notes. "So, are you thinking that this Clayton guy beat up David Kim and killed Tom Wise?"

"The timeline works," Eddie replied. "He was in the right places at the right times. Plus, his phone goes dark around the times that those crimes happened. There's also some suspicious calls and texts right around the dates of those incidents. And, we've got the gun oil residue in Wise's mouth that just doesn't jibe with a drug overdose suicide. Travers confirmed that they're treating the Wise investigation as a homicide."

"Okay. What about the 'Urgent' text messages? New

information? More like a change of plan from the sound of it. Maybe this Clayton guy wasn't sticking to the plan?"

"It's possible."

Shaw sighed. "Fuck, Eddie. None of this is clear-cut. Not at all. Why don't you talk to David Kim first? See if his 'hit-and-run' was this Clayton guy?"

"Well," Eddie responded, "Kim's definitely antagonistic to us. Uncooperative. He's already claimed he didn't see who hit him. The fact that we have a suspect isn't likely to change any of that."

Shaw was nodding along with Eddie.

"I still think the best next step is to talk with the senator. See what he has to say. Then we can regroup," Eddie said.

Shaw's eyes were closed, thinking. After a few moments, he replied, "Makes sense. You're right." He handed Eddie back his notes. "Great work, Eddie. I mean it. Let me know once you've talked to Harlan."

CHAPTER FOUR

Joe Harlan Senior was sitting in his new office looking at a photo on his desk. It was of him and his son, Joe Junior, at a campaign event about six months before Joe disappeared. The senator had just gotten off the phone with Liz Bareto, who was flying up for the weekend, and as he'd put the phone down, the image had caught his eye. The photo reminded him that he and Liz were connected by the fact that they'd both lost sons before their time. It was the biggest negative in his relationship with her—every time he saw Liz, she reminded him of the son he'd lost.

It had only been three months since he'd met Liz for the first time in Austin, Texas. Another fast and furious courtship for Harlan—another notch on his bedpost. He enjoyed her physically, and even enjoyed her company when she wasn't obsessing over her son's death and who the culprits might be. Although Harlan had learned from Slipknot that Roy and Susie had probably been involved, and Deb Wise had probably done the boy in, he didn't plan to share that with Liz.

Nothing to be gained by that. And how would you explain where you got that info? He thought. *Besides, not knowing gives her a reason to wake up in the morning. Something to fight for.*

As he looked at the picture of his son, he wondered at how his son's death had been the catalyst that brought Liz into his life.

Harlan had always loved his son, though he recognized early on that the boy had issues. It wasn't that Joe was a bad kid—in his father's opinion at least. He just loved pussy. And, when he drank, the worst in him came out.

When Joe was younger, he'd shown signs of being different,

sexually. Harlan Senior had been slightly amused when he'd caught Joe— then just seven—masturbating. It was shortly after his mother had passed from cancer. It seemed that he was a bit young for that, but then again, he was going through a lot. And different people develop at different speeds, don't they?

At fourteen years old, Harlan had caught Joe getting a blowjob from the maid. He'd walked in on them in the laundry room. Of course, he'd fired her and reprimanded Joe. But, before he'd fired her, as she'd begged for her job, she'd told Harlan Senior that Joe had threatened to get her fired if she didn't acquiesce and had been paying her twenty dollars per session. Harlan Senior had chosen to believe that the maid was just lying to try to save her job. When he'd confronted his son, Joe had denied everything she'd claimed. But the doubt lingered.

Two years later, after Joe had started driving, Harlan Senior got the call that changed his opinion about his son.

It was early evening, around 7:00 p.m., and Joe was supposed to be at home after a late football practice. The legislature was in session, and Senator Harlan was at dinner with some lobbyists when his mobile vibrated. It was the then-Austin Police Chief Albert Gaines.

The senator made his excuses and headed down to the police station. Chief Gaines was waiting for him. The police had found Joe parked on a side street up near Rosewood and I-35, an unsavory neighborhood.

"With a hooker," said Gaines.

"I see," said Harlan Senior.

"When the officer saw Joe's name and age, he thought it best to bring him in. He hasn't been arrested, technically, and isn't going to be. But he was with a girl that's well-known to our guys. Drug addict. Lots of priors. Just really nasty, Senator."

Harlan nodded slowly. He didn't know what to say, or what Gaines was after—something specific, or just banking a favor?

"I remember being young and horny," said Gaines. "But this girl, like sticking your dick in the sewer. He wasn't using a condom, either."

"What is her... background?" asked the senator, trying to delicately fish out a very specific piece of information.

"She's white, if that's what you mean." Gaines opened a file folder on his desk. "Twenty-seven years old. In juvie when she was thirteen for selling drugs. Arrested a few times since then for hooking. In and out of rehab a couple of times for heroin. Bad news is, heroin means needles. I'd have Joe get tested if I were you, just to be safe."

Harlan Senior's stomach sank. He could see headlines, various and sundry:

Senator's Son Arrested with Known Drug Addict
Senator's Son Arrested with Prostitute
Senator's Son Dies of AIDS

None of them were pretty.

"I am stunned, Al. I don't know what to say. He's never done anything like this before, obviously. Never any indication."

"Hey. These things happen. I just... it doesn't make sense to let one mistake ruin the kid's life. This kind of thing, I mean, being who you are and all, if it got in the press, it'd be no good for him... or for you."

"I understand, Al. Thank you so much for your discretion."

Gaines smiled. "What are friends for, Joe?"

Harlan Senior had driven Joe home. He'd yelled; he'd lectured; he'd questioned his son, trying to understand what he thought he was doing. Joe had stayed mostly silent. In the end he'd cried.

"I don't know what's wrong with me, Dad. I don't want to. I want to be good. Sometimes I just feel like I *have* to do bad things. Like I can't control it."

Harlan Senior had held his son. "It's alright Joe, we'll find help."

Joe had begun seeing a therapist shortly thereafter. The senator had set it up so that it would be under the name John

Hughes. He'd wanted to be sure that none of this could come back to bite him on the ass.

The senator with the unstable son, the sex addict son.

When the whole Kristy Wise incident had happened, Harlan's worst nightmares had come true. All the headlines, worse than he'd imagined. The scrutiny. The accusations. The questions about his fitness as a father, having raised Joe as a single parent. He sometimes wondered if maybe he hadn't done enough—too much time spent on career, not enough on his own flesh and blood.

Part of that was what had driven him to hire Slipknot. He felt he owed it to Joe to find out what had happened if he could, and to make it right.

What a clusterfuck.

While Slipknot had gotten a confession out of Tom Wise—that Deb Wise and Susie Font had orchestrated the whole thing, that Tom Wise had hung Joe's penis on Harlan's front door—the confession was useless, as a legal matter. As Harlan understood, it had been obtained at gunpoint.

And then the stupid sonofabitch went and killed Tom Wise!

Still, the senator felt that he had done right by his boy. Deb and Tom Wise were now both dead. The information Slipknot had obtained tying Cruise and his wife to the whole mess was tainted at best, unreliable at worst.

And Slipknot wasn't really all there, was he?

That Halloween night, when Cruise had called Harlan from Slipknot's phone, the senator knew that he'd never hear from Slipknot again. He'd let things cool down a bit, and then he had reached out and made peace with Cruise. An uneasy truce, perhaps, but he hoped it would be a permanent one.

And, for whatever reason, Liz seemed much more at peace lately, as well. She still spoke of her own son, but she, too, seemed to have come to terms with the past. It had felt to Harlan like maybe everything in his life was finally normalizing once again. He was settling into his new job. Things were looking up.

But, now this...

Harlan turned back to his computer and the email from

Detective Eddie Garza that he'd been contemplating when Liz had called. Garza wanted to schedule a time to speak "informally" about Joe's case.

What the fuck does that sonofabitch want now?

Harlan typed up a reply, giving Garza a date after the holidays.

CHAPTER FIVE

Liz Bareto had been on pins and needles for several weeks. After receiving the anonymous package containing the syringe that possibly ended her son's life, she'd immediately contacted Maximiliano Ureña, the private investigator she'd been working with on Liam's case. M had come to her house and inspected what she'd received.

"And you're sure you don't want to just turn all of this over to the police? Or the FBI? It's what they do—"

"The police have been completely useless, M," she interrupted. They were sitting in her living room, the package on the coffee table in front of them. "It's been years since Liam died, and now I finally have proof that he was killed. They didn't discover it. It came *to me*. Someone wanted *me* to have this, not the cops."

The investigator nodded. "I understand. But if we go to the police—"

"Do you work for me or don't you?" Liz interrupted him again. "Well? Do you?"

M nodded.

"Then, we're going to do this my way. I want it checked out, and if there's anything there, *then* I'll go to the authorities... on *my* terms."

The private investigator sighed, then nodded. "Well, we can have all this analyzed. The letter, the box, everything, and see what prints and such we find on it. Trace materials and so on. And the syringe of course."

Liz shook her head adamantly. "The only thing I'm interested in is the syringe. Was it the murder weapon? Whose fingerprints are on it? Whoever sent it to me was good enough to go out of their way to risk a lot to get it to me. I think I owe it to them to do as they say and just test the syringe. Don't you?" She took the investigator's arm, and hissed, "I want to know if that syringe killed my boy, and who used it!"

In the end, she and the private investigator agreed to send just the syringe out for testing first. They would keep the box and letter that came with it in a large Ziploc bag to preserve them in the condition they were in when received. Just in case. But Liz had no intention of having them tested. She believed that her beau, Joe Harlan Senior, had acquired the evidence and sent it to her. And she didn't want to do anything to put him in jeopardy... at least not without first letting him know.

So many times, she'd come close to bringing up the subject with him. To thanking him. To asking him how he had come upon the syringe. But she also knew that his new role with the government was very sensitive. She didn't want to make waves or put Joe in a compromising position. She had no idea what it had taken to get the syringe. What favors he'd had to call in. And if he'd felt the need to send it to her anonymously, she didn't want to seem ungrateful by breaching that anonymity.

Liz wasn't stupid. She'd considered the possibility that the package hadn't come from Joe, but from somewhere else.

But who?

Eddie Garza makes no sense. He'd have had it analyzed himself. He wouldn't have sent it to me.

Some other random person who stumbled on it? Why? Why would they bother—take the risk—to get it to me?

It had to be Joe. After all, he told me in no uncertain terms, "They will be avenged Liz. I swear it on my life."

The analysis was taking forever. Liz believed that it should just take a matter of days. Weeks at most. But M had informed her that the average turnaround time in Florida for a basic forensic biology analysis—when there was a homicide suspect—was two to three months.

The wait time seemed ridiculous to Liz, but M insisted

that multiple tests needed to be run—DNA to determine if the syringe had been in Liam, analysis of any contents of the syringe, fingerprinting—and they needed to be done such that the results were beyond question.

Liz entrusted the matter to her private investigator and called him daily to check on the status. Still, she was on pins and needles.

CHAPTER SIX

After Eddie had arranged his interview with Harlan, he'd recalled Liz Bareto's email. It had been a while since he'd seen her. Ever since she'd gone to Austin chasing down Senator Harlan, he'd heard very little from her. Eddie had to admit that he was a bit jealous. It was silly, really. He was married, relatively happily. But there was just something about Liz.

Garza opened her recent email with the new "lead" regarding the dead congressman in Spain. He'd decided to read up on it, as it would give him an excuse to call her back and reconnect. Maybe he could turn it into a coffee date...

Eddie followed the link she'd provided—*Former Congressman Found Dead*—and read the article. It was an odd coincidence, to be sure. But, so what? Even if there was anything linking Cruise to Getz, it was way outside Eddie's jurisdiction.

While he ate a sandwich at his desk, Eddie piddled on his laptop, link-surfing, bouncing from article to article about Getz. After reading everything that seemed of interest about the former congressman's death, he began to delve into his past and how he had ended up in Spain.

In the end, it boiled down to corruption. Getz had been in the hip pocket of a number of mortgage lenders and entities that pushed to create and securitize sub-prime mortgages. He had been sued as part of a class action lawsuit brought by homeowners in 2011. While the whole mortgage fiasco was what led to his resignation from Congress, there had also been other minor scandals, infidelities, accusations of inappropriate sexual conduct, and so on. Once Eddie had a decent sense of who Getz was and how he had used his time in public office, he didn't have much pity for the dead man.

Eddie was about to let it go and get back to work when he bounced back to Getz's Wikipedia page and scrolled down to the *Further Reading* section. What jumped out at him was that a number of the articles in that section were authored by a single writer: William Applegate. Eddie scrolled up and saw that many of the *References* on the page also linked back to articles by William Applegate. And, because William Applegate was highlighted in blue, Eddie clicked on the hyperlink and found himself reading Applegate's Wikipedia page.

William Applegate... retired Wall Street Journal reporter... received a number of awards for investigative reporting... freelance writer... divorced... former member of the Vizcaya Museum and Gardens board of directors.

That last entry rang a loud bell for Eddie Garza. He did a quick search and discovered that the retired reporter lived in Coconut Grove—less than fifteen minutes from where Eddie was sitting. Down near the water.

Now that's *an odd coincidence, Eddie...*

Eddie checked his calendar and saw that he had a light afternoon ahead of him. The odds that it—the whole *Getz thing*—was a dead-end were almost 100% in Eddie's mind. But, if he looked into it, he could report back to Liz on what he'd done for her. It gave him an excuse to call her. And, it got him the hell out of the office early.

Eddie called it a day at 3:00 p.m. to give himself plenty of time to swing by Applegate's residence on his way home. The drive to Applegate's condo took almost forty minutes, as Eddie failed to account for the fact that mid-afternoon was school dismissal time, and there were several schools on the way to Applegate's home.

Applegate's retirement digs were nice in Eddie's estimation. The development was on the water down near Mercy Hospital, hidden on a side street. From what Eddie could see as he stood at the main entry gate and pressed the buttons to call up to Villa Two, all of the condos appeared to have a bay view.

"Can I help you?" a staticky male voice asked through the intercom.

"Detective Eddie Garza, Miami P.D. I wanted to speak with William Applegate."

The metal door next to Eddie emitted a mechanical buzzing sound and a loud *clack.* Eddie pushed and entered, following signage to Villa Two. As he climbed the last steps, he saw a partially open door, which he approached and knocked on.

"Come on in!" a voice shouted from inside.

As Eddie entered, he saw that his assumption was correct. He was standing in an open kitchen-living-dining room with large windows and a sliding glass door facing a balcony, and beyond it the bay.

"Beer?" Applegate asked, offering Eddie a sweaty can of Bud Light.

"Sure. I'm off duty."

Eddie took the can with his left hand and then shook Applegate's offered right hand. The man's hand was rough and dry, which seemed right to Eddie. He had a full head of white hair that he wore brushed back away from cornflower blue eyes. His skin was dark—not just tanned, but Miami Gold; the boater's tan. Eddie guessed the man spent a lot of time on the water.

"You can call me Billy. William's just for print. Come on..." Billy walked toward the open sliding glass door. Eddie followed. The condo was sparsely decorated, and Eddie was willing to bet Billy lived alone. The only feminine touches were a few family photos that Eddie quickly scanned on his way out to the small terrace. One photo was of Billy, an attractive woman, and two young adults—at a graduation ceremony. The rest appeared to be photos of the two young adults as children.

"To what do I owe the pleasure, Detective?" Billy asked as he took a seat on a chair and picked up a half-smoked cigar from an ashtray on the table in front of him and played with a lighter to get the cigar burning again. A small sofa facing the bay sat perpendicular to Billy's chair, and Eddie took a seat. Although it was December, winter hadn't yet hit. It was 82 degrees out on the terrace with a light breeze.

"Great view," Eddie said, looking straight out at the bay.

"It is." Billy turned to look. "It gets shallow down there," Billy used his cigar to indicate the water close to the docks belonging to the condo, "but deep enough for a small center console. That's mine over there. With the green bimini."

"Nice," Eddie sipped from the beer, as Billy took a puff from his cigar. "So, I assume you read about Getz? Drowned in Spain." Eddie studied Billy for a reaction.

"In the Bay of Pollença." Billy nodded matter-of-factly. "Yep."

"What do you think?"

A smile crawled across Billy's face. "Well, that's about as open-ended as they come, Detective." Billy picked at his tongue with his index finger and thumb, removing a bit of tobacco. "What do I think about what?"

Eddie smiled. "Well, I read about it online. And I saw that Getz... well, it seemed like you did a lot of writing about him. Thought you might have an opinion about him dying."

"Good riddance, I guess. Guy was as corrupt as they come. Shady deals. *Quid pro quo*. You name it. I don't think the '08 financial crisis could have happened without his help. Best thing that happened for U.S. politics in a while was Getz resigning. But, as far as him dying? He drowned, didn't he? Out for a swim..." Billy studied Eddie for a reaction. "Or... is there more to the story?"

Eddie shrugged. "Just a hunch, I guess. Did you still keep up with him? After he retired?"

"There wasn't much to follow—public information, I mean." Billy shook his head. "After he moved to Spain, he kind of dropped off the radar. Though, I suppose that was the point."

"Did he still do any business in the U.S.? Anything that you came across?"

"Last time he popped up on my radar was... in 2016? Maybe

‘17? He was supposed to give the commencement speech at his law school—University of Arkansas.” Billy chuckled. “Some protestors threw balloons at him. They were full of shit.”

Eddie coughed, choking on a sip of beer he'd been taking, and asked hoarsely, “The protestors or the balloons?”

“The balloons,” laughed Applegate.

Eddie chuckled and coughed some more, clearing his throat. “Have you heard of a company called Cruise Capital?”

Billy shrugged and shook his head. “Nope. Should I have?” He puffed from his cigar.

“Not really. No.” Eddie shook his head. “Like I said, just chasing a hunch.”

CHAPTER SEVEN

The best way to tell that it was winter in Miami was by how early the sun set. The temperature was no indicator. Even though there was a bit of breeze coming in from the sea, it was still in the eighties. But, by five-thirty in the afternoon, it was dark.

Roy Cruise was almost home. He'd taken off work a bit early to go to the gun range. His main objective had been to pick up some recent purchases. But once there, he'd taken the opportunity to do a bit of shooting.

As he drove through the gate into his subdivision of Lago Beach, he felt safer—at home. Though it was dark out, the neighborhood was lit up by strategically placed security lights and by Christmas lighting and decorations that gave everything a homey feel.

For a while, after returning from Spain, Roy had been on edge. Even at home. They had barely landed, and while he was still trying to get the adrenaline from killing Getz out of his system, they'd been attacked in their own home. Although it had ended well—thanks to Kristy Wise—and he'd gotten rid of the body, Roy didn't feel safe. Knowing that Harlan had the balls to come after them like that worried Roy.

Roy had previously emailed Harlan—while still in Spain—proposing a meeting at the senator's Austin office. His hope had been to deny any knowledge regarding Joe Junior's death, and to make peace with the senator. At that point, Roy knew that his partner David Kim had gotten beat up by a guy asking questions about Joe Harlan Junior. Roy suspected Senator Harlan was behind it and was probably coming for him and Susie. He'd confirmed his suspicions when he used the dead assassin's phone to dial the only recently called number on the phone and Senator Harlan answered.

From that point forward, as far as Roy was concerned, all bets were off. He had to make sure things were safe for Susie. She didn't need added stress during her pregnancy. So, Roy had begun planning how to eliminate Harlan.

That is why he was surprised when earlier that month on December 3rd, his assistant buzzed him in his office, and announced, "Roy, a Senator Harlan is here to see you. He's not on your calendar, but he insists that you'll be happy to see him."

Roy had sat motionless for several beats, shocked. Then cleared his throat and said, "Put him in the Bay View," referring to a mid-sized conference room at Cruise Capital that had a view of the bay. As he stood and tried to guess at what the senator had planned, Roy removed a small key from his pocket and opened the bottom right drawer of his desk.

Is he here to kill me?

Or just to talk?

If it's to talk, assume he's wearing a wire.

From the drawer, Roy removed the handgun that he'd begun carrying since returning from Spain. It was in a small holster. He looked at it, thinking.

How do I inconspicuously carry this into the fucking conference room?

Roy slipped the handgun into his laptop case. He placed his laptop on top, then put a legal pad on top of that. He placed a thick file folder for a deal he'd been reviewing on top of everything, then made his way to the conference room. As he pushed the door open, he could see through the glass that the senator was standing facing the widows, admiring the view. Roy studied his silhouette, but didn't see the outline of a concealed weapon printing through the senator's suit jacket. Roy put everything down on the table, positioning the laptop case so that he could get to the handgun if necessary.

"Mr. Cruise," the senator said as he turned. "You stood me up for our meeting November 5th."

"I had a feeling you wouldn't want to meet."

The senator moved toward the table and took a chair opposite Roy. "Didn't your parents teach you that it's rude to leave people hanging?" The senator smirked, then looked up over Roy's shoulder. As Roy was about to answer, he heard the conference room door opening behind him. The hair on the back of his neck stood on end.

Shit! The bastard distracted me.

Roy turned abruptly, his hand reaching for his laptop case, only to see his assistant Eve entering with a cup of coffee. Eve was a piece of work. Long-ago divorced, she'd raised three boys as a single mom. She was in her late fifties, but looked to be forty-something. She was Roy's eyes and ears at Cruise Capital. She placed the coffee in front of the senator, who thanked her and studied her appreciatively as she walked away. Eve asked, "Can I bring you anything, Mr. Cruise?"

Roy shook his head and took the seat across from Harlan as the senator sipped from his cup and eyed the stack Roy had placed on the table. The glass conference room door made a slight *poof* sound as it closed behind Eve.

"As the Martians always say, Mr. Cruise, 'I come in peace.' No need for that," Harlan gestured at the stack with his head. "I'll come right to the point." The senator looked down at his hands for a moment, pursed his lips slightly and cleared his throat, then looked Roy in the eye. "We have both been visited by tragedy. We both know what it is like to lose a child. And... well..." Harlan sipped from his coffee. "I understand from your last phone call to me, that a gentleman known to me—but I assure you, acting on his own and without my consent—may have visited you, and that it ended badly for him." Harlan paused and studied Roy, who nodded once, saying nothing.

"Well now, Mr. Cruise, my understanding from this gentleman, which I will not ask you to confirm or deny, is that Debra Wise was behind what happened to my son, Joe. Oh, the husband Tom may have played a small role," Harlan waved a hand at the air, "but in the end, the instigator was Deb Wise."

The man paused for a moment, but Roy made no move to comment on any of what he had just said.

"Ironic, isn't it, that she would eat a bullet?" Harlan titled his head, as if cracking his neck. "I say *ironic* because that happened without the aid or intervention of my friend. I assure you, I have no idea who did it or why Mrs. Wise was killed." Harlan looked sad, though he chuckled and said, "As the Good Book says, 'Vengeance is Mine, so sayeth the Lord.'"

He shrugged, then leaned forward putting his elbows on the conference table, the coffee cup and saucer sitting between his two open arms. "My point, sir. The reason that I am here is to tell you to your face that *I am at peace*. As far as I am concerned, Joe's death has been avenged. I want to know nothing further about it." Harlan raised his hand for emphasis, "I bear you neither good will nor ill." Then he pointed at Roy and hissed, "I simply want you the fuck out of my life."

Harlan sat back in his chair, took a sip of coffee, then said in a normal tone, "I have come to ask whether you want the same."

Roy sat for several moments eyeing Harlan. "I think we can agree on that one point."

"Well then," Harlan stood, "I give you my word, on everything I hold sacred, that I will leave you and yours in peace, so help me God. Will you do the same?"

Harlan held out his hand and stood waiting, staring Roy down.

This guy's very old school.

Roy stood slowly, not taking his eyes off Harlan.

"Why come all the way here for this, Joe?" he asked.

Harlan kept his hand outstretched and said, "Didn't seem like something to be done by phone. And, as I said, Joe has been avenged. So, I'm through with this whole mess. But, putting myself in your shoes, to be quite blunt, I'd be on edge. I'd be wondering whether 'Harlan's sending someone else after me. Or my wife.' If I were you, I'd want to get ahead of the curve by trying to take me out. I assure you, you'd fail. Especially given the level of security my new role comes with—a nice perk."

Roy feigned ignorance of Harlan's job change, raising his eyebrows, but he was all ears. The man had unexpectedly retired from the Texas Senate a few weeks prior, citing "health concerns." There were rumors that he'd been tapped for some sort of NSA or possibly CIA role, but nothing Roy had been able to confirm as of yet.

"But, like I said, I'm done," Harlan waved his hands casually, "with all of this. And I'd sleep better at night knowing that you aren't plotting my death."

He once again held his hand out to Roy, who this time reached out and firmly shook Harlan's hand, saying simply, "Peace."

After Roy told Susie about Harlan's impromptu visit, she asked the same question that Roy had puzzled over after the senator left the Bay View Conference Room.

"Do you believe him, Roy? Can we trust him?"

CHAPTER EIGHT

Roy pulled into the garage. He brought two large bags with him into the house and unpacked them on the kitchen island.

"Hello, helloooo," Susie called out.

"In the kitchen! I come bearing gifts," he replied.

Susie waddled in and gave her husband a peck on the lips. At almost six months pregnant, she was showing and just beginning to experience discomfort and back pains. She was wearing blue denim pregnancy pants and an oversized white linen top. She was barefoot, as was her preference. Her hair was thick—she'd been letting it grow long—her breasts full, eyes sparkling. Roy recalled how her first pregnancy had also agreed with her. Susie was glowing.

"What have we got here?" she asked, looking at the packages on the island. "Baby shower's still two weeks away," she smiled, "and I don't think I registered for these."

Roy laughed. It was obvious from the boxes—three handguns and a lot of ammunition. In addition to the smaller Glock 26 subcompact that Roy normally kept in the safe but had begun carrying regularly since returning from Spain, he had purchased two standard size Glock 17s and another Glock 26 for Susie to carry.

"These two," he indicated the larger pistols, "are going in the safes." Roy had installed a quick access safe in the master bedroom that was big enough to accommodate the larger gun and opened by means of a mechanical push-button combination. "One in the new safe. And one in the office safe. And this little guy," he said, holding up the smaller gun that was almost identical to the one they already owned, "is for you to carry." He offered it to his wife, butt first.

Susie studied the smaller gun while her hands unconsciously went to her belly, protectively. She sighed, then reached out and took the small pistol from her husband.

She held the gun in her right hand, feeling its heft. "It's got a nice weight to it. Same as the old one? As far as functionality, I mean? It feels heavier..."

"Identical," he replied.

Susie drew the slide, held the gun up, and pointed it out the window, assuming the Weaver stance. "Kinda stiff. Needs oiling and some use, I guess."

She placed the gun back on top of its box.

Roy replied, "Look Susie. I think—I really hope—that Harlan is out of our lives for good. I think I believe him. But I'd feel better knowing you had this handy, just in case."

Susie nodded and replied, "Is it okay if you carry the new one? If I'm gonna carry, I'd prefer the old one. Since it's already broken in."

"Sure. I'll trade you. Where should I put it?" he asked, removing their old gun from his computer bag. It was in a black nylon holster.

"Just drop it in my purse." Susie pointed at the breakfast island, where a mid-sized black Gucci bag sat on one of the four chairs.

As Roy complied, Susie moved toward the refrigerator. "You hungry? I'm famished."

Susie began making dinner while Roy put the two larger guns in their respective safes. On the way back to the kitchen, he stopped by the dining room and got a bottle of Barolo out of the wine fridge. As he carefully uncorked the bottle and poured himself a glass, Susie looked on with a bit of envy.

"The guns... the ones in the safes. I put them away loaded, okay?"

"Got it," she replied, "and the ammo?"

"All in the office."

She nodded, then held out a hand and said, "One sip." He handed her his wineglass, and she took a small mouthful, swirled it, then spat it out in the sink.

"Damn," she said. "Great bottle."

Roy took a swallow and nodded.

CHAPTER NINE

For the first time in years, Kristy Wise was happy. It was Tuesday, December 31st. New Year's Eve. Looking out the window to her room, she could see Beaver Creek Village down below, all lit up for the holidays. Christmas lights were everywhere, and she could make out the movement of holiday merrymakers in the plaza. Not so different from the last time she had been here, with her parents. With the Rosens. Still, so much had changed.

Kristy was already all dressed up for the evening. She'd taken a cue from Alfie's cousins, Alma and Bella—nothing too fancy. Jeans, Uggs, a black cashmere turtleneck. They were all to have an early dinner together with Alfie's uncle and aunt, then the young ones—*los jovenes*—would go off and ring in the new year with friends. Alfie's family owned a house up on the mountain just above Beaver Creek Village, and she'd been invited to stay in the family home. When he'd initially proposed spending the new year together, she hadn't expected it to be a family affair. Once she understood what was involved, she'd experienced some trepidation.

Alfie had lived with his aunt and uncle from an early age, and his two cousins were like sisters to him. For Kristy, meeting them involved the usual "Will his family like me?" insecurity. But, of course, that was amplified by the additional meet the "girlfriend who was allegedly date-raped, whose mother was recently murdered, and whose father then committed suicide" baggage. When she'd thought about it, she'd felt like curling up in a ball in her closet.

Had it not been for Alfie's pigheaded insistence, she would have begged off. She was glad she hadn't. She had been accepted by the entire family with open arms.

Would they be so nice to me if they knew the whole story?

When she'd returned to Austin from Miami, she'd done so intent on revenge. She'd learned in Miami, from the man she'd killed at the Cruise's home, that Frank Stern had raped her the same night as Joe Harlan Junior. Frank had supplied the roofies that had made it possible, and he was also the source of the drugs that had later landed Bethany in the hospital. He needed to pay. Kristy had already been planning that revenge, with Bethany's help.

After hearing from Susie about how she and Roy had been so careful in planning the murder of Joe Harlan Junior, she'd worried that her plan for Stern might be too slapdash. That she hadn't prepared enough. She needed help from someone she could trust. And while she knew she could trust Bethany with her life, she needed someone to help her execute the plan who was unknown to Frank Stern. Someone he wouldn't recognize. She had turned to Alfie. And he'd come through.

Now, she needed to share the latest with him. There hadn't been time yet. But, given his involvement, if there was any risk that they might get caught, it was only fair that he know. Kristy picked up her phone and scrolled to the text message she had received from Pippa Warren.

Pippa: *Well-played! I hope the bastard rots in hell.*

Kristy had received it earlier that morning. She had yet to reply. She'd needed to talk it over with someone first. Bethany had told her to just blow it off.

"Frank and Pippa broke up. And Pippa's a fuckin' idiot, Kris. You know that."

"But it's clearly a tease. She knows something, she's not sharing what, and she's talking like I know and I had something to do with it, whatever *it* is," Kristy replied.

"Well then, your other option is to call her. Dial 'er up and play dumb. See what she has to say. You know she's dumb as a box of rocks. But if you call her, call in the evening.

At that point, she'll be either drunk or high. You'll get more out of her..."

Kristy was worried. As she locked her phone screen, she looked at the photo of the three of them—Alfie, Bethany, and Kristy—that Bethany took the night Kristy had first met Alfie. It had been taken less than three hundred yards from where she was standing now. So much had happened since then.

Kristy sighed.

What the hell does Pippa know?

She hated not knowing. It worried her. It ate at her. Especially because it wasn't just her that was at risk. She needed to talk it through with Alfie. Together, they could decide what to do.

CHAPTER TEN

Alfie was wearing a plaid wool shirt with jeans and snow boots. After finishing his MBA and starting work, he'd shortened his blond hair. Not military short by any means, but too short to put it in a ponytail. It was still long enough in back that it brushed the edge of his shirt collar, which was a Dress Gordon Tartan that made his blue eyes pop. He was sipping on a rum hot toddy and had taken the news of Pippa's text message with aplomb.

"So call her," he shrugged. After three years living in Austin, his British accent was lighter than when Kristy had first met him, but it was still noticeable.

"And say what?" Kristy asked.

He nodded. "It's simple. You have no idea what she's talking about. So, you ask her what she's referring to. Get her to talk. Deny everything."

Kristy dialed the number, placing one Airpod in her right ear and giving the other to Alfie, who sidled up next to her, his right cheek against her left. He smelled of shampoo and rum, and his stubble pricked her cheek. Alfie never wore cologne.

"Hello Kristy!" answered a voice she immediately recognized as Pippa Warren.

"Hey Pippa. Happy New Year!"

"You too!"

Kristy could hear a television in the background. "Listen, I was just calling 'cuz I saw your text and... well, I didn't quite know what to make of it?"

"Are you sure? Or are you just bein' coy?" Pippa had a slight

East Texas drawl that came out when she was being extra friendly. And when she drank.

"No coy here. Really. But it sounded interesting—you got my curiosity up. Who do we want to rot in hell?"

"Frank, of course! Frank Stern. Are you bullshittin' me? You really don't know nuthin'?"

"No bullshit, Pippa," Kristy lowered her voice, conspiratorially, and asked, "What happened?" Kristy could hear the TV sounds fading, as though Pippa were walking to another room.

"Well, you know I broke up with Frank a while back? Piece of shit was cheatin' on me with some MILF up in north Austin. I let him have it. Told him off. Made all sorts o' threats. Well, a coupl'a weeks ago, he calls me up like at five in the mornin' all pissed off, claimin' I stole his money and his drugs from him. Bunch a crap. He was kinda slurrin'. I chalked it up to him bein' wasted or high. Hung up on 'im. And that's that.

"Well, just yesterday, he calls me back, apologizin'. Wantin' my help.

"Says he's in debt to his supplier. He bought some time, but he's gotta pay soon, and he needs everything back. He needs his money and drugs. I'm thinkin' he still thinks I did it, but he's tryin' to soften me up. So, he explains what happened. He was at a bar. And he hears from Joe Harlan—not the dad," she paused for emphasis, "but the *dead one*, you know, dickless Joe..." She laughed. "Frank claims he starts gettin' texts from him. They go back and forth. And Frank sets up a meetin' with 'im at the bar. Supposably, o'l dickless was gonna meet Frank.

"So, Frank's there waitin' for 'im. Well, next thing you know, this other guy strikes up a conversation with him. With Frank, I mean... All he remembers is he was blond, blue eyes, had an English accent, and claimed he was into start-ups. Guy buys him a coupl'a drinks. Well, Frank thinks he roofied him. 'Cuz next thing he knows he wakes up at home and all his shit's gone!"

"No fuckin' way?" Kristy noted that one conspicuous detail about Frank's condition when he awoke was omitted.

"Yes fuckin' way!" Pippa replied. "So, of course, I told him

I had nuthin' to do with it and I had no idea who could'a done it. But, when he mentioned the blond guy with the English accent, it reminded me of that friend of Bethany's—the one you showed up with at my house the night she OD'd. I just put two and two together, you know..."

Kristy did her best not to hesitate in replying. "Wow. That's a crazy story, Pippa. And I... you know I have no love lost for that piece of shit. But I really don't know anything about his stuff... I mean, like, who stole it or whatever—"

"Really? Nuthin'?" Pippa replied skeptically, her voice rising in pitch at the end of each word.

"No. I mean, I remember the guy you're talking about. But, he's a straight-laced type. He wouldn't be into stealing drugs or money..."

"Yeah," Pippa conceded. "I remember he was kinda a goody-two-shoes. Cute and all, but yeah..."

"I don't know what to tell you—"

"Well, shit... girl. It's cool. I don't need to know nuthin'. Hell, I don't *wanna* know nuthin'. Consider this me tellin' you that somebody out there is fuckin' with Frank Stern. And if you know who they are, tell 'em Pippa said, 'More power to ya!' And if you don't, well at least now you know that someone stole all of Frank's shit and... you can share in the joy!" Pippa laughed. "It's the holidays, right?"

Kristy laughed with her.

After hanging up, Kristy said to Alfie, "She was so fucked up that night. How could she remember you?"

"She was fucked up when you saw her, Kris, back at her apartment. When I got there earlier, before Bethany went to the hospital, she'd had a couple of drinks, but she was pretty damned sober. In fact, she's the one I talked with most about calling 9-1-1."

"Well, shit." Kristy shook her head. "The last thing I wanted was—"

"Shhh..." Alfie shushed her gently. "You're not in this alone. We're in this together. It doesn't sound like she even remembers my name. And she definitely sounded happy about what happened to Frank." Alfie took Kristy's hand in his and gave her a peck on the lips. "Let's not worry for now. There's nothing we can do about what she thinks she knows."

CHAPTER ELEVEN

Joe Harlan was seated in a large conference room. He had just reviewed Detective Eddie Garza's email for the umpteenth time, hoping to extract from it some inkling as to what the call was about.

Just a few questions relating to your son's case.

It annoyed Harlan not to know what had triggered the interview. He was curious to hear what Detective Garza had to say. But if it had anything to do with Tom Wise or Slipknot—any of that whole mess—he planned to play dumb. He'd long since destroyed the burner phone, so there was nothing of consequence connecting him to Slipknot. As he sat there mentally reviewing his "story," the conference room phone came to life, a woman's voice announcing, "Detective Garza is on line five, sir."

"Thank you, dear," Harlan said, then cringed. That "dear" thing didn't go over well in D.C. Everyone here was so touchy. He had to work on that.

Hashtag Me—Fucking—Too... he thought.

Harlan shook his head—old habits—then pressed the button.

After some introductory chat, Detective Garza began, "Thanks again for taking the time to talk with me, sir. I'm following up some leads and wanted to see if you could answer a couple of questions for me, informally for now."

"However I can assist, Detective."

"Does the name Ronald Clayton ring a bell?"

Harlan sat back in his chair. Eddie could hear it creak.

So, this is *about Slipknot. Goddammit!* Harlan thought.

The senator scoffed, "Ronald Clayton. My goodness.

Absolutely. Though I haven't heard that name in years. We met way back—when I was in the military. In *El Salvador*." Harlan pronounced the name of the country in Spanish.

"Do you recall when you last had contact with him?" Garza asked.

"With Clayton? Well, it would have been years ago, Detective. Decades. But, what does he have to do with Joe?"

"Well, sir, we have reason to believe that he paid a visit to Roy Cruise and his wife at their home. And he hasn't been seen since."

"Well, I'll be," Harlan feigned astonishment and shook his head, though there was no one present to see. "Clayton? At Cruise's? But, why?"

"Well, that's just it, sir. When we searched Clayton's home, it appears that he was investigating your son's disappearance. He had files, photos, notes..." Eddie paused and looked at the copy of Clayton's file on Joe Harlan Junior that sat on the desk in front of him.

Harlan leaned forward, closer to the phone, and spoke deliberately, "Well, I haven't the slightest idea. Files and photos of Joe, you say? Had he uncovered anything new?"

"Nothing that we didn't already know. Are you sure you haven't contacted him or been contacted by him recently?"

"Of that, I'm sure, Detective."

"Well, we have his phone records. And, there is one odd text message there, from him to you." Garza was looking at the transcript.

"To me? Ronald Clayton? Impossible. I would remember that, Detective." Harlan paused. As Eddie remained silent, Harlan continued on to what he believed would be the obvious next question an innocent person would ask, "What did the message he supposedly sent me say?"

"It said, 'Mission accomplished.'"

"Well... I'll be damned!" Harlan exclaimed in a stage whisper. "Now," Harlan paused for a moment, and actually searched his phone, finding the message. "Hold on now." After a few moments, he continued, "Well, here it is! Halloween night, or morning, I guess... just after midnight. I did get that message. Completely out of the blue. But I had no idea who it was from. I saw it the next day, and I replied at 9:03 a.m. 'Who is this? Wrong number?' And I never got a reply."

Harlan paused, smiling smugly.

"Yes sir," Eddie replied, "we saw that as well. In Clayton's phone log."

"So, you're telling me that was Ronald Clayton? That he sent that message?"

"Well, it was sent from his phone, yes sir."

Harlan sat in silence, waiting. Then he said, "Well, I had no idea. I thought it was just a wrong number. How did he get my number? Do you have any idea what he meant? What mission? He never replied to my questions, you know..."

"We don't know what he was referring to, sir. Not yet. I have my suspicions, but..." Eddie changed tack, "Do you, by any chance, have another phone, sir?"

"Well, I have my home phone, and my office number, then there's the number you called here—"

"I mean a mobile number, sir. Another mobile phone?"

"That, I do not, Detective." Harlan smiled ear to ear. He sensed that Garza was running out of runway. There was a pause.

"It's just that we also have records showing that he was in communication with someone else in Austin. Well, at least a phone number with an Austin area code. Is there, perhaps, someone in Austin who you know—a mutual contact or acquaintance—that might have been in contact with Clayton?"

"No one that I can think of."

Garza sighed. "You know, sir. This is off the record. But, with all the research he was doing, I think that maybe Clayton found something implicating Cruise—connecting him to your son's disappearance. That he went to the house to confront him. And that Cruise... made him disappear." Eddie paused.

Harlan sat in silence.

Eddie went on, "If you have any knowledge, or if, after you

think on it, you recall any contact with Clayton that might shed some light on what he was up to, or what he found out, it could get us closer to finding out what happened to Joe. And to getting justice for him."

Harlan had to give Eddie credit for trying a more emotional appeal.

"There is nothing I'd like more than to finally know what happened to Joe, Detective. Nothing more in the world. And if you have evidence against someone, anyone, I'll be there to do everything I can to help you. But I'm afraid that I have no idea what Clayton was up to."

"I understand." Eddie was about to wrap up the call, then added, "One last question, sir—you said you met Clayton in the military?"

"That's right. *El Salvador.*"

"I had no idea that you'd served, sir."

"Oh yes, graduated the Academy in 1980. I went to law school after I got out of the Army."

"And you met Clayton there, in *El Salvador*?" Eddie used the Spanish pronunciation as well.

"I did."

"Was that your first deployment?"

"It was, actually. Why do you ask?"

"No reason. Just curious. Well, thank you for your service, sir."

CHAPTER TWELVE

Eddie updated Shaw on his conversation with Harlan. They were seated in a conference room at the State Attorney's office. It had been a little over two months since Ronald Clayton entered the Cruise house, never to be seen again.

"He was just too slick, you know? Like he'd rehearsed," Eddie editorialized. "The normal thing would have been for him to say, 'Well, if you know Clayton texted me, then you also know how I replied.' Something like that. But instead he pretended like he was looking the message up on his phone. I dunno—something about it just didn't ring true. And then, he met the guy on his first deployment. Maybe Clayton wouldn't call him 'Cherry' now, not to his face—but that's definitely military slang for newbies."

Shaw accepted as true that Harlan was lying—because Eddie's intuition said so. Shaw had been doing this kind of work long enough to understand how intuition worked. With all of Eddie's experience, his intuition was like a supercomputer processing millions of inputs and coming to a conclusion. Eddie's efforts to justify that conclusion were just that, an attempt to explain to Shaw—and to his own rational brain—why *he believed* what his gut was telling him. Even if the logic rationalizing the intuition was weak, that didn't change the value of the output.

"Do you think if we press harder, we might get something more out of him? Or if we offer immunity?" Shaw asked.

Eddie shrugged. "Hard to say. I don't know what he stands to lose, in his new job and all. But, if it's to put Cruise away, maybe."

"Then, as far as other possible witnesses to what happened

to Clayton, all we've got is Kristy Wise?" It was stated in the form of a question, but it was rhetorical. They both knew the answer.

Eddie nodded. "And Cruise and the missus..." he chuckled.

Shaw rolled his eyes. The privilege that protected one spouse from testifying against the other was understood by both and didn't need to be mentioned by name.

"So, it's all down to this Wise chick," Shaw said. "What do you know about her?"

"Not a lot. I think Travers has gotten to know her pretty well. He might be able to shed some light."

"Will he take a call?" Shaw asked, motioning with his head at Eddie's mobile phone on the table in front of them.

Eddie raised an eyebrow, scrolled through his contacts, and called Travers on speaker.

"Detective Eddie Garza! Please tell me you're not calling from the shitter again?"

"Actually, Art, I'm calling from the State Attorney's Office. I have one of our prosecutors, Attorney Spencer Shaw, here with me," Eddie deadpanned.

As Eddie spoke, Shaw shook his head slowly and rolled his eyes, then added, "Hi Art, nice to meet you. And don't let Eddie fool you. It's well known here in Miami that he does his best work on the toilet."

"Hey," Eddie chimed in, "for me, it's all about the *outcome*—you know, *delivering* results. What's important is *what comes out* in the end."

The three laughed, then shifted to more serious matters. Eddie and Shaw gave Travers a summary of where things stood with Ronald Clayton's disappearance.

"So, Art. You know Kristy Wise pretty well. Do you think she'd be cooperative? As a witness?" Eddie asked.

"Well..." Travers paused, thinking. "It's hard to say really. How far are you prepared to go? Would you offer her immunity?"

Eddie looked at Shaw and shrugged. Shaw pursed his lips and nodded.

Travers continued, "I mean, if this guy Clayton entered the

house the same night as Kristy, and didn't come back out due to some sort of foul play—if she knows anything about it, that makes her an accessory in some shape or fashion. This young lady has seen plenty of how the legal system works—and doesn't work. I'm pretty sure she's not gonna talk to me on the record without talking to her lawyer first. I'm just guessing, but... I'm pretty sure."

"Immunity is doable," Shaw said.

"Okay, fine," Travers replied. "What I'd suggest then is that I connect with her. See if I can get her to tell me anything, kinda casual-like. And if she lawyers up, then I'll have her attorney call you direct?"

Shaw nodded at Eddie, who replied, "Sounds like a plan."

After they hung up with Travers, Shaw said, "So, Eddie, I've been thinking about Cruise. I re-read the transcript of your interview with him—about Harlan's disappearance. What was there about it that stood out in your mind?"

Eddie thought for a moment, then said, "Bottom line, that he had no motive. No connection to the kid. No reason to want him dead. It's what killed the case. We had all these little bits of circumstantial evidence that—with a motive—might have turned into something. But he had no motive. No motive, no case."

"I think it's that *plus*... See, Eddie, I've tried to put myself in this guy's shoes. And the thing I don't get is, why didn't he just plead the Fifth? Just refuse to answer any questions? Wouldn't that have been safer?

"I think I know why he didn't. Assume for a moment that I wanted to kill this Harlan kid in premeditated cold blood. As a lawyer, the first thing I'd worry about is my motive. If I have a reason to want this kid dead, my odds of getting away with it just fell by at least half. Probably a whole lot more.

"I think Cruise had no motive. He made a big deal about that with you because I think it's true. I think he was clear on that point from the start. And, because it was true, it gave him freedom. He put together a very careful plan, and he stuck to it—no surprises, and most importantly, no witnesses. That's why he was comfortable answering all your questions. He could tell you a version of what happened that you really couldn't poke any holes in.

"But I think this Clayton thing is different. I don't think Cruise planned on it. Clayton comes to the guy's front door, and meanwhile, Kristy Wise jumps their fence. And in a costume? I'm willing to bet that Cruise and his wife weren't expecting either Clayton or Wise to show up at their house. Cruise has no idea how much info we have on Clayton and why he came a callin' that night.

"If we have evidence, which we do, that Clayton was investigating Cruise and found something incriminating, then *Cruise has a motive to kill him*. And if Clayton showed up unexpectedly, *Cruise had no plan*. And if Kristy Wise showed up unexpectedly and saw what happened, *there's a witness*.

"Can he trust Kristy Wise? Can he be sure what she'll say if she's called in as a witness?"

"It is a very different scenario," Eddie agreed.

"Call the sonofabitch up, Eddie. Let's bring them both in for questioning. Him and his friend David Kim. But keep it real casual. Tell him we want to question him about Kim's hit-and-run. And then, once we've got them at the table, we'll poke and prod a little and see what they cough up. Call Cruise directly. If anyone can trip him up, I bet you can."

CHAPTER THIRTEEN

While Billy had helped me pick out my office space years earlier, he'd not been in to see me there since our divorce. As a result, it seemed strange to me to have Billy show up at work. He'd popped in unannounced, and I had him wait in my private office until I had an opening for him. He then explained that he'd wanted to see me to tell me about his surprise visit from Detective Garza *in person*, in case they "were listening." Bugging his phone, I suppose. After years investigating corrupt politicians, Billy had seen a lot. He tended to be a little paranoid.

When Billy initially told me about what Jeff Getz did to him as a child, I didn't tell him anything about what I was planning. To me, what Getz did hurt not only Billy, but I still believe the damage Billy suffered from it doomed our marriage to fail. I suppose I wanted revenge on Getz for both of us—for our entire family really.

Getz drowned less than six months after Billy told me, for the first time, what happened to him as a child. A few months later, at Christmas, when we got together with the kids, Billy took me aside to tell me that Getz had turned up dead. Billy had followed all the news. It had ultimately been ruled an accidental drowning. The only odd fact was that Getz's girlfriend swore that the swim goggles he'd been found wearing weren't his. She'd claimed that the two of them used the same brand. The police had apparently discounted her opinion, so she'd taken to the press with the information.

As Billy told me all of this on Christmas Eve, he studied me. Watching for a reaction. At least, that's how it felt to me. I'd already had a few glasses of wine. I was a bit drunk. It was stupid. But I never violated any confidences. I simply told Billy that he wasn't the only one with connections.

"I know some pretty bad people too," I told him. He nodded, his eyes small, lips tight, expressing something between skepticism and respect. I left it at that, but I still cringe when I think about it.

We hadn't discussed Getz again after that night. His visit to tell me about Detective Garza was the closest we'd come to addressing the topic.

"It felt like a fishing expedition," he summed up. "Very informal. I mean, I'll give the guy credit for instincts. But I don't think he's got anything more than a hunch."

"It worries me that he even found you, though. Don't you think that's odd?"

"He said it was because I'd written so much about Getz. That's not unreasonable, Cat."

I hated it when Billy called me that. It was a familiarity that I felt he'd long ago lost the right to, but I let it go.

He continued, "After he left, I went online and fished around to see what I could find—the latest on Getz's disappearance—which would be the logical thing for me to do as a journalist after getting a visit from a cop. I also trolled around looking at this company he mentioned, Cruise Capital."

He studied me, but I maintained a poker face. Billy didn't know anything about Susie and Roy. He didn't even know they were my patients. Best to keep it that way, I thought.

"The owner's a guy named Roy Cruise," he continued. "Lives not too far from here, in Lago Beach. I looked online for anything tying Cruise Capital and Getz together. There's absolutely nothing connecting them. But, it's all strange enough that I thought you should know..."

I thanked Billy for the information. He agreed to let me know if he heard anything further from the police, and I let him find his way out of the office.

I knew I needed to tell Roy about the visit. My only doubt

was whether I should wait until our next therapy session. This seemed like something he would want to know immediately.

I must confess that, as I'd gotten to know Roy better through our work together, I'd begun to look forward to our weekly sessions. To spending time with him. I considered calling him to tell him about Garza's visit to Billy, or maybe to meet him somewhere to give him the information. But, in the end, I knew I was just making an excuse to spend extra time with Roy, and I decided to wait.

CHAPTER FOURTEEN

When Roy's assistant Eve buzzed him and advised that Detective Garza was calling, Roy wasn't surprised. He'd already been to therapy that week and gotten an update from me on Garza's visit to Billy. The police were poking around again. Roy knew it was time to lawyer up.

"Of course, Detective. I am always happy to cooperate in any way that I can," he replied to Garza's request for a meeting. Roy didn't even bother asking Garza what he wanted to talk about. That was better left to legal counsel. "Let me touch base with my lawyer and have him get back to you with dates."

"Aw, come on, Roy. It's just a few questions. Why don't we just get a beer and chat? I know a great pool hall in Little Havana."

"I'm avoiding beer, Detective. Carbs, you know. But I'll have Moran get back to you."

"Okay," Garza sighed. "Well, if we're gonna be formal about it, then I'd like to talk to you and your buddy David Kim, too. Just to see if he recalls anything else about his hit-and-run. Maybe his memory's clearing up?"

After speaking to Eddie Garza, Roy immediately called his friend and attorney, Mark Moran. Roy had first hired Moran years earlier when Garza had questioned Susie and Roy in the death of Liam Bareto. Moran was a well-respected criminal defense lawyer. As they'd gotten to know each other, he and Roy had discovered they shared a passion for good scotch and boats, though Moran was more of a freshwater boater and fisherman while Roy loved the sea.

Roy gave Moran a quick summary of his call with Garza, as well as an explanation of what had happened to David, and told him that it sounded as though the detective wanted to question them about the incident.

"Let's meet this Friday at my office and talk through everything," Moran suggested. "Just so we're prepared. Meanwhile, I'll call Garza and firm up a date for these interviews. And I'll try to see if I can get any additional insight into what he's looking for. We'll schedule the interviews for my office if that works for you?"

They checked their calendars and the best date for them both was Monday, February 10th.

That afternoon, Moran called Roy back. "According to Garza, he just wants to follow up on your buddy's hit-and-run. Sounds fairly innocuous, man. But we'll see."

Roy nodded. He wasn't completely satisfied with Garza's response. It had been several months since the hit-and-run, and the police hadn't previously reached out to question him. Plus, Garza's recent visit to Billy Applegate asking about Getz made Roy think Garza was up to something.

That evening, Roy told Susie about Eddie's call.

"Do you believe him?" she asked.

"I dunno. He's a cop. They all lie. Maybe it is about David. Maybe it's about Getz. Who the fuck knows. Maybe it's about Harlan Junior again."

"Well, you'll know soon enough. And remember, 'you have the right to remain silent.'" Susie smiled lightheartedly. But she could tell Roy was worried.

That worry became more evident during our therapy session the following Thursday. Roy grilled me again about everything that Billy had told me about his visit from Garza.

"It worries me that he tracked down Billy, Catherine. That's not good. Do you think Garza knows about the connection? Between us? Are you sure he didn't mention you at all—to Billy?"

"He didn't ask about me. At all. And he only mentioned Cruise Capital. Garza didn't even mention your name specifically. Billy was very clear about that."

"And Billy—"

From the look on Roy's face, I knew where he was headed,

and I cut him off, "Billy knows *nothing*. Not about you. Not about Susie. He'd never even heard of you until Garza brought up Cruise Capital. I haven't told Billy anything. Ever. I swear."

Roy seemed to accept that and sat shaking his head. "I just don't get it. What is he playing at? What if all of this is actually about Getz?"

"Billy felt confident that Garza was just fishing. That he really didn't have an angle."

I wanted to help. To offer suggestions. But I felt out of my depth. I understood that the police connecting me and Roy and Billy could be problematic. I did remind Roy that everything we discussed was privileged. That seemed to give him some comfort.

The following day, Roy and David met with Moran. There was little to discuss. Roy was out of the country when David's accident happened. And, contrary to what Roy knew to be the truth, David told Moran what he'd told the police, that he remembered nothing about the hit-and-run.

David still vividly recalled the threat the man in the green jacket had made about talking to the police. He had no idea what had actually happened to Mr. Ronald Clayton. He did not know that the man formerly known as Slipknot was feeding fish two thousand feet under the Florida Straits. Nonetheless, David Kim saw nothing to be gained by changing his story at that point.

CHAPTER FIFTEEN

It was a big day for Liz Bareto. It had started like any other Friday: Pilates at the gym, then a shower. By nine o'clock, she was at her kitchen table having a yogurt and catching up on the news when her phone rang. It was M—her private detective. The DNA results were back and in her email.

She opened the email, and read and re-read the report through tears. No fingerprints. Not on the syringe. Not on the Ziploc. Negative results on the contents of the syringe. The lab had been unable to identify any residue from anything that may at one time have been placed inside the syringe or which the syringe had been used to inject.

But, the needle on the syringe had tested positive for Liam's DNA. That syringe had been in her baby's arm.

Her ex-husband. The police. They were all wrong. There was no doubt now. That thing had killed him! She had proof.

Finally, she had proof!

"I'm not an obsessed mother who just *couldn't let go!*" she shouted out loud to no one. "I was right! Liam was *muuuurdered!*"

Liz screamed at the top of her lungs. An animal, primordial, painful scream.

She stood and began pacing the kitchen frantically.

She was fighting through a horrible mix of emotions. Joy at having finally discovered the truth. Rage at knowing with certainty that her baby had been killed. Sorrow at realizing that he could still be alive if it weren't for those *murderers*!

Liz wanted to tell everyone. She wanted to call her husband and rub it in his face. She wanted vindication. She wanted *them all* to know that she'd been right, and they'd been wrong. And, she wanted the full weight of justice to slam down and crush her son's killer.

In her excitement, she dialed Eddie Garza. She could tell him. At least him.

"Hello, Liz," he answered.

As soon as she heard his voice, she knew it had been a mistake to call him. Four years. It had been over four years since Liam had died, and she had made more progress on the case than they had. For all their training, all their resources, the police were useless. The system was useless.

Besides, the only people in the world who could have wanted Liam dead had a rock-solid alibi. Out of town. A DNA test didn't change that. The police weren't going to do shit.

"Hello, Eddie," she said, trying to sound normal, casual. "It's been a while since we spoke, and I just wanted to touch base. Make sure you got my email about Spain. The congressman?"

That was quick, girl! You're getting good at lying...

After four years, Eddie could now admit to himself that there was something about Liz Bareto that got his balls twitching. The case against Cruise and his partner David Kim had had its ups and downs. But, staying connected with Liz made it worthwhile to Eddie. There was something about her that he couldn't put a finger on, but, oh how he wanted to...

"I did, Liz. And it's odd. Definitely. I chased down a few leads. I even tracked down and spoke to a journalist who's an expert on the guy. But, it's complicated, what with it being in another country and all."

In spite of herself, Liz scoffed.

So typical. More excuses. Too much work, no doubt.

Eddie picked up on the sound, and continued, "Don't be that way, Liz. I'm making progress. I think things are starting to come together. Maybe we could get together for coffee and I can catch you up?"

"Oh, Eddie, I'm so tired of your disappointments," she said. It came out more bluntly than she'd intended.

Eddie became defensive. "Look. I think things are going to start to heat up here. I think we may finally have something on Cruise. If everything goes right, we may be able to get a warrant soon."

"How soon, Eddie? Because my son died over four years ago, and it doesn't feel *soon* to me."

"Look, Liz," the volume of Eddie's voice dropped. "That surveillance I told you about—it paid off. This coming Monday, we're bringing him in again for questioning. Him and David Kim both. Just sit tight a little longer. I promise."

Liz had almost forgotten. Back in October, when Cruise and his wife were in Spain and Tom Wise died, Eddie told her that the police were going to start filming the comings and goings at Cruise's house and office. Maybe there was something to this after all.

"I'll call you once we're done with the interviews and let you know what happened."

"Well, don't make me sit by the phone all day waiting, Eddie. You promise? Maybe we can get that coffee then..."

"That's a plan. We're meeting at Cruise's lawyer's office at ten o'clock. As soon as we're done, I'll let you know how it went."

As Liz hung up, a very simple plan came together in her mind. She'd tried approaching Susie Font before. The woman had always managed to evade her and avoid answering her questions. When she'd confronted her at the entrance to her subdivision, the woman had gotten security involved. On the radio show, her friend Veronica Rios had protected her.

But Liz believed she could get through to her. Susie Font was a mother, like her. She'd lost a child, like her. Liz believed she could crack her. And now she had more than questions and accusations; she had evidence. All she needed to do was get Susie's undivided attention.

PART TWO

Rebecca Forsyth
Madrid
2003

"It's not a question of if, but of when." Jules Fonseca was leaning over the bathroom sink, her head close to the mirror as she carefully lengthened her eyelashes. She was speaking in English, her Argentine accent barely perceptible. "I mean, let's face it. It's not an aberration, it's a fucking crime... that so few countries have elected a woman as president, prime minister, whatever. But one day, women will rule the world." She paused, then sighed and said, "I suppose it's just another way that Argentina is ahead of everyone."

Her roommate, Rebecca Collier, sat about fifteen feet away in the small sitting area of their dorm room, sipping on a glass of white wine and rolling her eyes. Jules was from Argentina, and she believed that her country led the world in everything.

"Ahead of everyone? You mean like ahead of Israel, with Golda? Or like Indira Gandhi in India? Or maybe you're thinking more like Thatcher in Britain? Shipley in New Zealand?" Rebecca smiled.

Jules stopped applying makeup and turned to scowl at Rebecca. "Fuck you! None of those women had an impact on western civilization even close to Eva Perón." She shook her head and turned to the mirror. "Fucking American know-it-all," she said under her breath.

"Hey, I heard that! And America's not so far behind. We've got Hillary. One of these days, she'll run. Then you'll see!"

"Oh, yeah! I'm sure that your dad can't wait!"

They both laughed.

Rebecca Forsyth grew up as Rebecca Collier, the only daughter of Dr. and Mrs. Raymond Collier. Her father was a proctologist, a Baptist, and a Republican—and avid about all three. He was very conservative in his principles, but very creative in his thinking. To the above list can be added that he was also an inventor. From what Rebecca explained to me, he invented some sort of disposable medical device that makes it much easier to get a really good look at your colon during a colonoscopy. Odd, but true. Although Dr. Collier's royalty for his invention was small, at two dollars a pop multiplied by about eight million colonoscopies per year—you can do the math.

Her father's invention took off when Rebecca was in high school. As a result, Rebecca told me that she had the blessing of knowing what it was like *not* to be rich—of growing up relatively normal. She'd gone to public elementary and junior high schools.

When her father "made it," everything changed. Almost immediately, they moved into a much larger house. Her mother stopped cleaning, as that was for the maids. Rather than continue with her friends to the public high school she'd been planning to attend, her parents moved Rebecca to a private school. And the old VW Bug she'd been eyeing as a gift for her sixteenth birthday, as her first car, was abandoned in favor of a new BMW 3 Series—more reliable and with the latest safety technology.

Some of these changes were difficult for Rebecca. One that wasn't was the vacations. She and her parents had always taken them together, once a year. And with her father's new wealth, they were able to travel extensively. By her senior year in high school, Rebecca had travelled Europe, Asia, parts of Africa, and South America. She loved to travel. So much so that, when it came time to select a college, she applied to and was accepted at the Instituto de Empresa—also known as IE.

Rebecca loved Spain, and everything about the Spanish culture. And she loved that Madrid was a two-hour flight from almost every major airport in Europe. She looked forward to experiencing Spanish culture while at IE, along with having the freedom on weekends and holidays to travel and explore countries she hadn't yet visited with her parents. When she announced that she'd been accepted to IE, her mother was not thrilled. Gayle Collier had grown up in Kansas City. She loved to travel, too. But she didn't see why her little girl needed to move halfway around the world to go to college.

"Come on, Jules! How much longer?" Rebecca had just about drained her wine glass. "It's ten-fifteen! We were supposed to meet everyone at ten!"

Rebecca was getting pissed. Jules was always late.

"Relax!" Jules replied. "They said at 'around ten.' *Around ten* means eleven. If we leave now, we'll be early." Her friend stepped out of the bathroom and, striking a pose, said, "Voila! Now, pour me a glass of wine."

The event *de nuit* was a little get-together at the apartment of a girl in Jules' study group—Rosalind. When they arrived, there were about twenty-five college kids crammed into the tiny flat drinking beer, wine, and GTs.

Among those Rebecca recognized, she was thrilled to see David Grant. His friend Alan was with him. Rebecca had met Alan Forsyth on the first day of school. She was a design major and he was studying business, but it turned out that Alan's friend David lived in Rebecca's dorm. Alan and David were both British.

From the moment she first met him, Rebecca had crush on David. He was tall, with sandy blond hair and chocolate-colored eyes. His face was strong, angular, with a dimple on his chin and matching dimples on his cheeks when he smiled. And Rebecca just loved his voice—deep, masculine, with a refined British accent. Rebecca's cheeks burned and her belly did a weird hummingbird flutter when he was around.

Alan, on the other hand, wasn't really Rebecca's type. He was smaller, chunkier, rough around the edges. He played rugby. He was loud. He seemed to love to be the center of attention.

In addition to David and Alan, Rebecca saw several girls

from her design program at the party, including a girl from her study group named Jillian. Rebecca greeted those she knew and was introduced to those she didn't. She mingled.

At close to midnight, Rebecca was seated on a small sofa talking to Jillian when she felt a push against her shoulder. She turned to see that David had sat himself down on the armrest to the sofa, right next to her. She felt that familiar hummingbird flutter in her belly.

"Hello, petal," he said.

Rebecca looked up at him, excited. However, the thrill passed quickly as she saw the vacant, drunk look in his half-shut eyes. Her brows furrowed as she replied, "Hi, David."

"What're you lovelies discussing?" he slurred, pointing at the two young women with his half-full glass of gin and tonic, spilling a bit on his pants leg.

Jillian—a fellow Brit—rolled her eyes at Rebecca, then smiled patronizingly at David and replied in her clipped London accent, "The weather, dear. It's quite warm for October, don't you agree?"

David swayed slightly and pursed his lips, as though he were contemplating a response, then put his hand on Rebecca's shoulder, and leaning into her, said, "You haf lofly eyes, you know? I find them fascinating." He paused to belch, covering his mouth with his free hand. Then he reached out with the same hand and tried to stroke Rebecca's hair. She pulled away in disgust.

"Aw, come on. I see how ya look at me. Don't be shy."

Rebecca scooched over on the sofa, closer to Jillian, and turned to face David. As she did, she saw a hand reach out and take his glass from him. They all turned and saw Alan.

"Easy goes it, mate. I think maybe we should call it a night."

"Oi, don' be a cunt, Alan. We're having a great time," he indicated at the girls with his left arm, and both Jillian and Rebecca had to dodge to avoid him accidentally hitting them.

"I can see that, but I think you've had too many of these, and—"

"Aw, bugger off!"

Alan took a step back as David staggered up from the armrest.

"I'm 'ere, havin' a nice time, talking to these ladies, and you come and fuck with me? Go cockblock someone else. And gimme my drink!" David reached for the drink, but drunk as he was, lost his balance and fell forward over the coffee table. Alan reached out and caught him, awkwardly breaking his fall while the contents of the glass he was holding spilled all over the floor. David took this as an attack and began to struggle drunkenly against Alan.

By this point, everyone at the party was silent, watching as the two friends awkwardly grappled to the sounds of Queen's "Don't Stop Me Now." Alan finally managed to push David into an upright position, and stepped back from him as David swayed, trying to keep his balance.

He pointed at Alan and yelled, "Don't ever fuckin' touch me, you piece of shit! I don't need y'ur bloody help!"

Alan stood back with his hands raised before him defensively.

"An' don't fuckin' tell me not to drink! Save that shit for your fuckin' father!"

Alan turned beet red, but said nothing. David swayed a bit, then looked around and scratched his head.

"Ah, fuck all of you!" He turned and headed for the door, and as he did, slurred at Rosalind who stood nearby, "Thank you for y'ur hospitality, my dear. Is's been lovely."

Alan followed him carefully. As David opened the door to leave, he turned and saw Alan close behind him.

"Stay the fuck away, you twat!"

David left, slamming the door behind him. Alan apologized to Rosalind, handing her David's glass, which he was still holding, and said, "I better make sure he gets home alright."

Two days later, Rebecca ran into Alan walking down Serrano Street on her way to class. They were heading the same direction, though she saw him before he saw her. When she greeted him, he turned beet red again.

"Quite a mess the other night, that," he said.

"It was good of you to take care of him," Rebecca said softly. "You're a good friend."

Alan shrugged, his eyes restless. "He's a good bloke. Just hits it a bit hard sometimes."

Rebecca forced a smile, though her brows furrowed. She wasn't quite sure what to say in reply. Alan seemed uncomfortable with silence and spoke rapidly to fill it.

"I've got some experience with that, I suppose. Like he said. My dad likes the drink a bit too much. Of course, I guess you heard that. Bit of a wanker sometimes, David. He didn't need to mention that. But I suppose it was the gin talking." Suddenly, Alan's eyes widened and he stammered, "He wasn't… I mean, he didn't step out of line… with you and your friend? I meant to ask, but... He can sometimes, and I was worried. That's why I stepped in. I mean… you just… you seem like a very nice girl… woman, I mean… and I just didn't want for him to say anything to… offend you."

It was Rebecca's turn to blush. "I really appreciate that, Alan. That was very gentlemanly of you."

Alan slowed up, and Rebecca realized he was stopping in front of a small café. "I always stop here for a *cortado* before class. Care to?"

It turned out that Mondays, Wednesdays, and Fridays, Alan had a ten o'clock class, as did Rebecca. Over the course of the next several months, they made it a habit of meeting before class for coffee at the little café. Although at first it was a quick ten-minute thing, it slowly evolved until, one November morning, she found herself meeting Alan and ordering her usual *café con leche* forty minutes before class.

Rebecca enjoyed their time together. There was something driven yet needy about the little Brit. It didn't take her long to learn all there was to know about him. She discovered that if she wanted to know anything about him or what he thought about something, all she needed to do was ask a question to introduce the topic, and then shut up. Alan was possessed by a conversational form of *horror vacui* that could not abide silence. He was an open book.

She learned that Alan, like her, was an only child. His mother died when he was young. He'd gone to public school—which in England meant private school—on scholarship. That was where he'd met David. This explained to Rebecca the obvious cultural disparity between the two friends. David came from a wealthy family; his father was a member of parliament. Alan's father had worked with horses until he'd suffered an accident. He'd been kicked in the back by a mare, which had put him on disability and exacerbated his drinking problem.

After her first semester of college, Rebecca went home for the holidays. Over the Christmas break, she kept busy catching up with friends, and her uncles, aunts, and cousins wove in and out of her days. Still, in the few moments she was alone, she found herself thinking about Alan—missing their conversations. It struck her as odd, but she didn't give it much thought. It was just that their morning coffees together had become a part of her daily routine. She was sure that was all it was. Until, on Christmas Eve, she received a text message.

Alan: *Merry Christmas! Missing you.*

Rebecca smiled. She was halfway through replying when she suddenly stopped. She realized that her cheeks were burning and she had that weird hummingbird flutter in her belly.

When she returned to university, she was anxious to see Alan. To renew their morning ritual. But she was also nervous. Things had changed. At least, for her they had. What if he didn't feel the same way?

They arranged via text message to meet at their little café the morning of the second day of classes. When she walked in, she saw that he was already at the counter, waiting with his coffee and hers.

"Hello, Alan."

He turned his head, and when he saw her, he smiled. As he stood, he brought his hand forward, and in it was a single, long-stemmed red rose.

Rebecca accepted it, blushing and giggling. "That's so sweet. It's lovely."

"I really missed you. I mean… " His face was red as he hesitantly leaned forward. Rebecca wasn't sure what was about to happen. A typical European air kiss? A Spanish double-cheek kiss? Or something else?

She hesitated. He pulled back, then chuckled. She giggled.

"Well, this is complicated," he smiled.

He leaned in again. She looked him in the eyes, then met him halfway. It was a chaste kiss. Brief. His lips were soft and dry. But the moment they touched hers, Rebecca felt an electrical charge shoot from her lips, through her body, to her fingers and toes, and heard a buzzing sound in her ears.

CHAPTER SIXTEEN

Sometimes I think that there were many points along the way where any one of us—Susie, Roy, Kristy, me—could have done things differently and reduced the amount of destruction we caused. We could have made different choices. That is what my rational mind tells me.

But there is another part of me that disagrees. That part of me believes that this whole mess was inevitable. That each of us was bound to act as we did based on how we were hardwired.

I realize that this second notion sounds fatalistic. That fatalism probably comes from too many years spent living in South Florida. There is a primordial influence here in this land of voodoo and alligators that, much like the humidity and heat, permeates everything. Choices that elsewhere are clearly a matter of free will, seem to be mulled with a strong dose of determinism, the closer one gets to the Caribbean.

Maybe that's why dominos figure so strongly in the culture here. Of course, dominos is first and foremost a game. But, give any child a set, and the first thing they do is line them up and knock them down. To me, there is something about dominos toppling that reflects that Caribbean fatalism. So much so that it has been elevated to an art form. I love seeing those elaborate trails of rectangular tiles lined up to within kissing distance of each other. There is nothing random there; nothing superfluous. Each tile is placed exactly where it needs to be.

They remind me of Nazca lines.

There is a glorious, pre-orgasmic tension to seeing dominos lined up before they fall, like a spring wound up tight and ready to be released. Then the gentlest touch, like the finger of God in Michelangelo's *Creation*, brings their potential connectedness into reality. The sharp *clack clack clack clack* as they fall announces that something amazing is happening; colors appear as different trails spring away from common starting points, then converge, only to twist and turn off again in new, different directions.

That change in progress is a thing of beauty. But, it is a beautiful lie. What happens is not transformation, but corruption, because the dominos must fall as they've been arranged. Nothing new is created. The initial, precise pattern simply collapses, and becomes a messier shadow of its former self.

I realize now, looking back, that my life's journey—connected as it was to Susie and Roy's, and to the lives of Kristy, Tom, Deb, the Harlans, and Liz Bareto—was like those dominos. In the mess we created, I believe the initial impetus was Joan Diaz, that little girl who was thrown from the cliff in Texas. Over the years, as a result of that one act, our multiple paths diverged and converged. I was drawn into that process. I became a part of it, but I believe that I was ultimately transformed by it, not corrupted.

You see, in life, sometimes it feels as if free will only exists at the point of that initial nudge that starts the dominos falling. As if, once the dominos get going, where they will fall is pretty well determined. But life differs from those hardwired dominos in one significant way. In life, an external event can interrupt the preordained flow and set a whole new bunch of dominos falling.

I think it's those unexpected events that can short-circuit our hardwiring and create windows of opportunity where we can choose how we move forward. Where we can truly change. That's where we can draw the line between fatalism and free will. I think it's the choices we make in those moments that can transform us, and determine whether we live as lemmings or as gods.

One of those unexpected events for all of us happened on Monday, February 10th. That day would mark a major turning point in my world. It marked the convergence of paths—and was, in fact, the culmination of several of the stories that had crisscrossed their way through mine. After that day, as they always do, the paths continued to move forward like so many falling dominos. But, on that specific day, their direction changed radically—one single event set a whole new bunch of dominos tumbling.

MONDAY FEBRUARY 10, 2020

CHAPTER SEVENTEEN

Susie couldn't sleep. She was twenty-six weeks along in her pregnancy, and the baby was beginning to make her physically uncomfortable. Not that she minded. She was lying in bed, looking out the window at the moonlit terrace and the early morning sky. It was still dark out. She touched the screen on her mobile phone, which lay on the nightstand, and it lit up, advising her that it was four a.m.

Roy was lightly snoring next to Susie. She got out of bed, careful not to wake him, and quietly padded to the terrace just outside their bedroom. There was an almost full moon out that reflected off the canal beyond their boats. She leaned with her elbows on the railing, taking in the view.

She scanned the backyard of their two-acre property, the swimming pool, jacuzzi, the sculptures, their yacht and fishing boat, the garage that housed her Bentley and his Range Rover, and half-chuckled. It seemed like she had it all. But did she, really?

She'd been thinking about that a lot lately. About what really mattered to her in life.

The thought had been gnawing at her for some time. After Camilla's death, she'd thought that revenge would make her feel better. That it would fill the emptiness inside her. It hadn't. After all the killing, she'd felt nothing. She hadn't known what to do. Where to seek solace.

Religion was not an option. Although Susie had been raised Catholic, as a teenager, she had come to see religion as bullshit. In her opinion, the whole focus on delayed gratification—rewards in the afterlife in exchange for suffering in the current—was just a transparent dangling carrot. Suffer this "shit" now in exchange for "glory" later.

The meek shall inherit the earth. Susie didn't buy it.

So, she had gone to the other extreme, like her friend Deb. Deb Wise had belonged to the "fuck it all" clan. She had never been interested in singing hymns with the angels in heaven. She'd always wanted to live in the now. Susie had tried that approach. She had pushed for more in life. And she'd discovered that the more you pushed, the more you got.

Losing Camilla had gutted her. And everything Susie had done to try to "fix" things had only made her feel worse. She rubbed at her belly, attempting to visualize the baby girl that lay less than an inch from her hands. Everything else was empty lies. This baby would finally make her happy.

Susie could smell the ocean on the breeze that blew through the palm trees and over the terrace. She turned her back on all their things, resting her hip against the railing, and looked through the sliding glass door into the bedroom and at the shape of her sleeping husband.

She loved him, albeit in her way, which was the only way she knew how. He was a good provider. They'd built a good life together. And to think she'd almost lost all of it. When he'd found out about Joan—that Susie had been involved in his sister's death—she'd thought for sure that it was all over. That she would lose everything.

The timing of her pregnancy couldn't have been better. As she looked in at Roy, with her hands resting next to their baby, she knew that this was what she needed to focus on. She would commit herself to these two people. The three of them could be a perfect family. She knew they could make her happy again.

Susie shook her head and sighed. It was Monday morning, the day of Roy and David's interview with Detective Garza, and she was worried about the police.

What could they want this time?

At least she was in the clear. They weren't asking to question her. She felt a pang in her gut as she thought of her lockbox downstairs in their office safe—the fish knife, the photo of her and

Deb at camp, the letter from Deb. She needed to get rid of all that stuff. It was time. She'd do some cleaning today. Susie sighed again and headed quietly back into the bedroom, lying down next to Roy.

She didn't realize it, but Roy had been watching her all the while. He'd closed his eyes and feigned sleeping when he saw the woman he loved returning to bed.

CHAPTER EIGHTEEN

It was a clear and sunny day in Miami, with very little wind. It was still—eerily so. Susie and Roy were having breakfast at the small table on their covered terrace. She was having tea, fruit, and oatmeal. Roy knew he needed to be at his sharpest. He'd opted for decaffeinated coffee as he didn't want to be jittery, and he ate two slices of toast and a hardboiled egg for breakfast. Roy and David's interviews were scheduled to begin at ten a.m. at Moran's office. They had agreed to meet there at nine o'clock for a final prep and discussion.

"What have you got going on today?" he asked Susie, who sat across from him sipping tea and reading the news on her iPad.

"Quiet morning," she said, looking up. "Going to try and do some organizing around the house. Then we have the doctor's appointment..."

Roy smiled. He'd intentionally scheduled the interview knowing that Susie had the appointment at three that afternoon. He'd discussed it with Moran, and they had agreed that if things ran long with the police, it gave Roy an easy out to leave and reconvene the interview another time. A natural backstop.

"Sounds good. Well, we'll see what these assholes want. I'll swing by here to pick you up around two-fifteen," he confirmed while rising from his chair. He was wearing grey slacks with a pale blue dress shirt and no tie. He stepped into the house through the open sliding glass door that led to the kitchen and got his jacket, a blue and brown plaid blazer in silk and wool. Then he returned to the terrace, and bent down to give his wife a kiss before heading out.

"Love you," she smiled. "Do what you do best, babe. Knock 'em dead."

"Will do," he smiled back.

Susie poured herself another cup of tea and finished reading the news.

The coronavirus was ripping its way through China. There were over 40,000 cases already reported. And the Friday before, Dr. Li Wenliang, the Chinese whistleblower doctor, had died of the disease.

A hero, that man.

The good news was that, so far, the only U.S. cases of the virus had been imported from China. There was no local spread. Still, the whole thing made Susie nervous. The elderly, the ill, and the very young were always the most susceptible to these things. She was hopeful that it would all be resolved long before her due date.

She idly swiped through entertainment news, not that she was interested. She had decided to clean out her lockbox and wasn't looking forward to throwing out the items with more sentimental value. She was avoiding the inevitable. But, she could feel the lockbox calling to her. She sighed.

Might as well get this over with.

Her plan was simple. The camp photo and the letter from Deb, she would burn. The fish knife, she planned to carefully clean with bleach and then throw in the canal. Susie walked down the terrace to their outdoor kitchen and turned on the grill, as she thought it would be the best way to incinerate what was left of the paper items after she burnt them in a small metal bowl.

Then she went inside, walking through the kitchen and, remembering that she needed the key for the lockbox, headed upstairs and retrieved it from the shoebox where she kept it hidden. Once she had the key, she went into the office and opened the safe. There, inside, on the second shelf sat her lockbox. Roy had put one of the new Glock 17s on top of it.

She removed the gun and placed it on top of Roy's desk, carefully pointing the business end at the wall. The gun was loaded. She knew that. But, even if it hadn't been, she'd have done the same.

Susie religiously followed the rule to always treat any gun as if it was loaded.

She then retrieved the lockbox and sat down on the sofa to open it and remove the items she needed to destroy.

CHAPTER NINETEEN

Earlier that morning, Liz Bareto had left her home and driven to Matheson Hammock Park. She was familiar with the spot, as she had been there numerous times with Liam. The county park was home to the Fairchild Botanical Gardens and to a large public marina. Liz was interested in another area of the park, however—the parking lot next to the iconic Red Fish Grill. The restaurant had been destroyed by Hurricane Irma and had not reopened for business. Only a skeletal structure remained. The parking lot next to it ended on a small beach where paddle boards and kayaks were usually available for rent, and where local kite-surfers parked before heading out into the bay.

On this windless February Monday morning, the parking lot was empty. Liz parked near the water and removed an inflatable paddle board from the trunk of her white Audi. She plugged an air pump into the car outlet—she still remembered when these were used for cigarette lighters—and in ten minutes was standing next to a fully inflated paddle board.

Liz assembled the collapsible oar and then removed a light jacket, under which she was wearing a shortie wetsuit, a one-piece with short sleeves and legs that ended above her knees. She kicked her flip-flops into the trunk and pulled on a pair of rubber booties. She then carried the paddle board the short distance to the shore, placing it in the water with a loud plop. Liz carefully climbed onto the board in a kneeling position, with the oar next to her.

Shit... did I lock the car?

Liz opened the fanny pack at her waist and removed the key fob, pointing it at the car and clicking. The car lights flashed.

Satisfied, she dropped the keys back into the fanny pack. They made a soft *clink* as they landed next to her handgun. She zipped the fanny pack, carefully stood up, and began paddling.

Liz knew she was taking a chance. But she believed the risk was low based on information Eddie had shared and what she'd cobbled together with some pointed questions she'd asked her private investigator.

Back in October, Eddie had told her that the police would be monitoring the comings and goings from Cruise's house and his office. But, he'd also stated when they last spoke that they might be able to "get a warrant soon."

How could that be? Surveillance but no warrant. Liz had asked her private investigator, who'd explained that surveillance of public spaces could be done without a warrant. It made sense—Eddie had said "comings and goings."

Liz was betting that there would be no surveillance of the Cruises' dock. She'd Googled their address and carefully studied a satellite image of it. The Cruises' home was surrounded by houses on all sides. Private property. The police wouldn't have been able to put cameras there without a warrant—so she believed.

Liz wanted to get Susie Font alone. She wanted to show her the syringe. She felt confident she could get her to confess. She wanted the truth, mother to mother. And if Susie confessed, then Liz would go to the police. That's what she told herself, although there was a small part of her that really didn't know what would happen next.

Liz believed that the gun was a necessary evil.

First, for protection. These people are killers. I'm sure of it. And, I'm not bringing a syringe to a gunfight!

More importantly, Susie Font may need a little convincing. She may not want to simply share the truth with me. But she'll think twice if I'm armed...

I bet she'll start talking when she sees the gun.

Liz had checked the gun several times that morning, almost obsessively, to make sure the clip was full. To make sure she'd properly chambered a round. She'd been to the gun range a few times. She knew how to fire the damned thing. But, she was no expert.

As she paddled along the canal that led to the Cruises' backyard, she lost herself in thought. Memories. She'd paddled along here with Liam when he was young. First in kayaks, with him trying to row but not really helping. Later, when he'd been old enough, they had paddle boarded down these canals, ignorant of the fact that these people, this family that would have such a terrible impact on their lives, lived so close by.

Liz reached the end of the canal and followed it to the right. According to Google, the Cruise house was about halfway down on the left. She'd been paddling for almost twenty minutes when she saw two boats come into view—one of which, the larger yacht, was named *Lady Suze*.

Liz pulled the paddle board up behind the yacht. She carefully climbed onto the transom of *Lady Suze*, then onto the dock. She removed the leash from her ankle and used it to tie the board up to a cleat. Liz then made her way up toward the house. As she walked across the terrace, she passed a small table that still had the remnants of a breakfast on it. Just past the table, she saw an open sliding glass door, beyond which lay the home's kitchen.

CHAPTER TWENTY

As Liz Bareto walked through the sliding glass door and into Roy and Susie's home, 1,100 miles away, Kristy Wise was jogging up the sidewalk to her front door, keys in hand.

Tom and Deb Wise's house had changed very little since their deaths. In fact, externally, the only significant change was the "for sale" sign in the front yard. It had been a mild winter in Austin, Texas, all things considered, and the Saint Augustine grass around the house had gone dormant, turning a yellow brown that matched the color of the wooden privacy fence that ran along the sides of the house.

Just as the house had not changed on the outside, it was almost unchanged inside, as well, the main difference being that only Kristy Wise lived there now—alone. Upon first returning from her visit to Susie and Roy in Florida, Kristy had considered moving to an apartment. She'd thought she'd be uncomfortable living alone in her family home—which was now also the house where her father had died. But, after shopping around and seeing a few apartments—studios, small spaces, sterile, lacking personality and any historical connection to her—she had decided to stay in her parents' house until it sold.

She had to admit, she was getting used to living in the place by herself. Being in familiar surroundings somehow made it easier to accept that her parents were gone. She'd continued to use her old bedroom upstairs. She hadn't really changed anything, except that she had begun to use her father's office as her own.

Kristy had finished college, but wasn't job hunting; she had her hands more than full. At first, she'd had to deal with numerous estate issues after her parents' deaths. She had used Tom's office for that, and then settled into it more permanently because all of the documents regarding the real estate Tom had managed to accumulate over the years—all of which now belonged to Kristy and needed to be managed—were in that office.

Kristy's parents' bedroom remained untouched. All their clothes were still in the closets. Kristy went into their bedroom once in a while, when she felt lonely. To think. To remember them. At times, she wondered whether it was normal.

"Don't they say, 'Let the dead bury the dead'? I'm sure that's what my mom would tell me," Kristy had told Bethany more than once.

Bethany disagreed on this point. She'd told Kristy that what she was going through was normal. That she shouldn't rush the process of letting go.

"You need to grieve. It's so much loss all at once, Kris. Remember, the dead aren't really dead until we forget them. When the time comes to let go, you'll know."

Consuelo also added to the sense of continuity, though Kristy caught the maid looking at her sadly from time to time. And then there was the superstition. Consuelo was constantly making the sign of the cross every time she passed through the living room where she had found Tom Wise's dead body.

All told, not a lot had changed—as far as the eye could see. Kristy was adjusting to her new way of life. That said, she still had the house for sale, although she had intentionally over-priced it. She wasn't in any hurry to leave, as she didn't know where she would move to once it did sell. She assumed she'd stay in Austin and see how things evolved with Alfie. But, she didn't want to pressure him or their relationship with any talk of living together.

This morning, Kristy had just gotten back from a run. She entered the house, locking the door behind her, and was going to go upstairs to shower before meeting Alfie for lunch when her phone lit up—it was on silent mode, so it vibrated gently but didn't ring.

Detective Art Travers

Or as Bethany referred to him, the devil you know...

What could he want? Kristy wondered.

"Kristy, I wanted to see if you would be willing to come in and chat with us a bit," Travers said, doing a good job at sounding nonchalant.

Kristy changed directions and headed toward the kitchen to get some water. "What about, exactly?"

"It's nothing serious. Just checking some boxes," the detective told her. He sniffed at the end of the phrase.

"Okay." Kristy shook her head. *Liar*, she thought. She was standing in her kitchen, and removed her running shoes by using the toe of one shoe to hold down the heel of the other, and then step out of them. First one. Then the other.

"Let's chat now," she said. She opened the fridge and got a cold can of sparkling water.

There was a pause, and some background noise that sounded like Travers possibly changing ears with his phone. "If possible, we'd prefer to do it down here... at my office."

"We? At the police station?" Kristy shook her head. "Detective Travers, that sounds very formal. Like more than checking boxes." She sighed. "Look, Art. I'm happy to talk with you—you've always been a straight shooter with me and you know I appreciate it. But, since I can't ask my folks what they think about this, let me get back to you."

When they hung up, Kristy immediately called Harold Riviera, the attorney who had represented her father when he'd been charged with attacking Joe Harlan Junior. Riviera confirmed that she'd done the right thing in contacting him, and told her that he would contact Travers to get more details about what the police wanted to "chat" about. Then he would call her back so they could decide what to do.

CHAPTER TWENTY-ONE

As Liz entered the kitchen, her adrenaline spiked. It suddenly hit her that she was actually doing what she had planned. Her surroundings were strange to her. She felt as though she had walked onto the set of a movie where she didn't belong. She stopped for a moment, breathing slowly in and out, taking everything in.

Oh fuck. What am I doing?

She suddenly felt vulnerable. She was in *their* house. What if the interview had been cancelled? What if Roy was home too? These people were killers. They had gun licenses. She was trespassing. Liz realized that, if it turned out that she needed it, it would take her too long to get to the gun in her fanny pack. She was walking into the house completely unprepared.

Her hands shook as she carefully and quietly unzipped the fanny pack at her waist and removed the 0.38 caliber handgun. It felt cold, heavy, and alien in her hand. She stood still in the kitchen—holding her breath—listening, and thought she could hear movement coming from deeper in the house.

She moved quietly from the kitchen into a long hallway down the middle of which ran a Persian rug runner. Her booties, still wet from paddle boarding, were making a very slight, wet rubbery squishing noise on the tile floor. Liz stepped carefully onto the runner, which muffled the sounds of her footsteps. As she advanced down the corridor, she heard a sharp *clack* come from a room further down and to the left. She advanced to its doorway, breathed in and out one more time, and entered.

Before her was what looked like a home office or small library. There was a desk at one end flanked by shelves of books. A sofa sat below windows that overlooked the front lawn. And on that sofa sat Susie Font.

"What the hell," Susie hissed, "are you doing," her eyes scanned Liz's body, taking in her wetsuit, her rubber booties, the fanny pack, "in my—" Susie stopped mid-sentence as her eyes settled on the gun in Liz's hand.

"What's the matter? Cat got your tongue?" Liz smiled nervously, studying the woman. The woman she believed had contrived to kill her son. She was wearing blue jeans and a pale blue blouse. She was barefoot. Liz noticed that she had very small feet. Her toenails were painted bright pink. For some reason, that detail stood out in her mind.

As she studied Susie, all of her speeches, all the words she had rehearsed, escaped her momentarily. She felt devoid of emotion, but also of reason. She couldn't think. Then she remembered how the speech she had rehearsed started.

"I know everything. I have it. The syringe. It tested positive for Liam's DNA. It's all over now. You're going to go to prison. And then you're going to die."

Susie sat staring.

What the fuck? How in hell would she get a hold of that? It's a bluff.

Or, Deb could have kept it—for misdirection. Or insurance. But Deb's dead... Tom? Or Kristy?

Kristy... fuck...

"Did you know that, in Florida, you get a choice? Death penalty-wise, I mean. Lethal injection or electrocution? It's up to you. Have you given it any thought?

"You could flip a coin. Or, maybe you could ask your darling husband what he thinks. But then again, he may have to make the same choice. Wouldn't that be interesting? A couple's execution. Kind of like a couple's massage..." Liz stopped. She was rambling. Holding the gun made her feel powerful. She was the one in control now. She wanted to taunt Susie. To make her suffer. But the woman wasn't responding. She hadn't said a word. Liz wanted her to react.

"It's not a hypothetical question. Which will you choose?"

Liz stood, waiting.

Stall. "I… I don't know what you're—"

"Save it! Don't lie to me, you fucking bitch!" Liz screamed, her face contorted in anger.

Oh, fuck. She's losing it.

Liz reached into the fanny pack and pulled out a Ziploc bag with a syringe in it. It wasn't *the syringe*, as that one was still making its way back to her from the lab. She'd brought a fake for effect. To illicit a confession. She threw it at Susie, but missed. It fell short, on the floor at Susie's feet.

"Pick it up!" she yelled.

Susie did, holding it like a live spider, at arm's length.

Deny. Deny. Deny.

Susie's eyes welled up, and she said, "I swear, I didn't—"

"Don't lie to me! Do I look stupid to you! If it wasn't you, then tell me—who would want to inject air into the body of a comatose twenty-four-year-old?!" Liz stared at Susie, her chest heaving with rage. "Who!?"

Maybe if I appeal to her emotions.

Susie began to cry. To buy time.

Should I tell her I'm pregnant? To get her sympathy? Or will it remind her of the child she lost?

Fuck.

Susie needed to act. She could tell the woman was slowly coming unhinged. And, she wasn't sure that even a confession would save her.

The Glock—it's on Roy's desk.

The sofa Susie was seated on was up against the wall, perpendicular to the desk. The gun was probably five feet away from her. Liz hadn't taken her eyes off Susie since she'd come into the room. Susie was sure she hadn't seen the gun.

"Oh, this is rich. Don't you think I've cried?" Liz shook her head at Susie. Her voice was frighteningly calm all of a sudden. "You think I care about your tears? I only care about one thing. I want the truth. I want you to admit it. Admit that you killed my Liam."

"Look. I don't know—"

"Liar!" Liz screamed.

Susie put up both hands defensively. "Wait. Wait. Hear me out."

I just need a short distraction.

"Go ahead..." Liz replied.

Susie jerked her head, looking over Liz's shoulder—then immediately made as if to hide the fact that she'd heard or seen something. Or someone.

Liz reacted, turning suddenly toward the doorway behind her, holding the gun in front of her. As she did, Susie threw the lockbox at the wall to her right, hoping to further distract Liz with the noise. She jumped up off the sofa toward the left and grabbed the Glock from the desk.

Only one shot was fired.

Outside the house, I don't know if birds scattered from the trees, the way they do in the movies. The back door was still open, so the sound of the gunshot definitely would have carried.

Yet afterwards, when they were questioned, none of the neighbors reported having heard anything. Maybe it was due to the thick walls and hurricane windows of their own houses. Or maybe the sound registered, but only subconsciously, and was quickly rationalized away—like the sound of a car backfiring. After all, who would be firing a gun in the middle of the morning in such a nice neighborhood?

CHAPTER TWENTY-TWO

Eddie Garza was seated at one end of the table in the large conference room in Mark Moran's office, next to the seat at the head of the table which was vacant, awaiting a witness. A court reporter sat off to the side next to his stenograph. Both were waiting. On the table were a few fresh legal pads, a small pen holder with blue and black pens, and a little crystal bowl full of peppermint Life Savers.

It was 10:15 a.m. when Roy, David, and Mark walked in.

"Sorry we're late, Detective," Mark said. "My fault. I got an unexpected call right before ten. Don't hold it against us." He smiled.

"Of course not." Eddie was standing. He shook Moran's hand, then Roy's and David's.

Moran stood behind the chair directly across from Eddie, and pointed David to the witness chair at the head of the table. Roy sat one seat down from Moran, farthest from the action.

"Are we doing this under oath?" Eddie asked.

Moran shook his head. "Come on, Detective. Really?"

"Hey, can't blame a guy for trying."

The court reporter went on the record at 10:18 a.m.

Eddie had a notepad in front of him that he referred to as he questioned David Kim about the night of his hit-and-run. At what time he'd left work. How he had gotten home. At what time he recalled entering the parking garage. What he remembered after parking—which was nothing. David's recollection had been consistent since he'd awoken in the hospital and given his first statement.

"I remember parking. And, that's it. I don't even remember getting out of my car. Next thing I know, I wake up in the hospital."

It was a lie. He knew it. And Roy knew it.

As he asked questions, Eddie ticked boxes next to handwritten scrawl on his notepad. Roy discreetly tried to read it from where he sat, but was unable to. As he proceeded, Eddie seemed uninterested in David's replies. Like he was going through the motions.

Maybe this isn't going to be a big deal after all, thought Roy, maintaining a poker face.

At 10:43 a.m., Eddie concluded his questioning of David Kim, and they went off the record.

"Short bio break. Then we can resume with Roy?" Moran proposed.

"Sure."

Fifteen minutes later, they were on the record again. Roy was now in the hot seat. And, almost immediately, it was obvious that something was afoot. The questions Eddie had for Roy had nothing to do with what he'd asked David about.

"Mr. Cruise, we've met before. I interviewed you before regarding Liam Bareto and Joe Harlan Junior. You recall that?"

"I do."

"Where were you on October 31st, 2019. Halloween night?"

Roy's face remained placid. Inside him, alarms were blaring. He looked at his lawyer, who shrugged. He looked back at Eddie and replied, "It was a weird day, actually. I was in Spain and in Florida." Roy chuckled. "My wife and I were on vacation in Spain. We flew back that day. So, we started the day out in Madrid and ended the day in Miami."

"I see," Eddie said. "So, you slept that night—Halloween night—in your home, here in Miami?"

"That's correct. Though, I don't see what that has to do with David getting hit by a car."

"I agree, Detective," Moran chimed in. "Seems like you're heading somewhere else."

"Just indulge me a bit." Eddie smiled. "You know. Background stuff."

Roy looked at Moran, who shrugged and nodded. "Okay. Just a bit."

"So, Halloween night, you slept at your home in Miami?"

"I did," Roy sighed.

"And, exactly how many people were in the house that night?"

Roy started visibly at the question. Moran noticed and broke in, "Hold on. Way out of bounds, Eddie. I can give you some leeway, but unless you explain what you're after, I'm instructing Mr. Cruise not to answer that question."

"You gonna do what your lawyer tells you, Cruise?"

"I sure am, Detective. That's why he gets paid the big bucks."

"Okay. Let's try something else," Eddie said. He hadn't looked down at his notepad once since he'd begun questioning Roy. "Let's talk about Cruise Capital, Mr. Kim's place of employment. Your company. The company you founded and so very humbly named after yourself. Do you guys have many offshore investors, Mr. Cruise? Non-citizens that place their money with your firm?"

Roy blinked several times. He thought he knew where Eddie was going... Getz. He replied, "Some."

"Any in Europe?"

"Some," Roy snapped back.

"Any in Spain?"

"Possibly," he replied again, less quickly.

"Mallorca?"

Roy looked over at Moran, and shook his head and rolled his eyes while shrugging, conveying with extreme clarity to everyone present, *What the fuck?*

Eddie didn't wait for an answer, but leaned forward, and asked, "Have any died recently?"

Moran sat forward and was about to speak when Roy raised his hand to stop him.

Roy slowly sat back in his chair, scratching his head. He looked carefully at Garza, sizing the man up, then replied slowly, articulating each word, "How recently, Detective? In the last thirty minutes? The last fifteen—"

"Don't be a smartass, Cruise!" Garza shouted, red-faced, interrupting Roy, who ignored him and continued.

"—minutes? Or even more recently?"

"Now hold on a minute, Detective," Moran jumped in. "I don't know where you're going with this whole thing, but you said this interview was about David—Mr. Kim's hit-and-run. This is totally out of line. Totally out of line. You're all over the place."

Roy began laughing out loud at the exchange. David Kim had shrunk into his chair at the end of the table.

"Please," interrupted the stenographer. "I can't keep track when you yell over each other."

Eddie raised both hands in a conciliatory gesture. "Alright. Let me try and refocus. This fancy office of yours," he said, looking at Moran, "has got me all star-struck." Garza pulled a manila folder out from underneath the notepad he had been using during his questioning of David Kim, and from it extracted two sheets of paper, placed them side by side on the table, and passed them across to Roy.

"Who is this?"

Roy sat staring at the pictures. Moran looked at them from the side, while David stood and walked around behind Moran to be able to see. They were the same photo—one from a distance, and one zoomed in closer up. The photos were of Roy's front porch, where a man stood. In the zoomed photo, the man's face was clear as day in the porch lights.

"Now, while you're thinking, Roy, let me describe what I'm seeing, for the written record here. Mr. Kim is standing behind Mr. Cruise, and looking at the photos, and he's suddenly very pale. In fact, if I didn't know better, I'd say he was about to puke. You may wanna sit down, buddy.

"Roy, you look like you've seen a ghost, literally. A dead guy. Funny? Huh? Not laughing now?

"And Moran, my friend, you look like you're wondering what your clients lied to you about." Eddie scoffed. "So, now, so as to not get 'out of line' again," Eddie made bunny ears, "answer the question, Cruise. Who is this guy in the photo that entered your house on Halloween night and then disappeared off the face of the earth? Or maybe, into the sea about a mile off Key Biscayne?"

Roy didn't look up from the pictures, but Moran was already in motion. He had placed a hand on Roy's arm, to keep him from speaking, and said, "Detective, you seem to have a bit more of an agenda than what you represented to me before we agreed to this meeting. I need to take a break to talk with my clients before we can agree to proceed."

Moran started for the door, but Roy didn't move. He had looked up from the photos, and was staring Eddie Garza down.

"What's wrong, Roy?" Eddie taunted. "You were so confident in all our prior interviews." Eddie held his hands in the air and imitated Roy in a sing-song voice, "*What possible motive could I have, Detective?*" Eddie laughed out loud, then leaned forward and almost whispered, "So, are you gonna go and chat with your lawyer outside, or are you afraid to get up 'cuz you just shit your pants?"

Roy glared at Garza a moment longer, then shook his head and said, "I'll be back in a moment, Detective Garza." He reached out and pushed the bowl of Life Savers toward Eddie, and added, "Have a mint. Your breath stinks." He then rose from his chair and left the room.

Garza watched him go, smiling. When the door closed, Eddie blew into his hand and sniffed. Then he grabbed a mint.

CHAPTER TWENTY-THREE

The three silently trudged back to Moran's office. It was a spacious, rectangular office with a large glass desk and two client chairs at the end with the window and the view—and a sofa, coffee table, and two more chairs at the end by the door. Moran entered and went to his desk, where he quickly flipped through phone messages while Roy flopped heavily onto the sofa. David pushed the door to, then leaned up against it.

"So, any idea what all that was about, gents?" Moran asked, looking up.

David looked over at Roy, who had leaned forward and was resting his elbows on his knees, hands clasped together. Roy looked up at Moran, but said nothing. David cleared his throat and Roy turned to gaze at him. David raised his eyebrows with a look that said, *Now what?*

"Can you give us a minute, Mark?" Roy asked.

Mark looked at the two, then walked over toward them, and said, "Look guys, I'm not gonna give you my whole 'what should you tell your criminal defense lawyer' speech right now. But, I will say that this is obviously a set-up. Garza clearly lied about the purpose of these interviews. But hey," he shrugged, "that's what cops do. They lie. The issue is, right now, we're at a complete disadvantage. We're flying blind. It's not a good place to be.

"You guys can go ahead and chat. I'll be right outside." He looked from one to the other, then added, "However, my recommendation as your lawyer is going to be that we call it quits today—and neither of you says another word to *anyone* outside this room about anything having to do with Harlan, or Halloween, or the guy in the photo, or anything else you haven't told me about, until the police give us a lot more clarity about what they've got and who they're after."

He let the words hang in the air for a few moments, then moved toward the door. David stepped aside to let him out. Moran left the office, closing the door behind him.

David began to pace rapidly in the space between the sitting area and the desk. "That was the guy, Roy! The one that beat the shit out of me," David said in almost a whisper. Then he stopped and looked at Roy, "And you know him?"

"No," Roy shook his head, then seeing the look of doubt on David's face, added, "I mean, I met him—once—when he showed up at my house that night. I figured that's who he was."

"Why didn't you tell me that he came for you? What did he want?" David suddenly shifted gears from the specific to the more general, and continued in a louder voice. "Look, Roy, what the fuck is going on? For real? I mean, all of this." David gestured in a large circle with both arms. "I've been loyal, man. Totally upfront with you." He sat down in one of the chairs across from Roy and lowered his voice again, "Hell, I just lied to the cops, man. About not remembering *my hit-and-run*." He shook his head, and said almost to himself, "That's gotta be illegal..."

David stopped, waiting for Roy to respond.

Finally, Roy sat up and said, "David. I'm trying to protect you here..."

David scoffed, throwing his arms up in the air, "Well thanks for that! I feel so safe! This is bullshit, man! I fucking *knew* it! What've you gotten me into?"

"Wait, David. Listen. Remember, I'm a lawyer. You," he paused for effect, pointing at his friend, "have done nothing wrong. Think about it. You know where you've been and what you've done. Have you committed a crime here at all? Hell, at any point in your life?"

David swallowed hard, but he was attentive, listening.

Roy continued, "The only thing that's happened so far," Roy pointed with his thumb back toward the conference room where they'd been interviewing, "is that you got the crap beat out of you, and you have amnesia. That's what you just told them. And there's no one that can prove otherwise."

"Then what about Halloween?"

"What about it? Were you there? At my house?" Roy snapped.

David shook his head.

"Then you've done nothing wrong. You don't know anything about it. So, you can't tell them anything about it. And I'm not going to fuck your life up by telling you about it. That's the end of it."

David seemed unsure, so Roy asked, "Where were you? That night? Halloween?"

"With Rosa," David said reluctantly, "at her sister's party."

Roy chuckled, shaking his head, "How's that for a fuckin' alibi? 'I spent Halloween with my cop girlfriend and twenty of her sister's friends.'"

David half-smiled, in spite of himself. He saw Roy's point. He sat for a moment, processing. Some of the tension seemed to leave his shoulders as he did. Then, his forehead furrowed and he asked, "Dude... what kind of fuckin' mess have you gotten yourself into?"

Roy was about to answer when there was a knock on the door. Both men looked up as the door opened. Moran poked his head in, then said, "Garza just left."

He was looking at Roy as he entered the office.

He didn't close the door.

"You told him we were done?" asked Roy.

Moran shook his head.

"He got a call, Roy. There was a shooting. At your house."

CHAPTER TWENTY-FOUR

Old habits die hard. Billy Applegate was no exception. For years, he had made his living as a journalist. And he had received several awards over the course of his career for his in-depth investigative reporting. In retirement, Billy continued to do freelance work to supplement his income.

That Monday morning, he was at his computer working on a piece regarding yet another corrupt politician, when a news alert popped up.

Billy was subscribed to numerous news sites and apps, and alerts were common. This one was local. The location caught his eye, and he clicked on the link to open the article.

> **Police on scene at shooting in Coral Gables**
> **CORAL GABLES, FLA.** — Police and emergency vehicles are at the scene of a shooting in the wealthy neighborhood of Lago Beach in south Coral Gables. Authorities say that they responded to a 9-1-1 call reporting an accident at approximately 11:00 a.m. Monday morning. Emergency personnel entered the house by force, where they discovered that the accident involved a victim with what appeared to be a gunshot wound to the chest. Police are on the scene and report that a woman in undisclosed condition was taken by ambulance to the Ryder Trauma Center at Jackson Memorial Hospital. Ryder is a world-

> renowned Level 1 trauma center located in Miami-Dade County and is equipped to handle gunshot victims. Police could not confirm the identity of the victim, but advise that no shooter has been identified.

It was the neighborhood that rang a bell for Billy. Lago Beach. It was the one where he'd learned that the owner of Cruise Capital lived, back when he'd done his research after Detective Garza's visit.

Billy later told me that he clicked on the little arrow icon to forward the message, and was halfway through typing in my email address when he thought better of it. Instead, he picked up his phone and called.

I was in the middle of a session with a patient when my phone buzzed. I had it on silent mode. I saw that it was Billy and let it go to voicemail.

CHAPTER TWENTY-FIVE

It took Eddie Garza almost half an hour to drive to the Cruise residence. He made several phone calls on the way. First, to a junior officer who he instructed to download the surveillance video of the Cruise property from that morning. Eddie knew that if there was any video of a vehicle or vehicles arriving at or leaving the property, the sooner they got a BOLO out on them, the better. He then contacted the police captain on the scene, who gave him a quick rundown of what had happened and what they knew about the victim. Finally, he called Shaw, who didn't answer. Eddie left him a voicemail summarizing what he had learned so far.

When he pulled up to the property, several police cars were still on site, though EMS and Fire were already gone.

The whole thing was a fucking mess. Of all the calls he might have gotten about the Cruise residence, he never would have guessed this would be the one.

While Eddie had seen the Cruises' home countless times via surveillance camera, seeing it in person still made an impact on him. The home was massive—a mansion, really—sitting on a corner lot and completely fenced in, with manicured podocarpus bushes lining the entire fence. Eddie walked up the ten steps to the front door. A duty officer at the door took down his name and the time and handed Eddie latex gloves and shoe covers. Eddie put them on, then entered the house.

Directly before him, across a massive foyer of marble tile that peeked out from beneath tastefully placed Persian rugs, was a spectacular floor-to-second-story-ceiling window that offered a view to the backyard, pool, and canal, beyond which Eddie saw Cruise's two boats docked. Two chandeliers that looked like melting ice hung from the ceiling some thirty feet above at staggered heights, around which wrapped a staircase that was like something out of a movie.

Eddie's moment of appreciation was interrupted by an officer—the police captain he'd spoken with by phone—who said, "Eddie Garza! You slumming it today?"

"Yeah. Real dump, right? I don't know how people can live like this!" Eddie shook his head. "Probably, what—only nine bathrooms? Maybe ten?" He rubbed his cheek, feigning pity. "I mean, where do you go to take a shit if you're in the conservatory and you have guests?"

The captain laughed and, as Eddie walked toward him, he signaled that he should follow him.

"Everything's over here. I got a call from Naylor," the captain said over his shoulder. Ted Naylor was the Chief of Homicide. "He said this one's all yours. Possibly related to something you're working on?"

"Well, Santa didn't bring me anything I asked for this year, so we'll see if today's my lucky day."

They walked down a large hallway hung with what looked to be expensive oil paintings toward a doorway which led to a room that overlooked the front of the house. Several forensics specialists were on about their business, taking photographs, collecting evidence, and dusting for fingerprints.

As they approached the door, a young officer shouted down the hall, "Cap! The grill out on the terrace is on. Burning real hot. Do I turn it off?"

The man Eddie was following glanced at Eddie, who nodded.

"Yeah," the captain shouted back, "but gloved hands! And make a note as to which burners were on. And get the damned thing dusted for prints."

The captain stood in front of a doorway and signaled to Eddie that he should enter.

"We've got a gun, but almost for sure it's not *the gun*. It hasn't been fired. Fully loaded, one in the chamber. The vic was laid out on the rug. Phone—land line—was laying on the floor next to her. But she didn't use it to call 9-1-1. Or, if she did, then she wiped it down afterward. Not a print on it."

While the officer spoke, Eddie poked his head into the room and looked around. A beautiful room. Polished wood floors covered by a massive Persian rug—a large dark stain marred the end of the rug near the desk. A lot of blood lost. The desk was at one end of the room. There was a sofa against one wall in front of a large window overlooking the front yard. There was also a little bar with crystal glasses and an assortment of fine alcohol. Cruise looked to be a scotch drinker.

"Can you believe that shit?" Eddie asked, pointing at the bar. "Only Macallan 15? Where's the twenty-five-year-old?"

Everyone in the room laughed.

"I told you, you're slumming it," replied the captain. "But, if it's any consolation, I did ask them to wait and let you do the honors." The captain made a flourishing motion with his arm, indicating that Eddie should enter. Eddie raised an eyebrow, then carefully stepped into the office. As he did, one of the specialists looked up and pointed Eddie toward the far end of the room. Next to the sofa, on the floor, lay an unopened lockbox.

"All good?" Eddie asked, to confirm that photos had already been taken of the box to preserve evidence of its position and condition.

"Go for it. Here's the key. Found it on the rug."

Eddie carefully righted the box on the floor. He pushed the key home and turned it, feeling the mechanism give through his latex glove. He gently lifted the lid, then shifted to the side to let the technician photograph the contents as they lay in place. Then, he removed and bagged each item, one by one.

A small linen bag. It looked to be handmade and appeared to contain hair. Possibly a child's?

A photo of two young girls. Old from the looks of the hairstyles, their clothing, and the condition of the print. The photo was on old school camera stock.

A small box, containing one ladies' ring. Possibly diamond.

A small box containing what appeared to be a child's teeth—baby teeth.

A baby's hospital ID bracelet. The name on it read Camilla Cruise.

A plastic Ziploc bag containing a dirty fish knife.

A manila envelope containing a handwritten letter. Eddie carefully removed the letter from the envelope and scanned. It was to Susie Font, from Deb Wise.

Eddie read the letter.

"So, how's it lookin', Detective? Today your lucky day?"

"Oh, yeah." Eddie nodded as he re-read the letter. "Christmas, my birthday, and Valentine's day combined."

CHAPTER TWENTY-SIX

Roy was sitting with David in a waiting room at Jackson Memorial.

The two had driven together from Moran's office to the hospital. Traffic was light, and in David's Porsche 911 they got to the hospital in record time. The attending nurse advised Roy that Susie was in critical condition, but that the team was doing everything they could for her and the baby. She parked them in the waiting room and advised that the doctor would be out as soon as possible to update him on their condition. All she could tell him was that Susie had suffered a single bullet wound to the chest and that she'd lost a lot of blood.

"They're getting the best possible care, Mr. Cruise."

Roy's mind raced, alternating between worry for Susie and the baby, and incoherent rambling speculation as to who could have done this. His immediate conclusion was Joe Harlan.

Fucking lying sack of shit!

He couldn't fucking let it go!

I should have known! I should have been there!

He wondered if the whole interview by the police was part of some elaborate plot to get him out of the house so that Harlan could get at Susie. A conspiracy. With Harlan possibly working in some sort of secret government job, anything was possible.

In his more lucid moments, Roy recognized that he was in shock. Emotionally, he bounced between denial and bargaining.

Please let them be okay.

I'll do anything, God.

Roy hadn't prayed in years. Not since Camilla had died.

He paced the waiting room because, whenever he tried to sit, his hands and legs shook uncontrollably. At one point, David asked him if he should ask the nurse to get him something, to take the edge off. A Valium. Or a Xanax.

"Xanax?" Roy laughed out loud, recalling the Xanax they'd given Harlan Junior. Then he shook his head and continued pacing. He didn't notice the worried look David gave him.

Fucking Harlan!

Fucking Deb Wise. How'd she con us into this fucking mess?

Oh God, I can't live without them.

"She'll be fine, man. Susie's a fighter," David seemed to keep repeating.

The clock on the wall stood still. From time to time, the PA blared out names of doctors being called to go who knows where.

Moran arrived about twenty minutes after David and Roy. He sat with David while Roy continued pacing.

Minutes turned into hours. As they did, the more time passed, the more fearful Roy became. Several times, Roy went to find a nurse, but was repeatedly told to stay in the waiting room. There was nothing new to report.

How complicated can it fucking be?

It's a fucking bullet. You remove it, stitch her up, and done.

Roy became more insistent. The nurse said her hands were tied. He asked to see her supervisor. The supervising nurse repeated the same stupid, placating drivel. Roy demanded to know the name of the doctor. There were apparently several working on Susie, but he insisted that there had to be someone—one doctor—in charge. He wanted a name.

If that bastard fucks this up, I'll fucking kill him!

After almost five hours, the door to the waiting room opened and a middle-aged man in scrubs entered.

"Mr. Font?"

For fuck's sake. This clown doesn't even know my name. Who's running this sideshow?

"It's Cruise. I'm her husband."

The doctor began to explain what had happened. The

clinical aspects of the wound. Roy tried to stay focused, but the more the doctor explained, the more frustrated he felt.

"Can you do this in fucking English, doc? I'm a lawyer, not a surgeon."

It was important for this quack to know that Roy was a lawyer. He needed to know there would be consequences to his career if he fucked this up.

The doctor continued, repeating much of what he'd already said, but using other words. Entry point. No exit wound. What had been done so far, surgically. What had been required. Their condition was fragile. Touch and go.

And then, Roy heard them. The five words no man ever wants to hear.

"Mr. Cruise, if it comes down to it, who do you want us to save—*the mother or the baby?*"

PART THREE

Rebecca Forsyth
Madrid
2005

After that first Christmas break, Rebecca and Alan began dating exclusively. He was an ideal boyfriend in almost every way. Rebecca's only complaint was that he refused to join her on her travels through Europe on holidays. After his first few refusals, she was able to get him to confess why.

He couldn't afford to.

Alan worked part-time at an English pub in a suburb of Madrid. He explained that all the money he was making went to pay bills, and the little extra he made he was saving for graduate school. He knew that a college degree alone just wasn't "enough" anymore.

In December of their junior year, Rebecca planned a surprise for Alan for their second anniversary. She was leaving for Florida the following day for Christmas, and they were having a romantic dinner at her apartment since they would be apart for three weeks during the holiday break.

"Close your eyes," she said.

Alan frowned. "Come on Bex, we agreed, no gifts..."

"This doesn't count. Because it's not for you, it's for me," she said coyly. "A gift—from me, to me."

He furrowed his brows, then reluctantly closed his eyes.

Rebecca tiptoed to the counter and retrieved an envelope from her purse. She opened it and carefully arranged its contents in her hand, fanning them out like playing cards. Then she held them out over the table between them, and said, "Okay. You can look."

Alan opened his eyes. In her hand were plane tickets to the Czech Republic.

"We're going to Prague! My treat!"

Rebecca's expression fell as she saw Alan's face transform and contort. He'd been pleasantly complying with her request, smiling. But, suddenly, his mouth became tight, his nostrils flared, and his eyes blazed.

"What the fuck? Do I look like a charity case to you? We said no fucking gifts!" Alan stood abruptly and headed for the door.

Rebecca was stunned, her mouth gaping as she tried to understand his reaction.

"I won't be looked down on! Fuck you and fuck your fucking charity!" He opened the door and slammed it behind him so hard that the door didn't close but bounced off the frame and swung back open again into the small foyer.

Rebecca jumped up and chased after him.

"Wait! Alan!" By the time she reached the hall, she could see that he was already two flights down the stairs ahead of her and taking the steps two at a time.

"Alan!"

She followed after him, but he was faster than she was. By the time she reached the street, he was gone.

Rebecca didn't hear from Alan for the entire holiday break. She called. She texted. She left voicemails apologizing. Nothing.

On Christmas Eve, she texted him.

Rebecca: Merry Christmas! Missing you. 💋 💋

She received no reply.

When she returned from Christmas break, she arrived at her apartment to find Alan waiting for her. He was unshaven. And his clothes were rumpled, as though he'd worn them more than one day. He was holding a single red rose. He smelled, of sweat and alcohol. She was furious.

"Get out of my way!" she almost screamed. "I called you. I texted you. You didn't even wish me *Merry Christmas*—"

"I'm so sorry!" Alan's eyes watered. "I was wrong, babe. So wrong. I missed you so much! I'm sorry. I overreacted. I was childish—"

"You were an asshole! A complete fucking asshole and—"

"You don't understand. It's that I... I love you." A tear rolled down his cheek as he said it. "I want to take care of you. And provide for you. And I hate the idea—"

Rebecca's heart melted. So that was it, what was at the heart of things. She put a finger to his mouth, quieting him.

"I love you too," she said.

From that point forward, Rebecca and Alan began to travel together regularly. Rebecca was happy to pay for the trips. And she noticed that Alan was always very frugal about their arrangements. He always ordered the cheapest item on the menu. He insisted on walking if they could avoid paying for a cab. He carried their bags to avoid having to tip the porters.

Rebecca relished their trips together. Spring of their senior year, they had just returned from a weekend trip to Poland when Rebecca was on her way home from class and came across Jules Fonseca—her first-year roommate—walking in the same direction. It was a gorgeous day. Rebecca had just received a text from her Aunt Chloe, her father's sister, and was about to open it when she spotted Jules. They'd lost touch after first year once they no longer roomed together.

"Hi Jules," Rebecca said brightly. "How are you?"

"Fine." Jules' face was tight.

"Is everything okay?"

"Seriously?" Jules scoffed, rolling her eyes.

Rebecca's smile drooped, confused at the cold response. "What do you mean?"

"You drop me the second you meet a guy, and now, three years later, you have the nerve to act all chipper and ask how I am?"

"What? What did I miss?"

"You started dating Alan and you just... disappeared. I thought we were friends."

Rebecca thought back. Alan had become a very big part of her life very rapidly, it was true—perhaps even to the exclusion of other friends. Maybe all friends. Alan did monopolize her time. And, when he went out with his friends, she took advantage of the free time to read and get things done for school. She realized that she'd really shut down her social life for him. But it wasn't like she'd been trying to be an asshole to anyone.

"I didn't mean to, Jules. I'm sorry. Honest."

Jules shook her head. "Too late for sorry, petal. But, if I were you, I'd keep an eye on Alan."

"What's that supposed to mean?"

"Oh, God... Really? I know love is blind, but apparently it's stupid, too."

"What?!" Rebecca almost shouted.

Jules waved a hand in the air and walked off.

Rebecca marched home and slammed the door to her apartment, fuming. She'd been mulling over what Jules had intimated. Was Alan being unfaithful? She scoured her memory for signs. Inconsistencies. She couldn't think of any. Her phone pinged. Aunt Chloe—*again*.

"Oh, for fuck's sake!" she shouted.

Rebecca called her aunt, who picked up on the first ring. Ten seconds later, Rebecca's life had changed forever.

The next seventy-two hours were a blur.

She called Alan on the way to the airport. She didn't remember the call clearly. "Dad's dead. Mom's in ICU. I'm flying home. Gotta be with her."

By the time Rebecca landed, her mother was gone as well. Her parents had been driving home from dinner at their favorite restaurant. The other driver ran a red light. According to the police, no one involved in the incident was drunk. Just bad luck. Her father had died on impact. Her mother succumbed while Rebecca was flying over the Atlantic.

Her Aunt Chloe was there for Rebecca. She handled the

funeral arrangements. She organized everything. Rebecca had nothing to wear. Her Aunt bought her a black dress at Nordstrom's. She rode to the funeral home in a large black limousine with her Aunt Chloe and her husband, Greg.

"We need to meet with the lawyer tomorrow," Aunt Chloe said. "I know it's terrible, dear. But life goes on. You're a very wealthy young woman now. You're going to need someone to help you with all that. To manage your money. I already spoke with Greg, and he's happy to help, aren't you?"

"Happy to help," Greg replied. "I've already been looking at options to make sure you're protected. You'll never have to work again."

Rebecca sat silently. Inside, she was fuming. Her father had never trusted Greg with a dime of their investments. He'd loved his sister Chloe, but always said that she was a blind fool and that her husband was an idiot. Rebecca would be damned if she let him help with anything.

"I'll talk to the lawyers tomorrow," she replied. "Alone."

They rode the rest of the way in silence. When they got to the funeral home, Rebecca did as instructed by the funeral director. She stood at the entry to the chapel as a line formed, accepting condolences. Friends of her parents. Relatives. Faceless suits and black dresses passing by. And then, suddenly, there was Alan. She collapsed into his arms and wept. He promised her that he would always be there. That she would never be alone. And she believed him.

CHAPTER TWENTY-SEVEN

Holy shit, Eddie!" Shaw exclaimed.

The detective had just given him a rundown of everything that had been found at the Cruise residence. After finding what he had in the lockbox, he'd coordinated with Shaw to get a search warrant *ex parte* for the entire premises. The mother lode of evidence was in the lockbox. The only other evidence of interest in the house were several more handguns, and two laptops that were found in the safe.

The laptops had been sent off for analysis, and preliminary indications were that they had been configured as burners. Eddie didn't understand all the tech stuff, but they'd apparently been modified to run some kind of Linux thing, the USB ports had been superglued, and they were running a browser that crooks used to surf the darknet—something called TOR.

He'd brought Shaw photos of all the items from the lockbox. The prosecutor had studied them with interest. Eddie knew in his gut that he had the broad strokes of a solid case against Cruise and his wife. Now, he needed for Shaw, the man who would take the case to trial, to agree.

Shaw sat at his desk, re-reading the letter from Deb Wise to Susie Font.

July 12, 2018

Dearest Susie,

I'm dead.

If you are holding this letter, it's because that's what's happened. I asked my lawyers to send it to you as a part of my last wishes. I asked that it be sent unopened, but you can't trust anyone these days. So, I can't tell you everything I'd like, but I think you'll understand, all the same.

I hope that this letter finds you happy. You deserve to be.

I have to say that I've enjoyed my life. I've been fortunate to have found love, and to have been loved in return. You know what I mean.

There are obviously things that I would change about my life—things I did early on that probably kept me from enjoying your love and friendship as much as I could have. But that's all water under the bridge.

I just wanted to send you a note to tell you that I love you. That I will always love you, no matter where I am.

I'm glad that I was able to help you out when you needed it.

And I thank you from the bottom of my heart for returning the favor. You and Roy both. I can't imagine all that it took. But it's made a big difference in all our lives.

If you can, keep an eye on Kristy for me. She's not like us. She's fragile. And on Tom. He means well, and he tries hard. But he's no Roy.

Well, that's it. I've never been much of a writer. You know that.

Big kiss, girl. Be good. And sorry for all the headaches.

I hope I went in my sleep. I always thought that's how I would want to go. Not that I deserve to. But it would be nice, you know?

Love always,
Deb

"I can definitely make a motive out of this, Eddie. We still need to get forensics on all this stuff," he waved vaguely with one hand, "but if the results come back solid, we're in business." Shaw was nodding enthusiastically. "The only piece missing," he pursed his lips, "is a fucking witness."

Eddie's face fell, and Shaw noticed.

"Now, hold on, *Eduardo*," he raised a hand at Eddie, indicating *Stop*. "Don't go getting all mopey on me. This is all great stuff. But, to really hit a homerun with a jury, we need a storyteller. A witness that can tie everything together. It's not to say that what we've got isn't great. But... it could be *greater*."

Eddie nodded, but the gesture lacked enthusiasm.

"And," Shaw smiled, "today is truly your lucky day." Shaw clasped his hands behind his head and leaned back in his office chair while looking and nodding at his desk phone, the landline. "This morning, while you were playing cat and mouse with Cruise and Kim, I got a call from a guy named Harold Riviera. Ring a bell?"

Eddie nodded, the smile returning to his face. "He was Tom Wise's lawyer when we interviewed him on the Harlan thing... the first time around."

"Exactly. Well—among other stuff, I'm guessing—Kristy Wise apparently inherited him from her dead parents. She wasn't too keen on talking to your friend Travers without counsel. She called Riviera, Riviera called Travers, and Travers gave him my number. So, he called me asking what's what. 'Is she a target?' 'Can she get a deal?' The usual." Shaw cocked an eyebrow.

"What'd you tell him?"

"I gave him the high points on Clayton, and told him we'd deal if she was useful. But, I acted like I was reluctant. I told him that she's not a target, but that she's damned close... almost there. You know, to put the fear of God into the little bitch. And, with everything you found at the house today, I *know* we can get somewhere with her."

"What'd he proffer?"

Typically, before reaching an immunity agreement, the attorney for the witness and the attorney for the state, in this case Riviera and Shaw, discuss in broad strokes what the witness is likely to say when questioned. That way, the state knows whether granting immunity is worth it.

"Well," Shaw dragged the word out. "He's going to talk to her and find out. But, she's got to have details on Clayton. Hell, she was *on the property* when the guy showed up—or shortly after, anyway. She had to have seen something. So there's that... at a minimum."

"Makes sense. Absolutely," Eddie replied enthusiastically.

"So," Shaw said, smiling broadly. It was the happiest Eddie had ever seen him look. He opened his arms toward Eddie, palms facing upwards, and asked, "You up for a trip to the Lone Star State?"

CHAPTER TWENTY-EIGHT

After speaking with Shaw, Riviera called Kristy by phone and explained the situation. He caught her at home in the middle of unloading the dryer and folding clothes. So, she put him on speaker.

"Here's the deal, Kristy. These guys have been investigating Joe Harlan Junior's disappearance since it happened. It seems like they're finally pulling some kind of a case together against Susie Font and her husband, Roy Cruise. I don't know how much your parents looped you in on all of that back in the day?"

"Some," Kristy said, nodding as she folded a pair of running shorts.

"So, you know who they are. Have you met them? Been to their house?"

Upon hearing the last question, Kristy's stomach turned. She stopped folding and picked up the phone, turning off the speaker and putting it to her ear. "Yeah, I... I have."

"Well, it appears that a man named Clayton—" Riviera sounded as though he was checking his notes, "Ronald Clayton went into their house on Halloween night, and never came out. They think he's dead, and they claim you were there and know what happened. At this point, they say you're not just a witness. You're a subject as far as they are concerned."

Kristy winced at the news. It didn't sound good. "What does that mean? A subject?"

"'Witness' means you didn't commit a crime, but you know something. 'Subject' means they're not sure whether you committed a crime, but you know something. 'Target' means they think you committed a crime, and you know something. 'Target' is not where you want to be... But, 'subject' means that they haven't discounted the possibility of charging you with a crime."

Riviera paused for a moment to let that sink in.

"Shaw was really forthcoming," he continued. "Almost apologetic, actually. Which I understand, given everything you've been through. But, they'd like to interview you. He claims that they think the culpable parties are Cruise and Font, and that any involvement you had was probably incidental. They're the targets, in other words. Given that, I went ahead and told him that I wouldn't feel comfortable with you talking to them at all without immunity."

Kristy leaned against the dryer, and asked, "Why do I need immunity? Why can't I just refuse to talk? What is it—Fifth Amendment?"

"Well, to begin with, the Fifth Amendment only applies if you've committed a crime, Kristy. I mean," Riviera added, "you're right. You can't be forced to be a witness against yourself as to a crime you committed. But, that presupposes that you actually did something illegal..." the lawyer paused. "Do you think that might be the case?"

Kristy sat down on a small stool in the laundry room, and sighed. "Let's assume for the moment that it is. Then what?"

"Well, from what he told me, this investigation is apparently pretty far down the road. They already have a lot of evidence lined up against these people. They just need you to verify some of it. And, if we're operating hypothetically in a world where you may have committed a crime, then you definitely need to get an immunity deal before you say a word to them. If not, the evidence the police have could be used against you. Anything Cruise or his wife say could be used against you. This could get really ugly really fast, Kristy. You could become a target of the investigation."

There was silence on the line for several beats.

"What exactly does immunity cover?" Kristy asked a bit hesitantly. "I mean, how does that work?"

Harold noticed her change in tone, and replied, "I can explain all of that to you in detail. Bore you to death with it. I think it'd be best to do that in person. That way, you can tell me everything you know and we can make the best possible decision for you.

"This guy Shaw didn't sound enthusiastic about giving you immunity. If we're going to do it, we need to move on it before they lose interest or find another witness. But, in order to cut the best deal for you and keep you out of any possible trouble, I need to understand what happened and what you know."

Kristy hesitated a moment, then said, "I guess that makes sense."

Harold and Kristy agreed to meet at his office the next day. Kristy hung up and, instead of finishing folding the laundry, changed and went out for a run. She was too wound up to stay in the house.

CHAPTER TWENTY-NINE

Kristy made her way down to Riviera's office the next morning. She had known the lawyer for years. He'd represented her father when he was charged with attacking Joe Harlan Junior in a Whole Foods parking lot. Riviera was a former prosecutor and a well-respected criminal defense lawyer. He was known to be scrappy, no-nonsense, pragmatic.

Riviera was a sole practitioner—no partners—and had a simple, functional office he shared with other solo attorneys. The sign on the door simply read "Attorneys at Law" at the top, then listed several names below it in alphabetical order. Riviera was next to last, just before Straussberg.

They met in a small conference room with a lousy view of the next building over. For over an hour, Kristy explained to Harold just how she had come to be at the Cruise house on Halloween. How she had investigated her mother's death. Her conversations with Liz Bareto. Her trip to Miami. How she'd killed the Cruises' home intruder. And everything that Susie had told her. She told Harold everything, except what the dead man had said about Frank Stern, and what she'd done to Frank when she returned to Austin. No one needed to know about that. And it wasn't connected to anything in Miami anyway.

"That's everything that happened. And, for obvious reasons, I am really not interested in talking to the cops about all this."

Harold looked up from his notepad and nodded. "I know where you're coming from. But, talking *to them* is not a choice. They can force that issue."

"Then I'll lie," Kristy said matter-of-factly.

"You can't lie, Kristy. I can't represent you if you tell me you're going to perjure yourself. If they subpoena your testimony, whether it's in an interview or on the stand at trial, you have to tell the truth."

Kristy sat for a moment, dumbfounded. "I thought everything I tell you is confidential. That you can't tell anyone."

"It is. But if I know you're going to lie, I have to withdraw from representing you."

"Well shit, Harold! You could'a fuckin' told me that before I spilled my guts to you..."

They sat for a moment in awkward silence, Kristy glaring. Harold was struck by the similarity between Kristy and her late mother. Kristy, for her part, was wondering about her parents' choice of lawyer.

"What if my memory *changes*... after I *think things over* some more?" she asked.

"Look," he said, shaking his head, "even if I *could* let you... The real problem with lying is that we have no idea what they know. Maybe they have info from this Bareto woman, or surveillance footage, eyewitnesses you may not even know about, or your fingerprints in the house. We don't know. And they won't tell us. They'll hint. They'll partially show their hand. They'll even lie. But they won't tell us everything. If you lie, we won't find out until it's too late."

"Wait! Hold on!" Kristy was getting angry. "You're saying that *they* can lie to me to get me to talk, but if I lie back, *then I go to jail*?"

"I know. It sounds bizarre, but those are the rules." Riviera stood, and went to a small table for a bottle of water.

"This is so fucked up! Look, Harold, I have absolutely no interest in ratting these people out. I don't want to be a witness. I don't even want to be involved."

Riviera sat back down. "That's not the way this works. You don't have a choice. If you're interviewed by the police, you have two options: answer their questions, or go to jail."

"Since when do we live in fucking China? How can they put me in jail just for not talking?"

"*They* don't. But, they'll ask a judge to order you to answer their questions, and if you don't, the judge will hold you in contempt of court. And then you'll get thrown in jail until you answer. It's that simple."

"What about the Fifth Amendment? What if I plead the Fifth?"

"First off, the Fifth Amendment only applies to testifying about things you did that could be crimes. So, there's still a lot you'd have to answer anyway—a lot of what you know doesn't involve you committing any crimes. But, Kristy, they're offering you immunity. Once they do that, the Fifth doesn't apply."

"Then I'll fucking lie."

"Goddammit, Kristy! You're not listening." Riviera studied the young woman who was sitting with her arms folded across her chest, then he tried a different tack. He lowered his voice, and said, almost pleading, "Look, Kristy, you've got to trust me on this. You're paying me a lot of money for my expertise. I've been down this road a hundred times before."

"Fine. Talk."

"The authorities, they don't push cases to trial unless they've got rock-solid evidence. You can't refuse to testify if they offer you immunity. But, the good news is that *nothing you tell them*," he paused, letting the words hang in the air for emphasis, "can be used to convict you of a crime. And that's good. You don't want to be in their sights. If they're willing to cut you a deal, you take it, and you tell them everything. *Everything*. You answer all their questions." He paused again, then added, "I know I can get you a deal. A damned good deal."

"Why?"

"Because you're the perfect witness, Kristy. Can I be blunt?"

"Sure."

"You're young, attractive, articulate, educated. You just lost two parents. You were raped." Kristy noted, and appreciated, that Riviera did not use the word *allegedly*. "And you've held your head high through all of that. You've kept it together. You are highly sympathetic. Whatever you say, a jury is just going to eat it up. And they know that."

"This is bullshit, Harold. It's complete fucking bullshit," Kristy said, shaking her head. "What these people did, maybe it wasn't legal... exactly. But, that sonofabitch deserved it! And now, as if it's not bad enough that he raped me and the system let him get away with it, now the system is going to force me to help put away the people that set things right? That is so fucked up!"

"Kristy. The system isn't perfect. But, it's the best we've got. Your choices are: one, tell them what you know and avoid jail; or two, refuse to cooperate and risk going to jail yourself."

"Or I could lie."

Harold threw his hands in the air. He shook his head.

Kristy pondered. She stood and paced the conference room. Harold waited, giving her time to think.

"What does this 'deal' you're getting me look like?"

The lawyer suppressed a smile. This was the right choice, the best choice. He was saving her life. She just didn't know it yet.

"Immunity. It basically means that nothing you tell them can be used against you to convict you of a crime."

"So, if I admit to killing this Clayton guy..."

"It doesn't even need to have been in self-defense. Look, I think we have a very strong argument that what you did was justifiable homicide. But," Harold held both hands up, palms toward Kristy for emphasis, "with an immunity deal, it doesn't even matter. You confess to it, give them all the details, every single fact. Then, anything you tell them cannot be used against you. Free pass."

"What if I tell them something unrelated, like... that I shoplifted at Macy's?"

"Again, free pass."

"What if I tell them that my friend Bethany was with me and we did it together?"

Riviera shook his head. "No free pass for her. The deal applies only to you."

Kristy thought for a few moments on that point.

Riviera noticed, and asked, "Did your friend have something to do with—"

"No," Kristy interrupted, shaking her head. "No. She wasn't even in Miami. It was just a hypothetical. But," Kristy changed gears, "will the jury believe me if they know I killed someone? That doesn't make me seem very... sympathetic."

Riviera nodded. Kristy was beginning to understand how things worked.

"The game is always the same. The State will try to show that you're an upstanding citizen telling the truth, the whole truth, and nothing but the truth. They're going to try to make you look like Ms. Perfect. While the defense will try to show that you're not a reliable witness. They will claim that you have good reason to lie to get immunity. And they'll argue that you're willing to give the State whatever evidence they need—that you'll say whatever they want—to avoid getting prosecuted for other crimes."

Kristy stared out the window.

"Look, Kristy. It's 'come to Jesus' time. It's every man for himself now. What you saw is what you saw. And it's not *that bad* for them. Hell, you did the killing that night. I doubt the State's expecting to hear that. Immunity gets you completely off of that charge, forever. And, whatever Susie or Roy told you they did—"

"It was Susie. Roy didn't tell me anything. He was out in the boat dumping the body."

Riviera tried not to shrink at Kristy's cold and casual description of Clayton's burial at sea. "Right, sure. Whatever she told you they did, in the end, that comes down to 'he said, she said.' The jury may believe their version of events; they may believe yours. Cruise and his wife are adults. That's their problem. They can deal with it. Hell, Kristy... after everything that they did to avenge you, they would *want you* to protect yourself."

Kristy's mind was elsewhere. She'd already resigned herself to the fact that her lawyer was probably right. She hated it, but she didn't see that she had any other options.

She took a deep breath and said, "Alright. Cut me a deal."

CHAPTER THIRTY

What makes the *crack* of a gunshot so loud is not the tiny explosion of gunpowder that propels the bullet from the barrel of the gun. It's actually the sonic boom that occurs less than a millisecond later as the bullet accelerates and breaks the sound barrier.

Susie had heard gunfire many times before at the gun range, but always while wearing earmuffs. She'd never experienced that sonic boom in the confines of a small room with no ear protection.

It was shockingly loud.

Her ears were still ringing from the blast as she studied Liz Bareto. From the startled expression on Liz's face, Susie felt certain that she'd wounded her—she just couldn't see where. As Susie slowly raised her arm to fire again, she realized, to her surprise, that the Glock wasn't in her hand. Before she had time to wonder what had happened to her gun, a searing pain pierced her chest like a fiery javelin. It felt as if her left breast was on fire with a deep burn that scorched through her torso and into her back.

Susie looked down and saw that her blouse was stained crimson.

Oh shit... the bitch shot ME.

An unbearable pain throbbed inside her, alternating between a white hot poker twisting in her ribcage and molten metal burning her insides.

I can't...

* * *

Susie's hands felt sticky. She was on her back, shivering with cold. Liz Bareto was standing over her, gun in hand, looking down at her with wide eyes. Susie could see her Glock on the floor, several feet to her right. She willed her hand to move, to reach for the gun. If she had to die, she wanted to take this bitch with her. But, she was too weak. The pain in her chest was in charge, devouring all her strength.

She opened her mouth... but no sound came out.

* * *

Susie awoke to darkness and the sound of distant whispers.

Hello? Who's there?

Help!

I'm over here!

She waited for the voices to come to her, straining to make out what they were saying through the slow, monotonous *beep... beep... beep...* that seemed to be coming from something to her right.

Help!

Help me! she screamed, until she realized that her voice was only in her head.

Susie tried to open her eyes, but couldn't.

Wake up, Susie. Come on. Sit up. Open your eyes.

Nothing.

What's wrong with me?

Susie took mental inventory of her sensations. She could hear and smell. The air she breathed was cool and dry. She could feel her chest rise and fall. Feel the air in her lungs. She sensed that she was lying on her back, but her eyes wouldn't open. Her hands, her feet... nothing responded. She couldn't move. She tried again to speak, but nothing happened. She was trapped in the darkness. Her mouth was useless.

Oh God. I'm paralyzed. Oh God! No!

She tried to fight down the panic, concentrating, trying to open her eyes. Just a little bit. Trying to move her hand. A finger.

Nothing.

She needed help. She listened again, but the voices were gone.

No! Where did you go?

The only sound she heard was that soft, rhythmic beep.

Help! Somebody!

Anybody!

Help!

Nobody came. She was alone in the dark, and for the first time in a very long time, Susie Font was terrified.

* * *

Susie heard the soft swoosh of an automatic door and felt a slight change in air pressure around her. Then, at a distance, through the beeping, she heard movement and voices. Her eyes still refused to open, so in the darkness, she tried to picture the room around her. A door far away to her left. People directly ahead of her. Two of them. Women. And this time they were speaking at normal volume, distant but clear.

"Hey, girl. Long day?"

"Yeah. Pretty quiet, now. I'm ready to call it quits."

"It's like a ghost town in here."

The voices were coming closer.

"Yep. Had an MI come through earlier. Mild. And a stroke from yesterday that didn't make it. Just this GSW in here now."

Susie listened as the two women came up to her bed, their rubber shoe soles squeaking softly against the floor, their clothes rustling. She fought to move. To speak.

Hello...

"Oh! Is this the lady that got shot in Lago Beach?"

"That's her."

"How's it looking?"

Susie heard papers shifting, crinkling. Someone looking at her chart.

"Touch and go. Stable now... but she's pregnant."

"No shit?"

"Yeah. They're talking to the husband... about what to do..."

What to do?

What to do about what?!

Susie fought harder to move. To open her eyes. To raise her eyebrows. Anything that would indicate to these two bitches that she was awake!

"I'd hate to be in his shoes..."

I'm right here, goddammit!

I can hear you!

Susie exhaled in frustration.

Wait!

She tried holding her breath.

That, she could do!

Susie held her breath, then let it out all at once, making a sighing sound.

She felt a cool hand on her forehead.

"Poor thing," one of the women said. "You stay strong, girl. We're gonna take good care of you."

CHAPTER THIRTY-ONE

As a therapist, one learns to practice detachment. This, of course, is complicated if you allow yourself to become too close to a patient, which is what happened after Roy killed Getz for me. I have always been very careful about drawing the line between the professional and the personal, but I'm only human. You will have to judge for yourself whether what I did was wrong.

Back in November, we were in my office for Susie's weekly session. She announced to me that day that she was pregnant. She told me about how she made the decision without telling Roy. About seeing the doctor and the Clomid pills—her 2.5 milligrams of salvation in a tablet.

I congratulated her, of course. And she thanked me, for helping her to get to a place where she could even consider having a child again.

"There was a point, I know I've never told you," she paused, "where I was very close to ending it all. I was so miserable. The pain was bigger than I was. It became 'me.' It's all that was left. A deep hollow-out-your-guts ache that would wake me up at night. I had no appetite. I loathed everything around me. Even Roy.

"Especially Roy."

I sat still, silent. Waiting for her to continue.

"It creeps up on you, you know, the idea of killing yourself. You're suffering every day, every moment. Every breath is painful. The things that used to give you joy seem putrid and corrupt. So, you think, why not just end it all? With each passing day, it becomes a little more doable. A more realistic option. At a certain point, it just becomes a question of how.

"My choice was a handgun." She smiled sadly, saying, "I held that gun in my hand. Loaded. I even put it in my mouth. It tasted metallic and oily. I was that close. I had even imagined my funeral. Everyone turning out to mourn me. All of them understanding that losing a child was just too much to bear.

"You have kids, don't you Catherine? You can relate.

"Camilla was just seventeen years old when it happened..." She looked at me for a long moment. "When... she died.

"She was exceptional. A bright, witty girl. She had chestnut hair, and green eyes like her dad. But she had my cheekbones—my bone structure. And she had a beautiful laugh. She lit up a room," Susie laughed, "and I know, I'm her mom! What am I gonna say, right? But it's true.

"Like mother like daughter," she laughed.

I like to think Susie was being facetious, though sometimes she crossed the line into narcissism.

"She had a beautiful, kind soul. Kindness radiated from her. She gave me joy, and hope. And she loved horses. Especially Beau. Whenever she had any spare time, she was at the stables riding, grooming him, cleaning up. I remember when she left that day she was running late to meet her instructor."

Susie's eyes began to water. She wasn't looking at me anymore. She had a far-off look. I could tell she was deep in her memories. "Ever since she was small, we played this little game. A ritual. Whenever we said goodbye—when I went to work, or out to dinner, or dropped her off at school.

"I'd kiss her on the forehead and say, 'You be good, missy.'

"She'd kiss me on the cheek and say, 'You be better, Mommy.'

"Then I'd kiss her cheek and say, 'You're the best.'

"After she left that day, I went into our home office to get some work done. Suddenly, she was back. At first, I thought something was wrong, but I quickly saw that she was carrying a duffle bag she must have forgotten.

"Then she said, 'Since I had to come back, I thought I'd say a proper goodbye.

"And she laughed that beautiful laugh of hers, and then she

turned it around on me, our little game. *She* bent down and kissed *my* forehead. I remember her hair smelled like peppermint.

"'You be good, missy,' she told me.

"I kissed her cheek and said, 'You be better.'

"Then she kissed my cheek and smiled, and said, 'You're the best, Mom.'"

A tear rolled down Susie's cheek. I could feel my own eyes watering, and I swallowed hard, my chest tight.

Susie sniffed and continued, "After she left, I sat for a few moments just wondering where the time had gone. One second, she was an infant in my arms," Susie looked down, putting her hand over her heart, "at my breast, and a flash later, she was bending down to kiss *my* forehead and driving." She looked up at me. "Someday sooner than I'd like, she'd get married, make me a grandmother...

"I heard the door slam. I heard her car leave. I went back to my work.

"Fifteen minutes later... she was dead."

Susie paused. The tears were flowing now. She wasn't trying to stop them. She took a deep, trembling breath and continued, "After a few months wallowing in and out of more stages of grief than I knew existed, I found myself sitting back in the office in that same chair, with the gun in my hand—thinking about her, about the ache in my soul, and about our last goodbye.

"It took just a few seconds to perform our little ritual. If we hadn't done it, maybe she would have been further down the road? Maybe Bareto wouldn't have hit her? Maybe she'd still be alive?

"As I was about to pull the trigger, the memory of our last moment together overcame me. I could see her, standing there right in front of me, smiling at me with love, saying, 'You're the best, Mom.' And there I was, with a gun in my mouth.

"It was ridiculous. I dropped the gun and cried and cried. I didn't pull the trigger because I'm better than that, you know? I'm not a quitter."

Susie looked over at me. She shrugged. Her face was dark now. Her eyes narrow and hard.

"And why should I be the one to die, when that little

bastard who killed her was still alive? That's when I decided that Liam Bareto had to pay. That's when all this—" she waved an arm, "shit started and snowballed into what it is now; not just Bareto, but Harlan, Getz..." Susie shook her head. "I risked it all, Roy, my freedom—everything—for my happiness. Because I deserved to be happy again.

"After taking all those risks, and still not finding what I wanted, I realized that I'd been happiest when I had a child. And..." she placed her hands on her belly, "...that's when I decided to try again."

She smiled at me, and said, "This is going to make me happy."

It was a breakthrough of sorts. Susie was finally overcoming Camilla's death. Unfortunately, what was apparent to me was that Susie's suffering at losing Camilla was all about Susie, as was everything that happened after. For Susie, the baby was simply another means to the same end.

CHAPTER THIRTY-TWO

The day after she got shot, I told Roy about that session with Susie. We were in the Jackson Memorial waiting room. He had called me about an hour earlier and asked me to meet him there. When I arrived, he was there with two men whose names I had heard, but whom I had never met: J.C. Cohen, his business lawyer, and Mark Moran, his criminal defense attorney. Both of them handed me business cards. Out of habit, no doubt.

Roy explained to me that Susie's condition was critical but stable. She had not, however, regained consciousness and was not improving as rapidly as they had hoped. The baby was in distress. A choice had to be made.

They could perform a Cesarean to save the baby. At twenty-six weeks, the baby would be born premature, stood a good chance of making it. The odds of Susie surviving the procedure, however, were very poor.

The other option was to do nothing. Susie's odds of surviving were good, but they would lose the baby.

Roy's lawyer, J.C., had brought the hospital a copy of Susie's Living Will, which empowered Roy to make decisions regarding her health in the event of her incapacity.

"From a legal perspective, Roy has complete authority," said the lawyer. "The hospital's attorneys have confirmed this. So, at this point, which option to pursue... isn't a legal matter."

Moran nodded solemnly in agreement.

"Can we have the room?" Roy asked.

The two attorneys stepped out. Roy closed the door behind them and stood before me.

"I needed someone to talk to. Not just a therapist. But, a friend. I..." Roy's eyes were moist with tears. "I don't know what to do," he said with a sigh.

"Talk to me as a therapist first."

He began to pace, slowly. "How do you even weigh two lives? Susie... she *is my life*. Everything. We've been through so much together. The baby... she's mine... I love her too. I want us to have her. But, that's just it. I want *us* to have her."

He took a deep breath, then exhaled—blowing air through his mouth in frustration. "How can I possibly choose between the two?"

He continued, "If only the baby survives, when she grows up, I'll tell her that her mom died in childbirth. It's tragic, but shit happens—she'll learn to live with it. Hell, she won't know any other reality.

"If only Susie survives..." Roy stared into the middle distance. "I know what losing a child did to her before. And—with Camilla—well, that was an accident. At least, nothing we influenced. But, this... if Susie is in there..." he pointed vaguely at the wall, "... if she got shot—because of something she did, or we did... and that costs her the baby... I don't know if she could live with that.

"What's worse, if I choose her... instead of the baby... I don't know if Susie would ever forgive *me* for making that choice."

He stopped pacing.

The therapist in me understood Roy's conundrum. It was obvious that he had given it a great deal of thought.

He is an amazing man, Roy. Perceptive. Analytical. Articulate. He'd suffered so much due to the loss of his sister, Joan. Even though he was still dealing with those issues, he'd had the strength to forgive Susie for her involvement in that crime, because he loved her. Roy had done a lot of things out of love for Susie. He'd gotten a raw deal from life in many ways. He deserved so much better.

My heart was breaking for him, but I tried to put that aside and give him purely professional advice. And I was doing my damnedest to be objective.

I don't believe that my advice to Roy was clouded by any selfish desire on my part. I will not deny that, by this point, my feelings for him had blossomed into something more than friendship. But nothing could ever happen between us.

He was married.

That said, I wasn't oblivious to the fact that the decision he had to make might change that.

These things are never black and white, are they?

It was probably a breach of therapist/patient confidentiality, but that's when I told Roy about my session with Susie, when she'd told me she was pregnant and confessed that she'd almost committed suicide. I didn't share everything. It was a more idealized version of what Susie said than what I shared with you, in the sense that I didn't tell him my impressions or conclusions regarding her motivations. But, I think I got the gist of it right—the important parts.

In conclusion, I told him, "This baby, she exists only because Susie realized that, for her, the baby mattered more than anything else. The baby is critical to her happiness." I took Roy's hand, and said, "I think you're right. If you choose the baby and Susie survives, you'll have them both. But, if you choose Susie over the baby, there's a good chance she may never forgive you for that. If you choose Susie... you may lose everything."

Roy sat motionless for a long time before asking, "And as a friend, what does Catherine think?"

I pulled my hand from his, to catch a tear that was running down my cheek. I sniffled, fighting back more. Roy looked at me, and I saw something in those green eyes of his. It's odd, I can't explain what was different, but he wasn't looking at me as his therapist.

"You have to save the baby," I said softly.

CHAPTER THIRTY-THREE

Susie heard the now familiar swoosh of the automatic door followed by the light squeak of rubber-soled shoes, this time accompanied by a sharper *clap-tap clap-tap*. Then she heard rustling noises, and finally a discussion in hushed tones.

She tried again to open her eyes. To move her fingers. Toes. Anything. Her body still refused to cooperate.

She held her breath, then exhaled, making a sighing sound.

The voices abruptly stopped.

Then the *clap-tap clap-tap* resumed, getting louder, coming closer—until it stopped, and she felt a presence standing over her.

"Susie..." Roy breathed in deeply. "Oh God, Suze—" His voice cracked.

Susie's heart leapt. She felt hope for the first time since she'd been shot.

Roy! Oh baby! I'm here. I'm okay.

Thank God, it's finally you!

I can hear you!

Oh God, Roy! I love you!

Susie looked so small to him there in the hospital bed. Childlike. So vulnerable. How could he survive losing her?

Sorrow clamped down on his chest, constricting his throat and squeezing the air out of him. He couldn't breathe. Looking at Susie, realizing that he might never see her beautiful eyes again, never hear her laugh again, never embrace her again... Roy felt the room collapsing in on him. He wanted to crawl into the bed with her. To hold her. To smell her hair. To feel her heart beating against his chest.

"Oh, Susie..." he choked.

Yes. Roy! I'm here, baby. Talk to me!

Susie held her breath, then exhaled, making a sighing sound—trying to communicate with him.

"Susie..." A sob ripped through Roy. He felt his soul tear in two. His knees buckled as he clutched desperately to the bed railing for support. "Oh, God..." he mouthed repeatedly. But no words came out—only an anguished, animal sound of pain that he repeated between sobs.

Roy, honey... you're scaring me, Roy...

It's okay. I'm okay. I love you. Don't cry.

Everything's going to be alright!

We'll get through this.

Please don't cry, baby! You're scaring me!

When he was finally able to regain his composure, Roy stood up straight, wiping his eyes and nose on his sleeve. Susie seemed to be sleeping peacefully. Chest rising and falling gently. Pulse throbbing along her slender neck. All of these little signs of life were reduced to numbers and graphed on the monitor that beeped softly next to her bed.

Susie felt him take her hand. It was cool against her skin. She tried to squeeze back.

"How did we end up like this?" he whispered.

It was that fucking bitch, Liz! She shot me!

We've got to hunt her down, Roy!

Make her pay!

"So, listen, honey," Roy said, squeezing her hand. "The baby's in distress. The doctor says that she may not make it unless they do a Cesarean.

"But—" he choked on the words.

But... but, what?

What, Roy?

"Oh God," he continued, exhaling hard. "You're weak, sweetie. Maybe too weak. The doctor says you—" he exhaled hard again. "The doctor says you may not make it."

What? What the fuck, Roy?

"The other option is to just let the baby go."

What do you mean "other option"?

"They can save you. But I know you. I know what losing Camilla did to you. I know you could never forgive me if I sacrificed the baby to save you."

Forgive you?

Roy—

"So, I need you to fight, Susie. You're tough. I know you can do it. I know how much you want this baby. I know how much she means to you..."

She does, but—

Hold on...

Are you choosing the fucking baby over me?

"In case you don't make it, I want you to know how much I love you. I'll always love you. You'll always be with me."

What the hell? You can't do this to me, Roy!

I can have another baby! We can fuckin' adopt!

It's my baby, Roy! I decide!

Fuck the baby!

Susie felt a kiss on her forehead. *No!* She had to stop this. She needed to communicate. She needed to get through to him.

She held her breath, then exhaled, making a sighing sound.

"Oh, Suze..." Roy said. "If you can you hear me—"

Yes! Yes! I can... I CAN FUCKING HEAR YOU!

Ask me a question! Ask anything!

Susie held her breath, then sighed again.

"I want you to know..." Roy sighed, " ...how much I love you. I'll always love you."

Susie held her breath longer, then exhaled again, sighing louder.

"Doc?" Roy called out, hesitantly.

Yes! Call the doctor!

Ask me a question!

Susie held her breath, then exhaled.

Squeaky shoes approached.

"Doc, I..." Roy said, "I think...I think we're ready."

No! For fuck's sake!

ASK ME A QUESTION!

Susie stopped breathing and exhaled several times.

Roy paused, studying his wife's face. "Is she okay, Doc?" he asked. "Her breathing—"

"She's okay for now, Roy. Irregular breathing is common in a coma. But we should get her into the OR before the baby suffers any more distress."

No! You stupid sonofabitch. I'm here!

Get me the fuck out of this! Wake me up!

Don't you dare fucking operate on me!

Save me!

Save me, Roy!

SAVE ME!

Susie struggled to move. Struggled to open her eyes. Struggled to scream.

She felt Roy kiss her and squeeze her hand, then heard the *clap-tap clap-tap* of his shoes moving away from her, receding as it was replaced by the bustle of several nurses around her bed.

You sonofabitch!

This is about your sister, isn't it?

You vengeful fucking bastard!

Susie Font screamed with all of her might as she felt herself being wheeled across the room and through the swooshing automatic door.

She screamed as she was pushed along the corridor and into the elevator that took her down to the freezing operating room.

Susie screamed at everyone around her, until a thin plastic mask was placed over her mouth, rendering her unconscious.

CHAPTER THIRTY-FOUR

Susie Font was pronounced dead on February 11th at 3:42 p.m.

Her daughter had been delivered successfully via Cesarean section twenty minutes earlier and was transferred to the neonatal intensive care unit.

Her father named her Joan.

CHAPTER THIRTY-FIVE

Kristy was standing on her back deck sipping a beer and working with a butcher knife. She'd organized a small get-together at her house—just a few friends for drinks and dinner. She'd picked up some ribeye steaks, but had also purchased a whole beef tenderloin that was on sale and was cutting it into steaks. She was working at a small counter next to the grill. There was still a winter chill in the Austin air, and she'd lit up her small fire pit to keep warm. It sat about ten feet away and gave off a cozy glow. As she cut the meat into pieces, the knife reflected the firelight through sticky streaks of blood.

Everyone was arriving at seven p.m. She'd told Alfie to come over early at five-thirty to help her get organized. Yet, she'd gotten started even earlier, and as she worked, she was talking with Bethany, explaining to her a concern she had and asking her opinion. She'd wanted to talk to her before Alfie came as the issue concerned him, and she thought she knew how he would react.

Kristy had already explained to Bethany what she'd learned from Riviera.

"That's great news, Kris! This means that you can tell them what happened at the Cruises' house and you're off the hook—a clean slate! What more could you ask for?" Bethany always saw the bright side of things.

Kristy opened the cooler with her knife hand and pulled out another beer. Her other hand was covered in blood. She used a paper towel to hold the can, popping it open with her clean hand and taking a swig, then placed the can on the counter. "I don't think you're hearing me right... what about Frank? What if, somehow, they ask about him?"

"Not likely, man. He's got nothing to do with what happened in Miami, does he? It probably won't even come up."

"But he's got to do with Joe. And the guy at the house in Miami—Clayton—he was asking all about Joe. It's all connected. If they ask me about Frank, that's a big problem. Anything I tell them is a clean slate *for me*, but not for anyone who helped me. Don't you understand?"

Bethany shook her head. "All that happened was Frank got slipped some roofies, and 'someone'—" she made bunny ears, "stole his drugs and his drug money. I mean, I know it's *technically* illegal, but... really... is stealing illegal stuff *really* stealing? I mean, *really*?" Bethany smiled.

"But Riviera said that if I lie, the cops can use that to kill my immunity. What happens if I don't tell the police about Frank, and then somehow it comes out? I think they could use that to invalidate my whole immunity deal."

Bethany shrugged. "I'm no lawyer. You need to ask Riviera."

"I can't. He didn't ask about Frank; I didn't tell him. But he told me so many times that I can't lie—I can still fucking hear him saying it—so, if I ask him about Frank, then I'm stuck. Then, I can't lie about it. I would *have to* tell them at that point."

Bethany understood Kristy's dilemma and pondered, "Shit..."

"Look," Kristy continued. "I think you're right. They're not even interested in Frank. They don't know anything about him. I don't think he's reported anything stolen—"

"Obviously not."

"—so, yeah. It's best just to ignore that whole part of the story. These cops are from Florida, anyway. And apparently all they're interested in is Susie and Roy."

Bethany pursed her lips, mulling over Kristy's words, following her logic.

"Riviera says that, as long as what they get from me is 'good stuff,' they won't be interested in making me look bad. The more it looks like I was just an innocent bystander caught in the drama, the better. I'm just gonna make sure they focus on everything that happened on Halloween. But, if they ask anything about Frank, I'm gonna lie."

Bethany smiled broadly and said, "That's my girl!"

CHAPTER THIRTY-SIX

Eddie Garza was sitting at the airport, waiting for his flight to Austin. Kristy Wise's interview was set for the following morning. Eddie had originally been scheduled to travel with Spencer Shaw, but a last minute court hearing had required Shaw's attention. He'd re-booked onto a later flight that same day.

As Eddie sat waiting, and thought over all of the developments of the last several days, he decided to call Liz Bareto. He realized that he'd forgotten to call her after Roy's interview, though understandably. A lot more had happened the day of the interview than expected. But, in the back of his mind, he thought it odd that Liz hadn't called him to follow up on the interview, either.

That morning, a news article had come out reporting that Susie Font was the woman who'd been shot in Lago Beach, and that she had died from complications. Eddie felt he was free to share general information about the case with Liz, now that the major details were public knowledge. Eddie always tried to be careful when he shared investigative information with Liz. And even though he sometimes erred on the side of oversharing, Liz had always been discreet.

She picked up on the third ring.

"I've got you on speaker, Eddie, 'cuz I've got my hands full. Been a bit under the weather," she advised. Liz was sitting on her sofa with her mobile phone on the coffee table. She'd put Eddie on speaker because she was on edge, she had been since the shooting, and worried that he might notice the tremors in her voice.

"Sorry to hear that. And I apologize for not calling sooner, but... well... I don't know if you saw the news, about Susie Font?" he asked.

"I did," she said, trying to strike a balance between curiosity and surprise. "I assume her husband was out of town?" she scoffed weakly.

"Actually, he was in the same building as I was."

"So, she was shot the day of the interview? I mean, I didn't know if the interview had gone forward. When you didn't call... I mean... I wasn't sure if the shooting happened before or... or if something had changed."

"Nope. Cruise and Kim showed up. We were in the process of interviewing Cruise when I got the call."

"Are you sure it couldn't have been him? The man has a way... you know..." Liz stammered. She worried that somehow Eddie knew, or perhaps suspected, what had happened. She had gone back and forth over whether to call him about Roy's interview. In the end, she hadn't trusted her nerves to hold up. Now, she regretted that decision, as not calling was clearly out of character for her. "Are there any leads? Wasn't the house being watched by the police?"

Eddie's stomach tightened.

Liz knew about the surveillance.

His mind raced, kicking into detective mode.

She knew about the timing of the interview.

Why didn't she call me to follow up?

Oh fuck...

Eddie's hand trembled slightly, and his mouth was suddenly dry. He realized he wasn't talking to Liz Bareto, his friend. He was talking to a suspect in the murder of Susie Font.

"Uh, yeah. It was. By video, actually. Cameras outside... All of that's still being checked out. It takes time, you know?"

Liz was silent, though Eddie could hear some movement at her end.

"Well, it's terrible," she said. "I read that the child survived. I didn't... I didn't know she was pregnant."

Oh, God. That sounded... remorseful.

"Yeah. Tough break. Anyway," he added, "I just thought you should know. In case you hadn't seen the news."

"Nothing more on Getz? Or from the interview?" The questions sounded perfunctory.

"No. No. Nothing—" Eddie was grateful to be interrupted by a flight announcement over the PA. When it was done, he said, "Listen, I gotta catch a plane. I'll call later. When I have more... I'll call you later, okay?"

They hung up.

Eddie's mind raced. His palms were sweating. He fought back a wave of nausea. He grabbed his carry-on and dragged it behind him to the restroom. Eddie walked rapidly, while breathing in and out slowly through his mouth to fight the nausea, even as he mentally checked the boxes.

Motive? Absolutely... Liz has been after these folks for years. Did she learn something new from Senator Harlan? Or from Kristy Wise? Something she didn't tell me?

Opportunity? I told her about the fucking interview! She knew that Cruise would be out of the house. And that there was surveillance, so she could've dodged it...

Means? A gun. Easy enough to check. I'll do that when I get back. Discreetly.

But, Liz? She's... she's Liz... fancy lady... She's not a vigilante.

And she's always suspected Cruise, hasn't she? Not the wife.

Besides, Cruise goes to work most days. The fact that she knew about the interview... if she was gonna do it, she could have done it any day. It's not really a big deal that I told her about the interview... not really.

But, it wouldn't look good...

The bathroom was packed. There were lines for the urinals and the stalls. The nausea was passing. Eddie walked to an open sink. His pale face stared back at him. He ran cold water and rinsed his face.

Forget it for now.

I'll follow up when I get back from Austin.

Eddie shoved the "Liz issue" into a little compartment in the back of his mind.

One day at a time...

CHAPTER THIRTY-SEVEN

It was late afternoon. Roy was wearing hospital scrubs and a mask. He had just walked out of the NICU, after checking on the baby. She was amazing. So tiny. Just barely over nine inches long and just shy of two pounds. She seemed so frail. She was beautiful. And yet, over the wonder of it all hung Susie's death, her absence, like a venomous green cloud.

Although he was still processing everything that had happened, and still in a state of shock, his brain had already begun spitting out hypotheses, mostly late at night when he couldn't sleep. While he didn't discount the possibility of a home invasion gone wrong, ten o'clock in the morning on a Monday was not your typical prime-time burglary hour. Besides, nothing was apparently stolen. No. The attack on Susie—on them—felt personal.

He had begun working backwards, from victims to suspects. There was no doubt whatsoever in his mind that whoever had done this to Susie would pay dearly. He just needed to know who.

The first and most obvious suspect was Senator Harlan. He was the closest to knowing what Roy and Susie had done to Joe Junior. He had already come after them once. He was at the top of the list.

Next was Liz Bareto. Less likely. She'd been stewing on the sidelines for years. Roy couldn't imagine what could have happened to convert her from an annoyingly obsessed PTA mom to a homicidal shooter. He'd had some exposure to her over the years. She didn't seem the type. But, it was possible.

Then, of course, it could be that an interested party had

somehow made a connection between them and Jeff Getz. But who? And how? That was sheer speculation at this point.

Roy was in a small dressing room peeling off his scrubs when he felt his phone vibrating in his pocket. He pulled the elastic band of the scrubs away from his waist and retrieved his phone from his pants pocket.

UNKNOWN

"This is Roy Cruise."

"Mr. Cruise," Roy heard that *click* and change of tone that one hears when a caller picks up a telephone receiver, switching a call from speaker to handheld, "please don't hang up."

Roy froze. He would recognize that Texas drawl anywhere.

"Harlan..."

"I had nothing to do with it, Cruise. I gave you my word, and my word is my bond. I am calling to offer my condolences. And, also, to assure you that I have kept and intend to continue to keep my end of our bargain."

Roy sat down on a bench in the changing room. He looked around, confirming that he was alone. All of his senses were on high alert. Roy had built a career on his bullshit monitor—knowing when people were telling the truth, when they were lying, when they were stretching the facts. He brought all those skills to bear as he engaged with Harlan.

"Why should I believe you, Joe? I mean, it's not like you'd call up to confess."

"Roy, I'm one phone call away from the President. You think I'd risk all of that...?"

Roy analyzed and digested—not just what Harlan said, but how he said it. Tone. Pauses. He scanned his memory through past conversations with the man and compared what he was hearing now to how he'd spoken in the past.

"Some might argue that that would actually put you in a position to get it done and not get caught. Using some government goons."

"Oh, for fuck's sake, Cruise. This isn't *Mission Impossible.* We live in the fucking United States. You know better than that."

Harlan sounded matter-of-fact. Not at all like he'd sounded when Roy spoke to him on Halloween. Roy waited.

Harlan continued, "As a gesture of good faith, I can tell you that I recently received a call from Detective Eddie Garza. He was asking specifically about your Halloween visitor. The authorities are investigating his disappearance. Garza told me that he believes that Clayton discovered something about you that you didn't want known, and when he visited your home, you killed him. I denied all knowledge, and will continue to do so—about that, anyway. Though that is a lie, of course."

Roy's ears perked up. The man had just admitted to lying to the police. But, it could be a trap. If he was recording the conversation or working with the authorities, this is where he would ask something incriminating of Roy, in exchange.

"And...?" Roy asked.

"And nothing. As I said, I am sorry for your loss. I lost my wife young. It was the most painful loss of my life. Even... even more so than Joe."

"Well, thank you for that. And, yes, the police are poking around about your friend. They had a picture of him standing on my front porch. Any idea how they got that?"

"None. I didn't even know he was going to visit you. That sonofabitch was a loose cannon."

Both men were silent for several moments, then Roy said, "Well, I gotta go."

"Look, Cruise. We're never gonna see eye to eye on a lot of things. And, I admit, I fucked up, with Slipknot. That got outta hand. It wasn't my intent, but... but, as far as I'm concerned, that never happened. Anything else the police ask me about Joe, I'll answer. But, as far as Slipknot is concerned, and his," Harlan cleared his throat, "disappearance, I know nothing."

"Yeah, sure."

"Like I said before, you stay out of my life, I'll stay out of yours."

"Yeah. Fine," Roy replied.

"I'm not a bad man, Roy. I suspect you're not, either. I think we just met under the wrong circumstances," Harlan said. "I'm sure you can understand. When you have a child, you'll do anything for them. Even if maybe it's not... not the most advisable course of action."

"Yeah," Roy replied. "I get it."

"Very well, then. Good luck with your little girl. God bless."

Roy sat for a few moments processing the conversation. Sampling conclusions. Harlan sounded genuine. Of course, he was a lawyer and a politician. He'd been trained to lie and did it for a living every day. Still, after weighing everything he'd heard, Roy tended to believe what Harlan had said.

Shit... if not him, then who?

Roy sighed, and finished stripping off his scrubs.

CHAPTER THIRTY-EIGHT

Tuesday morning, Garza and Shaw met for breakfast in their hotel in Austin, Texas. The night before, they'd had drinks with Art Travers. On their second beer, Shaw had sprung the news that he didn't want Travers attending Kristy's interview.

"It's nothing personal, Art. I just want to keep the number of folks in the room down to a minimum. And, I want to raise the intimidation factor. You're a familiar face. That'll be comforting to her."

Travers was silent, listening. He and Eddie had been working the case since Senator Harlan first called Travers to report that he hadn't heard from his son, who'd been visiting Miami. For Shaw to exclude Travers from the interview was a kick in the balls. Eddie felt horrible.

"I know you understand, Art," Shaw continued. "You know how this works. I want her to feel like she either talks, or the full power of the State of Florida is going to be unleashed against her. I want her to feel out of place, disoriented. I want her fucking scared."

Travers reluctantly agreed to sit out the interview. He finished his beer and made his excuses.

After much negotiation, they'd agreed to do Kristy's interview at Riviera's office, with a stenographer and a video camera. The interview would be conducted under oath. Shaw talked Eddie through how he intended to handle the interview.

Shaw had spoken with Riviera the day before. Harold had explained, in broad strokes, what Kristy could testify to. Shaw hadn't told Eddie any of the details yet, but he was excited. If he handled the interview well, he knew he had a slam dunk conviction on his hands. There was also going to be a huge surprise in her testimony, but Shaw held that back—he wanted to see Eddie's face when he heard it.

At nine o'clock, they left for Riviera's office. When they arrived, they were shown into a large, glass-walled conference room. The stenographer and videographer had arrived moments earlier and were getting set up.

"Would you mind sitting in the hot seat? Let me mic you up so I can check my levels?" the videographer asked. Eddie obliged and began to recite the Gettysburg Address. Meanwhile, Shaw helped himself to coffee, then sat down at the table and began organizing his outline, photos, and various documents that he had pre-labeled as exhibits.

Eddie was about halfway through his second rendition, "... testing whether any nation, so conceived, and so dedicated, can long endure—"

"All good. Thanks, man!" the videographer interrupted.

The stenographer said, "Start in about ten minutes."

The videographer nodded and replied, "I'm hitting the head."

"I could go to the ladies before we start."

They left Shaw and Eddie in the conference room, seated at the far left end of the table with the windows to their backs, facing the glass wall with a view of the hallway. Eddie helped himself to a cup of coffee and returned to his seat. Shaw was making some final notes when Eddie said, "There they are." On the other side of the glass wall were Kristy Wise and Harold Riviera.

"So, that's Kristy Wise, huh? Damn... I can see why Harlan went astray," Shaw commented. "I'd fuck that in a heartbeat."

Eddie bristled, but said nothing.

Kristy was in black pants, a pale blue blouse, and flat shoes. Riviera was in a dark blue suit, white shirt, and a fierce red tie.

As they entered, Eddie made introductions.

Moments later, the videographer and stenographer returned. The videographer sat Kristy at the head of the table and attached a mic to her blouse collar. He then went to the other end of the table, put on headphones, and checked the video and audio output for her, Shaw's, and Riviera's mics.

"All good here," the video guy said.

"Okay," said Shaw, "Could I ask you two to leave the room for a few moments while—"

"Sure," the videographer replied. The stenographer was already on her feet. The two exited and waited outside, just down the hall where they could still see but not hear what was happening in the conference room.

Shaw smiled at Kristy and began, "Ms. Wise. May I call you Kristy?"

She nodded.

"Kristy. Let me thank you for agreeing to be here today, on behalf of the people of the State of Florida. I know that sounds corny, but it's true. You agreeing to be here today and tell us the truth about what happened, what you saw, what you were told—all of that is going to allow us to put someone who broke the law behind bars.

"I wanted to talk to you first, off the record, because I want to make sure that we," Shaw pointed back and forth between Kristy and himself, "are on the same page about our agreement. I know. We've got it in writing..." he picked up the first document on the stack in front of him, "and it's going to be an exhibit here today. But, I want to make sure we both are clear on what it means. So, why are you here today?" Shaw paused, looking up.

Kristy said, "I'm here to—"

"Sorry, that was rhetorical," Shaw interrupted. "You are here today because... you basically got lucky. I am going to see to it that Roy Cruise gets the death penalty. But to do that, I need one witness." Shaw held up his index finger. "One sympathetic person who can tell the story to the jury. I already have all the evidence. But, you see, I'm a perfectionist. I want it all. That means one solid witness that can tell the entire story from start to finish. That's you.

"See, we've had Cruise's house under audio and video surveillance since October 27th. We know everything. We know about the relationship between Susie and your mom..."

As Shaw began to recite everything that "we know," Kristy

felt her stomach tightening. She fought to show no emotion. But she was surprised at everything that the police seemed to have figured out.

"We know about the exchange—the *quid pro quo*. Like that goddamned Alfred Hitchcock movie. We know about how they killed Harlan. And cut of his pecker. Hell, we've got..." Shaw flipped through documents, until he found the right one, a photo, and held it up for her to see, "...the goddamned knife."

Shaw paused. "We know about your father. And let me say," Shaw pursed his lips, "I am very sorry for your loss. Your father and mother both." Shaw shook his head sadly, then continued, "Your father's death was not a suicide. The gun oil in his mouth..."

Shaw paused, then removed another photo from the stack.

"I know you've seen this man before. This same man attacked Cruise's business partner in Miami. A week before your father died. And then he came here, to Austin... A very busy man, this one." Shaw shrugged. "Not a good person, this guy."

He passed the photo across to Kristy. As she studied the photo, he continued. He'd carefully scripted and repeatedly practiced the entire monologue.

"We've got lots of pictures. Hold on..." Shaw shuffled through the documents, pretending to search for another. He knew exactly where he'd placed it. "Look at this one," he said, holding it up for Kristy to see, then placing it on the table and sliding it toward her. It was the photo of two young girls at camp. Eddie and Shaw had been unable to figure out definitively who they were. Eddie thought one of the girls looked like a young Susie Font, but it was hard to tell. Shaw studied Kristy's face as she looked at the photo, and he saw that her face registered recognition.

Bingo, he thought. He knew now that she'd be telling him who they were shortly.

"So, you see, I have all the pieces. And there are people that'll be going down over this—death penalty down. I'm glad that you're not one of them. But, you understand, and I know Harold explained, all of that depends on you answering all of my questions completely and honestly. I just want to make sure that we're clear on that, because the consequences of not doing so," Shaw said, then paused, "of leaving some detail out of your answer or lying to us... that'd be some really bad shit. You understand that, right?"

Kristy nodded. She swallowed, and replied, "I understand."

Shaw was pleased with himself. He'd laid out the skeleton—an outline of what he thought had happened. He knew that he couldn't prove it all without Kristy's testimony. In fact, some of it was just plain speculation. But he also understood human nature. He knew that she would mentally fill in the blanks, thinking that the police could prove much more than they actually could. And, it would make it easier for her to confess everything if she felt she was only verifying what the police could already prove anyway.

Shaw sat studying her for a few moments. Then, slowly, he began to nod. He smiled and looked down the hall, indicating to the stenographer and videographer that they should return.

Two hours later, the interview was complete. Shaw took extensive notes. As they wrapped up and said their goodbyes, the stenographer asked Shaw, "Is this a rush? Where should I send the transcript?"

"No. No hurry. Call me when it's done," he replied, pointing at the business card he'd given her at the beginning of the interview, "and I'll let you know where to send everything."

The stenographer looked at the videographer and shrugged.

CHAPTER THIRTY-NINE

Kristy Wise's interview could not have gone better. Shaw was one sharp bastard. When Eddie had heard him lay out their case—the skeleton parts—he'd easily been able to fill in the blanks. Shaw had made it sound like they had much more on Roy Cruise than they really did. And Kristy Wise had filled in those blanks beautifully.

But, Kristy's testimony was not what Garza had expected.

"Holy fuck!" Eddie exclaimed once he and Shaw were in the rental car driving back to the hotel.

Shaw laughed out of excitement. "You should'a seen the look on your face, Garza. When she confessed to killing Clayton."

It was true. When Kristy had explained how she'd shot the home invader, Eddie had blanched. He'd felt like he was watching their case against Cruise go up in smoke, and with Kristy Wise sitting on complete immunity. But, Shaw was good at what he did. He'd maintained a straight face. Besides, Riviera had already explained to Shaw, at a high level, what Kristy would testify to, so he hadn't been surprised.

Shaw had continued poking and prodding. Not ten minutes later, Kristy had related her conversation with Susie, and Susie's confession to the murder of Joe Harlan Junior by her and by Roy.

"This is perfect," Shaw said. Then he repeated, in a shout that startled Eddie, clapping his hands together, "Fuckin' perfect!"

Eddie glanced sideways at the prosecutor. He looked like a kid at a ballgame, his favorite team having just scored a winning touchdown.

"And there's no way they'll see this coming, Eddie. Cruise

and his lawyer are expecting us to come after him for Clayton. They're gonna shit themselves when we indict him for killing Joe Harlan Junior."

Eddie smiled as they drove back to the hotel, and then on to the airport. At long last, he felt like they had that bastard Cruise in their sights. Still, there was an uncomfortable tightness in Eddie's neck. And the burn of acid in his belly.

On both nights of their trip to Texas, Eddie had not slept well. Sure, he'd overdone it on Mexican food one night and bar-b-que the next. And, without his wife haranguing him about his weight, he'd had a few more beers than usual. Still, even his usual dose of Pepcid hadn't gotten him through the nights. He'd tossed and turned, and been up both mornings at just after four a.m., unable to sleep anymore. It had nothing to do with Kristy Wise, and everything to do with Liz Bareto. On the flight back, he kept playing through different scenarios relating to Susie Font's death.

Forensics had confirmed that the gun found at the Cruise house had not been fired. There was no GSR—gunshot residue—found on Susie Font's hands. There were no powder burns on Susie's clothing, nor any stippling or tattooing of the skin at the wound site. The gun found at the scene, belonging to the Cruises, was a 9mm Glock. The bullet wound and fragments confirmed that Susie Font had been shot with one 0.38 caliber round. Susie Font definitely hadn't shot herself. The gunshot was taken from a distance.

The case was being investigated as a homicide. That said, it was a murder investigation that, so far, had produced very few leads. The telephone from the study had been taken into the lab for more detailed analysis. No fingerprints were found. The voice on the recording of the 9-1-1 call from the scene that alerted police to the "accident" was of a female caller. The woman sounded hoarse, strained, and distant, as if the caller was holding the receiver far from her mouth. All it said was, "Help me. I've been shot. I'm pregnant." The caller didn't hang up. The phone had been found out of its cradle, lying on the desk when the police arrived.

Eddie had listened to the 9-1-1 call recording over and over. It was poor quality audio, and wasn't clearly and irrefutably Liz—but neither could he rule out that it might be Liz disguising her voice. Roy Cruise had been asked to listen to the recording, and he'd stated without a doubt that the voice was not Susie Font's.

Surveillance video from outside the Cruise house showed no vehicles parking and no one entering or leaving the house during the relevant timeframe. That meant that access to the property had to have been via the backyard. Most probably by jumping the fence from a neighbor's yard.

The sliding door to the terrace was found open and was the most likely entry and exit path of the killer. The police had canvassed the neighbors within the subdivision and the properties directly across the canal. But, not surprisingly, on a Monday morning at around 11:00 a.m., no one had seen or heard anything of note. Not even the damned gunshot.

There were very few leads.

What Eddie wanted to find out was whether or not Liz Bareto owned a gun. It was something that had never come up in conversation. And she didn't seem like the type—under normal circumstances. But, Liz's circumstances were anything but normal.

Contrary to what you see on TV, there is no national gun registration database in the United States. There is no place to call or search to find out if someone has ever bought or owns a gun. But, there are ways of getting close.

When Eddie got back to the office, he logged into the database for the National Crime Information Center. This database gathers data on individuals, including criminal history records, outstanding warrants, and the like from law enforcement agencies across the country. The database can be searched to see if someone is a wanted fugitive or has a criminal past. And, whenever a person's name *is searched* in the database, that information is recorded as well—the date of the search, what was searched, by what agency, and so forth. Eddie checked the database search history for Elizabeth Anne Bareto, Social Security Number 462-76-0965.

In the last twelve months, Liz's name had been searched

twice. The first search was done in May of the prior year by Officer Pietro Sainz of the Coral Gables Police Department using an in-car computer. Probably a traffic stop.

The second search, however, turned Eddie's stomach. It was in October of the prior year by the National Instant Criminal Background Check System. The NICS was established by the Brady Handgun Violence Prevention Act and does only one thing—criminal background checks in connection with the purchase of handguns.

CHAPTER FORTY

Eddie Garza and Spencer Shaw were sitting in a mid-sized conference room that would soon become a part of Shaw's war against Cruise. Eddie stood at a dry erase board mapping out his vision of their case. He had carefully listed items of evidence found at the Cruise property as well as key points of evidence that had been provided by Kristy Wise during her interview.

From those facts, he was using a red marker to write a list of crimes on the board that he believed could be proven. Shaw was sitting at the far end of the conference table, leaning back with his hands behind his head.

"So, this is the full list, I think. We can go after him for," Eddie pointed at the dry erase board and read, "all of these.

(1) the murder of Joe Harlan Junior,
(2) mutilation of a dead human body,
(3) accessory to the murder of Liam Bareto,
(4) accessory to the murder of Ronald Clayton, and
(5) we can charge him with unlawful disposition of human remains—both Harlan's and Clayton's."

Eddie put the cap on the dry erase marker he'd been using and flopped into the chair next to the board.

"Well, that's the kitchen sink approach, right, Eddie? I mean, are you saying that we should actually charge him with all of that, or are you just saying that he's probably guilty in one way or another of all of those things?"

Eddie steepled his fingers, thinking, then replied, "Well,

I think we have the evidence for them all. What do you propose?"

"In my experience, Eddie, juries are made up of idiots. I know," he raised a hand, "it's not the politically correct thing to say. We are all equal in the eyes of God, and the law, and all that bullshit. But," Shaw chuckled, "God must be one nearsighted motherfucker... because I've seen enough juries to know that ten out of every twelve jurors are fuckin' morons.

"You'll get the three or four housewives that have nothing better to do, a couple of trades types—plumber, electrician maybe—then you'll have one or two semi-educated folks. And they're the ones that get elected foreman and run the show. It's a shitty system, but it's the best one there is. So, if we are going to win this thing, we need to keep it simple. Keep it focused."

Shaw walked across the conference room and picked up a black dry erase marker. He stood in front of the board reviewing Eddie's list of crimes. Then he reached out and circled "murder of Joe Harlan" and "mutilation of a dead human body."

"That's our case. See, Eddie, I don't like the idea of charging him with these body dumping crimes and lesser accessory charges. It gives the jury an easy out if they like him but they feel like they should convict him of 'something.'"

"Kind of like splitting the baby?" Eddie asked.

"Yeah." Then Shaw began to speak in a nasal tone, imitating a woman, "'Oh, poor Roy. He just lost his wife! And he has a baby to take care of... and the guy he killed was a nasty guy anyway! Let's just punish him a little bit...' And we spend all our time and tax dollars trying a capital case and end up with a fuckin' misdemeanor conviction for polluting the bay with a couple of corpses.

"But," Shaw pointed at Eddie with the marker, "we go for murder one, death penalty—for killing Joe Harlan Junior—and for the mutilation—for cutting off his dick." Shaw took a few steps toward Eddie, and added, "Because we gotta get that evidence in front of the jury." Shaw held the dry erase marker near his crotch as if it were his penis, then mimicked scissors snipping with his other hand and held the marker up, pretending to be in pain. He laughed and tossed it to Eddie who reluctantly caught it. "I mean, I want—" Shaw held his arms out wide and moved them in the shape of a large square, "to put a big-assed, blown-up picture of that kid's severed dick right in front of the jury. They'll all cringe at the thought! If we focus on that... we win!"

Shaw walked back toward his seat, saying, "Hell, we can even agree with the defense that Harlan was a shitty guy. But, who likes a mutilator? A dick-cutter-offer?" Shaw looked at Eddie. "It's uncivilized. It's inhuman. It's scary!" Shaw bugged his eyes and waved his hands crazily. "That's a simple story to tell. A four-year-old could understand *that story*. That's our case!"

Eddie nodded and smiled. Shaw was the expert. And he'd built a hell of a reputation as a trial lawyer. But, in his gut, Eddie didn't agree.

CHAPTER FORTY-ONE

In late February, Roy Cruise was indicted on two counts: murder in the first degree and mutilation of a dead human body. Shaw chose to seek the death penalty against Roy, should he be convicted. The indictment was sealed, pending Roy's arrest, which was planned for the following morning.

True to his reputation, Spencer Shaw leaked information about the arrest to a couple of trusted contacts in the media. Shaw planned to kick off the case with a bang and do what he could to begin to bias the jury pool against Roy. That meant getting as much news coverage as possible. He accompanied the police to the offices of Cruise Capital to arrest Roy.

Detective Eddie Garza flashed his badge at reception and, without a word, walked straight back to Roy's office, flanked by Shaw and two uniformed officers. As they made for Roy's office, Eve shouted, "Detective! Can I help you? Gentlemen, where are you going?"

Eddie didn't bother to knock on the office door. He opened it and stepped in, saying, "Good morning, Roy!"

The office was empty. Eddie, Shaw, and the two uniforms returned to Eve's desk.

"Can you tell me where Cruise is?" Eddie asked Eve.

"Good morning, Detective. Do you have an appointment?" she snipped back at him. She was clearly upset that the men had simply walked past her.

"Better. I have a warrant for his arrest."

"That's no excuse for bad manners, Detective. You've been

here many times before. I've always treated you with respect. Don't I deserve the same courtesy?" Eve chided.

"Well, I—" Eddie stammered before Shaw interrupted him.

"Listen, ma'am—"

"Quiet! I wasn't talking to you!" Eve glared at Shaw. "I don't even know who you are!"

"I'm—"

"And I didn't ask!" she cut him off again. Eve turned back to Eddie. "Now, Detective, let me see your warrant, please." Roy had instructed Eve on exactly what to do if the police came to the office that morning. She studied the document for a moment, then nodded as if she had confirmed that everything was in order, and said, "If you need to speak with Mr. Cruise, you'll have to go to the hospital. Or, if you like, I can call him and let him know that you're here," Eve said, reaching for the phone.

"Please don't," Eddie replied. "We'll go there. And please don't call him to let him know we're coming, either." Somehow, it sounded like a request rather than a command. Eddie added, "Officer del Rio will stay here to... keep you company." He nodded to one of the two uniforms.

The three took the elevator down to the lobby and walked empty-handed past two video cameras and reporters from the local news.

One reporter asked snidely, holding out a mic, "Mr. Shaw, what happened? Where's your suspect?"

Shaw was fuming and ignored the cameras. They headed to Jackson Memorial Hospital with several patrol cars and media vans in tow. As they drove, Eddie made a call.

"What the fuck, Wolfson? Cruise left the building!" He had the phone on speaker. Wolfson was the officer who had been charged with ensuring that Cruise was at his office for the arrest.

"I dunno, Eddie. He came into the office this morning at 7:30 in his Range Rover. It's still in the parking garage. I can see it from here."

Eddie hung up, and Shaw said, "He knows. Someone tipped them off, Eddie."

When the officers arrived at the hospital, they found their way to the NICU. As Eddie asked the duty nurse whether she had seen Roy Cruise that morning, Shaw's telephone chirped.

"Fuck," he said to Eddie. "Forget it. It's Moran."

Shaw and Eddie stepped away from the nurse's station, out of earshot of the two officers who'd accompanied them, and Shaw put the phone on speaker.

"Good morning, Spencer."

"Mark. How are you?"

"I'm great. How are you? Are you having a good day? Things going as planned?"

"What do you want, Moran?"

"Well, I'm calling because I'm here with my client, Roy Cruise. A little birdie told me that you might be looking for him. And, well, I'd just as soon not turn this into a media circus from the get-go, if you know what I mean."

"*Here,* where?!" Shaw demanded.

"Miami Dade County Jail, waiting for you to book my client, Spencer."

Thirty minutes later, Eddie and Shaw arrived. Roy was booked and processed, but Moran had already been working to have Roy's bond hearing set on an expedited basis. Because he was being charged with first degree murder, a non-bondable offense, an Arthur Hearing was required. In order to keep Roy in jail pending trial, Shaw had to show "proof evident, presumption great" that Roy had killed Joe Harlan Junior—a very high burden.

Roy had a number of factors in his favor. He had lived in Miami for decades. He was known for charitable giving to various non-profits in the area. He was employed—indeed, he was the owner of a significant business—and not a flight risk because he had a newborn child in the NICU. He had no prior convictions. He had no history of drug use. And—Moran argued—he was not deemed to be a danger to the community.

Shaw argued against releasing Roy on bond, and in support, submitted an affidavit from Eddie Garza outlining the evidence that had been found at Roy's house. Shaw presented no other witnesses and none were mentioned in the affidavit. In the end, Roy was required to surrender his passport, and bond was set at $250,000. While Roy was satisfied with the outcome, Moran was cautiously pleased.

"It's a win, and that's great. But, Shaw didn't push that hard against the bond, Roy. I know him, and that effort was really half-assed."

"What does that mean, exactly?"

"It means he has more evidence than he's letting on. He's playing hide-the-ball, Roy. He hasn't shown us his hand yet."

CHAPTER FORTY-TWO

The next day, as Roy parked his Range Rover at Mark Moran's office, he could swear that he could still pick up the faint scent of jail on his hands. He'd washed with several different kinds of soaps and hand sanitizers. Nothing helped.

Moran's office was on the fifteenth floor of a high-rise in Brickell, downtown Miami. After checking in with the receptionist, Roy went to the restroom and washed his hands again. The pump soap in the bathroom had a sickly sweet flowery smell to it. But, anything smelled better than jail.

When he returned, he was shown to a large conference room overlooking downtown, with a view of Virginia Key. The city below seemed unreal. Off in the distance, Roy could see Biscayne Channel—the same channel he had ridden through at night on a jet ski going to and from Bimini. That seemed like a lifetime ago. And there was something odd, otherworldly about being in a lawyer's office now, preparing to defend those actions. He'd been single-mindedly focused on his plan back then: Eliminating Harlan. Avenging Camilla. It all seemed absurd now.

Roy was wondering what Susie would think of the whole mess when he heard the door open behind him and turned to greet Moran. His lawyer didn't look very lawyerly. He was wearing dark blue, raw denim jeans, loafers with no socks, and a fitted, long-sleeved shirt with the sleeves rolled halfway up. His wavy ginger hair was combed straight back, his hairline slightly receding on the sides. He wore vintage-looking tortoise shell glasses and sported a Rolex on his left wrist, two-toned with a brown dial. He looked more like a startup CEO or venture capital partner than a trial lawyer.

After they shook hands and exchanged pleasantries, they sat down at the conference table, which was pristine except for a yellow legal pad and a plain Bic pen. Blue.

"Before we begin, Roy, I need to make something very clear. I want to explain to you how I like to work. I know you're a lawyer—"

"I was a lawyer," Roy corrected.

"Well, exactly. I don't want to tell you anything you already know or waste your time, but this is the first time we've gotten this far into the process together, so please indulge me. It's obviously my job to defend you to the fullest extent the law allows. I don't care if you're innocent or guilty. My job is to make sure that the State satisfies its burden and to keep them honest. They have to prove that you committed a crime beyond a reasonable doubt.

"Now, I obviously have no idea what happened here, what's true and what's not. I don't know if you did it or if you're being wrongfully accused.

"There are two ways to approach criminal defense.

"One is for you to tell me *nothing*, and I build our case based solely on what we learn from the State.

"The other approach is for you to tell me everything the way you remember it, and I use that information *and* what I learn from the State to build a defense."

Roy nodded and asked, "What do you prefer? What are the pros and cons?"

"Good question. I have no preference. I can prepare your defense based solely on what I learn from the State. And you tell me nothing. That has the advantage of us only focusing on the evidence they have—after all, if they don't have it, they can't use it against you. As you know, once we get discovery from Shaw, we'll see all their evidence against you. They have to turn it over by law."

At this point, Roy and Moran hadn't received any discovery from the prosecution, so they had only a general idea of the evidence against Roy—they had only what Shaw had revealed at the bail hearing and what was contained in the indictment. It was clear that Shaw was claiming that Susie and Roy had killed Harlan, and that they had mutilated his body. But the evidence they were relying on to prove it was vague. As Moran had insisted before, Shaw was playing hide-the-ball.

"But, beyond what they know," Moran continued, "if there is anything you know that would exonerate you, I may not find out about that from them. I can only find out about that if you tell me about it. Okay?"

Roy nodded. "That's clear. I get it."

"But, here's the crux of the matter: to the extent you tell me what happened, if we need to call you as a witness, your testimony has to be consistent with what you've told me," Moran explained. "I am an officer of the court. I cannot allow you or encourage you to lie under oath. If you give me any indication that you intend to perjure yourself, I have to withdraw from representing you. But, like I said—" Moran paused, looking hard at Roy, "I *only know* what you tell me. So, I can only know you're lying if you tell me one version of what happened, and then you tell me that you plan to testify to another version..."

Moran paused while Roy nodded, contemplating.

Roy had a big decision to make. How much should he share with his lawyer?

CHAPTER FORTY-THREE

After a moment of quiet reflection, Roy spoke.

"Assuming for a moment that I did it—that Susie and I killed this guy—you're saying that, for you to best do your job, I should tell you everything that happened, so that you can prepare the best defense?"

Moran nodded as Roy spoke. "Yes."

"But, if I plan to testify at trial—"

"Which you don't have to do. You have the absolute right *not* to testify, and that cannot be held against you..."

"Do you think I should testify at trial?" Roy asked.

"Well, it depends. It's the State's burden to prove their case. So, I would probably only recommend that you testify if things are looking bad for us—really bad. In that case, we might decide that having the jury hear from you could clarify things.

"You're a good-looking guy. You're likeable. You come across well. I think you'd make a great witness. And with everything that's recently happened—Susie and all—and a baby daughter, I think you'd be very sympathetic.

"But, of course, the State gets to cross-examine you. I know Shaw. His nickname is 'Shock-and-Awe'. He's aggressive. He knows where the line is between ethical and unethical, and he's a tightrope walker. He's a sharp sonofabitch. Merciless. I've seen him tear really solid witnesses apart."

Roy felt queasy for the first time since he'd been released on bond. "Tell me he's got some weaknesses."

Moran smiled. "So, I guess the short version is that I'd like to have the option to call you as a witness, and we would obviously prepare you for it. But, I would want to wait to make that decision."

"Okay. So, in that case," Roy concluded, "you're saying that if I do plan to testify at trial, then it's better—assuming I actually committed this crime—it's better for me not to tell you anything that happened, because then I can lie about it—"

"No, no, no. You can't lie, Roy. You can't tell me you're going to lie. I can't let you lie."

Roy nodded, "Let me phrase it differently. What you're *really saying* is that if I don't tell you what happened, then I am free to testify to whatever I want, because there's no way for you to know if it's a lie."

"Exactly." Moran nodded, satisfied that Roy understood.

"So, basically you're just telling me not to confess the crime to you if I plan to testify that I didn't do it."

Moran replied, "Those are your words, not mine. I could never say that—ethically."

"I had forgotten why I hate lawyers," Roy chuckled. Moran laughed with him. Roy's laughter died out and he looked at Moran thoughtfully. "Well, it's very simple, Mark. I don't want to hide anything from you. I'll tell you whatever you need to know. The complete truth. I have a daughter now, and I need to be free to raise her. I owe that to Susie. And to get out of this mess—I need you to prepare the best possible defense."

"Okay." Moran nodded. Then he picked up his pen, and said, "Let's start from the top, then. Did you and Susie have anything to do with this guy Harlan's disappearance or death?"

"Absolutely not. I've never met the guy. I've never even spoken to the guy."

For the next several hours, Roy walked Moran through his and Susie's trip to Bimini, leaving out anything and everything that had to do with Joe Harlan Junior. And at the end of the meeting, Roy told Moran the same thing he'd told Eddie Garza almost two years earlier.

"Bottom line, Mark, is that none of this makes sense. For a jury to believe all this horseshit, they need to hear why I wanted this kid dead. Money? Jealousy? Revenge? I had a great life. Hell, I still have a great life."

"That's what we're fighting for, Roy."

"Exactly. So, why in the name of God would I risk everything—risk my freedom—to kill some twenty-something-year-old kid I don't even know?"

Moran studied Roy's face carefully. Then he nodded and said, "You're right. Why would you?"

CHAPTER FORTY-FOUR

They say that "the lawyer who represents himself has a fool for a client." When he decided to lie to Moran, Roy knew he was at risk of violating that basic axiom. By withholding information from his lawyer, he was essentially self-managing a critical part of his own defense. But he was willing to take that chance.

It had been years since he'd studied law in Texas, but one thing Roy remembered clearly was how much he'd learned about trial law by simply reading the rules of procedure. The night before his meeting with Moran, Roy had sat down and read through the Florida Rules of Criminal Procedure—from cover to cover. Having gotten a sense for what awaited him, and what procedural tactics he could use to his advantage, he'd thought long and hard about whether or not to come clean with his lawyer.

Roy's decision to lie to Moran was based on wanting to keep his options open. Until he had a sense of the true scope of evidence that the prosecution had on him, he didn't want to commit to a version of the facts. He knew that he could always backtrack on his claim of innocence to Moran. But, if he told Moran any version of the "truth," he'd be stuck to that version when it came time to testify.

Roy also knew that there were several loose ends he needed to deal with. He did what he could to protect himself.

At our next therapy session, Roy explained to me what I should do in the event I was contacted by the police. To begin with, out of an abundance of caution, he suggested that I destroy all notes I might have regarding sessions with him or Susie. While those sessions were theoretically privileged, "Better safe than sorry." This, I did. All notes. All recordings. Gone.

He also advised that I contact an attorney of my choosing to be on-call in case I needed to assert the physician-patient privilege in connection with him or Susie. He gave me several names of criminal lawyers he recommended. Ironically, Melissa Losilla, who I'd previously consulted about my "Susie and Roy issue," was one of them.

He also advised me, though he told me to verify this with my own lawyer, that the physician-patient privilege survives the death of the patient. This is something I did not know. As executor of Susie's estate, Roy could assert the privilege on her behalf. He advised me that he fully intended to do so. So, bottom line, I should not speak to the police, should they come calling, about him or Susie. I should call my lawyer.

Next, he asked me one more time what I had told my ex-husband Billy about Getz, which was nothing. While I think he believed me, Roy wanted to be extra careful here. It bothered him that Detective Garza had visited Billy. While it might have been a coincidence, Roy wasn't satisfied with that explanation.

To be safe, he told me that he would advise Moran to hire Billy as a consulting expert to help with research on the case. Under Florida's Rules (and most states' laws as well as federal law), consulting experts do not need to be disclosed to the opposition. But, if they are "found" and questioned, they can rely on the work product privilege to refuse to testify about any case they have consulted on. While this plan wasn't foolproof, it gave Billy a leg to stand on in refusing to answer any questions if the police came knocking again.

The last loose end was Kristy Wise. Roy had no idea how to handle her. He wished that he'd spent more time connecting with her when she'd been in Miami. He had no sense how she would react to a call from him out of the blue. Or what she would say if the police came calling.

After much back and forth, he decided to let sleeping dogs lie as far as Kristy was concerned. After all, she'd only visited them in Florida for two days. And, she had killed Ronald Clayton. Roy concluded that, even if the police found her, her own self-interest would keep her quiet. And, aside from what had happened to

Clayton—which was Kristy's problem—she didn't know anything about what he and Susie had done to Joe Harlan Junior. For Roy, that was the key deciding factor—he believed that Kristy didn't know anything that could hurt him in connection with the State's allegation that he and Susie had killed Joe Harlan Junior.

This was a mistake.

PART FOUR

Rebecca Forsyth
West Palm Beach
2019

Alan Forsyth hated lawyers. They were leeches. All of them, to his way of thinking. They were only there when you were in trouble. And then they circled like sharks and took advantage of you.

Fuckin' rape's what it is!

Fuckin' highway robbery!

Nobody's time was worth a thousand dollars an hour. That was just insane! Alan could have two women at the same time for a couple of hundred dollars each. It made no sense to pay some hack more than twice that much just to "think." But, they had Alan over a barrel this time.

A week before, the police had raided his hotel and arrested him. He'd spent the night in jail and made bail the following morning. It wasn't a big sting. Only five girls arrested. There'd been a small article in the local paper—on page six. Thankfully, the reporting had focused more on the prostitutes who had been arrested, the Madame, and the potentially juicy list of clients that the police claimed to have uncovered. The hotel and Alan were only mentioned in passing. That was how he saw it, anyway.

Of course, there'd been an argument.

"Everyone *knows*, Alan! All of our friends have seen it. How can I show my face in public?" Rebecca asked. "I have a business to run!"

"It's all a big mistake. I swear. Fucking cops threw their

net too wide." It didn't sound convincing, even to him. So, Alan argued all the harder, "Come on. We knew when we bought the hotel that the neighborhood was a bit sketchy. Hell, that was part of the appeal. That's why we got such a great deal. We just got caught up in this whole thing by mistake. That's all. Dolphins in the tuna net, babe. The police are a bunch of fucking incompetents anyway."

"But they claim this investigation has been going on for over a year, Alan!"

"Why is it that you never trust me?" he exploded. "You agreed," he said, pointing at her. "You fuckin' agreed this was a good deal, and now that we hit a little bump in the road—"

"A little bump? You call conspiracy to commit human trafficking a little bump?" Rebecca squealed.

"Look! Stop! Alright! Just FUCKIN' STOP!" Alan screamed, spittle flying from his mouth. The violence of his tone silenced them both.

"They're charging *that woman—*" he pointed into the air, "with trafficking. The lawyer said *she's* the main target, and that this is all political anyway. All they really want is the names on her client list. The rest is bullshit. I'm not even an afterthought. I'm an afterthought of an afterthought."

"Well, you've got that part right," she replied, and stormed off.

Days later, Rebecca was still fuming. She hadn't spoken to Alan in almost a week. He'd been sleeping in the guest room. Normally, he'd have just gone and stayed at the hotel. But even after the police had let him "re-open," it was too quiet. His best bud, Dickie, was laying low. So were all the girls. Alan couldn't stand the quiet.

It was Tuesday morning. He was sitting in his hotel office, his large corporate checkbook in front of him. He wrote out the check, slowly. It pained him. Fifty thousand dollars.

Fuck me...

He sighed.

That's the amount the lawyer needed as a retainer to

represent him. He'd said he would charge a thousand dollars an hour against the deposit and agreed to return anything that was "left over."

Alan laughed out loud, sarcastically. *Good luck with that, mate.*

He did the math, balancing the hotel's checking account twice, and his stomach sank. When they'd bought the place, he'd taken a loan from the bank for the purchase and to fund the renovation. The renovation alone was going to cost almost two million dollars. Between one thing and the other, the project had been delayed. He'd paid almost eighty thousand for the architectural plans. Everything had been submitted to the city for approval. But, the permitting process had taken much longer than he'd been told it would. Over a year longer.

And, little by little, other "expenses" arose. It was all Dickie's fault, really. Rebecca didn't like him one bit. He was Irish and loved to party. Dickie also loved the ladies, and he loved him some cocaine. Little by little, he'd sucked Alan in.

Initially, Dickie had proposed a plan—a great plan, to Alan's way of thinking. Dickie had introduced Alan to Hillary Sesostris, the "alleged Madame." Alan had cut a deal to let her girls use the hotel for "massage clients" in exchange for a kickback on each client. Twenty percent. But, Alan had a hard time keeping track of the numbers. And he took payment "in kind" from the girls a bit too often. Little by little, money slowly leaked out of the renovation account.

In the past, he'd been able to convince Rebecca to dip into her trust fund to salvage his other failed business ventures. The horse farm. The custom jeep business. And the worst one financially, the composting company.

With each failed venture, things had gotten a bit more tenuous between them. And all the while, Rebecca kept running her shitty little interior design business, which somehow seemed to be growing. She'd started it just after they got married, and now, five years later, she had seven employees and had been featured in a couple of state-wide magazines. Alan couldn't understand who the fuck would pay someone to pick curtains and sofas. But, Rebecca had a way with the West Palm Beach rich bitches.

Their kind always stick together.

Checking his math, he saw that, after deducting bail and the lawyer's retainer, he was down to just under two hundred thousand dollars. That wasn't nearly enough to complete the project.

And with this fucking lawyer milking me dry, I'm fucked.

Alan locked up his office and hopped on his motorcycle. He was going to deliver the check personally, as the lawyer had told him he wouldn't do anything further on the case until he had the deposit, and Alan's arraignment had already been scheduled. As he rode his bike down South Olive Avenue, he was thinking through how he could convince Rebecca to dip into her trust again in order to save the hotel. The traffic stopped at a red light and Alan carefully wove his way between cars to get to the top of the intersection. As he did, he saw something that stopped him dead. There, just across the road, he saw his wife getting out of her car—a little red convertible BMW. It was her car; it was Rebecca. There was no mistake about it.

Alan's balls shrunk as he watched her pull open a glass office door and disappear into the building. The sign in front of the building said it all.

Horowitz and McNulty, Divorce Attorneys.

The light turned green, and Alan angrily shot out across the intersection, his Triumph doing a small wheelie. As he drove to his attorney's office, his mind raced. What to do? How to fix this? Without Rebecca, he was fucked. The hotel was in his name. The debt was in his name. And now he had the fucking legal case to deal with.

"FUUUUCK!" he screamed into his helmet.

As he rode, a familiar idea resurfaced. It wasn't new, by any means. He had toyed with it before, but he'd always pushed it away. It was risky. But, it was also stubborn. Little by little the plan had taken form. A piece here. Another tantalizing detail there. Where. How. Who would need to be there.

Alan did a quick shoulder check, then made a U-turn and headed home. Rebecca's car was not in the driveway and not in the garage. He went into the house and found what he was looking for. Rebecca's sewing kit. He carefully removed what he needed.

Alan then went to the guestroom closet. Had he not been sleeping in the guestroom for the past week, he probably would have forgotten where their scuba gear was. He turned on the closet light and located Rebecca's regulator. With the sewing needle and a thimble, he carefully made a small pin hole in the tube that ran from the tank to the backup regulator. He then replaced everything just as he'd found it and left the house.

After delivering the check to his lawyer, he returned to his office at the hotel and made a couple of phone calls, scheduling everything. Flights. The yacht. Then he made one final call to set everything in motion.

"Mike, it's Alan. Listen, I'm planning a little surprise vacation for Rebecca. With all the bullshit that's going on down here, we need to get away and just recharge. How do you and Sara feel about the Turks and Caicos? Our treat..."

CHAPTER FORTY-FIVE

Roy wore a charcoal grey suit, white shirt, and black tie to court. At his direction, and contrary to Moran's better judgment, they had filed a Motion for Speedy Trial and set it for expedited hearing. The typical time to trial for a felony in Florida was around 175 days. Roy didn't want to wait that long. He felt that the passage of time benefited the prosecution more than him. By filing the motion, they were entitled to go to trial within sixty days.

Roy and Moran sat in the gallery waiting for his case to be called. Shaw was already at the prosecution's table, as he had more than one case on the docket that morning. Judge Celia Goodwin sat on the bench.

The daughter of a retired congressman, Judge Goodwin had a reputation for being relatively even-handed. She was a former defense lawyer, and was known to lean slightly left. This was generally considered a positive for defendants. As Roy watched the cases called before his, he got a sense for her style. She was matter-of-fact. A bit abrupt at times.

The case just before his involved a discovery dispute.

The lawyer for the defense was irate. He complained, "This is the fourth extension Mr. Shaw has requested, Your Honor. Meanwhile, my client's sitting in jail, waiting to go to trial."

"Mr. Shaw?"

Shaw flipped through his trial notebook, then quietly read from a page, before replying, "Your Honor, I believe that the discovery Mr. Gross is waiting on was delivered to his office yesterday evening. I have a confirmation here from the courier service. They left it with the security guard."

"Security...?" fumed the other attorney. "At what time was this delivery, exactly?"

Shaw studied the note. "It says eight-thirty."

"At night? Your Honor, this type of gamesmanship is precisely what I've been dealing with since this case started. Mr. Shaw continuously—"

"I apologize," Shaw cut him off. "It was simply—"

"Mr. Gross," Judge Goodwin interrupted, "go back to your office and confirm you have everything you're supposed to. If you don't," she added, glaring at Shaw, "file a motion and we will deal with it. Mr. Shaw, is there some reason you didn't contact Mr. Gross to advise that the delivery was being made? An email, for example?"

"I didn't think that—"

"You preferred to waste his time, dragging him down here? And to waste the Court's time as well?"

"I apologize, Your Honor," Shaw replied without any hint of remorse.

The next case called was Roy's case, and he and Moran came forward to the defense table.

"Mr. Moran? I have a before me your *Rule 3.191(b) Demand for Speedy Trial*."

"Yes, Your Honor. Good morning. Just by way of background, my client's wife very recently passed away during childbirth. The child is in the NICU at Jackson." The judge looked up and studied Roy. He thought he caught a glimmer of sympathy in her yes. "Doing well, but still... you know, dealing with preemie issues. My client wants to get to trial as soon as possible. We're open to whatever date the Court has available within the sixty-day window."

"Well, that certainly is very sad. My condolences. But, that's all really irrelevant, Mr. Moran," the judge replied. "Your client is entitled to make this demand as a matter of right. Mr. Shaw?"

"Your Honor, we have no opposition to a speedy trial. But, I have a very full docket. I pretty much have a trial setting every Monday for the next several months. I'm looking at May at the earliest. And, to be fair, we haven't even responded to discovery yet.

In fact, we're probably going to need an extension of time to get everything we have to Mr. Moran."

Shaw was referring to the State's responsibility to provide the defense with copies of or access to whatever evidence it planned to present at trial.

Judge Goodwin glowered at Shaw. "Mr. Shaw. This is the third case today... the third time that you've indicated you need more time to provide discovery."

"It's a question of resources, Your Honor—"

"Mr. Shaw, when you decided to indict..." the judge looked down at the docket, searching for the Defendant's name, "...Mr. Cruise, did you have enough evidence to do so?"

"Yes, Your Honor."

"Then you need to get that evidence to his lawyer *now*. Period."

The judge looked down again at her trial calendar. "Mr. Moran, this is your client's lucky day. With this virus thing that's going around, our family has postponed our spring break plans. So, I have an opening on my calendar and can set your trial for March 9th..."

Moran looked down at Roy. Roy could see that Moran's face had flushed red. That was barely two weeks away.

"May I consult with my client?" Moran asked.

The judge nodded.

"That's really tight, Roy," Moran whispered. "This is a capital murder trial. I don't have to explain the stakes. Two weeks for prep is fuckin' insane."

While Moran whispered, Roy was carefully watching Shaw. He was studying a document, seemingly oblivious, unconcerned about what Moran and he were discussing.

Roy waited. And watched.

Shaw looked up and over at Roy, smiling a cocky smile. But Roy saw it, even though he tried to hide it. Shaw swallowed, hard.

"Do it," he told Moran.

Moran straightened up, tucking his tie back inside his suit jacket, and said, "That is fine with the defense, Your Honor."

Shaw replied forcefully, "Your Honor, two weeks isn't enough time to prepare for a murder trial! This is a capital case… I have a full caseload, and—"

"*And* you have an office full of attorneys, paralegals, and staff. And the weight and power of the State of Florida behind you. You'll be fine. If *you* don't have the time for this trial, find someone else in your office to handle the case. None of us is indispensable, Mr. Shaw.

"The *State versus Roy Cruise* is set for trial March 9th. And," the judge looked at the defense table, "Mr. Moran, if you have any issues regarding getting discovery from Mr. Shaw, please file any motions directly with my clerk. I am not going to have this trial date slide due to any shenanigans. That goes for both of you fine attorneys. Is that clear?"

"Yes, Your Honor," both Shaw and Moran replied in unison.

CHAPTER FORTY-SIX

Liz Bareto was sitting in her dining room. Although it was nine in the morning, it was dark inside her house. She had all the curtains pulled. On the table in front of her was a half-empty glass of red wine, and next to it were the syringe, in a plastic bag, and the lab report. She had received *the syringe* from the lab that morning, along with an original copy of the report.

Liz was in her pajamas and a robe. She had been for several days. She couldn't remember the last time she'd showered.

She'd been feeling miserable. She hadn't eaten in days. She had no appetite, and anything she did eat, she vomited back up. The only thing she could keep down was alcohol, and even the wine she drank to sedate herself seemed to lack flavor.

Liz had never intended to shoot Susie Font, much less kill her. She'd just wanted justice for Liam. For the truth to come out. She'd wanted a confession. But when the woman had distracted her and gone for that gun on the desk, Liz had tracked her movements with her own gun.

She'd shouted, "Don't!"

...and the gun had accidentally gone off.

When Liz closed her eyes, she could still see Susie lying on the floor, a deep red blossom slowly spreading out across her chest and staining her pale blue top as the life seeped from her body. The blood soaked the blouse, which stuck to Susie's body, making obvious what hadn't been when she was seated on the sofa. That she was pregnant. As she'd lain there bleeding on the rug, her mouth moved like a fish out of water trying to breathe.

Since the shooting, Liz's sleep had been constantly

interrupted by that image. So much so that she dreaded going to bed. She'd awoken sobbing and shivering more than once. The little sleep she had managed to get had been on her sofa—the few times she'd passed out drunk while watching television.

When she had gotten home after the shooting, she'd thought for certain that the police would come knocking at her door at any moment. She'd resigned herself to it, and had been waiting for them. With each day that passed, she felt a bit more relief. Her recent conversation with Eddie Garza had been close to normal. It didn't seem like he'd noticed anything unusual. Slowly, Liz was beginning to realize that she might actually get away with it.

She couldn't change the past. As her mother used to say, *What's done is done and can't be undone.*

Liz realized that she had a decision to make—turn herself in, or do her damnedest to get away clean. Little by little, her thinking had shifted towards not getting caught.

She'd surprised herself with how coolheaded she'd been at the Cruises' house. When she'd called 9-1-1 using the phone on the desk, she'd disguised her voice and wiped down the telephone after. She'd wiped down her handgun as well, before dropping it in the canal while she paddled back to her car.

There was only one piece of evidence she had not eliminated, and she was torn as to what to do with it. Liz realized that the syringe and the lab report were a problem for her now. True, they proved that Liam had been killed—that someone had used the syringe on her child. She wanted to turn them over to the police. But, that same syringe and lab report were now evidence against her. The report was dated almost a week before the shooting. Liz believed it gave her a clear motive for killing Susie.

She was trying to decide what to do about that evidence, and the letter and box it came in, when her phone rang. It was Joe. She was thrilled to hear from him. Perhaps 'relieved' was a better word, as she didn't have the energy to be enthused. She did her best to sound upbeat and sober when she answered. As they exchanged pleasantries, she realized that just speaking to him comforted her; it made her feel safe. They were kindred spirits. They'd been through the same hell of losing a child. Surely, he would understand what had happened.

"So, I'm guessing you saw that they're taking Cruise to trial, finally?" he asked.

"I did," she said, trying to sound chipper.

"Well, I was contacted by the prosecuting attorney, to testify. So, I'll be in Miami for a couple of days—"

"Well, you'll stay here with me, Joe. I won't have you staying at a hotel!"

By the end of the call, it was settled. And, for the first time since shooting Susie, Liz felt hopeful. She took the syringe and lab report and placed them in her buffet, in the living room, next to the letter and box the syringe had originally come in. She poured herself some more wine and plopped down on her sofa in front of the television.

Joe will know what to do.

CHAPTER FORTY-SEVEN

During the two weeks leading up to the trial, Roy Cruise spent his free hours visiting Joan. His only adult interactions to speak of were his therapy sessions with me and his time with his lawyer. He told me that our sessions were the only moments when things seemed somewhat normal, with some semblance of what his life had been like before Susie's death.

Roy lived in relative peace during those weeks, yet there was always the blade of a guillotine hanging over him—the upcoming trial. He tried to make the best of the time, enjoying the baby. He knew that his entire world hung in the balance, and that twelve jurors could drastically change his future.

For his part, Moran was putting in twenty-hour days. Trial preparation, and trial, is an exhausting process. The time constraints Roy had placed on his attorney had complicated matters. And Moran was not one to cut corners.

Part of what makes a successful trial lawyer is the insatiable desire to win—not just to win at trial. Every hearing, every motion, every phone call is a contest, a competition against the opposing lawyer. Trial law is a game of inches. The best trial attorneys judge their success solely based on the outcome of their most recent confrontation—everything that came before is history. This is why top lawyers have been known to come to blows over something as seemingly trivial as agreeing on the location of a meeting.

A week before the trial, Moran scheduled a meeting with Roy to discuss trial preparation and strategy. As a convenience to Roy, Moran agreed to meet at his house.

At 2:00 p.m., Roy saw Moran pull his Tesla into the circular drive. He went out to greet his lawyer. Roy walked Moran in, and the two settled down at the small, round table in Roy's study.

Contrary to what many television shows and movies would have you believe, when lawyers go to trial, they generally have a good sense of what evidence will be presented. This is because, as a part of the preparation process for trial, attorneys are required to exchange with one another any evidence that they intend to present to the jury.

When Moran initially received the State's evidence, he called Roy to let him know in broad strokes what had been found. Roy was blown away. He had no idea that Susie had been storing a time bomb in their house. Based on the State's disclosures, Moran had prepared his trial strategy in great detail—all of which was contained in a large notebook.

Moran had reviewed everything that Shaw had provided up to that point. This included what Eddie Garza had found in Susie's lockbox. But, it didn't include Kristy Wise's interview. Moran was right, though he still didn't know to what extent—Shaw was withholding the most important part of the State's case.

As the two sat in Roy's study, Moran removed the large red trial notebook from his briefcase and set it down on the table between them.

"So, how's it looking, Mark?"

"Well... we have some major problems, Roy."

CHAPTER FORTY-EIGHT

Roy swallowed hard. He'd been preparing for this moment, but that didn't make it any easier—especially since his life hung in the balance.

"There's good news and bad news," Moran told him. "The vast majority of the State's case is circumstantial, based on what they found in the lockbox and your safe. The good news is... the laptops came back clean. They may try to make something of the fact that they were configured as burners—"

"Like I told you, Susie used those for her research. Corrupt politicians and stuff..."

Moran nodded and handed Roy a sheet of paper that appeared to be a lab report. "And the fish knife they found doesn't have your prints on it."

Roy shrugged.

Moran nodded. "The bad news is, it has Susie's prints all over it. And the lab reports confirm that it also has Harlan's DNA on it. His blood, Roy."

"You're fucking kidding... What the fuck, Suze?" Roy said almost to himself. He stood up, holding the lab report, and walked slowly toward the window. "Why would she keep—" Roy felt queasy.

After all the planning. After the burner laptops and burner phones, the hours hiding in Starbucks and doing research via Tor. After all the careful cleanup. After *Roy's Rules for Murder*. Why the fuck would Susie have kept the knife? And why would she have kept it *in their house*?

Roy stared at the lab report for almost a minute, shaking his head. Then he turned and looked at Moran, and said, "You're telling me that Susie had something to do with this?"

Moran nodded, "So it appears."

Roy began pacing, shaking his head as he did. "When the fuck...? How could...?"

Moran studied him.

Roy stopped and stood still, staring out the window again. He hoped that his shock at learning that Susie had been so stupid as to keep the knife without even cleaning it would be interpreted by Moran as shock at learning that Susie had possibly been involved in a murder. Roy stood staring out at the yard. He was tired. Tired of lying. Tired of acting. He shook his head—pissed off, trying to estimate how much time would be appropriate for "the news" to sink in before he addressed Moran again.

Finally, he returned to the table and dropped the report on it. It was all gibberish to him. "Are we absolutely sure about these results? Could they have planted—"

Moran shook his head and pulled another sheet from the notebook. "What you're holding is *their* lab report. Here's the one done by our expert, who also examined the knife." He placed the sheet on the table and indicated different sections as he spoke, "There's Harlan's DNA. Twenty-two full and partial fingerprints, all belonging to Susie. And there's some fish DNA. Their report says 'fish'—our guy isolated it to yellow-tailed snapper.

"And, as you can see on this image here—this partial fingerprint of Susie's is made in blood—Harlan's blood. There's no way to plant that."

Roy leaned back in his chair, shaking his head in disbelief.

"Fuck me... I just can't believe that Susie could do something like this."

Moran looked hard at Roy, still studying him. He pursed his lips, then flipped to another section of the notebook. "The knife makes the case against Susie pretty solid, Roy. At the very least, it won't be hard to convince the jury that she was involved in the guy's mutilation. And, that strengthens the case against you by implication. The jury is going to want to know how she could do this without you knowing. Especially if the two of you were together in Bimini."

Moran paused. He studied Roy. Roy stared back, the voice in his head telling him to relax.

"Is there anything you want to tell me?" Moran asked.

CHAPTER FORTY-NINE

Roy had always known that at some point he might have to come clean with his lawyer. He had given the issue a great deal of thought. In the end, the only value to sharing the truth with Moran was if, somewhere in that truth, there was something exculpatory. Roy had been through the facts, and come to the conclusion that there was nothing there that could help his case.

"Mark, I've told you everything," he said. "You said there was good news?"

"I'll get to that in a second. As far as this knife, I've got some ideas. First of all, the timeline may help. You'll recall the penis turned up almost a week after Harlan disappeared, and that's once you guys were back in Miami. Susie could have done this after you got back from Bimini. Of course, the problem with making that argument is that the same logic applies to you, too."

Roy didn't seem to be listening. He was staring off into space shaking his head.

"Bottom line, I think we can deal with the knife, Roy. Deflect it onto Susie. And I've been through everything with a fine-toothed comb. As it stands, in my opinion, there is only one solid piece of evidence tying you to Harlan's murder."

Roy watched him, concerned. *The knife wasn't bad enough? There was more?*

The three rings of the notebook made a loud metallic snick as Moran opened them and extracted another sheet of paper.

"Well, 'solid' may be too strong a word. This letter that

Debra Wise sent Susie—that the cops found in Susie's lockbox..." Moran handed the letter to Roy. It was a one-page document, handwritten.

Roy skipped straight down to a portion of the letter that was highlighted in yellow.

I'm glad that I was able to help you out when you needed it.

And I thank you from the bottom of my heart for returning the favor. You and Roy both. I can't imagine all that it took. But it's made a big difference in all our lives.

If you can, keep an eye on Kristy for me. She's not like us. She's fragile. And on Tom. He means well, and he tries hard. But he's no Roy.

"That language is a major problem," Moran said. "It's a matter of perception. Those few sentences encapsulate what would be my theory of the case if I were Shaw—some sort of a *quid pro quo*. And it doesn't help us that the very next thought is about Kristy. It's not a slam dunk, by any means—"

"But, yeah, I can see how in the right context it could look bad."

"Do you have any idea what Wise is referring to here? What you and Susie did for her? Or what she did for Susie?"

"I have no idea, Mark. Absolutely none. Like I told you before, I've never met this woman. I didn't even know Susie knew her."

"Susie never even mentioned her?"

Roy shook his head.

"Well, the problem is that this is their motive. With this, the State can argue that killing Harlan was in return for a favor that Debra Wise did for Susie."

"But... this could be anything, Mark. This could be money. Maybe she loaned Susie some money, and then Susie returned the favor?" Roy suggested.

"Did she? Do you have any bank records that would show that?"

"I'd have to look and see, but who knows? What time period?"

"Any time period would help..." Moran replied as he scribbled on a sheet of paper and passed it to Roy. It said, *Check bank records for funds to or from Debra Wise.*

"I'll check on it," Roy nodded as he read the sheet, but in the back of his mind, he knew he wouldn't waste any time on it. There'd been no transfers.

"Do you have any sense of what they plan to argue? Shaw, I mean... what's the *quid pro quo*?" Roy asked.

"No. And that concerns me."

"Are we sure that this letter is even real?"

"Yes. The State has gotten a handwriting expert that's confirmed that it's Debra Wise's handwriting. And they've also got the Wises' estate lawyer, a guy named Pringle, who can testify that she gave it to him to send to Susie. It was in a sealed envelope when he received it from her, but when Tom Wise found out about it after she'd died, he demanded a copy. So, Pringle opened the envelope and gave him one, and kept a copy for his file. CYA."

"Fuck," Roy said flatly. "So, it's genuine."

Moran winced and nodded. "Yeah. But, stay with me, because we're not done yet. This is where I have good news for you."

CHAPTER FIFTY

Roy waited impatiently for Moran to continue. So far, everything he'd heard was bad news. He needed any good news he could get.

Fortunately, Moran didn't keep him waiting.

"While the letter from Deb Wise is probably genuine, that still doesn't mean the jury gets to see it. How much do you remember about the rules of evidence?"

Roy looked at Moran, eyes wide, and shrugged.

"This letter is classic hearsay. And I don't think that any of the legal exceptions apply. Of course, the fact that the State got a handwriting expert involved and interviewed Pringle means that they're going to try to get it admitted into evidence, so we'll be fighting over that—"

"You say you don't think the exceptions apply. What are our odds?"

"I haven't found any authority that says the judge should let the jury see that letter, but it's always a fight. Shaw's gonna try.

"The problem is that, if the trial judge lets it in, it hurts us—bad. And if the jury finds you guilty, even if the appeals court decides the judge was wrong in allowing the letter in, it's just one piece of evidence. There's probably still enough circumstantial evidence that the appeals court might not set aside the conviction, even if they decide the judge was wrong about the letter. Bottom line is, we have to fight tooth and nail to keep the jury from seeing this."

Roy stood and stretched his back. Then he began to pace. He did his best thinking on his feet. "So, what's their theory of the case? And what's our strategy?"

"Again, that's what concerns me. Their case has got to be about *quid pro quo*. That's the strongest angle here. But there's stuff missing. And I know Shaw. He doesn't like to lose. He *avoids* losing by not trying shitty cases. Shaw likes slam dunks. This case is not the type of case he typically tries. There are too many loose ends. That worries me."

"But you've seen everything they've got? Right? All their evidence?"

"Yep. And, based on that, all they've got is a parade of connections." Moran flipped to another page near the front of the notebook and removed a sheet he had created entitled *State's Key Facts*. He put it on the table between them.

State's Key Facts

1. Cruise Capital contacts Harlan to come to Miami.
2. Susie Font and Roy Cruise go to Bimini together.
3. Harlan arrives in Miami.
4. Harlan buys boat shoes.
5. Harlan disappears in Miami—never checks out of hotel.
6. Harlan cell phone contains contact for "Cruise Captain" which connects to a Seattle phone number on a disposable phone.
7. Strange text from Harlan to David Kim about not having dinner together.
8. Harlan penis appears in Austin, Texas on father's door.
9. Penis labeled "4 Kristy."
10. Debra Wise shot and killed—Roy Cruise in Austin.
11. Tom Wise shot and killed—suicide?
12. Susie Font shot and killed. Several items of evidence found in safe:
    a. Fish knife with Susie Font's fingerprints, Harlan DNA, and fish DNA
    b. **Letter from Debra Wise**

Roy skimmed through the list.

As he did, Moran said, "All of this evidence gets in. The only piece that we may be able to keep out is the letter, in bold there at the end. And, even if it gets in, it's still circumstantial. Their case comes down to, 'Susie did it, so Roy must have helped her.'"

Moran went on, "So, our story is going to be, first, that you have no reason to want this kid dead—no motive." Roy nodded as Moran continued, "Second, all of this evidence is circumstantial. And third, that while this evidence may indicate some wrongdoing by Susie, she has paid for that with her life. Our theory of the case, at the worst end of the spectrum, is basically, 'Maybe you can prove Susie did it, but you can't prove Roy did.'"

"So, do you think you're going to want me to testify?"

Moran took a deep breath. "I am currently leaning toward 'yes.' Aside from Senator Harlan, who can testify as to what Joe was like and give him some color, all of the State's evidence is very flat. Very impersonal. There are no eyewitnesses. It's a very clinical case for them.

"They don't have a storyteller. If we put you on the stand, we take control of the narrative. I think it's going to be important for the jury to get to know you. To hear *from you* that you didn't do it. And that you have no idea what Susie's involvement was. Hearing from you will make this real for them."

Roy nodded. "Okay, then."

Moran flipped to a page in the trial notebook entitled *Witness Questions - Roy Cruise*, and for the next several hours the two rehearsed Roy's testimony.

CHAPTER FIFTY-ONE

Eddie Garza popped into Spencer Shaw's office at noon for his witness preparation meeting. He was late by an hour, but the normally irascible Shaw was in a very good mood and didn't even comment on Eddie's tardiness.

Still, Eddie felt obligated to explain, "Sorry. Traffic."

"No worries, Detective. Come on down to the war room."

Garza followed Shaw down the corridor. The office was abuzz with activity. In one small office they passed, a pair of paralegals were working with blown-up excerpts of testimony from witness interviews. On the wall were several enlarged photos of the victim, Joe Harlan Junior: in one, he appeared to be giving a presentation to a mid-sized audience; in another, he was pictured with his father at what looked like a campaign event; yet another looked to be a high school yearbook photo.

"Quick question, Eddie," Shaw said, stopping at the door. The two paralegals looked over at the pair, "Your honest opinion, which photo of Icabod do you like best?"

"Icabod?"

One of the paralegals chimed in, "Icabod Crane. The headless horseman."

"Ouch!" Eddie chucked. He studied the three photos, then said, "I think the one of him giving the presentation." As he spoke, the paralegals smiled at each other.

"Why?" one of them asked.

Eddie crossed his arms over his chest, then replied, "He looks professional, clean-cut. Like someone who's going places. And... not at all like a rapist."

"Men generally seem to like that one," Shaw said. "The women tend to go for the father/son shot."

"Which are you going to use?" Eddie asked.

"Still trying to decide. Depends on the composition of the jury. Come on," Shaw continued down the hall.

As they approached a large conference room, they had to carefully negotiate their way through the hallway, which was stacked on one side with cardboard banker's boxes piled four high. There appeared to be around ten stacks.

Inside the conference room, documents and notebooks were spread all across the table. The wall's dry erase boards were full of lists—Eddie scanned and saw titles: *Witness List, Evidentiary Issues, Exhibits, Critical Facts, To Do*.

"We'll have to work in here." Shaw pointed Eddie to the far end of the table where there was a bit of clear space and two empty chairs. "Your timing worked out great, actually. I just finished up with our forensics expert. She's good to go if we need her."

For the next hour, Shaw walked Eddie through a rehearsal of his testimony for trial.

There are two types of testimony given at trial—direct and cross-examination. The former is friendly, the latter adverse. As Shaw would be calling Eddie as a witness, he was preparing Eddie for direct examination. This basically meant rehearsing a series of questions that told a story and presented the evidence Shaw needed from Eddie. The trick was to make sure that nothing was left out and, at the same time, make the questioning seem more like a conversation than a regurgitation of facts. It had to be interesting and genuine for the jury.

Through Eddie, Shaw planned to introduce evidence regarding critical elements of Harlan's time in Miami, as well as what the initial investigation had discovered linking Roy Cruise to Harlan. They worked for about an hour, practicing what Eddie needed to say until Shaw was satisfied.

All of Eddie's testimony was straightforward—all facts and no opinions—and as a result, little of what he had to say was open to interpretation. Regardless, Shaw spent a bit of time role-playing cross-examination questions which Roy's lawyer might throw at Eddie.

"Excellent work. You've clearly been through this before, Detective," Shaw complimented Eddie as they finished.

"Not my first rodeo."

As they were wrapping up, a junior attorney popped in and interrupted, "Excuse me, the courier is here for the boxes, but Marta said to double-check with you."

Shaw double-checked the time on his watch, then smiled and said, "Yep. All good to go. And make goddamned sure they are delivered *and signed for* before five p.m., okay?"

"Absolutely," replied the young attorney.

After she left, Eddie raised a curious eyebrow at Shaw.

"A little supplementation before trial for our friend Mr. Moran," Shaw said, pointing casually at the boxes in the hallway.

Eddie looked and saw a young man with a dolly loading up boxes four at a time.

Shaw continued, "We're sending a supplemental witness list and everything that we got from Texas—all the files that they had regarding Harlan, Debra Wise, Tom Wise, and Kristy Wise. From the police and District Attorney. We're turning it over this afternoon. As part of discovery."

"Shit, man. There's a ton."

"Thirty-seven banker's boxes," Shaw laughed. "I even got full transcripts of the Harlan trial as well as Tom Wise's trial for assaulting the kid—three separate copies. Mixed 'em all up in there. Just to beef it up. More documents for Moran to have to wade through over the weekend. It'll definitely cut into whatever he planned to use that time for. And..." he smiled, "Kristy Wise's interview is buried in there... somewhere."

"Wait! Hold on... you mean they still have no idea about Kristy's interview? Her testimony?"

Shaw shook his head, grinning. "Not yet. We just added her to our new list of potential witnesses today. Buried her name in with the names of all the boat owners you guys contacted back when you were chasing down the 'Cruise Captain' lead. We added around sixty new names to our list."

"Holy crap, Shaw... that's trial by ambush..."

"You're abso-fucking-lutely right, Eddie."

"But you should have turned all this stuff over to them way back. You're not going to get away with this..." Eddie paused, "are you?"

"Sure, we will, Eddie. We just received them yesterday from Texas. See?" Shaw opened a box numbered "1 of 37" and showed Eddie the first document in it, which was a copy of a shipping label.

Eddie looked skeptical.

"We'll be fine. The judge'll get pissed off at me, sure. But hey, that's life. It's all part of the game. If she thinks it's too unfair, she can always delay the trial. And if she doesn't, then we have the element of surprise. Trust me on the court stuff, Eddie. You handle the cop stuff."

CHAPTER FIFTY-TWO

Moran was heading home Friday afternoon. The trial was set for the following Monday, and although he was exhausted, he felt like he was ready. At home, a hot tub and a fresh bottle of scotch were waiting for him. Due to the long hours required for trial preparation, he had barely seen his wife and daughter in the last two and a half weeks, and was looking forward to unwinding, chatting, being normal for an hour or two before getting a good night's rest.

As he drove, he said, "Siri?"

He heard a pleasant *bleep*, then said, "Text Jessica, I'll be home in about twenty minutes. See you soon."

Siri repeated what he'd told her, and he confirmed, "Send."

He sighed.

It still bothered him that the State's case felt incomplete. But he'd been through everything, all of the State's evidence, repeatedly. He knew the evidence backwards and forward.

He had drafted several opening statements, both for the Defendant and for the State. Part of being fully prepared for trial involved not just presenting the best defense but being prepared for the State's best case. That meant going through the process of preparing the case for trial as if he were Shaw. He'd done it. And something felt wrong. Everything was just too circumstantial.

Enough for now. Tomorrow is another day.

His plan for Saturday was to be back in the office early to go through exhibit lists and finish the legal brief he was preparing for the court, seeking to exclude Deb Wise's letter as hearsay. They had to make sure the jury didn't see that letter. And then he would go through everything again to make sure he wasn't missing something critical.

As he sat at a light flipping through radio stations, his phone chirped, and he saw on his car's display that it was the office calling him. He clicked on his steering wheel to answer.

"We've got a problem, boss," said his paralegal, Jackie.

"Which case?"

"Cruise. We just got a delivery. Thirty seven banker's boxes."

"What?!" Moran growled, slamming his hands down on the steering wheel. "That fucker Shaw!" He took a moment to calm himself and took a deep breath. "Alright, I'm on my way back in. Who have we got that can start on them?"

Moran gave Jackie instructions to find every available paralegal and junior attorney in the office so that they could begin sifting through the boxes.

"Where are the boxes right now, Jackie?"

"Up front in reception. We're gonna take them back to the main conference room as soon as I hang up."

"Okay. Before you do, though, take pictures of them. I want some good shots of all thirty-seven boxes sitting there in our reception area, okay?"

Moran hung up with his office, and he immediately called Roy and explained what had happened.

"There's going to be something nasty in there, Roy, I just know it."

"I have no idea what it could be, Mark. None."

"Well, we'll know soon enough. I'll do a damage assessment and get back to you. We may want to request putting off the trial, depending on how bad it is and what excuse Shaw gives for the late disclosure."

"No dice, Mark. That's what he wants. No delays. No continuances."

"Well, let's not jump the gun, Roy. Let me at least find out what he's buried in there first. I'll call you once I know more."

CHAPTER FIFTY-THREE

Moran returned to his office and he, two associate attorneys, and two paralegals spent the next six hours scouring through the boxes. Although there were over 76,000 pages of documents, the team got through them surprisingly quickly. The first phase of review was simply organization—not detailed reading of every page.

After about two hours, they had categorized all the documents and, in the process, one of the paralegals named Ben said, "I think I've got it, Mark. Here... I've got a partial document starting at page twenty-seven—the header reads *Witness Interview of Kristy Wise*. The rest of it must be in here somewhere."

"Here," Moran said, "let me see."

Moran began to read the portion of the interview that they'd found while the team continued organization and analysis. About fifteen minutes later, José, one of the associate attorneys, exclaimed, "Bam! I've got it. *Witness Interview of Kristy Wise* pages one through twenty-six, and a copy of her *Immunity Agreement*."

"Okay. Make me a copy of the whole thing to read. Then please scan it and one of you start doing a transcript summary."

Moran had a knot in his belly. In the portion of the interview that he had already read, Kristy claimed that Susie confessed to her that she and Roy had killed Harlan. This completely changed the case. It was no longer a clinical, colorless case. The State had a witness. They had a storyteller. And what she had to say was damning.

Moran texted Roy.

MORAN: *Roy. We need to meet tomorrow morning. Kristy Wise was given immunity in exchange for her testimony. I have her witness interview. Emailing to you shortly. VERY bad for us.*

CRUISE: *Ok, Mark. 10 am? Here at the house?*

MORAN: *See you then.*

"Whoa," Moran heard Jackie say, "I've got another one."

Moran's stomach churned. He looked up from his phone. "Another what?"

"Witness Interview. Senator Joe Harlan Senior. And he's got an immunity agreement too."

CHAPTER FIFTY-FOUR

Roy poured himself a scotch and sat down on the sofa in his study. That they'd gotten to Kristy Wise was a disaster. But, after Moran texted him about Harlan's immunity deal, Roy began to feel the world closing in on him. There were too many loose ends. Too much evidence pointing at him and Susie.

Through everything they had done, there were only two occasions where Roy had felt that they were at risk of being caught. The first was when he saw the online news report that Harlan's penis had magically appeared in Texas. And the second time was when he went in for his first interview with Garza. In both situations, he recognized that it was fear of the unknown that gave him this feeling.

In the first instance, *How did the penis get there? Were there fingerprints?* In the case of being questioned by Garza, *How much did he know? How much had he been able to connect? Had they found anyone who'd seen him on the jet ski? Or seen them in Miami with Harlan?*

In both cases, everything had turned out okay.

Roy knew now that the only way to find out how bad the damage was, was to read through the interviews and see what Kristy Wise and Senator Harlan had to say. Moran had emailed the transcripts to Roy late Friday night, and Roy had been about to start in on them when he'd decided that a glass of scotch was in order.

As he read, he began to feel lightheaded.

At the beginning of her interview, after the immunity agreement was acknowledged, Kristy confessed to killing Clayton in their house. She testified to Roy's own confession to Slipknot that he'd killed Harlan and dumped his body in the Everglades. Roy barely remembered having said that. Afterwards, while Roy was off dumping Slipknot's body, Kristy testified that Susie admitted to her that she and Roy had killed Harlan.

Kristy also testified that her mother killed Liam Bareto, and that Deb was the woman in the ladyfinger photos.

Roy read the document through twice, underlining critical passages. As he did, he became at turns angry, then agitated. Finally, he went pale. When he finished, he stood up rubbing his eyes and refilled his scotch glass.

In spite of everything they'd done—everything *he'd* done—to avoid being caught... All the research. All the planning. *Roy's Rules for Murder*.

It was all for nothing. Susie had sunk him.

As careful as he'd been, while he was out on the water dumping that bastard's body, cleaning up Kristy's mess, Susie had spilled the beans to Kristy. He sat heavily on the sofa and took a big swallow from his scotch glass.

What was he going to do? If they convicted him? Who would care for the baby? Susie's parents couldn't do it. They were too old. And his business? That would go down the tubes, as well.

Oh, fuck, fuck, fuck, fuck, FUCK!

You've gotta get this shit under control, man... Take care of the baby, sure. But, first and foremost, you have to focus on the problem at hand. It's your word against Kristy's. How do you win this case?

He was going to have to testify. Of that, he was certain. And he was simply going to have to deny everything.

Roy reluctantly picked up Harlan's interview. Again, an immunity deal. Yet, Harlan's interview was a breath of fresh air. The senator denied everything. He denied having conspired with Clayton. He denied having any knowledge about what Clayton had been up to. Although the police had apparently found an extensive file on Harlan Junior at Clayton's house, the senator denied any knowledge as to how he had come by it. He even denied ever having met Roy.

It was a bunch of lies. All of it. Yet, the man was keeping his word to Roy, and Roy was oddly comforted by the knowledge that Harlan was lying to save his skin—just as Roy was. Clayton was, after all, responsible for Tom Wise's death. And for assaulting David Kim. The senator's denial somehow gave Roy more confidence in sticking to his own plan—deny, deny, deny.

CHAPTER FIFTY-FIVE

Eddie Garza spent the whole Saturday before the trial canvassing. He was off duty, but he lied to his wife and told her that he had to work on trial preparation for the Cruise case. Instead, he drove to the Old Merrick Bay subdivision, which was adjacent to the Cruises' subdivision of Lago Beach and shared the same canal system.

The day of Susie's shooting, the police had gone door to door questioning all of Roy Cruise's nearby neighbors. No one had seen or heard anything. And there was nothing on the surveillance video indicating that anyone had entered or exited the house after Roy left home for his interview.

Eddie wrote in his report that the most likely scenario was that whoever shot Susie had accessed the house by jumping the fence from one of the adjacent properties. This was quite probable.

However, there was another, less likely scenario. Eddie had located Roy's house on Google maps and seen that canal access was also a possibility. The simplest point of access was via Matheson Hammock Park, which was about a mile away. Before going there, however, Eddie wanted to see whether any homes along the canal had security cameras that might have captured something.

Eddie was *not* doing this off the clock because he was trying to cover anything up. If Liz Bareto had something to do with the shooting, he would treat her like any other suspect—that's what he told himself, anyway. But he was naturally worried that she had used the information he'd shared with her to plan Susie's murder, and he wanted to control all aspects of the investigation. After all, if Liz had nothing to do with the shooting, it would be stupid to draw unnecessary attention to her. Or to himself. Why expose their relationship, and everything that he'd shared with her, if she'd had nothing to do with Susie's murder?

She's been through enough, hasn't she?

So, Eddie went door to door chatting with homeowners. Asking about security cameras, and whether they'd seen anything unusual. He was having no luck.

He'd been to every house in the neighborhood that backed up to the canals, and spoken to most of the homeowners. Still, a few folks weren't home, even on a Saturday. Or maybe they just hadn't answered the first time he came by. He'd decided to make one more pass at the four houses where no one had answered the door, then call it a day.

Eddie approached the front porch of one of the houses, which was a one-story, ranch style home. The house was a bit run-down compared to the upgrades and renovations that surrounded it.

Original construction, no doubt.

There was an old Chrysler K car in the driveway that had been there when he'd stopped by earlier. As he stepped onto the porch, the front door creaked open. An elderly woman stood in the doorway. Though she had probably measured five feet and a bit in her youth, her back was bent by arthritis and she barely reached four feet tall. She leaned heavily on a cane, and her hands were twisted and deformed by arthritis, as well. She was so bent that she had to turn her head to the side to look at him. As frail as she looked, Eddie was surprised by the strength of her voice when she spoke.

"Second time's the charm, eh?"

"Good afternoon, ma'am. I'm Detective Garza." He held out his badge.

"I was wonderin' when someone would come to see me. I tried to get to the door when you came before, but I ain't as quick as I used to be. So, I set up by the door and waited for you. Come on in."

Eddie followed the woman into her house and saw that there was a wheelchair parked just inside the front door. The house was well kept, though there was a slightly musty smell to it. The woman walked slowly into the living room and even more slowly sat down in a very low chair.

"Before you sit down, could you do an old widow a favor? In that cabinet there," she pointed with a gnarled hand, "there's light bulbs on the bottom shelf. You mind getting one and swapping out the bulb in my lamp here?" She pointed at the floor lamp next to her chair. "These hands..." She held up two twisted claws for Eddie in explanation.

Eddie headed over to the cabinet to comply.

"Don't sleep so well anymore. Bed's too damned uncomfortable. Don't get old if you can avoid it. Only nights I do manage to almost sleep through, always gotta wake up to piss.

"So, I read a lot at night, when I can't sleep. Goddamned bulb went out Thursday, and my girl doesn't come but every Wednesday. And there ain't nuthin' but crap on the TV. You remember Carson? You look old enough."

"Yes, ma'am, I do." Eddie had found the bulbs.

"Now, *that* was entertainment. But, I guess even if he was still around, he wouldn't have much to work with. All these young actors these days are a bunch of faggots. Except that Matthew McConaughey. Him, I like."

While she talked, Eddie changed the bulb and confirmed that the light worked. He stood in front of her with the old bulb in his hand.

"Thanks so much for that. So, what do you want to know?"

"Well, a few weeks ago there was a shooting—"

"Sure. Down in Lago Beach. Like I said, I was wondering when someone would come out to see me."

Eddie raised an eyebrow. "How do you mean?"

"Well, I called the police and told 'em, I saw a woman paddlin' down the canal that mornin'. In and out. Right around the time. I assume that's why you're here? Figured out it was me?"

"I don't understand..." Eddie sat down on the sofa across from the woman.

"When I saw on the TV about the shooting, I called 9-1-1. Told 'em what I saw. The lady kept tellin' me it wasn't an emergency and to call some other number. But I told her I can't write nuthin' down with these hands, and I hung up. I figured you'd trace me down eventually. Goddamned guv'mint. With all these computers—don't have no privacy anymore. Took you long enough, though, din't it?"

"Well, can you tell me what you saw exactly?"

"Just what I said. It was Monday. Around ten-thirty in the mornin'. Not usually anyone on the canal Mondays. Mostly, folks come through on the weekend. But, hell, I ain't got nuthin' to do but read and look out the window. TV's no good ever since Carson quit. And I seen her. She came in on one of those paddle surfboards, then out. She was all dressed up in a rubber diving suit. Right around the time they said the young woman got shot."

"Would you recognize her if—"

The old woman blew a raspberry. "Sonny, I can't see crap. These old eyes... I could tell it was a woman on account of her hair and her tits. And she moved like one. Not like a man. That's all she wrote. So, don't go and think I'm gonna go look at some police line-up or nuthin'."

"You wouldn't happen to have a security camera or—"

"You're shittin' me, right?" The woman laughed. "Now, you can throw that bulb in the trash. It's in the kitchen, under the sink." She smiled toothlessly, then added, "You're a nice fellow. I bet you could use a cup of coffee. As a thank-you for your service, you know?"

Eddie stood and headed toward the kitchen. "I'm fine, ma'am."

"Well, how about makin' me a pot before you go? With these hands, it takes me twenty minutes. It's like a goddamned Jane Fonda workout. The coffee's in the cupboard. Folger's. Red can. Pot's in there to your right. Can't miss it."

CHAPTER FIFTY-SIX

Less than half a mile from Eddie, Moran had pulled up into Roy's driveway to strategize with him over the bomb that Shaw had dropped on them the prior afternoon. Moran had swung by on his way to the office.

"This last minute crap is bullshit, Mark," Roy said to his lawyer as soon as he was inside the house, as they walked to the study. "They're sandbagging us. Besides, this is all hearsay."

"Some yes, some no. Susie's... gone, Roy. That makes her an unavailable witness. And a lot of these are 'statements against interest.' A lot of what Kristy Wise says in that interview will be admitted as evidence. We can fight it, but we'll lose.

"I am going to prepare a motion to suppress your alleged confession to this Clayton character—I'm confident that we'll win that one. Even if what she says is true, he invaded your house, he was armed, he had Susie tied up on the floor—there's no way that gets in. It's clearly duress."

"Couldn't we use it to impeach Kristy's testimony? About what Susie told her?" Roy asked.

"You mean contradict her claim that you and Susie killed Harlan together by claiming—"

Roy finished Moran's sentence, "...by claiming that I killed him alone and dumped him in the Everglades. Yeah, stupid. Never mind."

"We can definitely keep your confession to Clayton out, but we still need to deal with Susie's confession to Kristy. And... well, it's fucking bad..." As Moran spoke, they were passing through the living room where Clayton had been killed. Roy stopped. He could see it all again. He felt clammy as the blood rushed from his head. Tears welled in his eyes.

He turned and looked at Moran, and saw the reaction on his face. Lips pursed. Eyes slightly narrowed. Something passed between them at that moment. An understanding. Moran knew that Roy was lying to him about pretty much everything. He knew that Roy had killed Harlan. And Roy knew that he knew. But Moran was his lawyer and his friend. He would take him at his word.

As they entered the study, Roy sat heavily, rubbing his eyes. "Holy shit, Mark. I'm fucked." He looked up at Moran, and for once, the lawyer did not disagree.

"Look, Roy. You've told me 'your version' of the events. You claimed you didn't have anything to do with Harlan. And, you *convinced me*. I *believed* you. I don't think Kristy's testimony changes anything. *You* never confessed anything to her. Our strategy still holds. But, barring a miracle, it does mean that you're going to have to take the stand. In the face of this," Moran indicated Kristy's interview transcript, "you have to address the jury."

"I figured as much."

"We also need to see what we can do to impeach Kristy. The fact that she's got immunity from killing Clayton in exchange for her testimony is a good start. What can you tell me about her?" Moran asked.

"Kristy? I barely know her. Barely talked to her. What she says in her interview is accurate—some of it, at least," Roy added the conditional because he was still maintaining the pretense of his innocence. "It's true that she showed up here at the house when we got back from Mallorca. Came into the house dressed like a fuckin' Mario brother. She caught Clayton in the act. He was getting ready to execute us both, me and Susie. And she killed him.

"Then, she stayed over a couple of nights before she went back to Texas. She's fucking sympathetic. She'll make a great witness. She's cute. Vulnerable. And on top of it, she's a rape victim. Both parents dead..."

" ...and under suspicious circumstances..." Moran added.

"Mark, I didn't have anything to do with *any of that*! I swear!"

"I believe you. And, they're not claiming that you did. They're smart. The implication is worse. They don't have to prove it. They can just let it sit there, like a rancid turd in the middle of the courtroom. And if we address it, it only stinks worse. Like trying to prove a negative. It puts us on the defensive.

"But tell me about her. Kristy. So, you think she'll make a good witness... What else?" Moran asked.

"I dunno. She and Susie talked a lot. She was here a couple of days. But, I wasn't around. I was working. Susie told me she was distraught about losing her parents. Naturally. Not much else."

"Why'd she stay so little?"

"No idea. It was kind of a spontaneous visit. And, after killing that guy in our living room... hell, I would've wanted to get back to Texas too... although..." Roy looked into the middle distance, recalling, "I do remember... I was setting the table for breakfast the night she arrived—it's something I do—and Susie asked her how long she was staying. And she said she had to get back because she and Bethany had some 'loose ends' to tie up." Roy shrugged. "I assumed it had something to do with her dad's estate or something? Maybe it was just an excuse? I dunno. I guess a couple of days was enough time for whatever she wanted to discuss with Susie."

"Do you have a last name?"

"Huh?"

"For this Bethany person?"

"No, but Google it. She was her college roommate—the main witness at the rape trial. She walked in on the whole thing. Called the police."

"Hold on." As Moran Googled *Kristy Wise rape witness Bethany*, he looked up at Roy, wondering, "You seem to know a lot about Kristy's rape case, the case against Harlan?"

Roy looked back at him, his face expressionless.

Moran shook his head with a wry smile and turned back to his phone. "Here it is. First result. Bethany Rosen?"

Roy made a face. "Sounds right."

Moran put the phone back down on the table and scribbled the name on his legal pad. "I'll look into it.

"Well," continued Moran, "the good news is that Kristy claims she killed this Clayton guy. It was smart of her—using the immunity deal as cover to protect herself from prosecution for that. She's apparently got a good lawyer. But, we can use that to discredit her—claim she was lying about what Susie told her to get immunity for killing Clayton... it's something."

"We need more, Mark. Figure it out."

"Yeah."

"Why don't you reach out to her attorney? See if he has anything to share?"

"Right now?"

Roy nodded.

Kristy's interview transcript identified all four attendees, and Harold Riviera was listed as Kristy Wise's attorney. Moran Googled him and dialed. Most criminal lawyers contract services to transfer calls to them after hours—their clients often get into trouble outside the usual nine-to-five. After telling the after-hours service that he was a new client, and that it was an emergency, he was transferred.

Moran pressed the *speaker* button on his phone and signaled with his finger for Roy to be quiet. "Just listen," he added softly.

A moment later, the line picked up. "Harold Riviera speaking."

"Hi Harold. Mark Moran. Roy Cruise's lawyer."

"Oh. Hello. I was wondering when I'd hear from you. What took you so long?"

"Well, I got the State's revised witness list and your client's interview transcript yesterday."

"Ouch! That sucks."

"Tell me about it." Moran paused. "I'm assuming that you and your client will be in Miami for the trial?"

"Flying out tomorrow."

"I don't suppose there's anything you can tell me that might be of use? That's not in the transcript?"

"You're asking me for ammo to impeach my own client, Moran?"

Moran didn't say anything.

"Look. For what it's worth, she didn't want to do the interview. She doesn't want to testify. She's not happy about any of this. The State threatened her, and she did what was prudent. Best for her. I think she really likes your client—well, him and his wife. Well, liked. Condolences on that. She was really sorry to hear the lady died. So, look, she's not adverse to Cruise. But she's not going to jail for him, either."

"So, nothing you can do to help us?"

"The interview speaks for itself, man. Look, she was very meticulous about her testimony. She was very clear that your guy never told her anything about anything. Everything she heard was from Susie. That's what she says happened, and that's not gonna change. That's the best I can do."

CHAPTER FIFTY-SEVEN

After meeting with Roy, Moran picked up a sandwich and went to his office to continue preparation for trial. It was almost three o'clock by the time he was able to sit down and focus on the Kristy Wise problem.

His team had been hard at work on the issue. Overnight, they had paid a service to scan all of the new documents into digital form so that they were fully searchable. In addition, Moran's team had assembled a two-inch binder that included all publicly available information about Kristy Wise.

Moran was searching for anything that could be used to impeach her—to raise questions about her credibility.

As he flipped through the notebook, he saw news articles about the rape. The trial. The attack by Tom Wise on Joe Harlan Junior at Whole Foods and that second trial. But nothing else.

He logged into his document database and began typing in search terms.

He scanned Tom Wise's interviews from the prior investigations. Nothing.

He skimmed through Tom, Deb, and Kristy's testimony from the trial transcript of the rape trial. Nothing.

He read through their testimony from Tom Wise's trial for assaulting Harlan Junior. All good background information, but nothing useful.

Every couple of hours, he would get up and walk around the office to stretch his legs and give his eyes a break. Trials are marathons, not sprints. He was deep into the thick of it, and he was beginning to feel it.

While reading through all of the materials, he got to know the different players in the underlying cases. Among them was Bethany Rosen.

This reminded him of what Roy had said, about Kristy returning to Austin to tie up loose ends with Bethany. It was something to go on. So, he typed in "Bethany Rosen" and up came a list of documents containing her name. Moran read through these documents one by one. The Bethany Rosen interview in *State of Texas v. Harlan*. The transcript of Bethany Rosen's testimony at trial. Moran found nothing that could be useful as far as the case against Roy.

Once he'd been through all the obvious documents—transcripts, interviews, and so forth—he started to dig into records that might yield information that wasn't witness testimony. His eye burned. It was almost three in the morning.

As he went through Shaw's documents, the next item he came to was a strange one—Kristy Wise's phone data files from AT&T. He checked the State's disclosure and saw that Shaw had provided those logs because they contained geo-location data confirming that Kristy had been in Miami the night Clayton disappeared. But, the data files had popped up in Moran's search because "Bethany Rosen" was listed in Kristy's phone contacts.

He jotted down Bethany's phone number, then ran it through the database.

No Results.

Moran's brow knitted. That seemed strange. No calls between Kristy and her friend.

Maybe the contact info is wrong...?

Hmph.

On a whim, Moran searched his database again for just "Rosen."

Many of the same documents came up as before, but as he scanned, he saw there was a new one. One he hadn't seen in any of this prior searches.

Notes: Detective Art Travers. Kristy Wise alibi.

He skimmed and saw that the document contained Travers'

notes confirming that Kristy Wise was at the Rosens' house the night Tom Wise was killed. Bethany's mother, Meredith Rosen, had confirmed that Kristy was at her home. Oddly, there was no mention of Bethany's whereabouts that night.

What the fuck? Moran thought. *Where was Bethany on the night Tom Wise was killed?*

Moran contemplated for a few moments, then switched tabs on his computer, opening Firefox. He searched "Bethany Rosen Austin" and scrolled down the search results. There were numerous news articles about the rape trial.

> Harlan Arrested... roommate **Bethany Rosen**, key witness... **Austin**
>
> **Bethany Rosen**, witness...
>
> Rape trial... witnesses **Bethany Rosen** and Frank Stern...
>
> Friends of rape couple... **Rosen** and Stern...

All the results ran in the same vein.

Moran scrolled to the bottom of the page, then clicked the link to the second page of search results. When he read the headline to the third result on page two, his mouth fell open. He clicked the link and read, wide-eyed. Then he scrambled to check his notes.

It made no sense.

Unless...

"Holy shit!" he whispered, almost to himself. A moment later, a shout of, "Holy fucking shit!" reverberated through the empty office.

CHAPTER FIFTY-EIGHT

Roy was asleep, in the middle of a recurring dream. A nightmare, really. He'd started having the dream shortly after he and Susie killed Harlan. He was in the ocean at night. He'd been in the midst of crossing the Florida Straits and had fallen off the jet ski. The water was cold. The waves were high. He couldn't see where the jet ski was. Visibility was miserable, and boats and freighters were coming his way. He was lost. And he knew he was going to die.

Roy sat up in bed, awakened by the sound of ringing. He grabbed his phone off the night table and looked at the screen. It was Moran. It was four in the morning. Roy slapped himself in the face with his free hand and swiped to answer.

Moran explained to Roy what he had discovered and what he thought they could do with the information.

"It's a longshot, Roy, but all the pieces fit. It makes sense."

Roy was out of bed, pacing barefoot in his pajamas. His belly tightened when he glanced back at the bed; Susie's side was untouched. Only his side was mussed. He walked out of their bedroom and into the hallway, turning on a light. He was wide awake.

"If you're right about this, Mark, it completely guts their case, doesn't it?" For the first time since he'd read Kristy's interview transcript, Roy felt hopeful about his chances at trial.

"I think we need to get a deposition done to confirm it. The judge is bound to give us time, considering how Shaw sandbagged us. Thirty-seven boxes the Friday before trial is complete bullshit. That's shitty, even for him."

There was silence on the phone for a few moments while

Roy processed, then he said, "Hold on—if we do this deposition, and we're right, then what does Shaw do? Dismiss the case?"

Moran pondered the question, then replied, "Probably not. He still has enough circumstantial evidence that there's some risk here. And just out of embarrassment or pride or whatever, he may not be willing to back down. But we can definitely get him to reduce the charges to manslaughter, or maybe even just straight conspiracy on the mutilation. That would get you out in twelve months, tops. Probably less. He doesn't want egg on his face. His reputation is extremely important to him. I think he'll make a deal."

Roy's voice was suddenly sharp, "I hired you to get me out of this mess, Mark. Not to send me to prison 'for a bit.' A plea deal is not gonna happen." Roy was thinking through his strategy as he spoke. "No, we're not going to ask for more time. We're going to file a motion to exclude everything he sprung on us. The judge won't grant it. But, she'll be much friendlier to us once she knows he screwed us around. And then," Moran breathed in on the other end of the phone line, knowing what was coming, "you're going to spring this on Shaw at trial."

"That's a *huge* risk, Roy. Huge. I mean, maybe we're missing something. I could be wrong. We both could be. Or, even worse, maybe he already knows and has a response prepared, something that minimizes the damage. Maybe it's a trap? I'm not willing to take that risk," Moran said.

"Well, Mark, it's not your fucking life."

CHAPTER FIFTY-NINE

"Thirty-seven boxes, Your Honor." Moran handed up the photo that Jackie had taken of the boxes sitting in the reception area to his office, so that the judge could see for herself. "Over seventy-six thousand pages, Your Honor. Sixty-five new witness names. All of this," Moran pointed at Shaw, "was delivered to my office this past Friday at five p.m. At the close of business. There's no excuse for this. The witness statements we found buried in there—two of which are critical to the prosecution's case and have *immunity agreements,*" Moran raised his voice for emphasis, "were taken *over a month ago!* This is nothing but a bald-faced attempt at trial by ambush."

Judge Goodwin nodded at him, then turned to Shaw. "Counselor. What is your response?"

"Your Honor. May I approach?"

The judge nodded, and Shaw walked up to the bench, handing her a sheet of paper.

"What Mr. Moran fails to mention is that, also contained in those boxes was what I've just handed to the Court—the shipping label that proves when *we received* the boxes from Texas. We only received them at our office this past Thursday. We made a copy, keeping the originals for ourselves, and turned a copy over to the defense as soon as was feasible. It was not our intention—"

"So, Mr. Shaw," the judge interrupted, "are you telling me that you did not have copies of the immunity agreements that you signed with these witnesses anywhere in your office files?"

"That is correct; they were exhibits in the interviews. The stenographers had them."

"May I see one of them?"

"I'm sorry?" Shaw asked.

"Actually, both. Do either of you—"

Moran was up on his feet, walking to the bench. "I have copies of both agreements, Your Honor." He handed them up to Judge Goodwin.

She took the two documents and flipped to the back of each where Moran had already highlighted the dates they'd been signed along with Shaw's signature on each.

"Mr. Shaw, your signature is on both of these agreements. From almost a month ago. Yet, you waited until Friday to disclose that these two people..." she turned to the front pages of the documents, "...Wise and Harlan, might be witnesses?"

"That's not true, Your Honor. Senator Harlan is the victim's father, and that was disclosed long ago. As far as Kristy Wise, I... well, your honor... it's hard to keep track—"

"Enough!" The judge turned to Moran. "I told all counsel when I set this case for trial that I didn't want *any* shenanigans. Apparently, I was not taken seriously. How much time do you need, Mr. Moran? To prepare for trial, given these new disclosures?"

"Well, that's the problem, Your Honor." Moran turned and looked at Roy, who nodded. "We don't want to change the trial date, Judge. We asked for an expedited trial setting. And we know Mr. Shaw didn't like it—you'll recall he objected to going to trial on such short notice—"

"I do," agreed the judge, glaring at Shaw. "Then, what's your remedy?" She held her hands in the air, feigning helplessness. "What do you want me to do?"

"Well, delaying the trial simply rewards Mr. Shaw for his misconduct. We'd like to proceed with trial, and we'd like the Court to order that the State cannot introduce any of the evidence that they just sprung on us at the last minute. Especially the witness, Kristy Wise."

"Your Honor, I—"

"Quiet, Mr. Shaw! I didn't ask to hear from you." She glared at the prosecuting attorney, and sat back, steepling her hands against her lips. The two lawyers stood in silence, watching as Judge Goodwin decided their fates. After almost a minute of silence, she leaned forward and addressed them.

"I agree with the defense, that you've," she looked at Shaw, "created a situation where granting them more time to prepare may be what you actually want to happen—to delay the trial." She shook her head, red blotches of anger appearing on her neck. "So, here's what we're going to do. I'm not going to deny your motion, Mr. Moran. I am going to take it under advisement. We will proceed with the trial.

"And, Mr. Moran, I will tell you right now that I'm *not* going to exclude *all* of the State's evidence across the board for two reasons. First, I think it's too harsh a remedy. And, second, I've offered you the opportunity to postpone the trial, a remedy that you have declined. But," she looked back at Shaw, "I agree with you that you've been wronged by this late disclosure. Your client has been wronged. And Mr. Shaw shouldn't get a free ride for his wrongdoing, either.

"So, here's what's going to happen. I'm going to carry your motion, and ask that you re-urge it as the case proceeds. As Mr. Shaw presents his evidence, you may object to any evidence that was disclosed in this last batch of boxes, and I will make my rulings as we go along, as I believe fairness dictates. Some of the evidence may be allowed, and some of it will *definitely* be excluded."

"Your Honor!" Shaw practically shouted. "That completely handicaps me," he was almost whining. "How can I present the best case for the State if I don't know in advance what evidence you may allow or exclude?"

"You've created this problem for yourself, Counselor. Maybe you should have thought through the consequences of your shenanigans before you pulled this little stunt."

"But, Judge—"

"But what?" Judge Goodwin almost shouted.

Shaw knew when to cut his losses, and backpedaled, finally saying, "That's fine, Your Honor."

The judge looked back and forth at the two lawyers, then

asked, "Is there anything else we need to address before we begin, gentlemen?"

"Just one other item, Your Honor." Moran handed a copy of Deb's letter to Susie up to the judge. "We believe the State intends to offer this document into evidence. It's hearsay and doesn't satisfy any of the exceptions."

"Very well." The judge scanned the document, then looked up and said, "Mr. Shaw, before you offer this letter," she said, holding it up for Shaw to see, "please approach the bench."

"That's fine, Judge." Shaw nodded.

"Anything else?"

The lawyers looked at one another, and both shook their heads.

Judge Goodwin sat up straighter and spoke over both of the lawyers' heads, addressing the bailiff at the back of the courtroom, "Sam? Call down to the central jury room and have them send us a panel, please? Gentlemen, we'll begin as soon as the potential jurors arrive."

CHAPTER SIXTY

Selection of the jury took the better part of the day. The courtroom was relatively empty save for Roy, Eddie Garza, the lawyers, and the potential jurors. A couple of reporters popped in, then left, each after speaking to the bailiff, no doubt to get a sense for when the jury would be impaneled and the real fireworks would begin.

Moran and Shaw took turns explaining the basics of the case, and asking questions aimed at identifying any jurors who might have potential biases in favor of one side or the other. Some lawyers see this process as an opportunity to give the jury a preview of their case, which it is. But, there is also risk to the process.

In order to identify biases, one must ask jurors very personal questions in front of the judge, the spectators in the gallery, and all of the other potential jurors. Moran was of the opinion that in this process, less is more. Shaw, on the other hand, believed that by asking the right questions, he could put himself in a position where the twelve people selected would be more inclined to convict than acquit.

Roy, for his part, had to sit up straight and seem interested and likeable for six hours until the lawyers finally whittled the fifty potential jurors down to twelve and two alternates. The two alternates had to sit through the whole trial but would get to vote only in the case of illness or other issues preventing one of the twelve primary jurors from completing the process.

At the end of the day, Judge Goodwin swore in the fourteen jurors.

"We will begin with opening statements tomorrow at eight o'clock sharp."

CHAPTER SIXTY-ONE

"You *what*?" Joe Harlan Senior was wide-eyed with shock.

He'd arrived in Miami that morning at the request of State Attorney Spencer Shaw. The trial against Cruise was going forward and Shaw expected to call Harlan as a witness the following day, the first day of trial. Harlan had decided to use the trial as an excuse to come to Miami a day earlier and hook up with Liz Bareto. Things had been a bit quiet between them. But, then again, Harlan was up to his eyeballs in work.

The plan was for him to stay two nights at her place, testifying at the trial the day in between. She had insisted they stay in for the evening. And everything had gone according to plan until about ten minutes after dinner. They'd had a martini before the meal she'd prepared of ribeye steaks with sweet potato fries and broccoli. And they'd shared a great bottle of Barolo he'd brought.

The conversation over dinner was light—catching up, current events. But then Liz had started acting strangely. Harlan knew something was up. She'd seemed slightly off since his arrival. He'd also noticed that she'd lost some weight. Something was amiss.

Harlan liked to believe he had a sixth sense for these things. When women started behaving oddly—losing weight, changing hair color, joining a gym—these kinds of things were all signs. And when they wanted to "talk," that usually meant trouble. He'd thought it was going to be about getting serious, spending more time together, him not calling enough, the usual crap. What she really wanted to discuss hit him like a jackhammer in the balls.

"You heard me, Joe," she replied. "It was an accident." Liz had explained how she'd gone to see Susie. How she'd planned to get a confession out of her. How she'd held her at gunpoint. And how, when Susie had gone for the gun on the desk, Liz had reacted unthinkingly, and accidentally shot her in the chest.

"Why the hell are you telling *me* this, Liz? I can't... I can't help you."

Liz's face twisted. "I'm... I'm not telling you because I want help, Joe! I'm telling you because it happened, and... I don't know what to do. If I turn the syringe over to the police so they can use it against Cruise, well... they might think I had a motive—"

"They *might think*?" Harlan shook his head in disbelief. "Are you fucking kidding?"

"Well, don't act all spanking clean and innocent now, mister. If you hadn't sent me the goddamned syringe in the first place, none of this would have happened!"

"What? I sent you..." Harlan sputtered. "I did *what*?!"

At his reaction, Liz seemed uncertain. "The package, with the letter. And the syringe that killed Liam."

Harlan shook his head at her, his mouth open, eyebrows raised. Liz stood up from the table and went to the buffet in her living room. Harlan watched her as she opened a drawer and returned with the envelope, letter, syringe in a plastic bag, and the lab report. She placed them in front of him. Harlan skimmed the letter without touching it, then looked up at her and asked, "You think *I* sent you this?"

Liz seemed baffled, but nodded.

"Why the hell would I... Where in the fuck... This wasn't me, Liz. I didn't—"

Liz's eyes narrowed, and her voice turned hard as steel. "Well, it doesn't matter," she interrupted. "What's done is done." She crossed her arms defensively across her chest. "So, you think that if I give them the syringe, it might implicate me? I shouldn't do it, then? Is that what you're saying?"

"What you should do... So... hold on now... nobody knows about this? At all? I mean, you didn't tell anyone that you think I sent you this..." he waved his hands at the objects on the table, "crap, did you—?"

"Of course not, Joe! What? Do I look stupid to you? I just thought—"

Harlan raised a hand at her and stood up from the table. He began pacing back and forth in the dining room.

"Joe, I—"

"Shhh!' He raised his hand again, index finger pointing up to shush her. He was clearly trying to process everything that he'd just heard. Finally, he stopped pacing. "I don't think it's such a good idea for me to stay here, Liz." He headed for the front door, beside which his roller suitcase was still parked.

"Wait, Joe! Nobody knows anything... I haven't told a soul, I swear!"

"Look, Liz," he began to tick off a list with his fingers, "Murder, breaking and entering, obstruction of justice, evidence tampering... I don't know what the *fuck* you think you're doing, but I can't be anywhere near this. Everything you said tonight... *everything*... it *did not happen*. I didn't hear any of it. I came by to say 'hello' to a friend. We had a very nice dinner. Then I left for my hotel. End of story. That's *all* that happened here." He pointed at her. "Remember that!"

Harlan walked out, closing the door behind him. Liz watched, teary-eyed, through the window. He marched toward the street, then stopped and stood in front of her house on the curb, his suitcase by his side. About seven minutes later, he got into an Uber and drove out of her life.

CHAPTER SIXTY-TWO

At eight a.m., there was a soft buzz of conversation in the courtroom. There were maybe ten people in the gallery waiting for the trial to start, most of whom were clearly press. Eddie Garza sat in the gallery as well. The jury had taken their seats, and the judge had explained that the trial would begin with opening statements.

Spencer Shaw was dressed in a dark navy suit with a white shirt and a solid red tie. He wore a lapel pin with the flags of the United States and the State of Florida crossed. His shirt sleeves ended in simple barrel cuffs. He wore no jewelry, and Roy noticed that the stainless steel Rolex he normally wore was missing. His shoes were spotless black patent leather—they looked to Roy like military dress uniform shoes, though Roy knew from his research that Shaw had never served. It was a subtle but probably effective ploy.

"You may begin, Mr. Shaw," the judge said.

Shaw carefully closed a notebook he had been reviewing, it's plastic cover reflecting light upon the table. As he rose and approached the jury, Shaw gave off the impression of a spry, energetic politician ready to give a stump speech. He stood before the jurors and clasped his hands like a preacher.

"Good morning, ladies and gentlemen.

"My name is Spencer Shaw, and I represent the State of Florida. And it is my sad duty to prove to you that the Defendant," Shaw pointed, "Roy Cruise, murdered a young man by the name of Joe Harlan Junior.

"We are met today in a court of law of the United States of America. And, as I look around, I see that all of the pieces are in their proper places.

"Judge Goodwin is duly presiding, and she has sworn an oath to apply the law in this case without bias. You, ladies and gentlemen, fourteen good and honest citizens, have been selected as the finders of fact, and have sworn an oath to uphold the law.

"I stand before you on behalf of and representing the State of Florida, and I, too, am sworn to uphold the constitution of our great state.

"And Mr. Moran will soon address you on behalf of the accused Defendant, Roy Cruise.

"Yet we, all of us, are only temporary pieces, playing our role, strutting and fretting our hour on the stage, so to speak.

"It is the courtroom we sit in today—no, it's more than that—it's the institution this courtroom represents, that is permanent. There are symbols all around us to remind us of that. The scales of justice, engraved in marble above Judge Goodwin's burnished bench. The flags of the United States and the State of Florida. All of these symbols are here lest we forget what this process, this system, stands for. They stand for something that is greater than any one of us.

"And that thing is the rule of law.

"Our founding fathers built this country on that principle. Millions of American soldiers have died defending it—our right to self-governance and freedom from anarchy.

"The rule of law means that no *person*," Shaw raised his voice when he said 'person', and looked at Roy, "can take the law into his own hands. We must all live within the bounds of the law. And if we cross that line, there is a system in place designed to punish offenders." Shaw pointed at Roy.

"We have all agreed to abide by these rules.

"If that system is violated, ladies and gentlemen, if the process is disrespected, then everything that America stands for is destroyed.

"The Defendant, Roy Cruise—and his wife—did exactly that. They spat in the face of justice, and in the face of the rule of law.

"The Cruises, you will learn, were very fortunate people in

many ways. Mr. Cruise and his wife met in law school in Texas. These are people who studied law and know how the legal system works. After some time in law, Mr. Cruise established what is now a successful investment firm—Cruise Capital—that he built from nothing to now managing over four billion, that's 'billion' with a 'B', dollars in assets.

"Mrs. Cruise—you may know her as Susie Font—was in television for years. At the time of the murder, they were citizens of the State of Florida and residents of Coral Gables, living in a private community called Lago Beach, to be precise.

"How could two people with so much going for them run afoul of the law? What could lead them to commit murder?

"It all begins with their daughter, Camilla Cruise. The evidence will show that, on March 30th, 2015, Camilla Cruise was in a terrible car accident. A young man named Liam Bareto was texting while driving and collided with Camilla's BMW X5. She was sixteen at the time. She died instantly. But Liam was left in a coma. This is undeniably a tragedy—for all concerned.

"But, what happened next... is an abomination.

"The Cruises were crushed by the loss of their daughter, as you can imagine. Who wouldn't be?

"They wanted justice. But, more than that, they wanted revenge. Rather than turn to the system, to the rule of law, to set things right, the Cruises took matters into their own hands. They contacted a friend, a childhood friend of Susie's. That friend, Debra Wise, came to Miami and went to the hospital where Liam lay alone, unprotected, in a coma. And she killed Liam in cold blood."

Shaw paused, letting the words hang in the air, looking each member of the jury in the eyes.

"The same day that Debra Wise killed Liam Bareto, Mr. Cruise and his wife were visiting Susie's mother. They were—logically—suspects in Liam's death. And they were questioned by the police. But it was a very short interrogation. You see, they had a perfect alibi—they were in another state at the time of the murder.

"Now, you may be thinking, what does all of this have to do with Joe Harlan Junior's murder?

"Well, Debra Wise asked the Cruises for a favor in return for killing Liam Bareto. You see, her daughter, Kristy Wise, was allegedly date-raped by a young man—a young man named Joe Harlan Junior.

"Joe was arrested. He was put on trial. And a jury of twelve honest citizens—just like you—found Joe not guilty.

"But, that wasn't good enough for Debra Wise, or for Roy Cruise and his wife. Although Joe was acquitted of the date-rape, these people thought they knew better than the judge and jury. They thought Joe was guilty. And they wanted revenge.

"And the Cruises owed Debra Wise a favor because she had killed Liam. Tit for tat.

"So, Roy Cruise and his wife killed Joe Harlan Junior. The evidence proving that they killed Joe is ironclad.

"Unfortunately, you will not hear directly from Debra Wise. She met a violent and untimely death. A gunshot to the head." Shaw looked Roy, and added, "Her husband Tom is also dead from an 'apparent' suicide, although the case is being investigated as a murder. And, Roy Cruise's wife, Susie, was recently shot in their home—and later died."

He paused, shaking his head at Roy. "None of those three murders has been solved." Shaw turned back to the jury; several members seemed to squirm in their seats, and a few looked askance at Roy.

"But Mrs. Wise's daughter, the alleged rape victim, Kristy Wise... she *will* testify before you. She will tell you how her mother—unbeknownst to her at the time—asked Roy and his wife to kill Joe Harlan Junior.

"Based on that request, Cruise and his wife concocted a plan to kill Joe, and at the same time make it appear that they were out of the country—vacationing in the Bahamas, as they often do—on their sixty-foot yacht. They once again set up an ironclad alibi.

"And they did it. They killed Joe. In fact, they did worse things to him than just killing him, and you will hear all about that too.

"And they almost got away with it. These are people who

studied law. They understand how the legal system works. They have more money at their disposal than any of us here today could hope to earn in a lifetime. And, they almost succeeded. Almost...

"Roy Cruise and his wife Susie became a law unto themselves—judge, jury, and executioner. But that's not how our system works. Ours is a system of justice, not revenge. And now, it is Roy Cruise's turn to face justice."

CHAPTER SIXTY-THREE

Moran jumped up as soon as Shaw finished. He wanted to give the jury as little time as possible to process what Shaw had just said.

Like many trial lawyers, Mark was slightly superstitious. He was wearing his traditional first-day-of-trial outfit. A khaki suit, with a pale blue shirt and a royal blue tie. Moran's light complexion, ginger hair, and blue eyes matched perfectly with the ensemble. Unlike Shaw, Moran wore French cuffs, and had not removed his wedding ring or his Rolex. He gave off the impression of a successful, capable, professional attorney. Someone to be trusted. Someone you would want to hire if you needed a lawyer.

As he approached the jury, he was careful to walk a line—one that he had previously studied from inside the jury box—that blocked the jury's view of Shaw to the greatest extent possible.

"Ladies and gentlemen of the jury, I will be very brief." He paused, slowly approaching them, looking them in the eye. His face was placid. He didn't quite smile. It was a look he had practiced in the mirror. One that conveyed confidence, competence, and compassion. It communicated, *You can trust what I say. I'm a good person.*

"The prosecutor and I, we don't agree on just about anything in this case. But Mr. Shaw was right about one thing—we live under the rule of law.

"And one of the principles which the rule of law has established is the concept of reasonable doubt."

He spoke quietly, reverently. As though he were sharing an intimate secret.

"We are all—each and every one of us—presumed innocent until proven guilty.

"And in order for the State to convict a person—any one of us: you, me, Attorney Shaw, Judge Goodwin, or anyone else—of a crime, it is the State's burden to present evidence proving that a crime was committed. And the State must present evidence that convinces a jury—all of you, each and every one of you..." he paused for emphasis, "unanimously... beyond a reasonable doubt. The State *must* carry that burden."

His voice rose a bit as he continued. "In this particular case, the State must leave you with no doubt in your mind—no reasonable doubt—that Roy killed Joe Harlan Junior. It is your sworn duty to hold the State accountable. Just as it is my sworn duty to point out to you the flaws, the failures, the errors in the State's case.

"I have seen the evidence, and I am confident that you will find that the State cannot meet its burden.

"In this particular case, the State cannot meet its burden for many reasons. The first and simplest is that my client, Roy Cruise," he pointed at Roy, "was not in Miami... he wasn't even in the country... when Joe Harlan Junior disappeared. And that's just the beginning. You will hear more, much more evidence, proving that Roy Cruise is innocent.

"Roy is on trial today for one thing, and only one thing. The State claims that *he is guilty* of the murder of Joseph Alan Harlan Junior.

"Now, it is undisputed that Mr. Harlan has disappeared. But, it is possible—and this is an important point that Mr. Shaw left out—that Joe Harlan Junior simply... ran away. The *State*," Moran almost shouted the word, "cannot prove that Joe Harlan Junior is dead!" He paused here, and several jurors looked at one another. One tried to look past Moran at Shaw. Moran took that to mean that, already, the jurors were wondering what else the State had failed to mention.

"Mr. Harlan was last seen—safe and sound—here in Miami on May 2nd, 2018. On that day and for several days after that, Roy Cruise was in the Bahamas.

"There is no evidence that Roy ever even met or spoke to Mr. Harlan.

"And there is absolutely no evidence that Roy killed Mr. Harlan.

"Mr. Shaw was correct to tell you that this is a case *filled* with tragedies. But, the prosecution's opening statement to you failed to disclose many important details. It is true, for example, that about a month ago, Roy's wife Susie was shot and killed." Moran paused, letting that sink in. "What the prosecution did not disclose to you is that Mr. Cruise was with me and Detective Eddie Garza..." Moran stopped and looked into the gallery, then pointed in Garza's direction, "...on the other side of town when it happened. Susie was at home." He paused again. "And, she was pregnant."

One of the female jurors put a hand to her mouth to stifle a gasp.

"One ray of sunshine in this case, perhaps the only one, is that the baby survived. A beautiful baby girl.

"Yes, ladies and gentlemen, the prosecution conveniently failed to disclose a great deal of critical information to you, and that is something that I will correct over the course of this trial, to ensure that you hear the whole truth. And the whole truth is that Roy Cruise did not kill Mr. Harlan.

"So, why are we here?

"We are here because *there is evidence* that Roy's wife Susie *may have* had something to do with Mr. Harlan's disappearance.

"In fact, it was during the investigation of Susie's death that the police found evidence tying her—Susie Font—to Joe Harlan Junior.

"It is the police and the prosecutor's job to solve crimes and to prosecute criminals. In this case, I agree that the State has the evidence to make a case of some sort against Susie Font. And every piece of evidence you will hear points at *Susie*. Not at my client. Not at Roy.

"But... Susie Font is dead.

"And, since Mr. Shaw cannot prosecute her, he is going after Roy.

"The State wants you to hold Roy accountable for a crime based on evidence that ties his wife to that crime.

"That is not justice. That is not the American way."

CHAPTER SIXTY-FOUR

"Mr. Shaw, please call your first witness," said the judge.

"The State calls Detective Eddie Garza."

After Eddie was sworn in, Shaw stood—carefully consulting his notes. To his right, he had a small stack of documents.

Shaw stood up straight and studied the jury for several moments, waiting until all their eyes were on him before he began, "Detective, how did you first come to meet Roy Cruise and Susie Font?"

Eddie began by explaining to the jury how Camilla Cruise died. He then detailed his initial investigation into the death of Liam Bareto and how, even though everything initially pointed to death from injuries sustained in the car accident, Liz Bareto ordered a second autopsy that revealed a needle mark on Liam's arm. Based on that, security footage was reviewed which yielded the ladyfinger photos, copies of which Shaw removed from his stack of documents and presented to the jury. Eddie also told the jury about his unsuccessful initial interviews of Susie and Roy.

"Since the Cruises were both in South Carolina when the Bareto boy died, they were ruled out as suspects at that time," Eddie concluded.

Shaw nodded knowingly. "So, all you were left with at that point was these pictures of this mysterious ladyfinger woman and an unsolved death?"

"And the needle mark. That is correct," Eddie replied.

"Very well," Shaw said. "Let's fast forward a bit from Liam Bareto's murder. Let's talk about Joe Harlan Junior."

Through Eddie's testimony and various documents, Shaw laid out a skeleton outline of the events surrounding Joe Harlan Junior's disappearance. He began with the phone calls from Cruise Capital that had brought Harlan to Miami. He then presented credit card receipts showing that Cruise Capital had paid for Harlan's flight and hotel room. Then surveillance footage from the hotel proving that Harlan had checked in to the Intercontinental Hotel on May 2, 2018.

Garza explained how Joe had purchased boat shoes that afternoon at Saks Fifth Avenue. And after his disappearance, further evidence the police had found, including Harlan's mobile phone contact for 'Cruise Captain'—a contact that he had spoken to twice while in Miami. The jury also heard about the strange text message exchange with David Kim about dinner.

Finally, Eddie testified to the discovery of Joe Harlan's penis nailed to his father's front door. Shaw put up a photo of the penis while Eddie testified. The men on the jury cringed. Most of the women looked away.

The detective then explained that Susie and Roy had once again been interviewed, and once again been out of town, this time in Bimini.

"Did your investigation end there—with the Cruises' alibi?"

"For a time. But, additional facts arose that led us to investigate further. You see, on September 12th, 2019, Debra Wise was found shot dead in Austin, Texas. And it turns out that the Defendant, Roy Cruise," Eddie paused and looked at Roy, "was in Austin at the time."

"And the Defendant is a gun owner, correct?" Shaw asked.

"That's right. And then, only weeks later, Tom Wise was found dead in his home. It just seemed like a lot of related deaths. So, we began to surveil the Cruise house at that point."

Shaw stopped Eddie for a moment. "Did you have a warrant for this surveillance?"

"None is required. We were only watching who came and went from the street. It's all in the public space."

"Okay. Continue."

"Well, on Halloween night, we identified a gentleman—who we later learned was Ronald Clayton—arriving at the Cruise house. But, based on our surveillance, he never left. Several days later, however, we found an abandoned rental car that was rented by him. This led us to his home in Georgia."

"And what did you find there?" Shaw asked.

"Extensive files, all about Joe Harlan Junior. Clayton was a private investigator. Although we weren't able to find any evidence as to who had hired him, it appeared that he was investigating the murder—"

"Objection, Your Honor!" Moran jumped up. "At this point, there is only evidence of Joe Harlan Junior's disappearance. There is no evidence that he is dead, much less that he was murdered."

"Your Honor—" Shaw began.

"Hold on, hold on. We're not going to do this one all day long. I am going to rule on this once and for all. I know, Mr. Moran, that you are going to refer to what happened to Mr. Harlan as a 'disappearance.' And the jury understands that it's the State's job here to prove that it was more than that."

The judge turned to face the jury. "The jury is full of good, smart people, and they know that it's up to them to decide what really happened. And I am going to instruct them that Mr. Shaw must prove that Joe Harlan Junior is dead. Just him saying so doesn't make it so, okay?"

Most of the jurors nodded in reply.

"But," she turned back to the lawyers, "the State is claiming that Mr. Harlan was murdered, and I'm going to let them call it that. However, the jury will have the final word. So, your objection is respectfully overruled. You may continue, Detective."

Eddie nodded. "Thanks, Judge. So, yes, from everything we found, it appeared to us that Mr. Clayton was investigating Mr. Harlan's murder. But, we don't know who for. And, the last place Clayton was seen alive was entering Roy Cruise's house."

Shaw paused, turning to look at Roy. Almost every juror followed the prosecutor's gaze, and Roy fought the impulse to shrink into his chair. He could tell that Shaw was done setting the scene. Roy braced himself. What came next was the physical evidence. And he knew that it wasn't going to be pretty.

CHAPTER SIXTY-FIVE

Shaw walked slowly back to his table and checked his notes briefly before setting up his next exhibit. It was the surveillance footage of Ronald Clayton entering the Cruise home. While the image was not great, there was one moment where Clayton turned to look back toward the street and his face was clearly captured. There was no doubt in anyone's mind that the man on the video was the same man in the driver's license photo Eddie had shown the jury.

"Would you say this was your big break in this case?" Shaw asked.

"No, sir. That came a little later. On February 10th, we got a 9-1-1 call—from the Cruise house. When officers and paramedics arrived on the scene, they found that the wife, Susie Font, had been shot once in the chest. She later died. It was as a result of that shooting that the case broke wide open. Because we obtained access to the Cruises' home and their safe."

Shaw paused, then asked, "And, what did you find?"

"Well, there was a Glock—a handgun. And there was a fish knife."

Eddie's usual rambling speech pattern suddenly changed. Roy was sure that he and Shaw had rehearsed this.

"A fish knife?" Shaw repeated. "Is this that knife?" he asked, walking towards Eddie with a Ziploc bag.

Eddie took the bag and carefully examined it. "Yes. It appears to be."

"Why, Detective, would someone keep a fish knife in their home safe?"

"That's a good question. It's unusual."

"Did you have the fish knife examined?"

"We did."

"And, can you please tell the jury what that examination revealed?"

Eddie paused, then turned to the jury and said, "First of all, there were fingerprints on it. Belonging to the Cruises." Eddie quickly corrected himself, "Specifically, Mrs. Cruise."

Moran had begun to stand to raise and objection, but at the clarification, he sat down shaking his head. The jury noticed Moran's sudden movement and head shaking.

"And then, there was blood." Eddie scanned the jury. "The blood was type A negative, and DNA tests confirmed that it belonged to Joe Harlan Junior."

Eddie looked back at Shaw, who stood still, nodding his head. Letting Eddie's testimony sink in.

"So, a fish knife with Mrs. Cruise's fingerprints on it, and the victim's blood, was found in the Cruises' home safe. Was there anything else?"

"Yes. A photo."

Shaw approached and handed Eddie a 4 × 6 picture.

"Yep. This is it. It's a picture of two girls that our investigation revealed are Susie Cruise and Debra Wise. It was taken at a camp when they were kids."

"Amazing, Detective. Is that all that you found?"

"No, sir, we also found—"

Moran was up and out of his seat. "Objection, Your Honor!"

The judge raised an eyebrow. "Grounds?"

"May we approach?"

The judge nodded, and Moran and Shaw approached the bench. There was a soft *tumpf* as the judge turned off her microphone so that the lawyers could sidebar out of the hearing of the jury. The court stenographer moved closer to take down what was discussed.

As Moran approached the bench, Roy flipped through Moran's notebook and came to Deb's letter. Keeping the jury from seeing it would go a long way toward gutting the State's case. The highlighted text stared up at him from the notebook.

I'm glad that I was able to help you out when you needed it.

And I thank you from the bottom of my heart for returning the favor. You and Roy both. I can't imagine all that it took. But it's made a big difference in all our lives.

If you can, keep an eye on Kristy for me. She's not like us. She's fragile. And on Tom. He means well, and he tries hard. But he's no Roy.

"Your Honor," Moran said in a low voice to ensure the jury could not hear him, "I believe that Mr. Shaw was about to have the detective testify as to the letter that we briefed the Court about."

The judge looked at Shaw and whispered, "Well?"

"That is our next evidence, Your Honor," he replied in a low voice as well. "I was only going to have the detective state that he found it before presenting the issue to the Court. I apologize—"

"You're already treading on thin ice with your last minute supplementation, Mr. Shaw. You pull another stunt like that and I'll declare a mistrial so fast your head'll spin, is that clear?"

"Yes, Your Honor."

For the next several minutes, the lawyers argued out of the hearing of the jury. Roy knew exactly what was going on. He carefully watched the judge's face as she listened to one lawyer, then the other. Moran's face was flushing red as he argued. Shaw was equally aggressive. It was apparent to everyone in the courtroom that something significant was being decided.

Finally, the judge raised her hand to both attorneys, indicating that she had heard enough, and spoke to the lawyers and the court reporter. Both took down notes. Then, the court stenographer moved back to her position and the lawyers returned to their tables.

Shaw returned to his table looking smug and satisfied, and reviewed his notes to resume questioning. Roy's belly sank.

Moran sat down, then scrawled on his legal pad and showed it to Roy. *We won.*

Roy breathed a sigh of relief. At least one obstacle had been overcome.

Shaw continued, "Detective Garza, we'll come back to that last item later. But, as a police detective with over thirty years' experience in the force, what did all this evidence mean to you?"

"Well, I now had evidence that Debra Wise and Susie Font had known each other for years. I had evidence that an at-that-point-unidentified woman killed Liam Bareto—the kid that caused Camilla Cruise's death—while Susie and Roy Cruise were conveniently out of town with a perfect alibi. I had a knife with Mrs. Cruise's fingerprints and Joe Harlan Junior's blood on it—a kid that came to Miami, all expenses paid by Cruise Capital. The same kid that was acquitted of date-raping Kristy Wise. And then that kid's penis magically ended up back in Austin, Texas. I had almost all the pieces of the puzzle—two revenge killings committed by two old friends covering for each other. It's a classic motive for murder—revenge."

"What do you think of the fact that, of all the players in this tragic drama: Debra Wise is dead; Tom Wise is dead; Susie Cruise is dead; and Roy Cruise is the last man standing?"

"Objection, Your Honor!" Moran was up out of his seat again. "The question—"

"I'm way ahead of you, Mr. Moran—"

"I'll withdraw the question, Your Honor," Shaw said, smiling. "I pass the witness."

CHAPTER SIXTY-SIX

Before Moran began his cross-examination, the judge ordered a fifteen-minute break. After the jury exited, Roy asked Moran what the judge had said about the letter.

"It was the best of all possible worlds. She's a smart judge," Moran said with admiration. "She ruled that the letter was inadmissible as hearsay *and* that, even if it was admissible, she wasn't allowing it in evidence as a sanction for Shaw's late supplementation."

"That's brilliant," Roy said. "So, even if she's wrong about the hearsay, she can do pretty much whatever she wants on sanctions. If she keeps doing that on all her rulings, there's no way any of her rulings against Shaw get overturned on appeal."

Moran nodded. "You remember more law than I thought."

Roy smiled. He was pleased that the judge seemed to be going their way. If only she'd do that with Kristy Wise's testimony. He sat back, allowing Moran to review his notes in preparation for his showdown with Detective Garza.

After the break, the jury returned to their seats, and the trial recommenced. Moran stood and walked to the side of his table. He held no notes, and seemed very relaxed with one hand in his pocket as he addressed the detective.

"I just have a few clarifications for you, Detective Garza. First, a very important one—so important that I want to ask it first to be absolutely sure we heard you correctly. When you testified as to the fingerprints on the fish knife, you said 'belonging to the Cruises.' But then, you quickly clarified your mis-statement by saying, 'specifically, Mrs. Cruise.' Just so we're all absolutely clear, can you please tell the jury exactly whose fingerprints were found on the knife?"

"Mrs. Cruise's."

"And only hers, correct?"

"That's correct."

"Nobody else's?"

"That's right."

"So, Roy Cruise's prints were not on the knife, correct?"

"That's true."

"Excellent. Because I have here the police expert's report—the expert you guys picked—regarding the fingerprints and it says that very clearly, that only Susie's prints were found on the knife." Moran handed it to Eddie and continued, "Now, let's discuss the three items you mentioned you found in the safe—the Glock, the photo, and the fish knife. Is it true that the photo and the fish knife were found in a lockbox inside the safe?"

"Yes, that's true."

Moran approached and handed a medium-sized metal box to Garza. "Is this the box?"

"Yes."

"How did you get the box open?"

"There was a key, found on the floor in the room where Susie Cruise was shot."

"Just to be clear—one tangent. At the time Susie Cruise was shot, isn't it true that you were with Mr. Cruise? In the same room?"

Garza hesitated, then replied, "That's true."

"Okay, so Roy Cruise didn't shoot his wife, correct?"

"No. He didn't."

"Alright, now, once you opened it, what else was inside this lockbox?"

"There was a ladies' diamond engagement ring, and a lock of hair that belonged to Camilla Cruise."

"What about prints? Fingerprints? Isn't it true that both Susie and Roy's prints were on the outside of the box, as though they had both handled it, but only Susie's prints were found inside the box?"

"Yes, that's true."

"Based on all of that evidence, who would you conclude owned that lockbox?" Moran asked.

Eddie paused, glanced at Shaw, then reluctantly answered, "I'd have to say Susie, Mrs. Cruise."

"And, to be clear, there is no evidence that Roy Cruise ever touched the photo or the fish knife, correct?"

"True."

"Or that he ever even touched the inside of the lockbox?"

"True."

"The handgun, on the other hand, was not in the lockbox, correct?"

"That's true."

"And it did have Roy's prints on it?"

"Yes."

"Did you check that gun—ballistically—against the weapon that killed Debra Wise?"

"Yes," Eddie replied reluctantly. "It didn't match."

"So, what we can say about the evidence you found is that it appears to tie Susie Cruise to Debra Wise and to Joe Harlan Junior. But, *nothing you found*," Moran said, raising his voice before he paused, "there is no physical evidence tying Roy Cruise to Deb Wise in any way, is that correct?"

"That is correct."

"Let's change gears for a moment, Detective. You understand reasonable doubt, correct?"

"Yes, I do."

"And, is it your understanding that reasonable doubt may 'arise from a conflict in evidence or a lack of evidence'?" Moran asked, reading from his legal pad.

"I do."

"Okay, then let's talk about lack of evidence. We've already established that there is no physical evidence tying my client, Roy Cruise, to Joe Harlan Junior. Is it possible," Moran's voice was rising as he spoke, "Detective, *is it possible* that Joe Harlan Junior... is alive?" The words echoed through the courtroom.

"What?"

"You heard me. Let me ask it another way. Do you have any proof that Joe Harlan Junior is actually dead?"

For some reason, Garza did not seem prepared for this question. "Well... there's the blood on the knife... and the fact that he hasn't been seen in a couple of years. And, of course, there's the question of his penis."

"Did you find his body?"

"No."

"And a man can survive without a penis, can't he?"

"Well, I don't know if he'd want to."

There was some snickering in the gallery, and a couple of the jurors smiled in spite of themselves.

"But it is possible, isn't it, Detective?" Moran asked.

Eddie became serious, and answered, "It is possible. Yes."

"So, to be clear—there is no physical evidence that Roy Cruise is connected with Joe Harlan Junior in any way, and it is possible that Joe Harlan Junior is not even dead?"

Eddie seemed very uncomfortable, but answered, "Yes."

"That's all I have for this witness, Your Honor."

CHAPTER SIXTY-SEVEN

"I have a few follow-up questions," Shaw said, standing up.

He approached Eddie and handed him a document. "Can you tell me what this is?"

"It's a Living Will. Signed by Cruise's wife. It gives Roy Cruise the right to make healthcare decisions regarding his wife in the event of her incapacity," Eddie replied.

"Where did you get it?" Shaw asked.

"From Jackson, the hospital where she was being treated after she was shot."

"And can you tell me why?" Shaw asked.

"Well, after the shooting, Cruise's wife was unconscious. A decision had to be made whether to save her or the child."

"I see." Shaw nodded. "And what happened?"

"Well, the Defendant authorized the doctor to try to save the baby. They did... save the baby... but his wife, Susie, died," Eddie answered.

Several of the women on the jury looked sadly at Roy. There were tears in his eyes as he looked at the detective on the stand.

"So," Shaw looked at Eddie, then at Roy, then at the jury, "what you're telling us is that Roy Cruise used that Living Will to kill his wife."

Moran flew out of his seat. "Objection! Your Honor—"Roy stared daggers at Shaw, his face turning red.

"Mr. Shaw!" The judge spoke loudly, over Moran. "That is a highly inflammatory question. I'll instruct the jury to disregard Mr. Shaw's statement."

Shaw nodded to the judge. “I apologize. Nothing further, Your Honor.”

CHAPTER SIXTY-EIGHT

"The State calls Senator Joe Harlan Senior."

Harlan wore a dark grey suit with a crisp white shirt and a blue tie. The clomp of his black cowboy boots—spit-shined—was the only sound in the courtroom as he approached the witness stand. There was a spring in his step; energy. The man was old, but fit.

When Harlan sat and faced the courtroom, Roy was struck once again by how much the father reminded him of the son. His stomach lurched at the sight and as he remembered the first time he had physically set eyes on Joe Junior, at the marina the day he and Susie had killed him. The same jaw line. The same eyes. But the father's eyes were different. There was something more behind them—intelligence, cunning—that had been missing in the son.

Harlan answered the State's initial background questions in his pronounced Texas drawl, directing himself to the jurors. He seemed calm, composed. Very professional. Very credible. This was clearly a man comfortable speaking to groups of people and persuading them.

Then, his testimony began in earnest.

"Tell me about Joe, Mr. Senator."

"Joe was a good kid. He was my only son, so our relationship was... you know, special. After my wife passed—she died of cancer—we became really close. And then, you know, after that business with Kristy Wise, the rape accusation and the trial, well, that was a tough time for him. For us both. But, I always told him that things would be okay. That justice would prevail. And it did."

As Harlan spoke, he scanned the jury, eyes periodically

resting on one member, then another. He was connecting with them. Building rapport.

Roy wrote on his notepad and slipped it to Moran: *Object to something. Throw off their rhythm.* Moran nodded.

Harlan continued, "But, that whole episode was really hard on him. Joe was always a kind soul. And a trusting soul. He had trusted Kristy, completely," Harlan paused, pursing his lips. "He told me at one point that he had fallen for her. That he was in love with her."

One of the ladies on the jury raised a hand to her mouth. Her eyes appeared moist. Harlan paused, sighing, and then continued.

"So, when things took the turn they did—what with the false accusations—well, that was exceptionally hard on him. Joe felt like he'd been betrayed by his girlfriend, the girl he loved. He couldn't understand what he'd done to deserve that. I mean, it's one thing for a young lady to change her mind after, you know, to... maybe regret... having intercourse. But it's another thing to wrongfully accuse someone of rape.

"And even though the jury found him innocent, well, he'd still been accused. You can't un-ring that bell. Joe had to deal with the media circus leading up to the trial. He changed universities because things became very uncomfortable for him at UT. After all of that, being found not guilty... well, it didn't magically undo all of the damage.

"And then, when the girl's father—Tom Wise—attacked Joe," several of the jurors looked at each other with shocked expressions, "that made things even worse."

"Can you tell the jury about the attack?"

"Well, Joe was at the grocery minding his own business, and out of nowhere, Tom Wise appears and attacks him, physically. You know, punching and kicking like a maniac. Joe was taken completely by surprise. Thankfully, several security guards were able to subdue the man. But I find it very hard to believe that this was just a coincidence. There is no doubt in my mind that the man was stalking Joe, waiting for the right moment, the right opportunity.

"The attack on Joe happened two years after the alleged

date-rape and months after the trial finding Joe innocent. What it made clear to me was that those people were not going to accept the decision of the jury. They wanted revenge—the parents, both of them." Harlan paused, clearing his throat. "I just didn't know how far they would go."

Moran stood. "Objection, Your Honor. Senator Harlan has no personal knowledge about anything done by the Wises. He's just speculating. The implication is inappropriate and assumes facts not in evidence."

The judge turned to Harlan and said, "Senator, I will ask that you please limit your testimony to only your first-hand knowledge. I know you are a lawyer by training, but I also understand that it's easy to get caught up in the moment. I will sustain the objection."

"Was Joe okay after the attack?" Shaw asked.

"Well, the paramedics came and took him to the hospital to deal with his physical injuries, but I think the bigger issue was on the inside. He didn't feel safe anymore. I mean, after everything he'd been through, he was acquitted and trying to get back to normal life, and then out of nowhere... I actually considered leaving Austin. I was ready to resign my office and move somewhere safe with Joe. But he wouldn't hear of it." The senator gave the jury a closed-mouth smile, then added, "He was a tough kid. Always thinking of others. But, I think maybe that's why, possibly, moving to Miami appealed to him."

"Speaking of Miami, sir, do you know the Defendant, Mr. Roy Cruise?"

Harlan looked at Roy for a moment. The two made eye contact. They had spoken several times by phone, and had met face-to-face on one occasion. Roy knew it and so did the senator.

The only question was whether Harlan was going to admit it.

CHAPTER SIXTY-NINE

The courtroom was silent for a few tense seconds before Harlan spoke. He glared at Roy as he answered Shaw's question. "We've spoken by phone, but no, we've never actually met."

"Tell me about that."

"Well, Joe came to me saying that he'd been contacted about a job by a company called Cruise Capital. They were interested in Joe because of his company and his experience. Joe was going to go to Miami to meet with Mr. Cruise and one of his partners about the job. He asked my advice."

"What did you tell him?"

"Well, it sounded like a good opportunity. 'Too good' is what I told Joe. I mean, Joe's company was just getting off the ground. They were doing well, but hadn't really proven themselves. But Joe convinced me that there was no harm in hearing Mr. Cruise out and seeing what he was proposing. That was Joe—a trusting soul, like I said." Harlan shook his head, his eyes tearing up. "So, he headed off for Miami. And that was the last time I saw my son," Harlan finished as his voice cracked.

"Do you need some water?" Shaw asked.

Harlan shook his head. "No. I'm fine," he continued, clearing his throat and speaking a bit louder. "So, Joe left for Miami on a Wednesday. But I didn't hear from him that day or the next, which was unusual. We were very close, and we normally talked every day. I was concerned, but you know, boys will be boys. But when he didn't arrive on his return flight, that's when I got worried. And I called Mr. Cruise's office."

"Can you tell the jury about that call?"

"Well, I think I left a message and he returned my call. Cruise told me he was out of the country. Said he understood I had called. That's when I learned that Joe hadn't showed up for his meeting with them. At least, that's what Cruise claimed. He gave me his mobile number in case I needed anything. It was a short call."

"Is there anything else you remember from the call?"

"Well, yes. He seemed very edgy, Cruise did. Very nervous. I thought it was odd, given that he was on vacation. He seemed like he was calling... like he had to, out of obligation. But he seemed to want to get off the call as fast as possible. It seemed very suspicious to me. When I mentioned that Joe hadn't come home, he just didn't seem surprised. It was like he knew something he wasn't telling me."

"Do you think that's because he knew where Joe was—"

"Objection!" Moran sprang up. "The question is leading and—"

"I agree," interrupted Judge Goodwin, "Sustained. Mr. Shaw, you know better than that."

"Apologies, Your Honor," Shaw said, though the sparkle in his eyes belied his words. Turning to Harlan, he asked, "Then what happened?"

"Well, I contacted the police, as it had been several days since I'd heard from Joe. They did a little investigating and found that he had arrived safely in Miami. He'd checked into a hotel down by a boat marina. I also saw on his credit card record that he'd bought some shoes." Harlan glared again at Roy and added, "Boat shoes."

"What was the next thing that happened regarding Joe's disappearance?"

Harlan fidgeted in his seat, and looked back and forth between Shaw and the jury. "This part is very difficult for me."

"Would you like a break before we continue?"

Harlan shook his head. "About a week after Joe disappeared, one of the detectives that was looking for Joe called me, then met me at a restaurant where I was eating. They had found evidence that Joe was probably dead." Harlan looked at the jury, one by one. Then slowly, he said, "Joe's penis was found nailed to the front door of my house."

Several members of the jury looked uncomfortable. Shaw put the enlarged photo of Joe's penis up on an easel again. The senator kept his eyes on Shaw, refusing to look at the image.

"And, on it, were written the words—'4 Kristy'."

The murmur of conversations could be heard from the gallery. Judge Goodwin smacked her gavel several times and said, "Please. I will not tolerate any disruptions in the courtroom."

As things quieted down, she said, "Please continue, Senator."

"Well, who 'Kristy' was—that was pretty obvious. The police did a DNA test, and it was..." Harlan paused, took several deep breaths, then said, "...it was my boy. They couldn't—the police—couldn't say whether it had been cut off when he was alive or... after." Harlan shook his head, then looked at the jury, saying, "It's a terrible thing for a parent to pray that their child is dead, but I did." Several female jurors were crying. One of the male jurors was wiping at his eyes. All eyes were glued on Senator Harlan. "I prayed that the sickos that did this to my boy at least killed him first. That he didn't suffer through that alive. Isn't that terrible of me?"

Almost all of the jurors were shaking their heads in response.

"Can you tell me what this is?" Shaw asked, approaching and handing Harlan what looked to be a picture frame.

Harlan held the frame, looking longingly at it for several moments. He sighed, then took a breath and was about to speak, but paused, shook his head, and looked away from the jury. He cleared his throat, then asked, "Could I get that glass of water, please?"

Shaw approached with a small plastic glass. The senator took a sip.

"Okay," he said, "thank you. So, this is a photo of me and Joe. It was taken about six months before he was murdered. I mentioned before that I'd considered leaving politics and moving away from Austin. Well, Joe had insisted that I continue my career. So, this picture was taken just after I announced that I would run for re-election to the Senate."

Shaw showed the photo to Moran, who indicated that he had no objection to the photo being admitted as evidence. In it, the two Harlans were both professionally dressed in suits and ties, and smiling at the camera. The senator was caught in a half-smile that didn't reveal his velociraptor teeth, his greatest physical flaw. Joe Junior seemed happy. The light caught him just so. He looked young, clean-cut, likeable.

Shaw passed the photo to the juror closest to him, who studied it, then passed it on.

"Is there anything else you believe the jury should know, Senator?"

Harlan looked at the jurors again. "My son deserves justice. If you have kids, then you can begin to imagine what I've been through. I would trade places with Joe right now. I would do anything to have him back. I know that's impossible, but justice can still be done. Please listen to all the evidence, and once you have, please find Roy Cruise guilty."

CHAPTER SEVENTY

Moran rose to cross-examine Harlan.

"Mr. Moran," said the judge, "it's twenty minutes to five, and it's been a long day..."

"I'll be done in less than ten minutes, Your Honor." Moran didn't want the jury to go home and think about what Harlan had said without getting his cross-examination in. Judge Goodwin nodded.

"Senator Harlan," Moran began, "have you met Roy Cruise, face to face, before today?"

"No."

"And you were in Austin, Texas at the time of Joe's disappearance, correct?"

"That is true."

"So, you have no firsthand knowledge about what happened to Joe in Miami, correct?"

"Correct."

"You cannot provide any firsthand evidence that Roy Cruise was involved in your son's disappearance or death, correct?"

"That is not true."

Roy felt a chill run down his spine. Moran paused. What had he missed?

"Okay, what firsthand evidence do you have that Roy Cruise was involved in your son's death?"

"Are you a father, Mr. Moran?"

"Objection, Your Honor."

"Sustained. Senator..." the judge began. Harlan didn't look at her. He glared at Moran, as the judge said, "Please just answer the question. You cannot answer a question with a question."

"Okay. I'll answer. I've been in politics for going on forty years—"

Moran interrupted, "Objection, Your Honor—"

"Counselor, allow the senator to continue for a moment, please," the judge said.

"Like I was saying, I've been in politics for over forty years. And I've been successful because I've learned to take the measure of a man, and that man is a murderer!" Harlan shouted, pointing at Roy.

"Objection! Your Honor—" Moran shouted.

"Sustained. Senator—"

"He killed my son!" Harlan shouted louder, still pointing.

The judge slammed the gavel several times. "Senator Harlan! Please, sir. I understand the emotional nature of the situation, but you of all people understand that a certain degree of decorum must be maintained. This is a court of law, sir!"

"I apologize, Your Honor," the senator said. But his expression belied any remorse. There was a glint in his eye, as though he were pleased with himself.

But Moran wasn't going to let him off the hook just yet. "Senator Harlan, you *are* a lawyer—correct, sir?"

"Yes, I am."

"Do you understand what firsthand knowledge is?"

"Of course, I do!" Harlan spat. "That's first-year law stuff."

"Then, isn't it true, isn't it a fact, that you have no firsthand knowledge of any evidence that Roy Cruise was involved in your son's disappearance or death?"

"You see, Mr. Moran—"

"Oh, no you don't!" Judge Goodwin interrupted him. "Not again, sir. I have given you plenty of deference, but that is a yes-or-no question, sir. And you will answer it as such. Which is it? 'Yes' or 'No'?"

The senator didn't look at the judge. For a moment, it seemed as though he may not have even heard her, based on the expression on his face.

Then, he simply said, "Yes. That's true."

Moran nodded.

"Senator Harlan, you mentioned in answer to a question by Mr. Shaw that you thought that working in Miami might possibly have appealed to Joe. Were things that bad in Austin?"

Roy saw where Moran was going with the question. He wondered if Harlan would take the bait.

The senator sighed. "You have to understand, Mr. Moran. Being a senator's son, Joe was always on display. And that comes with pluses and minuses. The whole date-rape mess, that was made worse by the fact that he was my son. The press was more interested—everybody was more interested—because of who he was. That kind of attention is very difficult for anyone to deal with, much harder for a young man. So, yes. It was very hard for Joe in Austin. People knew who he was. They stared. They whispered."

"And, you said that Joe didn't want you to end your career because of him, but... do you think that he was open to the possibility of moving to Miami? Of working for Cruise Capital and leaving Texas for Florida?"

Roy noticed that Harlan paused for a moment. Harlan's radar—his instincts—were sensing something, but Roy could tell that he couldn't put his finger on the trap. The senator answered more slowly, pondering, "Like I said, Joe was very selfless. He couldn't have lived with the idea of me leaving politics because of him. But I think he was open to the idea of... a fresh start."

"A fresh start. That would mean leaving Austin? Getting away?" Moran asked.

"Yes."

"Senator, you never saw your son's dead body, did you? It was never found?"

"No, it wasn't. I was never able to properly lay him to rest."

"But," Moran continued, "as Detective Garza testified, a man can survive a mutilation. A man can live without a penis. Is it possible, sir, that your son is still alive?"

"What?!" Harlan roared in reply. "That's ridiculous! Who the hell—"

"Objection!" shouted Moran.

"Senator Harlan!" Judge Goodwin interrupted. "Senator!"

Harlan turned to look at the judge.

"The defense has asked a legitimate question, and it again is a yes-or-no question. I have to insist that you answer it. Is it possible that your son is alive?"

Harlan turned to look at Moran, then back to the judge, then scanned the jury. He glared at Shaw, who appeared to be calmly reviewing his notes. Finally, he looked back at Moran, shaking his head, and said, "Anything's possible."

"So, it is possible, isn't it, that your son chose to get away from all the attention and limelight, and is alive somewhere? Maybe even somewhere in Florida?"

"Objection!" Shaw stood as he spoke, "Asked and answered."

Harlan's face contorted as he stared at Moran.

The judge looked at Moran for a response to the objection. Moran waited several moments, and just when it appeared judge was going to rule, he raised his hand and shook his head at the judge.

"Thank you, Senator. I have no further questions," Moran said and sat down.

The judge excused the jury for the day and called a recess until the following morning. As the jury filed out, Roy and Moran stood, somber. Watching them go.

Once the jury was gone, Moran spoke first in a whisper, "That wasn't good, Roy. The jury really liked him."

"I know," Roy sighed. He shook his head. "At least there's still no evidence so far that I actually *did* anything."

"But, he made it emotional, Roy. Did you see them, the jury? Joe Harlan Junior is now very real to them. And there's nothing more dangerous than an emotional jury."

CHAPTER SEVENTY-ONE

"I hope I'm not bothering you," Roy said. He was at my front door. He wasn't wearing his suit jacket and had loosened his tie. He had a bit of a five o'clock shadow and looked tired.

"Not at all. Come in."

The first time Roy visited me at home, I have already told you about—he had come by to "thank me" for everything I'd done for him and Susie. And he'd brought me a bottle of Macallan 18 and suggested that we should "go out on their boat" sometime. This was just after Susie had confessed to me that they'd killed Harlan Junior. I took that visit as a threat.

Our relationship had come a long way since that first visit. This time, Roy had come to ask a favor.

I was still in my work clothes, though I was barefoot. It was just past eight o'clock. I'd had some edamame for dinner, and was a third of the way into a bottle of red wine and feeling very relaxed.

"I'm having wine," I said, pointing him into the living room. "Can I get you a scotch?"

"Please."

The scotch bottle he'd brought me before was still in my kitchen cabinet, practically untouched. I poured him a glass and brought it to him on the couch. I sat down across from him on the love seat, folding my legs up under me.

Roy gave me a quick overview of the first full day of trial. He described it without emotion. Who said what; just the facts.

"Based on this first day, I think it's going as well as can be expected. Of course, before Shaw sprang his last minute surprise on us, I was feeling pretty good about my odds. Now..."

"Everything will work out, Roy. It's a close case, but reasonable doubt is reasonable doubt. You've got to think positive," I told him.

"I am. I know. But you know me." He smiled halfheartedly. "I've got to plan ahead, just in case. I've been thinking about things." He swirled the golden liquid around in his scotch glass for a few moments, then took a swallow. "Assuming this all goes south, I don't know what to do about the baby. I mean, foster care is out of the question. Susie's folks, well, they're way past their prime. They have health issues. Her dad has Alzheimer's. And her mom... let's just say that they're in no condition to raise a child. It's not a question of money. There's plenty of money—"

"Roy, if you're asking—"

"Let me, Catherine. I know it's a lot... to ask." He chuckled. "You know, I know *a lot* of people. Partners at work, clients, social stuff. But, going through this mess has made me realize that I don't really have any friends. And I don't have any family, either. I'm really all alone in the world." His eyes began to water.

My heart went out to him. I was torn between responding as a therapist and responding as a person. As a woman.

"I mean, Susie was it for me. She was everything. So, now, here I am, all alone. And now, I have this child that's depending on me. And I may go to prison—or worse. How fucked up is that? So, what I wanted to ask is whether—assuming this trial goes the wrong way for me—whether you'd be willing to raise Joan? You can work or not work. If you want, you can quit your practice. It's up to you. Like I said, there's plenty of money. I just need to know that, if I'm gone, she's got someone, you know?"

This was huge. I felt butterflies in my belly like I hadn't since I'd been a young woman. So many things were running through my head. Roy was essentially asking me to be the mother to his child. I understood the emotional and psychological significance of the request, even if he didn't.

When choosing a mate from an evolutionary perspective, the male seeks out a female who can provide healthy offspring. This is why men are attracted to signs of health and fertility: lustrous hair, large breasts, wide hips. The fact that Roy could see me as the mother for his child indicated to me that, on some primitive level, he felt that sort of animal attraction for me. And, beyond that, he recognized at a higher level that I would make a good mother, a good parent for Joan—and, most probably, a good mate for him.

"Roy, I would be honored." My heart was pounding. "But," I added, "it's not going to come to that. Trust me. It may sound sexist, but I have a very strong woman's intuition. I am not going to have to raise Joan for you. I can guarantee it."

"Well, thank you. Anyway. I'll have the lawyers draw up the papers, just in case."

Roy finished his drink, then made his excuses. He needed to rest up for the next day. I wished I could attend, but we'd agreed it was best for me to keep my distance from the courthouse. Still, I made him promise to call me with updates.

CHAPTER SEVENTY-TWO

"The State calls Toni Obregon."

Roy scribbled on his notepad and pushed it over towards Moran: *Who is she?*

Moran turned his head a bit toward Roy and replied, "Boat from Bimini."

A fifty-ish looking woman approached the stand. She was well-dressed, heavyset, and attractive. When she turned and faced the gallery, Roy saw that she had a broad, pleasant face and a big brown eyes. As the judge swore her in, he also noticed that she had a raspy, smoker's voice.

"Ms. Obregon, can you tell us your whereabouts on May 2nd, 2018?" Shaw asked.

"Sure can. My husband and me were in Bimini with some friends. We were staying at Fisherman's—the marina, that is, on our boat—*I Sea U*. My husband's a surgeon. Turns out we were docked right next to *Lady Suze*, which wasn't the first time I'd seen her—the boat, I mean. We'd seen her before in Compass Cay a few years back. And... well, sorry, I'm a little nervous. This is my first murder trial. What was the question?"

"You're fine, Toni. So, to be clear, you were in Bimini, docked next to the *Lady Suze* on May 2nd, 2018, the day that Joe Harlan Junior disappeared?"

"That is correct."

"Did you see Susie or Roy Cruise at any time that day—or at any point during your trip, for that matter?"

"Well, I am a bit of an insomniac. And, I am not ashamed to say I smoke—cigarettes. My mama smoked since she was fourteen, and she's ninety-two and still has three a day. So, I know I've got some anti-cancer genes that run in my family. Roly—he's my husband, the surgeon—thinks that doesn't exist. But I know it's a thing. I read about it on the internet.

"Anyhoo, when we're out on our boat trips, between the not sleeping and the smoking, I'm out and about a lot, and I see a lot of things. And, I remember telling Roly that there was something odd going on next door, that being on *Lady Suze*.

"You see, I did see our neighbors quite a bit during our trip. Roy and Susie. Coming and going. Saw them one night at the casino. Nice couple—nice looking. Met her. Never met him. Susie was just nice—a very nice lady. I thought it was odd that their daughter wasn't with them. Of course, since then, I've found out about the whole... tragedy." Toni paused, then looked at Roy, and said, "So sorry for your loss."

Roy's ears turned red. He pursed his lips and nodded to Toni in acknowledgement.

"So..." Toni paused, searching, then recalled the question she'd been asked and stated, "so, yes. I did see them both on that trip."

"And you just mentioned that something odd was going on next door? Can you elaborate on that?"

"Now, hold on..." Toni straightened up. "Don't be puttin' words in my mouth. What I said was that *I told Roly* that there was something odd going on next door. That was before I knew what was *really* going on. See, that day—May 2nd—I remember the day because it was the day before we left—I was up early as usual, I'd been up most of the night, in fact. And so, that morning I was down on the dock smoking at about four a.m. when I hear the door to *Lady Suze* slide open and close, and I seen Susie leave the boat. She was carrying a backpack and wearing a light sweater or sweatshirt, I think, for the chill. She didn't see me, and she headed on off the dock and turned right—headed toward the resort."

"Did you—"

"Now, hold on, again. I'm not done yet."

"Sorry, please continue."

"So, *that*, Susie going off alone, *that's* what I thought was odd. First time I'd seen her off on her own without Roy. And that was what I told Roly that day. That it seemed odd for her to go off alone.

"But that was only part of the story, see? After she left, I went on about my business. We were with friends at the Mega Yacht Marina and then at the casino most of the day. Came back to our boat around 11:30 that night—early for us, but that's cuz we were leaving real early the next morning, like I said.

"So, when we come back, the lights are on next door—on *Lady Suze*. I went on into our boat and got organized. Roly hit the hay. He sleeps like a log, that man. And I decided to have a smoke before calling it. Well, wouldn't you know—I was all out of ciggies. So, I decided to go back to the casino and get a pack, for the trip.

"Well, when I left the boat, I could smell smoke. Someone was smoking nearby. And I looked up, and there was Susie, on her flybridge. So, I asked her if I could come up, and I did. And we had a ciggy together. Then, I was going to head to the casino, but she gave me—offered, mind you—five for the road. She didn't have to do that... really nice of her.

"Anyhoo, like I said, I had told Roly earlier that day that it was odd that Susie had got up so early and headed out on her own. But, she told me—while we were chatting—that Roy had the vomirrhea... you know? Coming out both ends? Something he ate.

"Well, of course, then it all made sense! I don't know if you've ever been in a boat when someone's got it, but... oh boy... Not. Nice. So, it wasn't odd anymore to me, at that point. I could see her wanting to get some air, you know?"

Toni paused and looked at the jury, as if she'd suddenly realized they were there. Then she smiled warmly and shrugged.

Shaw reviewed his notes and, as he did, said, "Okay. So, to be clear, the day Joe Harlan Junior disappeared, you saw Susie Font leave the *Lady Suze* at 4:00 a.m. When you returned at 11:30 that night, the lights on *Lady Suze* were on. But, during the course of that whole day, you did not see her at all?"

"Yep. But, then, I was out and about."

"And when she left the boat that morning, she was alone?"

"Correct."

"And you did not see Roy Cruise at all that day?"

"That's true."

"Had you seen him the day before?"

"I think so. But it's been a while now. Almost two years, you know. But, I think so, because it seemed odd to me not to see them together. Odd enough that I mentioned it to Roly. And it would only have seemed odd if that day was different from the others."

"So, on the day that Joe Harlan disappeared, you did not see Roy Cruise all day on Bimini, correct?"

"Yes, sir."

"Thank you, Mrs. Obregon. Pass—oh, wait, one last question. When you went onboard *Lady Suze* to smoke with Susie Cruise, did you notice where the Cruises' jet ski was?"

"I thought you'd ask about that. Well, no, I didn't. And I told the Detective—Garcia?"

"Garza."

"Exactly. I told him that the jet ski—for most of the time we were in Bimini—they had it tied up to port, between their boat and ours. But that night, and the next morning when we were leaving, it wasn't there. But, like I told the detective, it could have been tied up closer to the bow, or maybe even starboard side. It's not—I didn't go looking for it. But it was odd that it was right there next to us almost every day except for that last day."

"So, you didn't see either Mr. Cruise or his jet ski that day?"

"That is true."

"Thank you. I pass the witness."

CHAPTER SEVENTY-THREE

Roy leaned over to Moran and whispered, "What the fuck was that?"

Moran kept a straight face, but replied, "Completely useless to them, I think. I'll be very quick."

He stood and addressed the witness, "Mrs. Obregon, I'm Mark Moran, attorney for Roy Cruise. Thank you for your testimony, and for taking the time to be here. I just have a couple of questions."

"Okay."

"First, based on what you've told us today, on May 2nd, 2018, Susie Font left the *Lady Suze* at 4:00 a.m. and the next time you saw her was at midnight that same day, some twenty hours later, is that correct?"

"It is."

"And, it is also the case that, based on what you know, on May 2nd, 2018, Roy Cruise was in Bimini on the *Lady Suze* suffering from 'vomirrhea', is that correct?"

"Yes siree."

"So, I take that to mean that you had seen him on Bimini?"

"Oh sure. Him and Susie. In and out of their boat. I saw them in the casino one night. He was definitely in Bimini when we were."

"And on the day of the 'vomirrhea', you have no reason, no facts or evidence, to indicate that Roy Cruise was anywhere else but on the *Lady Suze*?"

"That's correct."

"Thank you."

CHAPTER SEVENTY-FOUR

"The State calls Kristy Wise."

Moran stood. "Objection, Your Honor. May we approach for a sidebar?"

The judge turned off her microphone once again as the attorneys went up to the bench. Once again, the two lawyers went at it aggressively. The judge heard from one, then the other. At one point, Shaw seemed almost beside himself, and repeatedly interrupted Moran until it appeared that the judge scolded him. Finally, the judge seemed to call a halt to the arguments, and made her ruling.

Moran returned to the defense table and, as he sat, whispered to Roy, "She gets to testify."

At the words, Roy cringed. He'd hoped the judge would exclude Kristy's testimony based on Shaw's last minute stunt. No dice, apparently.

Up to this point, the entire case against him was circumstantial. Kristy's testimony would change that. He'd read and re-read the interview, and knew exactly what was coming. Despite that fact, all of what she had to say would be new to the jury, and Roy needed to react to it as though he were also hearing it for the first time.

He and Moran had spoken at length about how best to deal with Kristy's testimony. It was damning stuff. Roy's job, they had agreed, was to look sad and incredulous. Moran would object periodically, to throw off Shaw's rhythm.

As Kristy took the stand, she seemed slightly nervous. She wore a simple blue business suit. Her trial uniform. The same clothes she'd worn on the first day of the trial of Joe Harlan Junior so many years before.

Shaw stood as Kristy was sworn in, legal pad and pen in hand. After asking Kristy her name and where she lived, he began the questioning in earnest.

"Do you know the Defendant, Roy Cruise?"

"I do."

"Can you please tell the jury how?"

"We met at his house in Miami. His and Susie's. His wife. I was trying to find out what happened to my mother, and eventually I contacted them."

"Okay, but let's start at the top, please. How did your mother, Debra Wise, die?"

Kristy answered matter-of-factly, "She was shot in the head."

"And how did that lead you down the path to Mr. Cruise and his wife?"

"Well, when my mom died, she left me some letters—"

"Objection, Your Honor!" Moran stood. "Hearsay."

"Mr. Shaw?" The judge glared down at the prosecutor from her bench.

Shaw replied, "We are not offering any letters into evidence. I am just asking Kristy what she, did based on learning of them."

The judge studied Shaw for a moment, then said, "I'll allow it, but be very careful, Mr. Shaw. I've already ruled on this."

"Yes, Your Honor." Shaw turned to Kristy and said, "So, without telling us what any of the letters said, can you tell the jury what the letters motivated you to do?"

Kristy looked at Shaw quizzically, but nodded slowly and said, "Alright. Well, one of the letters was to 'Susie Font.' And I was trying to figure out what happened to my mom, when this lady—Liz Bareto—she sort of suggested that maybe Roy Cruise had killed my mom. So, putting the two together, I decided to contact them."

Shaw let the words sink in, then continued, "And, can you tell the jury who Liz Bareto is?"

"She's Liam Bareto's mother. The boy who killed Roy and Susie's daughter. He was texting..."

After starting out a bit tentatively, Kristy seemed to become more comfortable with the back and forth with Shaw. She explained what she knew about how Camilla Cruise died.

Then Shaw asked, "How did you meet Liz Bareto?"

"She was trying to find out what happened to her son. She didn't think he died of his injuries, but that maybe someone had... you know... killed him. When my mom died, she reached out to us—me and my dad. So, I spoke with her."

"And," Shaw said, turning to look at the jury, "do you know who, in fact, killed Liam Bareto?"

"Yes," Kristy said, her tone becoming tentative again, "my mother did."

There was silence in the courtroom. All eyes were on Kristy. Even Judge Goodwin turned away from her notetaking, hanging on every word.

Shaw presented Kristy with the ladyfinger photos, and Kristy identified the woman in them as her mother. As she answered Shaw's questions, everyone in the courtroom could feel the line of questioning about Liam Bareto building to a climax.

"Can you please tell the jury why your mother killed Liam Bareto?"

"Because Susie Font asked her to."

There were several gasps in the courtroom. Shaw waited for them to die down before continuing.

"How did your mother and Susie Font meet?" Shaw asked.

"Well, they'd known each other for a long time..."

Kristy explained how she had gone to Camp Willow and found a picture of her mother and Susie Font as young girls. Shaw put a massive, blown-up copy of the photo on an easel in front of the jury, and Kristy confirmed the identities of the two young girls. As the testimony continued, Shaw also seemed to grow in confidence. The story was flowing. He could sense that the jury was enraptured. He knew he had them in the palm of his hand as he turned the questioning to the critical matter at hand.

"Now, we are here today because Roy Cruise is charged with

the murder of Joe Harlan Junior. Can you tell the jury how you knew Joe?"

Kristy started at the insensitive manner in which Shaw asked the question. She stared daggers at him, and answered icily, "Because he raped me."

Shaw looked surprised, then stammered, attempting to maintain his composure, "I'm... um... sorry. Yes... I apologize for how I asked that. I know this is difficult for you." Shaw paused, making what he believed to be a sympathetic face, then stepped back to stand at the top of the jury box to make sure that there was no obstruction between Kristy and the jury. "Kristy, can you tell the jury who killed Joe Harlan Junior?"

"Yes. Susie Font and Roy Cruise."

"And how do you know this?"

"Because Susie told me."

Shaw stood in silence. Many of the jurors shook their heads. The few who looked over at Roy saw him sitting with pursed lips, looking sadly at Kristy and shaking his head in disbelief.

"Did she tell you why they did it?"

"Because my mom asked them to."

"Can you tell the jury in detail exactly how they did it?"

"Susie told me that what happened to me, being raped and Harlan getting away with it, was wrong. Unjust. She said that my mother asked her to do it because Harlan was too obviously connected to them—to my parents, I mean—too connected for them to kill him and get away with it. Susie agreed to do it because of what my mom had done to avenge Camilla.

"So, she said they got Harlan to come to Miami for a meeting of some sort. And then they drugged him, just like I was drugged. And then they killed him."

"How did they kill him?"

"I didn't ask."

"Did she give you any further details about how exactly they accomplished this or when?"

"No."

"What about the mutilation?"

"Susie said that she did it, cutting off his penis. Then she sent it to my folks, and they nailed it to the front door of his house," she replied.

"Who wrote '4 Kristy' on it?"

"I didn't ask. She didn't say."

"What did Susie and the Defendant do with the body?"

"She didn't say exactly. All she said was that he would never be found."

For Roy, the experience was otherworldly. His throat became dry and his eyes burned. He was doing his best to look "sad but incredulous." It wasn't hard.

The few times he sneaked a glance at the jury, they were all-eyes-glued on Kristy. Roy had a feeling of impending doom—which he had read was often associated with the onset of a heart attack. But, in this case, he felt certain that it was not his heart that was the issue, but actual doom.

"Lastly, Kristy, there is the matter of Mr. Ronald Clayton. Can you tell the jury about that?"

Kristy explained how she had come to Susie and Roy's house to meet with them. Shaw then played the surveillance video that showed Kristy Wise in a Halloween costume jumping the fence onto Roy's property. Kristy confirmed that it was her in the video. She told the jury how she had found Susie and Roy being held hostage and interrogated by Clayton, and how she had killed him.

"Why did you kill him?" Shaw asked.

"He was going to kill Susie, who was pregnant and tied up on the floor. And then he was going to kill Roy. I did it to defend them."

"What happened to the body? Clayton's body?" asked Shaw.

"Objection!" Moran flew out of his seat. "Irrelevant, Your Honor. The Defendant has not been charged with any crimes related to Ronald Clayton."

"Sustained. Please move on, Mr. Shaw."

"Very well. Just so that we are completely transparent with the jury, you have testified here today under an immunity agreement, correct?"

"Yes."

"Is everything you've said today the truth?"

"Yes."

"Did you change your testimony in any way because of your immunity agreement?"

"No."

Shaw looked through his notes, checking to see if he had missed anything. Seemingly satisfied, he summed up, "So, in essence, Susie Font confessed to you that, at your mother's request, she and Roy Cruise," Shaw paused, "killed Joe Harlan Junior to avenge your alleged rape." Kristy bristled at the word "alleged", but Shaw didn't notice and continued, "And they then cut off his penis, sending it to your parents, who hung it on the front door of his house with the words '4 Kristy' on it, correct?"

"Objection! Leading!" Moran said as he stood.

"Sustained," said the judge.

Shaw nodded, looked at the jury, then back at the judge, and said, "I pass the witness."

CHAPTER SEVENTY-FIVE

"Your witness, Mr. Moran," Judge Goodwin said. Despite her impeccably professional manner, her tone seemed to him to imply, *How the hell are you getting out of this one?*

As Moran organized his notes and half-stood to begin cross-examination, there was electricity in the air. The revelations from Kristy's testimony were shocking. And, there was a palpable sense of excitement as everyone wondered where the testimony would lead from this point. What would Moran ask the young lady in blue?

Mark buttoned his suit coat, then picked up his legal pad and his blue Bic pen, and walked around in front of the counsel table. The jury was to his right, and Kristy dead in front of him.

"Ms. Wise. Kristy. You've told us a lot here today. It's a lot to take in. I'd like to start where you ended, with your immunity deal. And, I guess my first question would be about the immunity agreement you made with Mr. Shaw. As part of that agreement, you confessed to a murder, correct?"

"Yes."

"You confessed to killing a Mr. Ronald Clayton."

"That's right."

"And, now, you can't be charged with that crime—is that your understanding?"

"It is."

"And am I correct in understanding that you killed Mr. Clayton by shooting him in the head with your own personal handgun?"

Several jurors winced.

"That's right."

"To protect Susie Font and her husband Roy Cruise, the Defendant?"

"Yes."

"Why didn't you call the police? After you killed Mr. Clayton?"

Kristy paused, silent. She had answered the exact same question in her interview with Shaw. Moran expected her to give the same answer, but her hesitation made him swallow hard.

"In the moment... I didn't want to go to jail, I guess."

Moran exhaled discreetly, with relief. "And you accomplished that goal, didn't you?"

Kristy tilted her head. "I don't understand."

"Well, based on the deal you made with Mr. Shaw, now you can't go to jail for killing Clayton. Right?"

Kristy nodded. She seemed attentive to Moran's questions, as though she wanted to make sure to answer accurately.

"Given your immunity agreement, I suppose you can understand how someone—how this jury—might be skeptical about your testimony? I mean, the State has basically agreed not to prosecute you for killing Mr. Clayton in exchange for your testimony condemning my client, Roy Cruise, correct?"

Kristy knitted her eyebrows but didn't seem to take umbrage at the fact that Moran was accusing her of lying. "Yes, that's true."

"Can you understand how someone might think that you'd be inclined to say whatever the State wants—whatever it takes—in order to avoid going to jail for killing Mr. Clayton?"

She nodded. "I do."

"I mean, you were willing to cover up the murder to avoid jail. By comparison, lying to a jury isn't that big a deal, is it?"

"I guess it's not..." she pursed her lips and shrugged. From across the room, she could see Shaw's cheeks turning red.

"But, you still claim that everything you've testified to is true, to the best of your knowledge?"

"It is."

"So, you're going to answer all of my questions honestly and truthfully also?"

Kristy sat up straighter, looking back at Moran, and nodded. "Yes, sir."

"Okay. So, we saw a video of you in a costume. What were you wearing exactly?"

"It was... I was dressed as one of the Mario Brothers. As Luigi, actually."

Moran raised an eyebrow. "So, you came to Miami to confront my client and his wife, to find out about your mother's death, and you thought the best approach was to jump their fence and break into their house, dressed as one of the Mario Brothers and carrying a gun?"

"Well, no. I was going to just ring the doorbell, but then I saw the guy—Clayton—when he was on the porch... and he didn't look friendly... he had a gun. So, I figured it was best to come in through the back."

"And the gun?"

"I always carry. It's my constitutional right."

Moran nodded. "And the costume?"

Kristy shrugged. "It was Halloween."

"Okay. Let's jump ahead a bit, then. So, Kristy, when you left Miami for Austin, do you remember what you told Susie Font and Roy Cruise?"

For the first time, Kristy hesitated, looking at Roy and then at Moran. Then she replied, "We said 'goodbye,' I guess. I... I don't know. I'm not sure what you're referring to..."

"Let me refresh your recollection. Do you recall telling them—Susie and Roy—that you were going back to Austin because you and your friend Bethany 'had some loose ends you needed to tie up?'"

Kristy's eyes widened. Her neck flushed. She looked at Roy, who stared back at her, his face placid. She looked at the jury, then quickly at the judge, and finally, nervously, at her attorney, Harold Riviera, who was seated in the gallery. He pursed his lips and shrugged, as if to say, "I have no idea."

Kristy turned back to Moran and stammered, "I... I may have said that."

"What did those loose ends have to do with?"

Kristy looked anxiously around the courtroom, as if looking for a way out. Then back at her attorney. Finding no help there, she looked at the jury, and then, finally, she turned to the judge and said, "I plead the Fifth."

"Objection—" began Moran, shaking his head.

The judge interrupted, raising her hand at him, and spoke directly to Kristy. "Ms. Wise, you are not on trial here, and you have an immunity agreement with the State. You cannot plead the Fifth. You have to answer the question."

Kristy sat, looking down at her hands, motionless.

Moran prodded, "You said you would tell me the truth, Kristy."

Kristy continued to stare down at her hands.

"Let's try this a different way. When you were in Miami, at my client's house, at that point, did you and your friend Bethany have loose ends to tie up in Austin? Yes or no?"

Kristy sat silent for several moments. Moran was about to object to her refusal to answer when she took a deep breath and said, "Yes, we did."

"And you told Susie that very thing, did you not? In my client's presence? Right in front of Roy?"

"Yes, I did."

"What loose ends were you talking about?"

Kristy stared down at her hands. Silent.

"Objection, Your Honor," Moran said.

"You have to answer the question, Ms. Wise," the judge said.

Kristy looked up at Judge Goodwin, studying her face for several moments. Then Kristy made a decision, her face hardened, and she simply said, "No. I won't."

The judge shook her head, then looked up into the gallery. "Counselor," she said, addressing Riviera, "do you need a moment to speak with your client?"

Riviera stood, buttoning his jacket as he did, and said, "If we could have five minutes."

"We'll stand in recess."

CHAPTER SEVENTY-SIX

As the jury filed out of the courtroom, Shaw looked back at Eddie and indicated with his head that he wanted to speak with him. Shaw then looked over at the defense table. Moran stood next to Roy as the last of the jurors exited, both of their faces expressionless.

Eddie came through the swinging gate from the gallery and approached Shaw, who maintained a smile on his face and asked in a low voice through clenched teeth, "What the fuck was all that about? Who the fuck is Bethany? And what 'loose ends' bullshit is so important that our star witness is fucking pleading the Fifth?"

Eddie looked perplexed. "I think she was the roommate... the witness in the rape case against Harlan."

Still smiling, still clenching, Shaw hissed, "So, what the fuck 'loose ends' are they talking about? Where is this going?"

Eddie shrugged. "Beats me."

"Well, find out. Call Travers and see what he knows."

Eddie pulled his phone out of his suit pocket and called Travers' mobile number. As he did, he heard, "Detective..." and turned to see the bailiff chopping his hand across his own neck and pointing with the other at the doors to the courtroom. In spite of himself, Eddie blushed at having forgotten that he was in the courtroom and hit END.

"Sorry," he offered, and said to Shaw, "I'll be right back," then headed out into the hallway.

Once in the hall, Eddie re-dialed.

He got voicemail.

Eddie hung up and called Travers' office number.

Voicemail again.

He hung up and texted, "Art. Urgent. Call me ASAP!!!"

CHAPTER SEVENTY-SEVEN

Riviera walked Kristy into a small conference room in the back of the courtroom which was used for lawyers to meet with one another or with their clients. Kristy took one of the four chairs at the small table while Riviera shut the door behind them.

"What's the problem, Kristy?" Harold asked, taking the seat opposite his client.

Kristy breathed in deeply, then said, "The problem... is that I left something out of my interview."

"What? But... why?" Riviera's mouth hung open. "We discussed this. You agreed. I told you to answer truthfully. Every question—"

"Because they didn't fucking ask, okay? Shaw didn't *even come close* to asking about it. And... it wasn't just about me. Someone else was involved too. And like you told me, the immunity only applies to me, so..."

"Dammit, Kristy! Involved in what?"

"Frank Stern."

"Stern?" Riviera hesitated for a moment before his memory kicked in and he remembered who Frank Stern was. "Frank Stern. Yeah. Harlan's friend. Okay... what about him?"

"The 'loose end' he was asking about. It's him. Frank Stern."

"Oh fuck, Kristy! What did you guys do to Stern?"

Kristy explained everything to her lawyer in broad strokes. She told Riviera what Frank Stern had done—not just to her, not just that he'd raped her—but to Bethany, as well. And then she explained, at a very high level, the revenge that had been exacted on Frank Stern. She purposefully and carefully avoided disclosing to her lawyer who, besides herself, was involved in exacting that revenge against Stern.

"Oh fuck..." Harold ran his hands through his thick black hair. Riviera looked at his client with new eyes. He knew that she was capable of killing. She'd shot Clayton. Still, that was in defense of others; Clayton was about to commit murder. Two murders. But what Kristy had done to Frank Stern was cold-blooded, premeditated, and... just nasty.

"So, who else was involved in this? This Bethany person?"

"I can't tell you... I won't... because I may want to lie about it. In there," she indicated the courtroom with her head.

Riviera shook his head in disbelief. He stood and began to pace.

"I'm sorry, I guess—"

"Shhh," he said. "Give me a minute. I need to figure out how to get your ass out of this fuckin' sling." He continued to pace. The immunity agreement would clearly not cover this new crime. Neither for Kristy nor for whomever else was involved. Once he had gotten his head around it all, Riviera stopped by the door and put his hand on the knob.

"Kristy," he said, "if all of this comes out in court, you're screwed. And whoever you did this with is screwed, too. Give me a minute. I want to talk with Moran."

Riviera walked down the short hallway and poked his head into the courtroom. He saw Moran seated, conversing in low tones with Roy. As he approached, Riviera heard the judge ask him from her bench, "Are we ready to resume, Mr. Riviera?"

"I just need to speak with Mr. Moran for a moment, if I may, Your Honor."

Moran had turned to see who the judge was addressing. He stood slowly and walked toward Harold, who led the way out of the courtroom and into the hallway. As he did, Shaw glared at them both.

As they exited the courtroom, Riviera saw Eddie Garza on the phone down the hall to the right, so he steered Moran to the left, to keep out of earshot of the detective.

“So, now you want to talk?” Moran half-smiled.

“Look, Mark, I apologize. I was looking out for my client. Shaw asked us to lay low, so that’s what we did.”

Moran stood, arms crossed over his chest, waiting.

“So, look. Kristy’s been through a lot. I’m trying to watch out for her here. And she’s going to answer your questions. But, she can answer willingly, or you’ll have an adverse witness on your hands. Up until now, I think she’s been pretty neutral in the way she’s presented your client. The way she’s talked about him. That could change.”

“You asked me out here to threaten me? Is this how you do things in Texas?” Moran asked.

“It’s not a threat. I just want to see if we can maybe get to a win-win. She’s going to answer your questions. She doesn’t have a choice. But if you can give me an idea of what you’re looking for as far as her testimony, what you’re trying to accomplish, maybe I can protect her interests—not violate her immunity agreement—and also get you what you need?”

Moran stood very still, arms still crossed over his chest, shaking his head slowly. Thinking.

“Look,” continued Riviera, “I’m only on the periphery here. But it seems like your guy and his wife had some sort of special connection with Kristy? And for fuck’s sake, *she saved their lives.* Why don’t you talk to your guy? I just need to know the direction the testimony’s going so that I can hopefully give you what you want and protect her at the same time. That way everybody wins.”

Moran nodded, then said, “Give me a minute,” and headed back into the courtroom. He had a good idea what he wanted to ask Riviera to do. He just needed to clear it with Roy.

Less than five minutes later, he returned with a thin manila folder.

“Look, Harold. I get where you’re coming from. But you know as well as I do that what Kristy has testified to is destroying our case. Thankfully, she’s the State’s only eyewitness. Without her, everything is just circumstantial.”

Riviera nodded along in agreement with Moran.

"I talked to Roy. He doesn't want to cause Kristy any trouble. He understands why she'd cut a deal to protect herself on the Clayton murder. So, there's no hard feelings there. He's allowed me to share this with you." Moran indicated the manila folder. "I just need her to say two things... and, I don't think that saying either of them violates her immunity agreement at all. In fact," Moran paused, staring Riviera hard in the eyes, "as an officer of the court, I believe them to be true."

Moran opened the folder and showed Riviera a single sheet of paper.

At first, Riviera just stood there looking at it. Then Moran pointed to the date at the bottom of the document. Riviera still didn't react. So, Moran explained what he believed the document proved. Harold was stunned. Once the implications sank in, and he got over the shock, his heart raced.

Moran then explained what he proposed to ask Kristy, and what he "hoped" she would say in response. Riviera understood the strategy. It made sense. He took the folder from Moran and said, "I'll be right back," and went back to the small room to confer with Kristy.

About ten minutes later, he returned to Moran, with the folder.

"She'll do it," he said, and explained to Moran the best way to accomplish their mutual objectives.

CHAPTER SEVENTY-EIGHT

Eddie had been pacing back and forth, sending texts to Travers and calling his mobile phone, hoping that he would reply. He had watched as Riviera and Moran huddled together down the hall. Moran had left, then returned with a folder. Then Riviera left with the folder and returned. Periodically, the two attorneys glanced in his direction.

Finally, Moran and Riviera finished their chat and headed back into the courtroom together. They glanced back at him as they crossed the threshold into courtroom.

Eddie knew what it looked like to get screwed by lawyers. This was it.

He began to walk toward the courtroom and re-dialed Travers' office number again.

"Hello."

"Art!?" Eddie stopped walking.

"Art Travers' *office*, yes. But not him. This is Detective Sampson—"

"Shit... This is Detective Eddie Garza, from Florida. We're in trial and it's urgent..."

Just then, another call came in on Eddie's phone—TRAVERS MOBILE.

"Wait. He's calling me back. Goodbye." Eddie touched his phone's screen to end the office call and answered the incoming. He was now standing at the courtroom doors.

"Art! Listen, I need your help—"

"What's up? A guy can't even shit in peace anymore," he laughed. "What's so urgent, Eddie? Verdict already?"

"Not yet, but getting there."

"How's it looking?"

"That's what I'm calling about, actually. Kristy's on the stand. Couldn't have gone better. We got everything in. Everything. She came across great. But now they've got her on cross, and they're asking her about Bethany? That's her old roommate, right?"

"Yeah. So? What are they asking?"

"Well, apparently, after Kristy killed Clayton in Miami, she told Cruise that she was coming back to Austin to tie up some loose ends with Bethany—"

"What...?" Art asked.

"Yeah, the question really shook Kristy up. She took the Fifth, but the judge ordered her to answer. She refused. So, now we're on break while she talks to her lawyer."

"And, when did you say all this happened?"

"Just now—" Eddie replied.

"No. The stuff about the loose ends and Bethany."

Eddie sighed, exasperated. He needed to get back into the courtroom. He tried to re-state the issue more clearly, "Listen carefully, Art... here in Miami, right after Kristy killed Clayton, she told Cruise and his wife that she was coming back to Austin to tie up some loose ends with Bethany. That's what Moran's asking her about. And she's really spooked."

"Are you sure, Eddie?"

"Why? What gives, Art?"

"Hell, Eddie. The thing is..."

Through the doors, Eddie heard the judge's gavel bang twice, and he heard the bailiff shout, "All rise!" He put a hand on the knob to the courtroom door as he listened to Art. And as his counterpart from Texas told him what he knew, Eddie's brows knitted, his mouth fell open, and his stomach knotted.

Eddie hung up and, as quietly as he could, re-entered the courtroom. Shaw made eye contact with him, and Eddie shook his head with lips pursed. He still couldn't believe what Travers had just told him. But if he had any doubts, they would be erased in a few moments when Kristy Wise told the jury the same thing from the witness stand.

CHAPTER SEVENTY-NINE

Kristy returned to the stand, and the judge called the jurors back into the courtroom. Shaw looked to the back of the room and saw Eddie's head shake.

What the fuck now? he thought.

Had he been focused on the witness, he would have noticed that Kristy's eyes were red—as though she'd been crying.

Moran stood and addressed her, "Kristy, are you ready to continue now?"

She nodded.

"Okay, can you tell me who Bethany Rosen is?"

Kristy seemed tentative in her response. Almost as though she were distracted, not sure of herself. "She's... my best friend."

"And she's the same friend who—this past October, just five months ago—you told Susie and Roy you needed to go back to Austin to see about some loose ends, correct?"

"Yes."

"Now, can you tell the ladies and gentlemen of the jury what happened to Bethany two years ago, back in March of 2018?"

Kristy breathed in deeply, and replied, "Well, I got a call from her sister Sophia, like at three in the morning. Bethany had gotten some bad drugs. She thought she was getting X—you know, ecstasy, Molly? But it turns out it was PMA. Beth took it and ended up in the hospital."

"And that was in March of 2018?"

"Correct."

"How long after that did your mother pass away?"

"That was more than a year later. This past September."

"And when did your father pass?"

"About a month later, on October 10th."

"So, very close after your mother?"

"Yes."

"All of that... that must have been very traumatic?"

Kristy's eyes seemed to water. She sniffed, cleared her throat, and replied, "It was terrible, yes."

"After that, did you seek any sort of counseling or therapy?"

"No."

"Okay. Now, it sounds like you had to do quite a bit of investigating to figure out everything that you did. Everything that led you to be at Roy's house on Halloween. You mentioned you got information from a Mrs. Liz Bareto. Did you have any other help?"

"Well, yes." Kristy looked at Riviera, then took a deep breath and said, "Bethany. She helped me with figuring a lot of this stuff out."

"How, exactly?"

"Objection, Your Honor." Shaw stood. "Mr. Moran is going really far afield here. None of this has any relevance to the issue at hand."

Moran shook his head. Shaw's objection was absurd. He was clearly just trying to throw off his rhythm. "Your Honor," Moran began. "The witness has testified—"

"I'll overrule the objection. But, please do move things along, Counselor."

"Thank you." Moran turned back to Kristy. "Kristy. You were telling us how Bethany helped you investigate your mother's death."

"Right..." she nodded. "Well, she encouraged me to talk to my dad to try and understand what had happened to Mom. And when he didn't want to discuss it, she encouraged me to talk to Liz Bareto, which is how I learned that Roy was in town when my mom got shot. That's really—well, that and the photo from camp—that's really what got me to go to Florida to try to get to the bottom of everything."

"And what did Bethany think about you coming to Florida?"

Again, Kristy looked at Riviera for a moment before answering, "She thought that was the best way to go... to get to the bottom of things."

"So, just to be clear, your mother died in a very tragic and traumatic way in September of 2019?"

"Correct."

"Less than a month later, your father died."

"Yes."

"And, Bethany Rosen helped you figure out exactly what happened to your mother, which is how you came to be here testifying today?"

"Yes, sir."

"Let me hand you what I've marked as Defense Exhibit 1. Have you seen this document before?"

Kristy handled the document as though it were a poisonous snake. "Yes, just a few minutes ago."

"Do you know what it is?"

Kristy nodded.

"You have to answer audibly for the court reporter, please."

"Yes, I know what it is. I do now."

"What is it?"

"It says 'Certificate of Death'."

"Whose is it?"

"Bethany Rosen's."

"What is the date of death?"

"March 11th, 2018."

"What does the document say regarding cause of death?" he asked.

Kristy's eyes watered. "Drug overdose... of para-Meth... oxy... amphetamine. PMA."

Kristy looked up at Moran, then at Roy. She placed the certificate in front of her, pushing it as far from her as she could.

"The night that Bethany overdosed, Kristy—she never recovered, did she?"

Kristy shook her head, tears streaming down her cheeks. "No," she finally managed.

"But, you have testified that since that date—since Bethany died—you have regularly spoken to Bethany, and that she helped you figure out what happened to your mom and dad. Is that correct?"

"Yes."

It was Moran's turn to pause for dramatic effect. He stood perfectly still, looking at Kristy with a combination of understanding and sadness. His next question was asked tenderly, at almost a whisper.

"So, all that time you were talking to her and she was helping you, Bethany was dead?"

Kristy nodded through tears.

"Do you want to change any of that testimony?" Moran asked.

Kristy hesitated, then said, "No, sir."

Moran stopped, looking at the jury. None of them were looking at him. All eyes were fixed on Kristy. Several women were crying.

"Okay. With regards to the death of Joe Harlan Junior, exactly what did Roy Cruise tell you about his role in that crime?"

"Roy? Nothing. We never discussed it."

"Then, where did you get all of this information?"

"From Susie Font."

"Anyone else?"

"No."

"So, everything you told us today, about how my client Roy Cruise was involved in killing Joe Harlan, all of that was told to you by Susie Font. Is that correct?"

"It is."

"Are you aware that Susie Font is dead?"

"Yes."

"Did she explain all of this to you—everything she told you—before or after she died?"

Kristy looked at her lawyer, and Riviera almost imperceptibly nodded at her. "Before... I think," she replied.

Moran breathed in deeply, then exhaled audibly.

"Kristy, as you sit here today, under oath, are you sure that

Susie Font told you all of these things about Joe Harlan Junior's murder before she died, and not after?"

Kristy hesitated, then said, "I... I think so, but no. Not really."

"So, to be absolutely clear..." Moran paused. "It's possible that Susie Font told you all these things, *everything* that you have said about Roy Cruise killing Joe Harlan Junior, after she died?"

"Yes. That's true."

CHAPTER EIGHTY

Moran walked back to the defense table slowly. As he did, Shaw turned and looked at Roy. Roy had glanced at Shaw several times during Kristy's testimony, to gauge his reactions. Did Shaw know about Bethany? Were they walking into some kind of trap? Shaw's face had initially turned pale at Kristy's revelations. Throughout most of her testimony, he'd been so enthralled that he hadn't noticed Roy watching him. As Kristy's testimony reached its climax, Roy saw the pallor in Shaw's face darken, as shock turned to anger.

Now, he was looking at Roy with hatred in his eyes.

Moran stood at his table and studied his notepad for a few moments. Then looked up at the judge. "I pass the witness, Your Honor."

"Mr. Shaw? Any re-direct?"

Shaw's face was beet red. He stood up and replied, "Yes, Your Honor."

Roy knew that Shaw was treading in very dangerous territory. None of what Kristy had just testified to was in her witness statement. Anything that he asked her about it now went against the trial lawyer's adage, "Never ask a question you don't know the answer to."

It quickly became apparent what Shaw was after. He walked up to Kristy holding a document. He didn't even ask the judge for permission to approach.

"You signed an immunity agreement, correct?"

"Yes, I did."

He handed her a document. "Is this a copy of it?"

"Yes."

"And, in that agreement, you agreed that you would answer all questions pertaining to the investigation into Joe Harlan's murder, correct?"

"Objection, leading," Moran interrupted. Shaw turned and glared at him.

"Sustained," said the judge.

Shaw snatched the document back from Kristy, and scanned through it, furiously flipping pages until he found what he was looking for. He gave it back to her and asked, "Can you tell me what it says in Section 14(f) please?"

"'Witness agrees to answer truthfully and to the best of his knowledge…'" Kristy paused and looked at the judge. "The agreement says 'his', but I think it means 'her'—me, that is."

The judge nodded.

Kristy continued, "…'to the best of his knowledge all questions pertaining to the investigation into Joe Harlan's murder.'"

"Exactly!" Shaw almost shouted. "Yet, you did not, during the entire course of your interview, ever mention Bethany Rosen, did you?"

"No. I didn't."

"So, you would agree, wouldn't you, that you violated your agreement, didn't you?"

Riviera stood up in the gallery. "Objection, Your Honor. Leading and calls for a legal conclusion."

Shaw turned and shot dagger eyes at Riviera.

"Sustained," the judge said.

Shaw's head snapped back around at the judge. He was livid.

"During the break," he pointed at Kristy, "you spoke to Mr. Moran, the lawyer for the Defendant, didn't you?"

Kristy shook her head. "No." Then, as Shaw was about to ask another question, she added, "I have never spoken to Mr. Moran. Ever. Other than the questions he just asked me here in court."

Shaw stood there, shaking his head, looking at Kristy with disgust. "Nothing further!" he spat, and returned to his table.

Moran stood and said, "Just two questions, Your Honor."

The judge nodded.

"Ms. Wise, is it true that you never mentioned Bethany Rosen when Attorney Shaw questioned you about Joe Harlan Junior's murder?" Moran asked.

"Yes." Kristy nodded. "That's true."

"Why not?"

Kristy looked at Shaw and replied, "He never asked."

CHAPTER EIGHTY-ONE

"Call your next witness," the judge said to Shaw.

Shaw was looking in his trial notebook, pinching the bridge of his nose with one hand. He looked up, then stood and replied, "The State rests, Your Honor."

"Very well, Mr. Moran. Do you have any motions you'd like to make, or are you ready to present your case?"

Roy and Mark had discussed their next steps—and what to do once the State rested—earlier that morning. They had three choices. Put Roy on the stand to testify, go directly to closing arguments, or present and argue a motion to dismiss the charges against Roy, claiming that the State had utterly failed to prove its case. The motion was unlikely to be granted, but arguing the motion would eat up enough of what remained of the day and give them time to strategize that evening as to whether or not Roy should testify.

They opted for the third path.

"We'd like to move to dismiss the charges, Your Honor."

Judge Goodwin excused the jury while Moran and Shaw argued over whether the judge should throw the case out based on the lack of sufficient evidence to even allow the jury to decide the case. In the end, the judge denied Moran's motion, and, it being almost four p.m., recessed for the day, advising everyone to return bright and early at eight a.m. the next morning.

Roy and Moran met back at his office. They sat down to talk strategy in the main conference room.

"I think that went about as well as it could have, Mark. I don't want to gloat—not because I'm superstitious, just because anything could still happen—but did you see Shaw? He was beside himself. After all the bullshit and last minute sandbagging, that fucker deserves it."

Mark had removed his jacket and tie. He looked tired, but satisfied. "I've gotta say, Roy, I'm 50/50 right now on whether to put you on the stand. That said, I love that the jury is going to spend tonight thinking about Kristy Wise talking to dead people. That's pretty much the last thing they heard."

All trial lawyers understand the primacy/recency effect. The theory states that things observed at the beginning and end of a learning episode are retained better than things that come in the middle. This is why the state always has an advantage in a trial.

The state makes its opening statement first, and so it is the first to present to the jury a version of the facts. Thus, the state's version of the case has the benefit of primacy. But, the state can also have the last word in a trial, and therefore gets the benefit of recency. Although the state presents its closing argument first, the state is allowed to present a rebuttal closing after the defense. Thus, the state has the advantage of both primacy and recency in opening and closing.

But trial lawyers also know that every day of a trial is a learning episode. The first thing and last thing that jurors hear each day also stick in their memories.

Moran continued, "Right now, the jury has heard a lot of circumstantial evidence tying you to Harlan's murder. And then they have the testimony of a young woman that ties it all together. But, that young woman may be mentally disturbed and isn't sure whether or not she heard the whole thing from your dead wife. That's not a bad place for us."

Roy leaned back in his chair, tilting his head back and looking up at the ceiling. He breathed in deeply, then exhaled blowing through his mouth. "We've gone over my testimony *ad nauseam*. I'm ready, if you think that's the right choice."

Moran nodded, his fingers steepled under his chin. "How about we sleep on it, and decide tomorrow morning, with fresh eyes?" Moran proposed.

Roy pointed at him and replied, "That... makes very good sense, Counselor."

The next morning, Roy arrived at Moran's office at seven a.m., just as he had every day of trial. Moran was in the same conference room Roy had left him in the prior evening. He looked rested and was in a fresh, dark navy blue suit with a pale blue shirt and a blue and grey striped tie. People tend to associate blue with reliability. Moran had also read somewhere that psychologists claimed that clothing that brought out your eye color—his were blue—engendered feelings of trust in those you interacted with.

Moran began, "The idea of putting you on the stand, it was mainly to contradict Kristy. To make her out to be a liar, or mistaken. The need for that was lessened by yesterday's testimony. But my fear is that, if you testify, we give Shaw a run at you. Your testimony could make things better for us or could make them worse. What do you think, Roy? I'm afraid I'm still at 50/50."

"Let's head down to the courthouse. I still haven't decided."

"When will you decide? Or, what..." Moran stopped mid-sentence. He understood what Roy was thinking. "You want to see the jury?"

Roy nodded. "Let's tell the judge we're ready to present our case. Tell her you're going to call me as a witness. Then let's watch the jury as they come in. They had all night to sleep on it—on everything, and especially what they heard from Kristy. When they walk back into the courtroom, I want to see how they look at me."

Moran nodded, sagely. He understood. It was risky, trying to read a jury. But in all his years of experience, he'd rarely seen a jury that was prepared to deliver a guilty verdict and could look the defendant in the eye.

CHAPTER EIGHTY-TWO

At eight o'clock sharp, the door to Judge Goodwin's chambers opened and she took the bench.

"All rise!" bellowed her bailiff.

"Good morning, everyone." The judge scanned the courtroom. "So, Mr. Moran. What have you got on tap for us today?"

"We'll only present one witness, Your Honor. That would be the Defendant, Mr. Roy Cruise."

"Very well. Sam," she called out to the bailiff. "Can you bring in the jurors?"

The bailiff disappeared for a few moments, then returned and bellowed again, "All rise!"

The jurors entered and made their way into the jury box and to their seats. Roy and Moran watched as they passed. Roy had his hands clasped behind his back, and counted on his fingers as he studied them.

"Please be seated," said the judge.

As Roy sat, he spotted Spencer Shaw looking at him. He looked better than he had the day before. And although his face was flat, Roy saw the glimmer of a smile in his eyes. Shaw was clearly looking forward to cross-examining him. Roy felt a surge of anger in his belly. He knew he could take that bastard on and win. There was no way Shaw could make him crack.

Fuck Shaw, he thought to himself. *This isn't about beating him. It's about the jury.*

Moran and Roy leaned in to one another.

"Well?" Moran asked.

"I counted seven that made eye contact with me. Two smiled, including the big guy."

Moran peeked over Roy's shoulder and saw that the jurors were eyeing them quizzically. Only one juror, the old Hispanic lady, seemed uninterested.

"I counted about the same." Moran sighed. "What's it going to be?"

"Mr. Moran, you may call your first witness," the judge said.

Roy looked up at the judge. Then over at the jury. Having heard the judge's words, the jurors all looked over at the defense table in anticipation of hearing from Moran.

Roy studied their faces. Nowhere on the jury did he see animosity. No accusatory glares. They seemed to float between friendly and indifferent—the looks they were giving him were, in his opinion, about the same as they'd been on the day they had walked in for jury selection, before having heard anything about him. They did not look like twelve people who thought he was guilty.

Roy whispered to Moran, "Fuck it. Don't put me on. Let's close."

"Are you sure?" Moran asked. "This is life or death."

Roy put a hand on Mark's arm and nodded. "It's up to you now. You've gotta bring 'em home."

"No pressure, right? Thanks for that, man." Moran stood. "Your Honor. The defense rests. We are ready for closing arguments."

Judge Goodwin raised an eyebrow and pursed her lips. "Very well."

When Moran said "rests," Roy snuck a quick glance at Shaw.

The man's face fell.

CHAPTER EIGHTY-THREE

"Mr. Shaw, the floor is yours," the judge said, flipping to a clean page in her legal pad.

Shaw stood. He was wearing a dark blue suit, white shirt, and blue and red striped tie.

"I would like to reserve time for a rebuttal closing, Your Honor."

"So noted, Counselor."

Shaw seemed deflated. Somehow smaller. As he began to speak, his voice seemed weak. His hands trembled slightly at first. But, as he gained momentum, he became more confident.

"Ladies and gentlemen, thank you for your time and patience. The State does not bring murder charges lightly. And this case is no exception. Let us consider first what is undisputed.

"Joe Harlan Junior was lured to Miami, Florida on the pretense of meeting with Roy Cruise. Joe disappeared on May 2nd, 2019 in Miami. He has not been seen since. About a week later, his penis was found nailed to his father's door. And here," he held up the Ziploc bag containing the fish knife, "we have a knife. It was found in the Defendant's house. In the Defendant's safe. It has Joe's blood on it. And it has the Defendant's wife's fingerprints on it... in Joe's blood."

Shaw walked slowly to the jury box. He stood for a moment, holding the Ziploc bag, then carefully placed it on the railing in front of the jurors.

"The question you must decide is, did the Defendant and his wife kill Joe?"

Shaw ran through all of the strange coincidences the

police had discovered: the text to David Kim, the "Cruise Captain" contact, the fact that while Roy was supposedly in Bimini the day Joe disappeared, he was conveniently ill and not seen there by anyone.

"You have heard from Kristy Wise. She has told you how it happened. She has told you what Susie, the Defendant's wife, confessed to her. And the reason why—the motive—the tit for tat." Shaw looked at Roy, then pointed at him. "They killed Joe. The Defendant and his wife killed Joe in cold blood."

To Roy, it seemed that Shaw's closing was completely ignoring Kristy's revelation about Bethany from the day before. But he knew Shaw had to deal with it somehow. Then it came.

Shaw slowly walked toward the jury as he asked, "Has Kristy been through a lot? Yes. Did she swear to tell the truth? Yes. But, consider this: Does she have any reason to want to hurt the Defendant?

"She actually killed to save his life. His life and his wife's. She told you how Susie and Deb were friends from childhood." Shaw reached into his suit jacket pocket and removed the photo of Deb and Susie at camp. "When Susie's daughter died, Deb murdered the boy who killed her. And, in exchange, the Defendant and his wife killed Joe. It's that simple.

"Sure. The defense is going to try to throw up smoke and mirrors to try to confuse things. Don't let them.

"Just because there is no body does not mean that there is no crime. That would reward clever murderers, wouldn't it?

"When I look," Shaw turned briefly toward Roy and pointed at him, "at Roy Cruise, I see a brilliant man." The jury followed his gaze. "A rich man. A successful man. But, I also see a man who lost his daughter and wanted revenge. A man who was willing to kill, and was almost smart enough to get away with it.

"Almost.

"Don't let him. Don't let him make fools of us all."

Shaw walked back to his table and sat down.

CHAPTER EIGHTY-FOUR

Moran didn't miss a beat. He stood and walked into the center of the courtroom, putting the judge to his left, the gallery to his right, and the jury five feet in front of him.

"Ladies and gentlemen. Thank you, for taking the time to serve on this jury. It is a noble and sacred task. A man's life, Roy Cruise's life, hangs in the balance.

"And in a moment, you will decide Roy's fate based on one specific question—did the State prove its case beyond a reasonable doubt?

"To answer that question, you must consider this. Can you imagine... another version of events, based on the evidence you have heard, that does not involve Roy killing Joe Harlan Junior?

"Let's try on a few.

"First, has the State proven that Joe Harlan Junior is actually dead? Is it possible that Joe Harlan Junior is alive? There is evidence that his penis was separated from his body. But is it possible that he was castrated, but survived? His own father came here and told you how Joe wanted to leave home and get away from Austin. He sat right there," Moran pointed at the witness stand, "and stated that *it is possible* that Joe is alive. The State has provided *no proof* that he is dead. No body. It *is* possible that Joe Harlan Junior is not dead. *That* is reasonable doubt.

"What if Joe is dead?" Moran pointed open-handed at Shaw. "Let's give the State the benefit of the doubt for a second, even though they haven't proven it. Could someone other than Roy Cruise have killed Joe? Remember, Roy *left the country* on April 28th and returned on May 5th. Joe disappeared in Miami on

May 2nd. Roy wasn't even in the United States when Joe was last seen alive. Could someone else be responsible for Joe's disappearance? Absolutely. *That* is reasonable doubt.

"Now, we do have the issue of the bloody knife, with Susie Font's fingerprints on it. But, only her prints are on it. Not Roy's. Roy's prints were not on the knife. They weren't even on the *inside of the box that contained* the knife! Could Susie Font have killed Joe? On her own? Or with someone else's help? Without involving Roy? Of course, that's possible. *That* is reasonable doubt.

"*The only evidence* that Roy had anything at all to do with Joe Harlan Junior came from Kristy Wise. *The only evidence.*

"Is it possible, ladies and gentlemen, that Kristy Wise invented the whole story? Could this well-meaning but psychologically unstable young woman have been bullied by the State into saying things that aren't true? Remember, in exchange for her testimony, she cannot be charged with a murder she confessed to you that she committed. Could that have influenced what she said here in court? I think that's possible. *That* is reasonable doubt.

"I'm not saying that Kristy is lying to hurt Roy. She may not even know she's lying. Consider this... *strange coincidence*. What did Kristy claim happened to Joe Harlan Junior? She claims that Joe was drugged and then attacked sexually. Isn't it strange, an odd coincidence, that what she claims happened to Joe Harlan Junior is exactly the same thing that happened to her? She was also drugged and attacked sexually. Is that *just* a coincidence? Or is *that* reasonable doubt?

"But, there's still more. Ladies and gentlemen. Will you be able to sleep at night if you convict Roy of murder based on Kristy Wise's testimony? She claims that she came to Roy's house, dressed as a Mario Brother and carrying a concealed handgun..." As Moran spoke, his voice rose in volume. And she claims she jumped over Roy's fence, entered his house without permission, and shot and killed Ronald Clayton. That alone is enough to make any reasonable person question her sanity.

"But then, on top of that, Kristy admitted to you that it's

possible Susie Font was already dead when she confessed to her that they killed Joe Harlan Junior!"

Moran paused, letting the words sink in.

"The State wants you to accept Kristy's version of what Roy did, based on a confession Kristy received from beyond the grave. She testified that her dead friend Bethany helped her investigate her mother's death... *long... after...* Bethany herself was dead. Kristy believes she talks to the dead, and that they 'tell her things.' Can we really send Roy to the electric chair based on her testimony?" Moran shook his head. "No. We can't do that. *That* is reasonable doubt.

"Roy Cruise sits before you, a man whose wife has been taken from him by violence. Whose baby daughter, Joan, is in neonatal intensive care. All he wants is to get back to her—to raise his baby girl. Instead, he has been forced by the State to sit here and face these terrible allegations—including the disgusting allegation—" Moran glared at Shaw, "that he killed his wife. Roy had to make the choice—a horrible choice, an impossible choice—between saving his wife, who was in critical condition, teetering between life and death, or their healthy baby girl.

Moran shook his head, and it appeared that he wiped away a tear. He slowly approached the jury box, and asked in almost a whisper, "What has the State proven? What can we truly say beyond a reasonable doubt?"

Then, in a normal speaking voice, he said, "The State has only proven two things." He held up his index finger. "First, we *can* say that Susie, the Defendant's wife, probably cut Joe Harlan Junior with a knife. His blood and her prints are on the knife. And," Moran said as he added another finger, "second, we *can* say that she hid that knife in a lockbox—her lockbox—a lockbox to which Roy did not have access.

"That is all that the State has proven beyond a reasonable doubt.

"Based on the evidence that the State has presented, you cannot convict Roy Cruise of murder."

CHAPTER EIGHTY-FIVE

Shaw stood slowly. He took his time. He knew that what he had to say would be the last thing the jury would hear—what they would take back with them into the jury room when he was done. He wanted to make it count and to be sure that it stood out in their memories. He needed drama.

He walked over to the jury box and stood before them, looking slowly from one juror to the next until he had made eye contact with each juror individually. Then, he began to speak.

"I'm not surprised by what Mr. Moran wants you to believe. He's not a bad guy. He's doing his job. The job he gets paid to do. Trying to keep his client out of jail. We can't hold that against him.

"But, this is not a complicated case. Not at all. Part of what makes it a simple case for a jury is that the murderer did such a good job.

"In many ways, Roy Cruise committed the perfect murder. Joe's body was probably dumped in the ocean, never to be found. Deb Wise—the person who asked Cruise and his wife to kill Joe—is dead, shot by an," he made bunny ears with his fingers, "'unknown gunman' when Cruise just happened to be in town. Her husband, Tom Wise, well—he's dead too. So, there are no witnesses available to testify on that end.

"Cruise's own wife, Susie, the woman who wielded the knife, well... she confessed everything to Kristy Wise. You heard that testimony. We could have called her as a witness, so you could hear everything she told Kristy straight from the horse's mouth. But... well... she's dead, too. She's dead... based on the Defendant's own instructions under a Living Will."

Shaw turned halfway from the jury to look at Roy.

"Roy Cruise." He shook his head and scoffed. "He's a very clever man. A very smart man. He's amassed a fortune. An amazing house. Two boats. Tremendous wealth.

"He's committed the perfect crime. And all the witnesses, 'coincidentally'," he made bunny ears again, "are dead."

"All except one. Kristy Wise. She told you what Roy's accomplice—his own wife—confessed to her. And you saw with your own eyes the kind of person Kristy is. You heard her testimony. Did she seem crazy? Did she seem irrational? Not at all.

"But, then..." Shaw moved his hands, imitating a magician, "Cruise worked his magic once again. The judge had us take a break—a recess—so Kristy could talk with her lawyer. Kristy went out into that hall," Shaw pointed at the courtroom doors, "and someone else came back from that break. A new witness. A new Kristy. Someone who—"

Moran jumped up, "Objection, Your Honor! I don't like objecting during closing, but Mr. Shaw is implying that—"

"I know exactly what Mr. Shaw is implying, and—" the judge turned to Shaw, "you are on very thin ice, sir. Extremely thin." She glared at him. Shaw said nothing, but his face was flushed deep red and his hands appeared to visibly tremble.

Judge Goodwin continued, "Ladies and gentlemen, I feel that an instruction is in order, as Mr. Shaw may have unintentionally implied something he knows not to be true. I say *unintentionally* to give him the benefit of the doubt and avoid holding him in contempt of court." Judge Goodwin nodded at her bailiff, and he came forward from the back of the courtroom and stepped through the swinging door from the gallery to stand just behind the lawyers' tables.

The judge continued, "Every witness in court has the constitutional right to be represented by counsel. And every citizen in our country has the right under the Fifth Amendment against self-incrimination. When Ms. Wise raised the issue, when she said that she 'took the Fifth,' the Court was bound by the law to allow her to consult with her attorney. And Mr. Shaw understands this perfectly—don't you, sir?"

Shaw stared at the judge for a moment, then replied, "Yes, Your Honor."

"And Mr. Shaw is not implying that allowing Kristy Wise to consult with her attorney was in any way inappropriate, are you?"

Shaw shook his head. "No, Your Honor. I was not."

"Very well. Mr. Moran, I trust that my explanation resolves your objection?"

"It does, Your Honor," Moran replied.

"You may continue, Mr. Shaw."

Shaw nodded. He breathed in deeply, then resumed, "The judge is right. Kristy was absolutely entitled to talk to her lawyer. And if I implied otherwise, I didn't mean to. But, here's the thing... when Kristy Wise first took the witness stand, she told you exactly what she told me. The truth.

"And then, after being out in that hall for ten minutes, *ten minutes*," he emphasized, "she came back in here like Bruce Willis in *The Sixth Sense*—talking to dead people."

Shaw paused, looked at Roy, then pointed at him and turned to the jury. "Think about it. *Every witness* to this man's crimes is dead. Deb Wise. Tom Wise. Even his wife, Susie Font. Every witness, except one. And he even managed to get to her *during this very trial.*

"He's looking at all of us... right now... all of you, like we're fools. Idiots. And he thinks he's going to get away with murder.

"Don't let that happen."

Shaw stood in front of the jury until he had looked each of them in the eye again, then he simply said, "Thank you." And he walked back to the prosecution's table and sat down.

It was nine in the morning, and the trial was done.

For the next forty minutes, the judge read the jury the charge and instructed them on how their deliberations should proceed. Then, she sent them out to deliberate. Roy and the lawyers hung around the courtroom, waiting. At eleven-thirty, the judge ordered lunch for the jury. At four p.m., the jury sent out a note asking if they could call it a day and resume the following morning at eight.

None of the attorneys objected.

CHAPTER EIGHTY-SIX

Roy visited me at home again the evening after the jury began deliberating. We sat out on the terrace, on my small sofa facing the water. He updated me—on what had happened at trial, and what he hoped the jury would focus on. On what he was thinking, about himself, about his future.

"I have to confess, after all of this—after hearing the State make its case—when it comes down to it, I think Shaw's right. I'm a murderer. I'm talking about on the inside. I mean, I know that *technically* I am. I've done the physical act. I have killed. But, what I'm trying to say is that... what I've discovered is that I'm good at it. I'm okay with it. It's who I am."

"Roy," I said, shaking my head, "killing is a choice. No one is a 'murderer' any more than a person is a thief or a rapist. We choose our actions. But one act doesn't define who we are."

"Maybe not *one act*. But what are we really, if not the sum total of our past, right? And, obviously, there are some acts that count more than others... I mean, none of us is defined by brushing our teeth or buying groceries."

I laughed. He smiled, then turned serious again.

"But," he continued, "I think there are certain things we do that can stake a claim on our souls." He paused, organizing his thoughts. "When you cross certain lines, when you break fundamental rules that have been drilled into you all your life—rules that define civilization—I think that can change you. Why do you think some soldiers have a hard time adjusting to civilian life after they've been in battle?

"I don't know, Catherine. Maybe some people can cross

over the line and then come back, but... Look, when this all started, I had no interest—absolutely none—in taking another life. I didn't think myself worthy to serve as judge, jury, and executioner. Susie pushed me—" he paused, swallowing hard, shaking his head. "It doesn't matter how I got there... the point is, I can't just passively accept what life throws at me anymore. The 'system' is a joke. Our 'leaders' are a joke. Sure, the rules work sometimes. But if they don't work for me, when I need them to, why can't I change them? Or ignore them? Why shouldn't I?"

"Roy," I chimed in, "all that you're saying is that we live in an imperfect world. That's no revelation. But jumping from... dissatisfaction with the human condition, to defining yourself as... what... a killer by nature? That's a huge leap."

Roy shook his head, "You're not understanding me, Catherine." He took a swallow of scotch, then continued, "You know the fable about the scorpion and the frog?"

I shrugged. I recalled the title, but not the details. "The Brothers Grimm?" I asked.

He shook his head. "Aesop." He turned toward me and told the very brief story.

"A scorpion asks a frog to carry him across a river on its back. The frog says, 'No, you'll kill me.' But the scorpion promises not to kill the frog, saying, 'Why would I do that? If I sting you, you'll sink and die, but so will I.' The frog is convinced by this logic and lets the scorpion climb up on its back. Halfway across the river, the scorpion stings the frog. 'Why?!' screams the frog, 'I'm dying, but so are you!' And the scorpion, sinking into the water, replies, 'I'm a scorpion. It's what I do.'"

He looked at me, waiting for a reply.

"What?" I asked. "You think you're the scorpion?"

Roy nodded. "I apparently have a talent for it. It's what I do."

"But, Roy," I replied, "that's a choice. You can—"

"That's precisely the point!" he exclaimed.

I smiled at him sadly, shaking my head.

"Look, Catherine. The scorpion and the frog make a deal—

that deal represents rules, the law. 'I will carry you. You won't bite me.' But, those rules require the scorpion to alter its natural behavior and let the frog live. Breaking the law means that the scorpion dies. But halfway across the river, the scorpion strikes anyway. Why?"

He looked at me, waiting for a reply.

"Why, Roy?"

"Because despite its deal with the frog, despite the law, the scorpion refuses to deny its nature—to give up its identity—simply to delay the inevitable. The scorpion knows it can't escape death. But it can *choose how it lives* until that moment comes, even if how it lives brings death to it sooner."

After a very long silence, I said, "Roy, you're going through so much right now. Too much. Let's try to pump the brakes here for a bit. Not make any rash choices... or judgments, okay?"

He smiled. "That's good therapeutic advice."

Though all my training ran counter to Roy's argument, there was a certain logic to what he was saying. I had crossed lines in my own way, with Getz. And I'd felt empowered by it. Yet, I felt that the path Roy was describing led to self-destruction. Susie had set him on that path. He'd given in to it, and now he seemed committed to it. But I knew that he still had a chance at salvation—a twenty-six-week-old premature baby, and me, if he would only let me in.

CHAPTER EIGHTY-SEVEN

The jury returned the next morning at eight a.m. and resumed their deliberations.

Eddie had decided to take advantage of the time and make a visit. He'd driven to Liz Bareto's house. He was familiar with the neighborhood. The Italian Village of Coral Gables. Eddie preferred the Chinese Village. The Chinese houses there were just so out of place that they made him laugh. They looked like eight miniature *P.F. Chang's* with colorful tile roofs in the middle of an otherwise normal neighborhood.

He'd been sitting for over an hour in his car, just down the street from Liz's house, waiting. He'd wanted to catch her at home, to talk. When he'd arrived at eight-thirty, her driveway was empty. So, he'd sat, waiting patiently.

About fifteen minutes earlier, she'd pulled up in her small white Audi sedan. She'd unloaded five bags of groceries—three trips in and out of the house. After she'd closed the door, he exited his vehicle and approached.

When she opened the front door, Eddie's world fell in a little bit more. He had never seen Liz look so haggard. She was pale, and appeared to have lost weight.

"Hello, Eddie," she said, then walked away from the open door into the house as she added, "Come in."

Eddie followed her into the kitchen. He'd never been in her home before. Liz busied herself unpacking groceries—quite a lot of fruit and greens, Eddie noticed. She went on as though he wasn't here, so finally he spoke.

"You look like hell."

"I've been sick," she said. "Ask my doctor." She placed citrus fruits in a large bowl on a breakfast table—oranges first, then lemons and limes. Apples went in another smaller bowl on the little island. Organic Fuji, according to the bag.

"How long?"

"In and out of it for a few weeks now. It's been miserable." Liz opened the refrigerator and began stacking small yogurt containers on a shelf.

"So, you came down with it... what, before Susie Font was shot?"

Liz didn't miss a beat, and placed the last two yogurts in the fridge as she said, "Around then. It's probably why I seemed so out of it the last couple of times we spoke. Dr. Melvin Martinez. Google him. Call him and confirm if you like."

Eddie nodded. "So, you've been home, in bed?"

"Yep. Today's my first day out in a while. You can see the amount of groceries I bought." Liz gestured. Then she pointed, "The receipt's right there next to you, on the counter."

Eddie glanced at the receipt. Then he eyed the eight bottles of pinot noir that sat on the kitchen island.

"Any visitors?" he asked while Liz folded up the empty bags.

"Nope. No alibis, Eddie. Just me, all by my lonesome." Liz studied Eddie as she continued organizing, then finally asked, "So, what brings you by my house this morning? You're more than welcome, but I'm still not quite at a hundred percent. I was going to go back to bed."

"Sure, Liz. I don't... you go ahead and get your rest. I... uh... I can call you some other time."

"Thank you, Eddie. I'll walk you out."

Eddie reached the front door and opened it. As he stepped out onto the porch, Liz said, "And in case you're wondering, I don't own a gun. Not anymore. I sold it at a gun show a while back."

Eddie suddenly felt lightheaded. He turned to face her.

"I don't remember the name... of the man that bought it." She scrunched her nose. "He paid me in cash. Very average-looking fellow. Dark hair. Dark eyes. Just... dark. I don't think I'd even know him if I saw him again. Couldn't pull him out of a line-up," she chuckled. "I don't think I kept the ticket stub. From the gun show. Early January, I think it was. Well before Susie Font was shot. I was there about two hours." She sighed. "I'm just not the type, Eddie. Guns and me, I don't think that was ever meant to be, you know?"

Eddie nodded slowly. He was standing just outside the door. "You haven't asked. About the trial, Liz. About Cruise."

She smiled sadly at him, and then she shrugged. "Everyone gets what they deserve eventually, Eddie. If the system doesn't get them... karma will. One way or another."

CHAPTER EIGHTY-EIGHT

At three p.m., the jury sent out a note. The bailiff delivered it to Judge Goodwin in her chambers. She came into the courtroom. She wasn't wearing her robes, but was dressed in a navy blue skirt with a white blouse. She carried the note in her left hand.

"Gentlemen," she said.

Moran, Roy, and Shaw all stood. Eddie was in the back of the courtroom speaking with the clerk, and came forward as well.

"It appears we've got a verdict. It's unanimous. The jury asked for a ten-minute break before coming in, so we'll be," she looked at her wristwatch, "bringing them back in at three-fifteen."

She did an about-face and returned to her chambers.

Shaw grabbed his mobile phone and headed out into the hallway. Eddie followed.

Moran and Roy huddled close to the defense table.

"Five hours yesterday. Seven hours today." Moran shrugged. "Twelve hours deliberating... could mean anything. The fact that they didn't send out any questions to the judge tells me that they've been fighting to get to a unanimous verdict."

"Eye contact will tell the story," Roy replied. "We'll see soon enough."

Moran nodded, then said, "I'm gonna go take a leak."

Moran walked down the hall and into the men's room. Shaw was washing his hands at the sink. Moran paused for a second, then went ahead and crossed behind him to the urinals.

"Tough case," Shaw said as he looked in the mirror, straightening his tie. "Nice job on that Bethany Rosen bullshit. I *did not* see that coming."

Moran nodded. "Funny thing is, if we hadn't gotten Kristy's interview at the last minute, I'd probably have insisted on taking her deposition. Then we both would have found out about it at the same time."

Shaw shrugged. "You know, even if he's acquitted, this isn't over. I can still charge him with Clayton's death. As an accessory. For dumping the body. Obstruction of justice, probably."

"And?"

Shaw stepped away from the sink, drying his hand with a paper towel. He looked at Moran, and said, "And all those charges could go away if he pleads guilty. Manslaughter."

Moran looked over at the prosecutor. "Spencer, you were so fucking sure of yourself that you only charged him with murder one. You didn't even give the jury that option."

"Yeah, well, it's on the table. Before the verdict comes in, of course."

"You a betting man?" Moran asked as he walked over to the sink next to Shaw to wash his hands.

Shaw laughed. "I'm a trial lawyer. What do you think?"

"Yeah—only bet on sure things, right?"

"Exactly," Shaw replied.

"Okay, well I'll make you a bet," said Moran. "I'll bet you a dollar."

"Go on."

"I'll bet you a dollar that I tell Roy what you just offered, and his reply is 'Go fuck yourself.'"

"Fuck you, Moran," Shaw said, and left the bathroom.

Shaw was in his place back in the courtroom when Moran returned from the men's room. Roy was seated at the defense table. Shaw watched as Moran sat down next to Roy and pointed at Shaw, then leaned in and spoke to him. They went back and forth for a few moments. Shaw watched closely. He saw Moran hesitate, then ask Roy a question.

Shaw read Moran's lips, *Are you sure?*

Roy nodded, and sat back and closed his eyes. He didn't look toward the prosecutor.

Moran wrote on his legal pad, then tore out the sheet of paper, folded it up, and passed it over to Shaw.

Shaw smiled smugly as he accepted it, then opened it.

On it were scrawled five words.

You owe me a dollar.

"All rise!" bellowed the bailiff, then he opened the door to the jury room. One by one, the jurors entered the courtroom. They seemed to be in a relatively good mood as they walked to their seats.

Roy was on edge. His neck and shoulders were tense. He felt lightheaded, and discretely put his thighs against the edge of the defense table, leaning against it for support. He watched them as they came in. One by one. Jumping from one face to the next. It seemed to take an eternity.

"Be seated," the bailiff intoned.

"Ladies and gentlemen of the jury," Judge Goodwin began, "have you reached a verdict?"

A tall man stood up and replied, "We have, Judge."

"Is it unanimous?"

"Yes, ma'am."

The bailiff walked over and took the charge from the foreman, then handed it up to the judge. Judge Goodwin spent a few moments reading over the charge to make sure everything was in order.

Then she handed it back to the bailiff, who returned it to the jury foreman.

"Will the Defendant please rise?" the Judge ordered.

Roy stood, Moran with him.

"Mr. Foreman, will you please read the verdict?"

The man began reading. In the end, all Roy remembered was hearing the words "not guilty" twice. Shaw asked that the judge poll the jurors, to ensure that the verdict was unanimous.

It was.

CHAPTER EIGHTY-NINE

By the time Roy and Mark got back to Moran's office that Friday afternoon, Mark's paralegal Jackie had opened several bottles of champagne. The staff were partaking from crystal flutes that Mark kept in the office for "verdict days." Jackie had also ordered in some light snacks.

When Roy and Mark walked through the office doors, applause and cheers erupted. There were handshakes and pats on the back all around. Though, Roy noticed that while the staff was very enthused—ebullient, even—in congratulating their boss, the congratulations he received were slightly more restrained.

He suspected that everyone in the room had read Kristy's interview transcript, and they'd all formed their own opinions about his guilt or innocence.

After the initial excitement died down, and Roy had stayed long enough to give Moran his due, he discreetly pulled him aside, telling him that he needed to go. "I want to get to the hospital and check on Joan, but thanks, again."

Moran patted Roy on the back and replied, "Come on, bud. I'll walk you out."

Mark set his champagne glass on the reception counter and walked with Roy out into the elevator lobby, which was empty but for the two of them.

"Crazy case, huh? I'm guessing not all of your trials are so dramatic?" Roy asked as he pushed the button to summon the lift.

Mark shrugged. "Each has its little moments. But, yeah, this one definitely a bit more so."

Roy smiled, then squinting his eyes, nodded back toward the office. "I'm glad they weren't on the jury. It sure felt like they think I'm guilty."

Mark raised his eyebrows, then said, "If they were a jury... well, reasonable doubt is one thing. What people think may have really happened is a whole other story. You probably ought to prepare for more of that as you get out and about again. Just the *possibility* that you might have killed Harlan will probably be enough to scare a lot of folks."

Roy nodded, then asked, "Are you one of those people? You saw all the evidence. What do you think?"

Moran chuckled. "That doesn't really matter."

"Do I scare you now? Indulge me," Roy said as the elevator pinged and the doors parted. It was empty. He stepped toward it and put a hand out, holding the doors open.

"Well," said Moran, "you know I've got a daughter. If anyone touched even a hair on her head... I wouldn't hesitate to rain a storm of pain down on them. And, from everything I read about this Harlan guy—and I read it *all*," he half-laughed, "I don't feel any pity for him. So... I get it."

Roy nodded. "We're good then?"

"Yeah," Moran replied, "We're good. But, the whole dick on the door thing," he added, shaking his head, "I'd have skipped that part. Way too risky."

Roy stepped into the elevator and pushed the G button. Before the doors closed, he pointed at Moran with his right hand, forming a gun with his index finger and thumb, and as he lowered his thumb, said, "Great minds think alike."

* * *

Roy pulled a chair up next to the incubator in the NICU. The baby was still so tiny. He was amazed by her. An itty bitty little person. She had just the thinnest of peach fuzz for hair. Her tiny lips were rosy and full. When she opened her eyes, they were the cobalt blue of a newborn—and alert, quick, inquisitive. Her tiny little fingers and toes—all twenty of them, he'd counted—had adorable little fingernails. She was innocent, and beautiful, and perfect.

"Hello, Joanie. How are you doing, teeny-tiny?"

The baby turned her head towards his voice. He was sure she recognized her daddy. How he longed to hold her. But she was still in an incubator to help with warmth and breathing. So, he settled for the next best thing. He had thoroughly washed and sanitized his hands. He'd brought her a gift, a tiny pink beanie that had the word "Miracle" embroidered on it. But first, he needed to touch her.

"Daddy's going to say hello, teeny."

Carefully, he reached inside. Her skin was delicate and pink. She was not yet plump, and still had a little plastic clamp attached to her umbilical cord. Ever so gently, he placed his left palm against the baby's head. The hair on Roy's arms stood on end as she snuggled up into his hand, seeking his warmth and love. Then, with his right hand, he extended his pinkie finger and gently teased Joanie's hand.

"Daddy loves you, teeny," he said in a low, calm voice.

After several attempts, she did it. Her tiny little hand gripped his pinkie! Tears rolled down his cheeks. Her little hand barely spanned the width of the first knuckle of his little finger.

"Daddy loves you—" Roy's voice cracked, "...so much."

Joanie squirmed against his hand, her eyes searching for his face. She paused, then seemed to look right at him. Her tiny nostrils flared slightly, and then her little mouth opened and she yawned an adorable toothless yawn that ended with a cute baby cough.

Only a few hours earlier, Roy had been waiting to hear from a jury that could have turned his and her life upside down. Things had worked out for them, but they wouldn't always. More so than when Camilla was born, Roy felt prepared for fatherhood.

The world was a nasty place. A dangerous place. Just look at how baby Joanie's life had begun. She had come into the world at the expense of her own mother's life. But, Roy would always be there for her. He would protect her. He would make sure that she wanted for nothing. And he would teach her the most valuable lesson he could impart—how to protect herself.

CHAPTER NINETY

Sunday morning, I woke late, around ten-thirty. There are certain magical mornings in Florida, when the sun radiates an incandescent yellow-orange light that illuminates the world like a movie set. When the sky is a cloudless cerulean blue and the wind is absent. Everything is still. Perfect. Beautiful.

As my first cup of coffee brewed, I looked out the window at my beautiful world. I was standing in the kitchen in my PJs and a robe. I hugged myself, trying to calm the angst in my belly. I had not slept well, again.

After the verdict Friday afternoon, Roy called me—to tell me what had happened, and what came next.

I have to admit, my feelings for Roy had been developing for some time. But, it was too impossible—he was married; he was a murderer; he was my patient; he was probably going to jail for a very long time. I realize now that I'd allowed myself to indulge the fantasy precisely because it seemed so improbable. A classic case of outlier complacency—the odds of anything happening between the two of us were so remote that it was safe to let myself pretend that it could.

But, after Susie's tragic death, the impossibility of it all changed. For the first time, my fantasy had hope of becoming reality.

You see, I had already reconciled myself to the fact that Roy was a murderer—that he had killed Harlan. Hell, I'd asked him to kill Getz. The fact that he was a killer wasn't an issue.

The fact that he was my patient... well, that wasn't a big deal, really. It wouldn't be the first time that a therapist and patient fell in love.

When he asked me to care for the baby, assuming a guilty

verdict, I knew that I had connected with him on more than just a physician-patient level. And when I realized how alone he was in the world, I was certain that Roy needed me. The real me. Not C.J. Martin, Ph.D., the therapist, but Catherine Jane Martin, the woman.

I took my coffee, went back out to the terrace, and plopped down on the little sofa where Roy had sat next to me just a few nights ago. The more I thought it through, the more I knew that it was real.

He had come to *me*. He had asked *me* to care for his child.

And who better to help him rebuild? To help him heal? Who knew him better than I did?

We just needed time.

He needed a period of adjustment. He'd lost Susie. Suddenly and tragically. Then, without sufficient opportunity to grieve, his life and liberty had been put on trial. He'd had to repress all those feelings about Susie in order to defend himself. But, if we could put all that behind us, we could begin to pick up the pieces.

The jury's verdict was the final piece of the puzzle. The final obstacle we'd overcome. Roy was free. With that, we could begin a new life.

I knew I could give Roy what he needed. Help him through his periodic bouts of the blues. I knew that I could be the third leg of the stool that made a family.

Me, Roy, and Joan.

As the sun peeked over the houses across the canal, its balmy rays lit up the terrace around me and filled me with warmth and hope. And, as if the universe were listening, at that very moment, my mobile phone rang. I looked down at the screen and my heart leapt. It was Roy calling. The man I loved was calling me.

"Hello, Roy."

"Hi, Catherine. How are you?"

The hair on the back of my neck stood on end. My mouth became dry. "My God. You sound terrible. Is everything alright?"

"Actually, it's not. I've been up all night. At the hospital. It's Joanie. The doctors say pneumonia." His voice trembled as he said the word, and my stomach clenched for him. But the healer in me kicked in immediately. This was the perfect place to start. He needed me. Even more now. Right now. And I would be there for him.

"Don't worry, Roy. It's very manageable these days. Especially in the NICU. The good thing is that she's in great hands. Don't stress about it. Would you like for me to come down there? Keep you company?"

"I... it's not me. Not stress, Catherine." There was a long pause, and then he stammered, "I... she didn't make it, Catherine. Joanie's gone."

CHAPTER NINETY-ONE

From looking at the call log on my phone, after talking to Roy, I'd apparently sat out on my terrace for almost an hour before I began to function normally again. I don't recall clearly what we said after Roy told me about Joan's death. I think that I insisted on going to the hospital or meeting him at his house. I don't remember which. I think he said that he needed some time alone. To process. I remember thinking that I was doing the right thing, giving him space.

Once I got myself together, at around noon, I tried calling him back. After several calls and text messages went unanswered, I got dressed and drove to his house. There was no answer at the door. I peeked in the garage window and saw that his car was gone. So, I waited.

At about one o'clock, it occurred to me to call the hospital. I got through to the duty nurse, then eventually to the department head. I knew people at that hospital. Roy wasn't there. I camped out on Roy's front porch, waiting.

After about an hour, it occurred to me to drive by Roy's office. I checked in with the security desk. The guard told me that Mr. Cruise had not been to the office in over a week. I convinced him to show me the log-in sheet. Roy hadn't signed in that morning, but David Kim had, and it appeared that he was still there. I called the main office number several times, choosing different options on the automated system until I finally got through to him. He came down and met me in the lobby.

"I spoke with Roy a few hours ago," David said. "He's really fucked up." He looked concerned. "We talked before... during the trial... about me stepping in to run the business if things went tits up." He paused, then apologized, "I mean, you know, if he was found guilty. After the verdict, I thought we were good. But he called this morning and told me about the baby, and then he said I should go ahead and assume I'd be in charge for the near term. So, I came in to get organized."

"What time was that?" I asked. "That you heard from him?"

David checked his phone, then held it out to show me. "Around eleven."

"And he didn't tell you where he was going? What he was doing?"

David shook his head. "Sorry."

David gave me his contact info and told me that, if there was anything he could do, to let him know.

I left and drove back to Roy's house. On the way there, I dug through my purse and found Mark Moran's card.

"Oh my God. That's horrible news... fuckin' guy can't catch a break." I could tell from his voice that I was the bearer of this bad news. Moran had not heard from Roy, but I asked anyway.

"But you haven't heard from him?"

"I haven't heard a peep from him since he left my office Friday."

"If you do, will you call me?"

"Of course."

When I got back to his house, I checked the garage again. No car. I sat down to wait on Roy's front porch. At five that afternoon, when Roy still hadn't come home, I called the police and had them track down Detective Eddie Garza. I explained who I was and why I was calling.

"That's terrible, Doc. When you see him, give him my condolences. Seriously. But there's really not much I can do."

"I'm worried, Detective, that with so much that's happened... I don't know what..." I paused.

"You think he's a danger to himself?" Eddie scoffed, though not in a mean-spirited way—almost with admiration. "I doubt that, Doc. That guy's been through hell. He's tough. He's a survivor."

I said nothing, and Garza ended our call saying, "If you haven't heard from him by this time tomorrow, call me back." To which I agreed.

As I sat, waiting, I racked my brain.

Where would I go if I were Roy Cruise?

Suddenly, I knew. I got in my car and drove, fast, heading for Pinetree Cemetery. I arrived just minutes before the gates closed for the evening and was able to persuade the guard at the gate to let me in. There were still several cars on the property, finishing up visits.

As I approached Susie's grave, I felt a smidgeon of satisfaction. I was right.

But I was late. There on the grave were a dozen fresh flowers. He'd clearly been there earlier. Very recently. He'd probably spent the day there. It made sense. He needed to grieve. He'd come to her to find solace. To grieve the loss of their child with her.

There was a part of me that didn't like it, that was almost jealous that he'd come to Susie instead of me. But, given the recency of Susie's death, the therapist in me knew that it made sense. How could he deal with the trauma of a second loss when he was still struggling to process the first?

I touched the roses. They were fresh and their petals were moist. They were beautiful.

I wished they were mine.

We'd probably just missed each other. I should have thought of this sooner. And, if I were Roy Cruise, from here... I would go home.

I got in my car and headed back to Roy's house. It was dark by the time I got there. Thankfully, the exterior lights were on. And several interior lights were on as well. I palpably felt my stress level drop. It's a beautiful house. Elegant, like him. I'd never seen it before by night. The warm light was welcoming. It was a good place to re-charge, to find peace. Despite its size and grandeur, it felt like a home.

I rang the doorbell.

No answer. I walked around to the side of the house.

Yet again, I peeked in the garage. His car was there. The Range Rover.

I walked around back to the terrace and looked in through the sliding glass doors and windows. The kitchen, the family room, the dining room... No one seemed to be home.

I sat down on the terrace at the breakfast table. I was exhausted. So much back and forth. I checked my phone. No messages. No missed calls.

I called Roy again. As the call rang, I sat back, rubbing my neck. Trying to get some of the tension out of it and my tight shoulders. And then, I noticed.

The boats.

Lady Suze was gone.

CHAPTER NINETY-TWO

Four days later, on Thursday afternoon, Eddie Garza left the office early and went home.

The period after a trial was always anticlimactic. After all the rush and tumble, transitioning back to the usual routine took a few days. He'd gone into work early that morning to attend a department-wide briefing on the coronavirus that was spreading across the country.

Just after lunch, he had received a call from Doctor Melvin Martinez. Liz *had* been sick. And it had gotten worse. It turned out that she had the bug. COVID-19. They'd put her on a ventilator, but she was too far gone by that point. She'd asked the doctor to call and let Eddie know, and to say, "Thank you." She'd died alone that morning in the same hospital that Liam had died in.

I dunno, Eddie thought. *Maybe she took some comfort in that?* He'd told the doctor the same thing.

Eddie had just seen Liz at her house the Friday before. Less than a week ago. It was hard for him to believe she was gone.

He was sitting at the small island in his kitchen. He'd poured himself a whiskey on the rocks. He was home alone. His wife and daughter wouldn't be back for a couple of hours.

Eddie raised his glass and, looking up into the distance, said aloud, "Here's to you, Liz Bareto. You were a real classy lady. And a fighter. A real fighter. Sorry things turned out the way they did. But, I guess you got the justice you wanted after all. See you on the other side." He took a sip of whiskey, then added under his breath, "Rest in peace, beautiful lady."

Since the verdict, Eddie had thought a lot about Susie's murder, and Liz, and what the hell he should do. Liz's death put an end to any worries he had that what he'd overshared with her might come back to haunt him.

Eddie sighed.

As part of his job as a homicide detective, he regularly saw people in extreme situations, pushed to do things that they would never consider on a normal day. He knew that to do the job well, you had to be able to see both sides of the coin. If you couldn't understand why someone would be willing to kill, what could push them to that extreme, then you'd never be any good at catching them.

Of course, the tricky part of the job was to lie down with all those dogs, but not get up with fleas. Eddie believed that, overall, he'd done pretty good at that.

Hey, no one's perfect, but all in all... I color inside the lines. No special favors... Never taken a bribe...

In his line of work, there were a lot of grey areas. It was a very good day when things were neat and clear-cut. But most days were not good days. So, it came down to having good judgment. Eddie had to make a lot of judgment calls. He felt he'd been right about Liz. If he hadn't more diligently pursued the leads he'd had about Liz, so what? She was gone now. It wouldn't have made any difference, really.

Eddie shrugged, staring at the whiskey glass in his hand. He took a swallow and then, putting the glass down, wiped the condensation from his hand onto his pants' leg.

In the end, Liz was right.

If the system doesn't get you, karma will.

He thought about Roy Cruise. Eddie was pretty sure that he'd killed Harlan Junior—and if not, he definitely knew about it when it went down. And for damned sure he dumped Ronald Clayton's body in the straits.

Yeah, Cruise got away with that—maybe more. But, the universe had rained a hailstorm of shit down on that guy. Whatever they'd all done—Roy, Susie, Deb Wise and her husband—did they really get away with it? Deb was dead. Tom was dead. Susie, dead. Their new baby, dead. And Cruise was left all alone, with no wife and two dead kids.

That is true and absolute misery.

As he sipped from his whiskey, Eddie looked down at the envelope he'd been using as a coaster. The ink where he'd scrawled the contact information for Cruise's therapist was bleeding from the moisture. He hadn't heard back from her, and had assumed that Roy had turned up.

Eddie took out his phone, and added her name and number to his contacts before the condensation from his whiskey glass obliterated the scrawl.

Just out of curiosity, Eddie opened a browser on his phone and searched for "therapist C.J. Martin Miami" and clicked on *Images* so that he could put a face to the name. The search results screen refreshed and displayed a number of images of Dr. Catherine Martin.

The first and most prominent was a typical professional headshot. She was an attractive woman. Probably mid-forties. Shoulder-length, jet black hair. Pale brown eyes. She looked like a therapist in the photo. She wore a black turtle neck, what Eddie liked to call "smart glasses," and had a reassuring look to her. Calm, cool, and collected.

Eddie was about to close the screen when he saw an older photo of the woman, of a younger Dr. Martin. He scrolled down and studied it. It looked to be a photo from a conference she had given, according to the caption. She looked content. Confident. No glasses. There was something about her face that seemed friendly and familiar. Intelligent eyes stared back at him.

Holy shit.

Eddie never forgot a face.

The woman he was looking at was the same woman he'd seen in a photo, standing with her husband—now ex-husband—and two kids, on the wall of Billy Applegate's apartment.

Eddie shook his head and chuckled.
Well, I'll be goddamned.
Mallorca...
Fucking Getz.

PART FIVE

Rebecca Forsyth
Turks and Caicos
2020

Rebecca Forsyth had a dry, cottony taste in her mouth. Her head ached. Her throat was parched. She was cold. She shivered as the wind blew over her wet body.

She was on a horse. Her hands were stiff from gripping the animal's mane. The musky smell of its damp coat was so strong that it almost gagged her. It was dark out. She was riding bareback, stretched across the horse's back, her arms and legs clinging to the animal as it loped down the beach, its hooves clopping mutedly.

The sand on Rebecca's face bothered her. It stung. In her eyes. Her nose. In her mouth, it was gritty and tasted of salt. She reached up to rub the sand out of her eyes, but a sharp pain startled her. She remembered, vaguely. Below her left arm. Her ribs. She'd been injured. The railing?

No matter how she moved, she felt the pain. Rebecca sighed. She felt tears welling in her eyes. Maybe they would help wash away the sand? She let them come.

As she cried, the sound of the tide rose and fell—like the slow, rhythmic breathing of the planet. At times, the clopping of the hooves seemed synchronized with it. She felt as though her body was aligning itself with the sounds, with the universe—everything was syncing up—her weeping, the waves, the planet breathing, the clopping of the hooves.

As Rebecca wept, she felt the tide rising all around her. The horse was no longer loping; it was swimming underwater. She was breathing underwater. It was amazing. She felt free, liberated, as she looked all around her.

Looking heavenward, her eyes traced dancing beams of sunlight up and away until they converged into a round disc of shimmering white firmament. As she gazed downward, the world fell away from her—the bright blue and the light fading... everything becoming darker, the further she looked. The only sound she could hear was the too-close, too-loud in-and-out of her own breathing, which she tried to control—relaxing, breathing slowly—in and out, like the tide.

Rebecca squinted, opening her eyes. A slender rail of light came at her from the side, then was gone. As her eyes adjusted, she could see more clearly around her. The semi-lit room she lay in came into view. The sound of her breathing—the sound of the tide—faded into and became the whir of the ceiling fan overhead. She saw that the pull chain hanging from the fan ended in a little wooden bulb that knocked rhythmically against the base of the fan... *clop... clop clop clop... clop... clop clop...*

Rebecca lay in bed, partially covered by a blanket. The sheets beneath her were damp. She was wearing a swimsuit and an oversized shirt as a cover-up. She rubbed her eyes and scratched her head. As she stretched and half-yawned, everything slowly came back to her. She remembered where she was, and how she got there.

All of it.

Her dream was already fading from memory, yet part of it made sense to her. The scuba incident the day before. She could understand how that had bubbled up from her subconscious. So much had happened...

And then, she remembered *it*—the list. It took no effort to remember the complete list, as it was very short.

Mobile phone.

Pay-per-view.

Room service.

As she carefully sat up, she felt something poke her right hip.

She reached down and retrieved her mobile phone from between her hip and the mattress.

The phone advised that it was 8:04 a.m. She checked her text messages and saw that the last conversation she had viewed was still open in the app.

Sara: *Everything alright?*

Rebecca: *Wiped out. Going to bed.*

Sara: *You're Sure?*

Rebecca: 👍

Sara: *Okay. G'night.*

There were no new messages. Not from Sara. And not from Alan.

Everyone must still be asleep.

She noted that her phone was at 7% battery. A surge of adrenaline fired through her body.

Shit!

The damned thing must have come unplugged while she slept. She reached out with her arm, patting around her on the mattress until she felt the charging cord. Grabbing it, she followed the wire to the end. She noticed that her hands still trembled slightly as she attempted to plug the charger into her phone. When she succeeded in pushing the micro USB home, her phone thanked her with a pleasant *bloop*.

Rebecca sighed and laid her head back against the headboard for a moment; the jumble of pillows under her shoulders held her neck protectively. The room around her was relatively modern, clean, done up in beiges and wood tones. A set of brown plaid curtains blocked out most of the daylight.

The only light in the room, other than the thin beam that intermittently peeked in through the curtains when the wind from the ceiling fan hit them just right, came from the television. She looked up and saw that the TV was patiently displaying the welcome screen of the hotel's pay-per-view channel. The remote was on the bed, where she'd left it. She quickly flipped through the menu to another movie—one she hadn't watched the night before, a rom-com of some sort—and pressed BUY. Rebecca muted the TV and dropped the remote on the bed as the opening scene rolled and the film began.

Oh, God! What a mess...

She tried to inventory what she was feeling. Was it regret, or fear? In the end, it didn't really matter. Not now, anyway. She pushed whatever it was down and away. She could deal with that later. Right now, she needed to focus on the list.

Mobile phone.

Pay-per-view.

Room service.

She glanced over at the night table. On it were a glass that was one-third full of clear liquid and a crushed slice of lime, four empty cans of tonic, and four tiny bottles—gin—also empty. The room smelled of food. She didn't have to look to know why. The late-night room service dinner she'd ordered sat half-eaten on the trolley that it had been delivered on, at the foot of the bed.

She reached out for the hotel phone, called *In-Room Dining*, and was greeted by a perky-voiced woman with an island accent. Rebecca ordered scrambled eggs, toast, bacon, a bowl of fruit, and a carafe of coffee. The woman advised her that the meal would arrive in about thirty minutes.

Rolling carefully out of bed, Rebecca padded barefoot to the bathroom. By sitting up straight on the toilet while she peed, she could see herself in the mirror above the vanity across from her. Her hair was a bit of a mess, but other than that, she looked great.

Normal. Perfectly normal.

Her suntan hid any signs of fatigue. She ran a hand through her black bob and almost smiled. Her hairstylist, Jean-Luc, had recommended the style—he'd called it "The Villain's Secretary" from a poster he had on his wall of Manga character hairstyles.

'Secretary' my ass... you look good... considering.

Rebecca washed her face, brushed out her hair, and applied just a touch of makeup. Standing back, assessing, she was pleased with what she saw.

Good enough to go and see Alan.

She picked up her phone and checked for messages as she walked back into the bedroom. Rebecca frowned upon seeing that she still hadn't heard from anyone.

Odd that Sara's not up yet.

By now, the crew should have laid out breakfast and the smell of fresh-brewed coffee should be wafting through the yacht. If they hadn't awoken on their own, the smell of coffee and the sounds of nautical activity about the boat making their way down to the cabins should have served as a snooze alarm. The crew was up for sure, but the guests...

Maybe after everything that went down last night, they're wiped out? Sleeping in?

Rebecca could understand Sara not being up. After all, they'd gotten an early start drinking the day before.

* * *

"The secret to *my* espresso martinis is that I use chocolate liqueur instead of crème de cacao." Sara Watts had just finished vigorously shaking a Boston Cocktail Shaker and was carefully pouring a frothy, coffee-colored concoction into two used martini glasses. Her feminine hands were steady as she poured, athletic forearms and biceps aiding in the task. Rebecca marveled at the vein in Sara's bicep. She could almost see health flowing through it.

Rebecca and Sara were standing behind the bar on the flybridge of *Gratitude*, a 110-foot Hargrave mega-yacht that the two women and their husbands had chartered for the week. At just past two in the afternoon, it was a little early for martinis of any kind. Definitely early for a second martini.

"Come on, Bex," Sara had chided, using Rebecca's nickname, "it's a fuckin' vacation."

Rebecca's mother would have grudgingly approved of Sara. She would have called her *a real pistol*. Sara was a tiny woman. Smaller than Rebecca at barely five feet tall. Thin, athletic, energetic—Sara's golden bikini looked as though it were painted onto her deeply tanned body. Sara had thick blonde hair cut to shoulder length, which hung flat despite the humidity. She'd pushed her gold-framed sunglasses up like a headband to keep her hair out of her eyes—quick, rich hazel eyes that drew you in. Everything about Sara matched and vibrated. She was a dynamo, a clockwork praline in assorted shades of caramel.

Even the drink she was making them matched her palette. She'd politely taken over control of the bar from the steward because she wasn't happy with his first round of espresso martinis.

"It's just a question of taste. His version was too bitter. The chocolate liqueur is sweeter. And it froths." She held a glass out to Rebecca. "See the froth? Like a tiny head of foam on a beer. This is how I like 'em."

Rebecca sipped appreciatively. "That... is amazing!"

Rebecca was wearing a strapless black bikini and oversized Ray Ban aviator sunglasses. Her white linen cover-up was draped over one of the barstools. She was taller than Sara, and less tanned since she was lighter-complected and more diligent with the sunscreen.

The two friends returned to their lounge chairs with their drinks. All around them stretched an expanse of bright blue ocean. Bluer than blue. They were on day five of a six-day cruise they were taking with their husbands through the Turks and Caicos. Their motor yacht was a "starter" mega-yacht with a crew of five.

That morning, Rebecca had gone scuba diving with Alan, and nearly died 120 feet below the surface. They'd returned to the yacht around ten a.m. and shared the details of their experience with Mike and Sara. While Rebecca was in no mood for more activities, Alan had tried to convince them all to take the tender out with the steward to do some fishing. In the end, Mike and Alan had gone out, leaving their wives to relax and take in the sun.

Sara was playing an eighties music playlist on the ship's

sound system via Bluetooth. David Bowie was singing "Modern Love" as the ladies sipped their martinis.

Rebecca lay back on her lounge chair and finally relaxed, the second martini working its magic. Through her closed eyes, she could see the bright orange light of the sun. She was calm, and for the first time in a while, she felt like she knew what she needed to do. The incident that morning had helped put everything she and Alan were going through into perspective.

Life is short. Too short to waste...

* * *

A delicate chime from the doorbell to her hotel room interrupted Rebecca's thoughts. The room service waiter was kind enough to remove the remnants from the prior evening before setting up breakfast. She tipped him well. It made sense to. But she wasn't hungry.

Once he was gone, Rebecca made several trips back and forth to the bathroom, carefully flushing half the scrambled eggs, a piece of toast, and most of the berries down the toilet. She started to drink a cup of coffee, but then thought better of it.

The last thing I'm gonna need today is caffeine.

She flushed the rest of the cup and half the carafe down the toilet as well. Then, she put her brush and makeup in her purse and left the room, heading down to the reception desk to check out.

"You have a nice stay, ma'am?" the young lady at the desk asked as she handed her the bill for the night's stay.

"Okay, I guess... everything was fine. I just couldn't sleep. I was up most of the night." She skimmed the bill and then paid.

Rebecca left the hotel and walked along the beach, making her way back toward the marina. She plodded through the sand, stopping occasionally to shake out her sandals. Though she tried to control her breathing as she went, as her destination came into view, she began to feel unwell. There was virtually no breeze and the day was already heating up. It was humid, and the sun scowled down at her from a cloudless sky.

As she approached the cluster of three large palm trees on the shore near the dockmaster's office, she began to feel lightheaded, nauseous. She felt bile rising in her throat. Rebecca looked around her. The beach near her was empty. She casually walked up next to one of the palm trees, using it for cover, and quickly glanced over the area in and around the trees. A sharp spasm shot through her gut. She felt herself begin to sweat. Her knees were weak.

Rebecca checked up and down the beach again, after which she turned as if she was going to pick something up, and discreetly vomited between two of the trees. She removed a sandal and carefully used it to brush sand over the area. She took several deep breaths to try to still her shaking hands, then moved on quickly, trying to put distance between her and the trees.

Rebecca continued toward *Gratitude* and was just passing the dockmaster's office when her phone pinged. It was Sara. She walked slowly as she texted with her friend.

Sara: *You up?*

Rebecca: *Walking back. See you in a few.*

Sara: *Coffee? Or Bloody Mary?*

Rebecca: *Ugh…*

Sara: *Got it. Coffee.*

Blue Haven Marina was about half full. There were a few fishing boats, a couple of motor yachts, and two mega-yachts: *Gratitude*—which was her destination—and a 200+ foot behemoth named *Fisher King*.

As she approached *Gratitude*, she saw that the crew was hard at work cleaning. Rebecca walked across the transom to the boat's sliding glass door. She saw that their scuba gear was still laid out in the cockpit. She cringed when she thought back on how she had almost died the prior morning.

Fuckin' wreck diving... what was I thinking? Fuckin' Alan...

She opened the sliding glass door and entered the boat, passing through the saloon into the dining room and the air conditioning. As the cool air hit her, she felt better. The dining table was set for breakfast—all the place settings untouched except where Sara sat.

"Good morning!" Sara half-smiled.

Rebecca sat down across from her and drank deeply from her glass of water. She looked up at Sara and replied, "I suppose."

Sara shook her head slowly.

"Mike?" Rebecca asked.

"Snoring. Out cold." Sara took a sip from her coffee cup. "We talked last night. After you left..." Sara sighed. "After we put Alan to bed. He was," she shook both her hands, "fuuucked up... started cryin' and shit. Apologizing..."

Rebecca raised her eyebrows and pursed her lips, but said nothing.

"Mike agrees, Bex. Alan needs to get professional help. You guys can't... *you* can't go on..." Sara paused. Rebecca felt a hot tear running down her cheek. She took off her sunglasses and dabbed at her eyes with her napkin. Sara was about to speak again when the two heard footsteps.

Mike Watts quietly entered into the dining room. He moved softly for a big man, giving off the vibe of a giant teddy bear. Although he was carrying thirty pounds of excess weight, shades of the college football player he once was still peeked out from underneath. He was freshly showered and wearing long board shorts and a boat shirt. When he saw the two women at the table, his face—slightly sunburned—shifted from cautious to somber.

"Hey," he said to both women, raising a hand and fluttering his fingers. Then he bent and gently kissed his wife Sara on the lips. He took the seat next to her and poured himself a cup of coffee.

"I was just telling Rebecca," Sara said in almost a whisper, "what we talked about." She paused, waiting for him to speak.

"Yeah." He shrugged. He had both hands on the table in

front of him, cradling his coffee cup between them. Mike breathed in deeply.

"Look, I'm no expert or anything. We're not," he said, indicating Sara with a sideways nod of his head, "and if you want us to butt out, just say so." He paused, not moving his head, his eyes bouncing between Rebecca's face and his hands. It seemed that he was hoping she would do just that, ask him to butt out.

Rebecca was moved by his concern. And Sara's. She shrugged.

Sara prodded Mike gently with her elbow. "Go on, Mike."

The big man cleared his throat. "Um, yeah. Seems like... well, alcohol doesn't seem to agree... or it brings out... doesn't bring out the best... in Alan, you know?"

"He took a swing at Mike, Bex," Sara said, looking to her for confirmation.

Rebecca remembered. Although it was a very serious and uncomfortable situation, or maybe because of that, Rebecca had to fight down a smirk. Alan was strong-willed. And he could be mean. But he was a small man, barely five-foot-seven, although his ego was well over six-foot-two. He was no longer in the shape he'd been in when he played rugby, back when Rebecca first met him. Alan versus Mike? Mike wins, hands down. Rebecca succeeded in fighting down the smirk and simply nodded.

"I'll talk to him. I will. Today. And thanks, guys. For being—"

The three looked up as they heard someone clear his throat. A head poked around the corner. It was the steward.

"Good morning, all! So, are you guys still wanting to go shopping?"

So fucking perky... thought Rebecca.

After a bit of discussion, they agreed to meet in fifteen minutes on the transom to go explore Provo—the local nickname for Providenciales. Rebecca told Mike and Sara that she would check on Alan to see if he wanted to join the group.

As she took the stairs down to the master cabin, her shoulders and neck tightened. She tried to control her breathing.

Standing in front of the elegant double doors, she wondered what she would find on the other side. For a brief moment, she expected to find Alan asleep, fully dressed and reeking of alcohol. She shook her head.

It's showtime.

She opened the door carefully, trying to make as little noise as possible. She breathed in the air. It smelled of lavender soap.

Just do what you would normally do, she thought.

The room was cool and dark. The blackout curtains were closed. Yet, as she stood in the doorway, she could see with the help of the little light that came in from the hall that the bed was mussed, but empty. Rebecca reached in and turned on the light.

She breathed in deeply, then, "Alan?" she called out loudly. She entered the room. It was empty. She checked the master bath, calling his name loudly again. Empty, as well.

Rebecca returned to the dining room. She walked to the kitchen, where she found the chef and captain finishing breakfast. Neither had seen Alan since the night before.

The captain used his VHF radio to contact the crew members, asking them if they'd seen Alan. While he did, Rebecca called Alan's mobile phone. No answer. The captain soon learned that none of the crew had seen Alan that morning.

As Rebecca made another search through the master suite, the captain and crew began to search *Gratitude*. When they learned what was happening, Mike and Sara joined in as well.

Alan was not on the yacht.

Two of the crew went for a walk around the marina, searching. Rebecca continued calling Alan's phone, which continued to go to voicemail.

Approximately forty minutes after Rebecca had entered the master cabin and found Alan missing, the captain contacted the local police.

CHAPTER NINETY-THREE

The time after Roy's trial and disappearance was difficult for me. But, in some ways, I had very little time to think about it or him. None of us did. About a week after his disappearance, the state of Florida went into lockdown. Like Sherman to the sea, the coronavirus scorched a path of death and destruction across the planet, and across America. In the space of two months, we had over 1.4 million cases of COVID-19 in the United States and almost 87,000 deaths. It was a nightmare.

For a time, I saw patients remotely, via telemedicine. When things finally began to return to normal, it was refreshing to meet patients face to face in my office.

Business picked up, as many clients were grieving or dealing with mild post-traumatic stress. Some had lost loved ones. Others were recovering from time spent in isolation. I took on quite a few new patients.

Around that time, I had received several calls to my mobile phone from the same phone number, a number that I didn't recognize, and therefore didn't answer. I assumed it was a telemarketer and thought nothing further of it. Whoever it was that called never left a message. I was soon to learn who the caller was.

It was a Friday. My last appointment for the day had cancelled, and I was happy to be able to leave work early. It was a beautiful day, and a nice walk through the neighborhood before figuring out dinner seemed like a lovely idea.

I had packed up and was ready to leave my office. I walked out into the reception area to lock the front door before leaving through the back door, as was my habit, when I jumped back and screamed in surprise after almost walking into a young woman who unexpectedly stood in the doorway.

"I'm sorry," she said, holding her hands up. "I didn't mean to startle you."

After a moment, I recovered and laughed at my overreaction. The woman smiled and moved tentatively toward me, then crouched. When she stood up, she held my keys in her hand. I hadn't even noticed that I'd dropped them. She had pretty hands, with slim, delicate fingers.

"Not at all," I replied. "I was just locking up. I… did you have an appointment?" I asked, flustered, and raising my phone to see if I had missed something on my calendar.

"No," she said with a shake of her head. "I tried calling, but I could never get a human. I hate talking to machines." She laughed nervously. "That must sound craaaaa-zy."

"All the best people are," I replied.

She looked at me quizzically, then smiled brightly. By this point, my shock was fading, and C.J. Martin, Ph.D. took over. "It's very common, actually. I hate leaving messages myself. I'm Dr. Martin, by the way."

I offered her my elbow and she bumped it with hers—the COVID-19 greeting still felt awkward, but better safe than sorry.

"I'm Rebecca," she smiled. "Rebecca For— Collier. Sorry. Rebecca Collier. I'm using my maiden name again."

CHAPTER NINETY-FOUR

Though I was still slightly off-balance, I was already forming a first impression of this young woman. She was professionally dressed. Her jewelry was discreet, but expensive. She clearly came from money. But, her speech patterns seemed somewhat juvenile. Immature. She seemed a bit flighty, happy-go-lucky. Dare I say, in a nice way—shallow.

"I'm afraid I was about to lock up for the day," I said, gesturing with the keys she had just placed in my hand.

"Oh!" She looked at her gold watch. "I'm sorry. Could you just spare a few moments? I came a long way."

We went back into my office and sat down. She took the patient's chair. She sat with her feet and knees together. Her purse on her lap.

"So, how can I help you?" I asked.

She suddenly seemed nervous. I sensed that she'd passed from an informal into a more formal, perhaps rehearsed, mode of communication.

"I need to ask your medical opinion. As a healthcare provider. So, what I am about to tell you, I am sharing with you for the purpose of obtaining medical care."

The hairs on the back of my neck stood on end. This sounded like trouble. She had something she wanted to get off her chest, and wanted to make sure that it was protected by the therapist-patient privilege. It sounded like she had talked to a lawyer—or maybe was one, though she didn't look it. I had travelled that road before and was not interested in adding any new drama to my life.

"Mrs. Collier—"

"Miss. Maiden name, remember?" she smiled.

"Miss Collier. My standard practice is to pre-screen clients. There is a process. I can't simply begin treating you. If you'd like to become a patient—"

She shook her head and interrupted, "I just need to make sure that what I tell you—"

"...is privileged." I nodded. "I understand how this works. But, again, there is a process to becoming a patient. I can't simply agree to treat you because you happened into my office. I'm sure you can understand that? Now," I stood. "If you'd like, I can give you the pre-screening paperwork and you can fill it out," I walked around my desk and retrieved a new patient packet, "bring it back in, or scan and email it if you like, and we can take things from there."

I stood before her, using my "stern but caring" face, and held the packet out to her.

She looked at the packet, then up at me. Then, she raised her chin and cleared her throat.

"He told me to give you a message."

I studied her face for a moment. She had very pretty eyes. There was a softness to them. Perhaps naïveté?

"Who?" I asked.

"He said to tell her—to tell you... Oh, I'm not being very clear, am I? Roy. His name was Roy. And he wanted me to give you a message."

I slowly took hold of the new patient packet with two hands, and brought it protectively against my chest. Then I sat down, and said to her, "Miss Collier. Sometimes, when the situation requires it, I conduct face-to-face patient pre-screening. I believe this is one of those situations. So, you may tell me what you came here to tell me. Everything you say will be part of that pre-screening process, and protected by privilege."

The woman looked a bit confused. Almost as though she hadn't expected to get this far, and now that she had, she wasn't quite prepared for what came next. So, I tried to help her along. "How did you meet him? Where?"

"It was in the islands. Turks and Caicos. He saved my life.

Twice." As she spoke the words, I could see that she was visualizing whatever had happened. There were tears forming in her eyes.

"So much has happened since then. It seems like..." she cleared her throat, "another life, you know? I first met him... I was scuba diving with my husband. There was a malfunction... I thought it was a malfunction... turned out it was intentional... anyway, we were diving, and at 120 feet, I ran out of air. I was swimming after him, Alan... my husband, trying to get to him for help, but he was too far away. I wasn't going to make it. And this guy suddenly appears out of nowhere and gives me his backup regulator to use.

"He saved my life. Took me up to the surface.

"His dive partner went and got Alan's attention, and they came up after us. If he hadn't been there, Roy... I wouldn't have made it."

As his therapist, it pleased me to hear that Roy had saved a life, particularly given his tendencies in the other direction.

"When we got to the surface, well, I was so grateful, so thankful. They—the two of them—helped Alan and me get out of our gear and back up into our tender. It turns out Roy was diving with one of the companies down there. They'd dropped in just a little after we had. It was lucky they did, you know?

"They were super-cool about it all. Roy made sure we were fine. He was super-chill. Alan was freaking out. Pissed off about my tank. Yelling at the steward from our yacht.

"Then Roy and the guy he was diving with went off to finish their dive. I didn't even get his name at that point, actually. But, he's got those eyes, you know?"

I nodded.

"Anyway, I was done... for the day. We went back to our boat—we were in the Turks with another couple, Mike and Sara. I spent the afternoon chilling with Sara and drinking martinis.

"That night, we all went ashore to go to dinner. And as we were walking down the dock to get our taxi, I saw him. He was on the transom of a yacht called *Lady Suze*. Of course, he was all cleaned up and not in scuba gear, but I recognized him by those eyes. Green. Very unusual green. And I told them—Sara and Mike—

'That's the guy that saved my life!' I don't know if he just wasn't into the attention or what, but when I pointed him out and he saw me, he seemed almost bashful. He sort of reluctantly came down to the dock and said 'Hello,' and *that's* when I got his name for the first time. Roy."

CHAPTER NINETY-FIVE

I exhaled slowly, trying to remain calm. I was anxious to know what Roy was up to, when she had last seen him, and if she knew where he was now or at least where had gone from there. I was ecstatic to know that he was alive and well. I had so many questions. But I fought them down, and simply nodded at her to continue.

"That first conversation with Roy was kind of awkward. I mean, what had happened had happened, you know? But we didn't really know anything about each other. I didn't really have a lot to say other than 'thank you' again.

"I remember, I asked him if he wanted to join us for dinner, but he begged off. So, we went ahead and did our thing. And after, when we came back to the yacht, I noticed that the lights were still on when we passed *Lady Suze*. But, no sign of Roy. We went back to the *Gratitude*, that's the yacht we were on, and went up to the flybridge for a nightcap."

Up until this point, Rebecca had been speaking rapid-fire, very animatedly. She took a deep breath and asked, "Could I get something to drink?"

"Of course," I replied, standing and heading to the small kitchen off of my office. "Water, tea, or soda?"

She stood and followed me. "Do you have anything stronger?" she asked.

I bent down and opened the lower cabinet, then stood to the side and let her see in.

"Vodka on the rocks would be fine."

I poured two and handed her one. She raised her glass, and I clinked mine against hers. "Cheers."

We returned to my office and took our seats.

"So, that night on the flybridge... well, there'd been the martinis earlier. And we'd had wine with dinner. Then more back at the yacht, Alan a few more than the rest. And, you have to understand, Alan and I were having some issues. In fact, that was part of the reason for the trip. Things had been a bit shaky—marriage-wise. I had even talked to a lawyer, about a divorce. Just preliminary, you know? To understand my options.

"Part of it was his drinking. His dad was an alcoholic. And he grew up around... well, things were kind of abusive, I guess. He'd dealt with it pretty well, I suppose. But, I can see in hindsight that he would lean on alcohol when things got stressful. And... around that time, things were *pretty* stressful.

"See, we'd invested in a hotel... it was a dump when we bought it, and the plan was to renovate it. It was sort of 'his thing'. I didn't really get very involved. But, then the place was raided by the police. They claimed it was being used for prostitution or escorts or something... We had to get lawyers involved. It was a mess. And it turned out that a chunk of the money that was supposed to have been used for the renovation—money we borrowed from the bank—was just missing. Gone. Needless to say, our relationship was not on solid footing.

"Well, that night, after everything from the diving 'accident'," Rebecca made air quotes, "sort of sank in, I was feeling... just really lucky to be alive, you know? And we were sort of rehashing everything—like you do, you know. And I said something offhand about Alan having checked my gear before we went diving. I honestly don't even remember what I said, and it wasn't accusatory or anything. Or at least it wasn't meant that way... but Alan *just went nuts*. 'How can you say that? You know I love you more than anything! I couldn't live without you!' You know, that kind of stuff.

"But then the whole thing sort of expanded and he turned it into the same old stuff he had been throwing at me for a while. 'You don't trust me. You think I'm not worthy of you. You're so much better than me. You think you deserve better.'

"We'd all had a lot to drink, I'll admit that. But this wasn't the first night on the trip that Alan had kind of blown up. So, Mike, our friend, stepped in to try and calm him down. And, Alan took a swing at him. And," Rebecca chuckled, "Mike's a *b-i-i-i-g* guy. That wasn't going to end well for Alan, you know? So, I stepped in to try and calm things down, and he—Alan—pushed me sort of, and I fell against the railing pretty hard. Turns out I bruised a rib." She pointed at her left side.

"Well, I got a bit hysterical at that point. The whole thing was getting out of hand.

"So, I left. I told them all I needed some air, and that I was going for a walk. Sara tried to come with me, but I insisted that I wanted to be alone. I told her to please help Mike get Alan to bed and make sure he didn't drink anymore.

"I walked out of the marina and down to the beach. It's kind of this whole complex; there's the marina, then a big beach, then this hotel. And, I was kind of out of it." She rolled her eyes. "I was a little drunk. But, there was more to it... not just alcohol, you know... a lot of shit going on?

"I was crying. I felt like the guy I married and the guy on the boat were two different people. And I didn't know if I could trust Alan after the money thing with the hotel. It wasn't his first business disaster, you know? It felt like everything was kind of out of control.

"So, I was about halfway between the marina and the hotel. There's this little area with some palm trees? And I was leaning against one of them, just trying to think everything through. And there it was. Clear as day. I needed to get a divorce."

Rebecca looked up at me and paused.

"I know that may sound flippant, but it's something I'd been thinking about for a while. There were lots of little things. And some big things. And I'd been lying to myself about everything getting better. And I'd give Alan another chance. And then another chance. And it suddenly clicked for me, that if we couldn't be happy and at peace and in love on vacation in a place as close to paradise as there is on earth, there's no way things were going to work out in the real world. I'd been fooling myself."

As Rebecca got deeper into her story, I began to realize that the flighty, happy-go-lucky, shallow impression she'd given me at first was at least part façade. Behind that softness in her eyes there was something more. There was nothing dumb about this young woman. Perhaps she was simply accustomed to acting that way. This one definitely had many layers to her.

I nodded, and said, "That's understandable."

She stood abruptly. "I need a refill. You?"

I looked down at my glass, which was untouched, and said, "Just ice."

She walked to the kitchen and kept talking. I could hear her opening the cabinet and the icemaker as she yelled back from the other room. "Is that normal? To just have an epiphany like that? About something so critical?"

"Well," I said loudly, so she could hear me, "major life decisions can be triggered by all sorts of circumstances. Your scuba incident could have been the trigger."

"That's what *I thought*!" she shouted. "Looking back on it..." She came back into the room, both glasses in hand. She didn't appear to have added any ice to mine. Only more vodka. "...sort of a 'life is too precious' kind of moment, you know?"

I nodded.

She handed me my glass, then sat down.

"So." She blew her bangs out of her eyes. "There I was, just past the dockmaster's office, leaning against this palm tree, this gorgeous moon shining down on the water and the beach, and I hear him. Alan. He scared the shit out of me. He'd followed me, and I hadn't heard him coming. And next thing I know, he's standing next to me."

She took a drink from her glass, downing about half of it. Then she looked at me, then at her glass, and said, "I don't drink usually. Not lately, anyway. It's just that, well... the shit gets real now."

I nodded.

"So, Alan's there all of a sudden, and he's got different modes, you know? Like all guys... angry mode, proud mode, smart-ass mode." She cocked an eyebrow, "...horny mode... well, now

Alan's in his penitent mode. He's apologizing to me for having yelled at me and so forth. He's never gonna do that again. Yada yada yada...

"It was a pattern. I'd dealt with 'remorseful Alan' a million times before. And I'd accepted his apologies. And his promises to change. All of it.

"But, I wasn't going to this time. Which is fine, I guess. But then, I did something terribly, terribly stupid." She shook her head, staring at the wall behind me. Rebecca bit her lip, raised both eyebrows, and said, "Right there, on the beach, him as drunk as he was... *fuuuuck...*" she hissed, shaking her head. Then she squinted her eyes as if she were in pain, and said, "I told him I wanted a divorce."

I pursed my lips, then asked, "How did he react?"

"Not well," she half-laughed, but a tear ran down her cheek. "It was..."

I sat quietly as my new patient wept. I offered her a box of tissues. She grabbed several and dabbed at her eyes and nose. She fought to stifle sobs, until she was able to control herself and continue.

"Alan went crazy. He started with all the usual accusations. That I'd never loved him, that I thought I was too good for him, and so on. And I just wanted to get away, you know?" She wiped away tears. "I just wanted peace, and to be done with it all. But, then he... I guess it was a combination of alcohol and anger or whatever... he said, to me, he said... 'You should'a died down there.'

"And when he did, everything just sort of stopped. Like, when someone's talking to you and you're half-listening, and then you register just the last thing they said to you and it's really bad, you know? And you kinda do this mental rewind, and play it back again, and then you just say, *what the fuck?*

"It was kind of like that, for both of us. I think he realized what he'd just said... and to me, it sounded like a confession. I mean, he'd checked my gear. He was the *fucking expert,* right? And I looked at him, expecting him to take it back, you know? Like, to say it was a mistake, or he didn't mean it, or he didn't mean *that,* you know?

"But, he didn't… he didn't backtrack at all.

"And I was like, 'Alan, wait.' But he didn't want to hear any of it.

"So, I took a step back, away from him, I guess kind of from shock, but I was also suddenly scared, you know? And I tripped on the base of one of the palm trees—there were like three of them clustered together—and fell flat on my ass in the sand.

"Well, I looked up, and Alan was coming at me. And my initial thought was that he was coming to help me up, you know? Like he was back to penitent Alan… But then, I saw it. His posture was kind of off; he wasn't positioned like he was going to pick me up. His right arm was kind of to the side. And he was pissed. I mean, his face was twisted. Angry. Fucking angry.

"And I kind of crab-walked backwards, trying to get away from him. And as I did, I could see that he had something in his hand. In his right hand, that flashed in the moonlight.

"And I realized that the sonofabitch was coming at me with a knife."

Rebecca almost whispered that last sentence. Her face had gone white. I could tell she was reliving the moment as she described it.

I prompted her, to bring her back to the present. "What did you do?"

"It's funny," she spoke slowly now. Deliberately. "I'd never been in a life or death kind of situation like that—being attacked, you know? And I'd certainly never thought Alan was capable of… that… at least not against me, you know?" She took a swallow from her glass. "When I realized what was happening, that my husband was crazy pissed off and was going to try to kill me, I just froze.

"I couldn't believe it.

"I wasn't afraid. Hell, that same morning, I'd almost died 120 feet underwater. *That* scared the piss out of me… literally." She chuckled. "But, this…"

She looked up at me, tears flowing. "I wanted to cry." Her voice was no longer juvenile or immature, but deeper, old and tired.

"It was so sad to me. That I'd given myself to this man, given him my love, my... everything... and that I'd been so wrong about him. I felt… hopeless. Lost. I think... I didn't care if he killed me."

Tears flowed down her cheeks.

"And all I could muster was to say was, 'Babe. Wait.'

She scoffed, "And the last words my dear husband ever said to me were, and I quote..." she pointed a finger in the air as she said them, "'You actually thought the tank was an accident, you stupid fuckin' bitch?'"

I sat expectantly. The words hung in the air.

"Next thing I know, Alan collapses sideways and hits the ground... hard. Like he was a machine and someone just turned off the power. He's just laying there in the sand." She looked off into the middle distance quizzically and added, "I think there was a *thunk* or something before he fell. There had to be. Anyway." She shook her head and continued. "Standing there, where he was... where Alan had been... is your friend Roy, holding this big-assed wrench.

"He looked like a fuckin' superhero—to me at least, at that moment...

"He asks me if I'm okay. And I guess I'm kind of in shock, a bit drunk still. And then he's, like, apologizing. And I start crying, and I tell him," Rebecca paused for a moment, then added, "You're only the second person I've ever told. Roy was the first. I told him, 'He was going to kill me.'" She looked at me sadly, and repeated in a whisper, "My husband was going to kill me."

"So, there we were. On the beach. With my 'I think he's dead' husband laid out on the ground and me sitting on my fat ass in the sand.

"Well, once he calms me down, Roy tells me to go and stay the night at the hotel, and to text Sara that I'm staying there to get some space. And he tells me to make sure to—" she ticked the three items off on her fingers, "'keep your phone on—because the police can see where you've been with GPS—order lots of room service, and use the pay-per-view.' Then, the next day, he said I should go back to the boat and act like nothing happened. 'Just do what you would normally do.'

"He made me repeat it back to him, like ten times: *mobile phone, room service, pay-per-view.*"

Rebecca shrugged, and concluded, "So, that's what I did."

"The next day when I went back to the ship, we reported Alan missing. The police looked for him. All over. They questioned me. But I had an alibi—I'd been at the hotel all night. Oh, I had to do the whole grieving wife, 'where's my loving husband?' thing... you know, like in *Gone Girl*? At least until I got the fuck out of there." She scoffed. "Never going back to Provo, no sirree.

"But, that was the end of it. Alan Forsyth, disappeared. Missinggg." She hung on the "g" at the end of the word.

We sat for a few moments in silence. It was a lot to take in. And I could tell from looking at Rebecca that, while it had been difficult to get it all out, she seemed a bit more at peace—one of the benefits of catharsis. She was holding her drink in one hand on her lap and running the index finger of her other hand slowly around the rim. I took a sip from the vodka she had brought me. It was cool and sharp. It burned my throat as it went down.

"And Roy," I asked, looking at her, "you said he had a message for me."

"Oh, yeah." She looked up at me and smiled. "So, two days after all this went down, after the questioning and everything, the police gave me the okay to leave the island and go home. We left *Gratitude* for the airport—me and Mike and Sara. As we left the marina, I stopped by *Lady Suze*. I told Sara and Mike it was just to thank Roy again about the diving, you know? It was mid-morning, maybe ten o'clock?

"Anyway, I called out, but no one answered. So, I went onboard and knocked on the saloon door. After a bit, Roy came up. He saw I was with Mike and Sara, and invited me inside so we could talk privately.

"I told him I was leaving, and he said he was getting ready to take off himself.

"And, I told him that what he'd said to do, that it had all worked. That the police had let me go. They didn't suspect me. They thought Alan may have run afoul of some locals or something. But, they had no real leads. And I asked him what he did with... you know... with Alan. He said it was better for me not to know."

Rebecca shrugged.

"So, I told him I didn't know how to thank him. And *that's* when he asked me to come and see you."

She smiled at me. "If you don't mind me saying... none of my business..." she raised a hand. "But I think he misses you." She bit her lip and raised her eyebrows. "There was just something about his eyes when he said your name. Sadness, you know?"

My belly tightened at hearing this young woman's opinion of what Roy might think about me. Funny. I'd worked with the man in therapy for years. I knew him much better than she did or probably ever would. Yet, somehow, her opinion—her impression—that he missed me... it mattered.

"Anyways, he told me, 'You can do me a favor when you're back in the States. Find Dr. C.J. Martin in Miami. Tell her what happened. And give her this message.'"

I leaned forward slightly in my chair. I was listening. But, in my mind's eye, I could see Roy—sailing the seas out there somewhere. He was tanned and smiling, his green eyes squinting in the sun.

"He said, 'Tell Catherine I was right, about me and the scorpion.'"

Rebecca pursed her lips and then shrugged, studying me.

"He said you would know what that meant."

EPILOGUE

I wish I could report that everything ended there. That there was no more killing, no more deception, no more breaking of laws. I wish I could tell you that those of us who survived this parade-of-horribles lived happily ever after.

But I'd be lying to you.

To be sure, Roy sailing off into the sunset did mark a waypoint on our collective journey. While he was off finding himself, I soldiered on with my therapy practice. Kristy Wise decided to stay in Austin to be with Alfie, who, for his part, continued to work in venture capital. And David Kim took the reins at Cruise Capital.

For a time, normality reigned in our world. And all the forces that had conspired against us seemed to go dormant. The police in Miami and in Austin focused their efforts in other directions, and Senator Harlan went back to doing whatever it was he was doing.

Yet, what I came to realize was that the interlude of calm that we experienced then was not an end state. It was only a pause.

This false peace that I took for a denouement was really a sort of a beginning for me.

The storm of misery that we had endured was not done with us. It was gathering strength, like a hurricane. We were blissfully and obliviously living in the eye of the storm, believing that it had passed while, all around us, it was circling, waiting, growing in ferocity.

You see, the storm is always there—just out of sight, swirling beyond the horizon. I think it's something we all know, instinctively, which is why most of us cling to the safety of the shore. We prefer to ignore the tumult, the violence, the destruction that is lying in wait—as if by ignoring it, we can will it out of existence. It is only when the tempest lashes out and violently invades our tranquil lives that we are forced to react, though for most of us, that simply means scurrying back to safety, seeking solace in civilization—in the social, legal, and moral rules that pretend to define a safe space for us. But that's just it. They pretend. There is no safe space in this world. My experience with Susie and Roy taught me that. And something more.

When I first learned what Susie and Roy had done, I didn't agree with the choices they had made. On the contrary, I was appalled by their acts and I was afraid for my life. Over time, I came to understand their decisions. So much so that I joined them and sought my own revenge. Yet, I did so half-heartedly, asking them to act for me. I was still missing the point. What I did was cowardly.

I see that now. And, I think I finally understand what Roy meant about the scorpion. I still disagree that he is a killer by nature. But, there is a fundamental truth to that fable, that Roy understood and embraced, which I have only recently come to appreciate.

Our world is not safe. It is a toxic swamp populated by predators and parasites. The odds are stacked against us from the moment of conception. We survive only because we fight—the elements, hunger, disease, each other. And, although civilization promises us safe harbor, that promise is a fairy tale. Only the storm is real. It comes for each of us. And we cannot win. We can only choose how we will suffer our defeat.

We can meekly take our beatings, and die like lemmings, finding solace in the belief that we shall one day inherit the earth.

Or, we can plunge into the chaos with eyes wide open, taking comfort instead from the bruises, scars, and broken bones which prove that we fought to live and die as gods.

ADDITIONAL CONTENT

Don't stop reading yet.

This is J.K. Franko and I have a small surprise for you on the next page.

After finishing *Life for Life*, many of my early readers emailed me, saying that they wanted to hear a little more about Roy at the end of the book. So, I decided to share a little extra bit with you, which you can read below.

Roy, Kristy, Catherine and the rest will return a little later in the Talion Series. I am already at work on book four, which should be released in mid-2021. You can read an exclusive preview on the following pages. The next book will go in a slightly different direction, bringing some new characters and crimes into the mix.

Thanks for reading the *Eye for Eye Trilogy*, the first three books of the Talion Series, and making it such a success. As you've probably noticed, I don't have the marketing muscle of a big publisher behind me, so word of mouth is how I sell books.

If you enjoyed the series, please write a review and tell your friends.

Feel free to reach out to me at jk@jkfranko.com. I love hearing from readers.

And sign up for my newsletter at www.jkfranko.com

Roy

Roy sat at the flybridge helm of *Lady Suze* as he navigated northwest. The yacht was on autopilot, cruising at 10 knots. It was late in the day and the seas were calm. He kept a lookout for other ships as he fought the hypnotic effect of the sway of the yacht as it cut through the ocean, the thrum of the dual CAT engines, and the comfort of the warm breeze in his face.

He was in a contemplative mood. Reflecting. He had come to realize that his entire life, ever since he'd lost his sister Joan, and with her his family, had been one giant attempt to recapture love and normalcy. Susie and Camilla had given him back what he'd lost. With them, he'd been truly happy. He'd felt whole again, for a while.

Losing Camilla had destroyed it all. And, he should have known from experience that he hadn't just lost Camilla, but that it was all over. No doubt due to that stubbornness he'd inherited from his grandmother, he'd fought to keep things alive with Susie. He'd thought that what they'd had before could be salvaged. Susie had known that about him. She'd convinced him that it could be saved. He'd been willing to do anything to try. He'd killed to keep it alive.

But, it was no use.

He didn't blame Susie for that. She had probably manipulated him to some degree. But there's always a bit of manipulation in any relationship, isn't there? And Roy believed, deep down, that she thought that what they had done would put them in a better place. It just didn't. That's all.

After Susie died, in their baby Joan, he'd still seen a final glimmer of hope. He'd hoped that the universe was going to give him another chance. Another chance with Joan... and possibly with Catherine.

It was stupid. He should have known he'd gone too far. They'd broken way too many rules for that ever to happen. There's no way that everything he'd done could be rewarded. It just couldn't end well.

Roy knew that you have to pick your battles in life. You have to choose what's a must-have and what's a nice-to-have. When it comes down to it, you can't have it all. Any fool knows that.

He'd had a lot of time to think about everything—and about Susie—while sailing the Caribbean. He'd made it all the way down to Grenada. His plan had been to navigate through to Trinidad before turning around and heading back to Miami. It's something he and Susie had always talked about doing. But Venezuela was going through bad times, and Roy decided to avoid the coast. One man, alone on a nice yacht with only a handgun, didn't have great odds against pirates. So, he'd turned around at Grenada to head home.

Ray was about a week out from Miami now, heading into the lower Exumas, trying to get to Abraham's Bay on Mayaguana before dark, to drop anchor overnight. He'd left Miami because he'd needed time to get his head together. And being alone on the sea gives you that. The weather had been amazing. The spaces vast, the waters beautiful blue, and the people generous, simple, and kind.

It's funny how, when you've lost someone you love, there are some things that you forget so quickly it's frightening. They just disappear like a morning haze. But then, other little things about them slowly begin to come back to you. Other memories percolate up. Those are permanent. Those are memories you'll keep forever. They're the ones that matter.

One of those memories came to Roy as he navigated that day towards Abraham's Bay. It was of the last time he saw Susie, on their terrace, at breakfast the day she was shot—before he'd left for that goddamned interview with the police. Susie had looked radiant that morning. Glowing. Literally full of life. Chestnut hair. Dark brown eyes. Lively, intelligent eyes. What a fucking woman! That's how Roy would always remember her.

As he savored that memory, that mental image of his beautiful wife, something came back to him. It hadn't occurred to him before, for some reason. But suddenly it was right there, front and center.

There are people who make a big deal about this kind of thing. A person's last words. They claim they're significant in some way.

As he navigated toward Abraham's Bay, Roy distinctly remembered what she'd said. The last words Susie ever said to him.

"Love you. Do what you do best, babe. Knock 'em dead."

He chuckled to himself, taking in the full significance of those words. She knew him so fucking well. He was a scorpion. There was no denying it.

After that little moment of reflection, he re-checked his heading. Everything was good. He took a quick look around with his binoculars. No boats in sight. He was about eight nautical miles from Abraham's Bay and the depth gauge showed 7,800 feet of ocean between him and the bottom of the sea.

Roy headed down into the crew quarters at the stern. Even though he'd set the A/C to sixty degrees, it was starting to smell a bit funky back there. He'd wrapped Alan Forsyth's body up in a tarp and used duct tape to seal him up with the dinghy anchor and a few old dive weights wedged between his legs.

Still, after three days... well, Alan was starting to smell a bit ripe.

Roy carefully maneuvered him out of the crew quarters, up onto the transom, and laid him on the edge at the very back of the boat, just above the water. Then he took a last look around just to make sure the coast was clear.

If you've never been in this part of the world, you really have to make the trip. It simply must be experienced firsthand, because words fail. As Roy chugged toward Abraham's Bay, all around him was an amazing multi-colored sky, a calm blue ocean, and not another human being for miles. The breeze smelled of salt and life. The day was ending, and the sea and sky seamlessly blended at the horizon into a beautiful blue dome like the ceiling of a cathedral painted in the purples and golds of salvation. The vast expanse of it all felt spiritual and left Roy almost breathless.

Carefully, he reached forward with one foot, and gave the duct-taped tarp containing Alan Forsyth's body a gentle push. It rolled over and neatly flopped into the sea. Of course, Roy took the yacht off autopilot and circled back once, just to make sure the sonofabitch sank.

You can never be too careful.

ACKNOWLEDGEMENTS

Thanks to my wife, Raquel for supporting this writing project for so many years, and for her advice as to all aspects. I could not have completed the *Eye for Eye* Trilogy without her.

Special thanks to my daughter Pi who brainstormed endings with me and to whom I am indebted for two of the major plot twists in *Life for Life*.

Thanks to all of my early readers and supporters—Mercedes Perote, Sara Bensadon, PhD., Colleen Marone-Calvo, and James Trezza. Thank you for your input and encouragement.

Thank you also to my focus group participants—Francesca Marturano Pratt, Cheryl Green, Renee Freeman Owens, Lisa Hall, and Nicole Sexton—who devoted time and effort to providing feedback leading to significant improvements in the story

AVAILABLE NOW FROM AMAZON

If you enjoyed

LIFE FOR LIFE

Book 3 of the Talion Series

Please leave an Amazon review so that others may enjoy it also.

To find out more about J.K. Franko, the Talion series and for access to exclusive additional content, register now at J.K.'s official website.

www.jkfranko.com

Made in United States
North Haven, CT
16 April 2024